CAPRICE

I do not know what aroused me but suddenly I was wide awake, my eyes staring into the thick darkness of the room, my ears straining to hear any slight sound, but the house was still. The room felt cold. Probably the fire had been out for hours and no chink of light from outside showed through the thick curtains drawn against the windows. I had no idea how long I had been sleeping but now that I was awake my dreams came back to me in a jumbled mass of improbabilities. Of one thing I was sure, no dream had been responsible for my racing heart and the cold chill of fear which lay over my body.

Sara Hylton

CAPRICE

**THE SHERIDAN
BOOK COMPANY**

This edition published in 1994 by
The Sheridan Book Company

First published by Hutchinson 1980
Random House, 20 Vauxhall Bridge Road, London SW1V 2SA
Arrow edition 1981

Printed and bound in Great Britain by
Cox & Wyman Ltd, Reading, Berkshire

ISBN 1-85501-644-3

PROLOGUE

From the ship's rail we are looking our last at the exquisite curve of the sickle-shaped bay which is called the East Port, but in my memory Alexandria will always lie all glittering blue and white in that god-sent Egyptian light which has shone on the land of the pharaohs through dead ages and unrecorded centuries. Alexandria, this brittle city of Antony and Cleopatra, will be our last view of Egypt and soon the shoreline with its white buildings and slender minarets will be only a white jumble on the horizon. Others are drifting away now to seek the comfort of their cabins or the lounges where afternoon tea is being served, but we linger on to savour for the last time the incredible beauty of an Egyptian sunset.

It is written that they who drink Nile water must return, but shall we ever come back, I wonder, to this land of golden sunlight, with its overpowering sense of history? This land which has held us enthralled as glittering days followed nights when we could hear the desert's stillness and see the moon hanging like a globe of pale light above the shifting sands? We are going home to a sterner land. To rolling moorland and towering crags, where streams of cold, clear water tumble down the rocks to swell the gentle rivers on their way to the sea.

It would be a lie to say that I am not afraid. I only have to think about that great house standing amongst the hostile crags to bring the shadows back into my eyes and that old sickening flutter to my heart. I try, constantly I try, because I must not hurt him by my reluctance to face the future in a house he loves as dear as life. Perhaps one day they will cease, those nights when I wake up screaming, my body cold and clammy, when only his arms, gentle and strong around me, reassure me that I have nothing to fear.

I did not realize three years ago that I was journeying into an experience which would almost cost me my life and rob me of my sanity. Men are able to fill their days with so many things and the estate is large. I know that as soon as our homecoming is known the tenants will descend upon us with varying requests and complaints, so there will be whole days when I shall be left alone to amuse myself as best I can. It is those days I fear most, particularly in the winter when the days are short and the evenings long. Will it be then, I wonder, that my eyes will peer into the shadows where the light from the lamps and the firelight cannot reach, when my ears will find themselves listening for quick, light footsteps behind me or the gentle swish of a gown upon the stairs? I cannot think it will be Caprice who comes to mock me with her light silvery laughter, but how can I be sure?

When I find him looking at me with anxious appeal in his dark eyes I smile brightly, confidently, in order to reassure him, for how can I tell him that I am afraid of Elsa still, with her Nordic beauty and her cold, blue eyes?

Looking back, it seems like a thousand years since that bleak day in the autumn of the year when I boarded the little country train that was to take me to Milverton. It was a raw, cheerless day, chilled by a fine flurry of snow, blustery, with a strong north easterly wind sweeping down from the fells. I remember that I was afraid on that day also, but it was a different fear, fear that I might prove inadequate for the position I had been offered, and which I most desperately needed. My father had died only a few months earlier and, apart from the princely sum of seventy pounds and the few personal belongings in my trunk, I was destitute. I did not know on that day that I was setting out upon a journey which was to end in a nightmare.

1

You will be met, the letter said. So I was anxious when the train from Medchester to Feltham was late. It had been snowing during the morning and, although the snow did not have any real depth, it lay like a thin white blanket over the wintry fields. It was wet, with little strength to cling to the trees which stood out stark and black against the red of the late afternoon sky. The train climbed upwards and I could now see the outline of Mower Gap, uninviting and hostile. I remembered it from my childhood, the formidable fell we always promised ourselves that one day we would climb, but never did.

A man sitting in the far corner of the carriage stared at me curiously, but I turned my head away. I had been raised by aunts who had instilled into me at an early age that one did not talk to strangers in railway compartments. He returned to his newspaper and I stole another covert look at him. He had a smooth, broad face and he was completely bald. He seemed to have a pink, naked look about him, like one of the country cheeses Aunt Maud always kept in her pantry. Just then he looked up and his eyes looked straight into mine. There was nothing childlike about his eyes. They were keen and piercing and I withdrew my gaze from his with considerable effort.

It was almost dark outside and the snow had started again. I could see it fluttering against the window like fine powder. The train was climbing so slowly that the wheels seemed to have difficulty in coping with the gradient. The high fells were hidden now and only the snow, swirling and drifting, could be seen outside the windows. The carriage was so dimly lit that my companion was forced to put away his newspaper and I fidgetted and played with the handle on my bag and the gloves which lay in my lap.

He consulted his watch, then drummed irritably on the

arm of his seat. When he saw that I watched him he said, 'I fear we shall be late arriving in Feltham. I do this journey three or four times in the year but it is always bad in the winter.'

I gave him a small, swift smile. The comments he had made were natural and hardly the words of a man with sinister designs upon me.

'Are you travelling the entire distance?' he asked.

'No. I am leaving the train at Gleave. I hope there will be someone there to meet me.'

'I hope so too, young lady. This is no night to be standing about on station platforms.'

He was looking at me even more curiously now. I looked away in confusion, and he said, 'Forgive my curiousity, miss, but are you by any chance a visitor for Milverton?'

My eyes opened wide for there was nothing about me to advertise the fact. My trunk was in the luggage compartment at the end of the train and there were no labels showing on my suitcase high up on the rack.

He smiled at my surprise. 'There is no mystery, my dear. I know the people at Milverton and I know they are expecting a companion for the young Mrs Lytton. I have friends in Gleave and it is too small a village not to hear some of the gossip when I visit them.'

'Why did you think that I am to be the companion you speak of, sir?' I wondered if my voice showed resentment that my role in life should be so apparent to a perfect stranger.

'Few people travel to Gleave at this time of day in winter,' he said. 'They go on to Feltham. I have become very familiar with these parts over the last few years and have got to know some of the people in Gleave. You, young lady, are a stranger, but I can assure you that your calling is not obvious.'

I looked at him sharply to see if he was amused by my touchiness, but his calm smooth face was bland and I could see no signs of sarcasm in those curious eyes of his. I wondered what his business was. I supposed he could be a lawyer or a doctor.

'When you say you know them at Milverton, do I take it you know them well, sir?' I asked him.

'Not at all well, but Gleave is a small village, little more than a hamlet and the Lyttons are an old county family of considerable standing. It is largely a farming community and the Lyttons own vast estates all round the vicinity. As I said, my friends know the Lyttons well, except for the young Mrs Lytton, and few people know her, poor lady.'

I needed to know many things about this family I was expecting to live with but I was reluctant to confide in a stranger. My appointment had been arranged through my father's lawyers who were also his executors. They had only told me that the young Mrs Lytton was an invalid and required a female companion who was young, cheerful and of an amiable disposition.

I looked unhappily at the man sitting opposite me and surprised a kindness in his face. Unbidden, the treacherous tears rose into my eyes and trickled down my cheeks.

His voice was very gentle. 'If it will help I will tell you what little I know of the family you are going to live with. It is indeed hard to go to strangers, and to be forewarned is to be forearmed, I think.'

I nodded mutely, afraid to trust my voice.

'Well now, let me see. It is a very large house and stands in its own grounds roughly three miles outside the village. Perhaps you are already aware of that fact?'

I had recovered my composure well enough now to answer him calmly.

'Yes, I know the house. I spent some time in Gleave as a child with my father's sisters who lived there. The ladies of Milverton in their carriage and the men on horseback were a familiar sight in the village and the house is very beautiful, particularly when one looks down upon it from the fells.'

He nodded thoughtfully. 'Ah yes, the fells. One cannot escape the fells in Gleave. The old lady, Mrs Lytton, is still alive but very frail since her stroke. I believe a nurse lives in to attend to her. Then there is Mr Thorn who is now the head of the family, and of course his wife. Mr Stephen and his wife also live there, and I believe Miss Rowena. She is Mrs Allington now but I have heard that she and her husband are none too comfortable. At least she spends most of her time at Milverton, but her twin brother, Mr Jeremy, is travelling abroad, which may be just as well.'

He was smiling, his eyes twinkling in his broad smooth face and I asked, 'Oh, why is that sir?'

'Mr Jeremy is a bachelor with the dubious reputation of being unable to resist a pretty face, and you, my dear young lady, have a very pretty face, if you will allow a prosy old bachelor to tell you so.'

I bit my lip, blushing furiously, and he permitted himself a dry chuckle.

My thoughts were busy with this formidable family I was on my way to live with, a family it seemed I had been aware of all my life yet never expected to know more intimately.

His voice broke into my thoughts.

'We have just passed over the causeway, we shall be arriving in Gleave in about ten minutes' time.'

'The causeway?'

'There is a new reservoir now which stretches on each side of the causeway, a man-made lake which is pretty on a summer's day but desolate and lonely on one such as this. It is indeed a long time since you were in Gleave not to know of it.'

He was right and, because I was going back there, the memories came trooping back to me one after the other.

In the main they were of summer days. My aunts had lived in a stone cottage at the top of the straggling village street. They were my father's sisters – Aunt Maud, his senior by seven years, Aunt Beatrice his junior by one. They had all been raised in Feltham but on the death of my grandfather they could not afford to keep his big house in good repair and they found the little cottage in Gleave. It was double fronted, and wallflowers grew in plots beneath the front windows. At the back was a large orchard with a swing hanging from the branches of 'Old Pear', and in the autumn, before I left the village, all the other children would be invited in to gather up the windfalls.

I could lie down in my little back bedroom breathing in the scent of honeysuckle, and in the mornings the warm scent of home-made bread from the bakery down the street drifted in through the casement windows round which the ramblers climbed. I remembered the small shops in that winding village street. The butchers, the baker and the little post office. Then there was the shop where the Misses Phipps sold laces and ribbons as well as the silks and wools Aunt Beatrice used to embroider her firescreen and, across from it, the antique shop where occasionally old Mr Tobias would let us wander around his treasures. Mostly they were composed of chipped and cracked ornaments and deeply scarred furniture, but I loved to handle the links of jet and amber beads, making up all sorts of colourful stories about the people whose treasures they had been.

I spent spasmodic intervals at the village school, dressed like the other children in sprigged muslin or starched gingham; then, just when it seemed my life was settled and running in normal channels, my father would come for me.

It was always the same. After two days of listening to Aunt Maud's scolding and Aunt Beatrice's tears, we would head for the railway station. In one hand he would be carrying my valise containing my freshly starched and laundered clothes, and in his other would be my hot hand, holding on to his for dear life in case he should be tempted to pay heed to them and leave me behind. Now, when I think about my early life, I realize how patient and kind my aunts were, and how warm was my welcome each time I returned to them. Dear Gleave, it surely was the only solid peace of earth my small feet ever found.

In case I have led you to think that my father was a wastrel, this was not so. He was a scholar, an archaeologist with a degree at Oxford, but destined never to make a fortune. Aunt Maud consistently maintained that he should never have married but, since he had and I was the unfortunate fruit of that marriage, she did what she saw to be her duty – when I was in England she gave me a home. In her fashion she loved both my father and me, but her nature was not as soft as his.

There were times when I could not join him on his travels. Those were the times I spent in Gleave, but there were those other times when we lived in ramshackle tents in whatever country he found an archaeological expedition willing to employ him. Before I was sixteen years' old I had lived in Persia and Greece, and I was with my father in Egypt when he died from a heart attack. I knew more about the Nile and the Euphrates than I knew about the fresh spring water that rippled down from the fells to find its home in the broad waters of the river that served the huge woollen mills in Medchester and, instead of the apple trees in the orchard behind the stone cottage, I had looked upon date palms and olive trees.

There were whole weeks when my father forgot my existence, when some small find would send him into realms of ecstasy as he poured over crumbling scrolls of papyrus or pieced together bits of old pottery. I have known the lamp in his tent to burn all night after the unwinding of an ancient mummy and in my heart I have hated that long-dead being for usurping a place in my father's heart which I felt should have been mine.

Even in the little time I spent with him in London his heart and his mind were far away from the cheap lodgings we were able to find in Bloomsbury, not far from the British Museum. Each morning we would sally forth to wander the vast halls filled with relics of an age long gone and he would read for me the hieroglyphics on some battered mummy case or bury himself in old manuscripts while I was free to wander where I willed.

I do not remember my mother because she died when I was three years' old, but great Aunt Tabitha, my mother's aunt, says I am very like her, and from an old, faded photograph my father kept in his wallet I think that perhaps I am. I am a little short of average height, fine boned and very slender. My hair is heavy. Dull-gold hair, too dark to be called fair, and too fair to be called brunette. I have always considered it mousy, but my father, who had a pretty turn of phrase, insisted that it was beautiful hair, the colour of rain-soaked corn. My eyes are grey, large in a rather oval face and, although there are some who have considered me pretty, I have never thought so. I know well the type of beauty I had always wished was mine and it is very different from that with which I have been blessed.

The train gave a sudden lurch which brought me quickly out of my reverie. The man sitting opposite me had risen to his feet and was reaching up to take my case off the rack.

'We have arrived in Gleave,' he said smiling down at me.

He opened the door for me and a flurry of fine snow

invaded the compartment, bringing with it the cold night air. I shivered and pulled the fur tippet I was wearing closer around my throat; then, thanking him for his courtesy, I climbed down on to the platform.

I was the only one to alight but I could see further up the train that my trunk was being put down on the platform. Hesitantly I walked towards the only building I could see, which appeared at closer quarters to serve as a ticket office and a waiting room. The door of the waiting room was closed but I could see firelight playing upon the ceiling through the grimy windows, and a gas jet glowed fitfully, sending its eerie light into the gloom. The train was moving now, pulling its way painfully along the station platform like some ageing dinosaur, so that in a few moments all I could see of it was the tail light disappearing into the tunnel ahead. I left my trunk where it was because I knew it was too heavy for me to lift alone and I did not think anyone would be foolish enough to try to steal it.

Gingerly I turned the knob on the waiting room door, but the wind snatched it from my grasp and both I and the snow were flung into the dimly lit room beyond. Two men sat round the fire – the porter and an old man wearing a peaked cap pulled down over his eyes and a dilapidated great coat with the collar pulled up over the striped muffler he wore round his neck.

They looked at me in astonishment – more, I suspect, because of the abruptness of my entry than from any other reason. Then they continued to sip the steaming tea they were drinking.

With difficulty I closed the door against the wind, and the coachman, for such I took him to be, eyed me from top to bottom before he said, 'I tak it yuer t' young wuman fur t' big 'ouse?'

'Yes, I am,' I answered. 'I have a letter to say that I am to be met.'

'Tha's reet. What thee forgeet to tell me was thet tha'd be arreevin' on t' last train.'

'I'm so sorry, have you been waiting long?'

'Only sin' two o'clock this art'noon.'

I apologized again. I know that country men are men of few words and since it was now after nine o'clock at night I suppose he had every right to feel aggrieved. At the same time I had not expected to be met by a disgruntled old man. It was evident that the Lytton family did not intend to put themselves out on my behalf. I stood beside the closed door wondering if I should sit until he had finished his brew, or mention my trunk standing out in the snow. I was just about to speak when the coachman drained his mug and rose to his feet.

'I suppose tha's gettin' a trunk out theer somewheer, thet's if oi con find it i' all thet snoa. Come on Nathan, oi'l need some 'elp wi' it, tha doesn't expect me to manage it on me own doest 'ee?'

I watched the ill-assorted pair as they struggled to open the door against the wind, and heard them go grumbling off into the night. I waited, my hands clenched in my lap, and in a few moments I heard them returning, puffing and blowing with the weight of my old trunk.

The porter came back alone. 'E's waitin fur thee,' he said.

My trunk had been loaded on to the rack behind a small carriage, and the coachman, if one could think of him in such distinguished terms, did not even bother to hold open the carriage door for me. Instead he sat aloft on his driving seat, holding the reins attached to an ancient and disgruntled horse, both of them wearing an air of dejected apathy. I pushed my case up before me, then, hitching up my skirts, I climbed into the ramshackle vehicle. The seats were narrow and none too comfortable, but by this time I was past caring how I travelled.

We rumbled along after a precarious start and I rubbed the windows so that I could see through them. It was very dark and the snow hid familiar landmarks. A few lights were lit in the main street and they shone through different coloured curtains closed against the night. The brief glimpse I had of the aunts' cottage, with its unfamiliar green curtains, brought the stinging tears into my eyes and for a few moments I gave myself up to the luxury of self pity. How I longed for my little room in Aunt Maud's house in Medchester which she had inherited from her eldest brother, even if it meant I would be subjected to her scolding! The steady clip-clop of the horse's hooves and the dull misery of the night had a hypnotic effect and I felt myself nodding. We had passed the village now and I could see nothing outside the windows of the carriage. To stop myself sleeping, therefore, I thought about all the strange events which had lead me to the position in which I now found myself.

There had been no money to bring my father's body home to England for burial so I had left him in the English cemetery in Cairo. I did not think that he would have minded because he had always loved Egypt. In some ways it comforted me to think that I had left his body buried in the same soil from which he had excavated so many of the treasures which had brought him joy.

I managed to get a passage back to England from Alexandria in a ship coming from the Far East and I returned to our old lodgings in Bloomsbury so that I could see my father's lawyers. Mr Runson, the senior partner saw me in his office, not because my father had been so important that I merited his personal attention, but because he had always enjoyed talking to my father, seeing in him an adventurous spirit.

I had sat in the large, leather chair across from his desk, watching his long, thin fingers leafing through the papers in front of him and wondering how anything to do with my father could possibly merit such careful scrutiny. The room had smelled musty, the smell of leather-bound ledgers and dried-up furniture polish; the only sounds had been the crackling of the papers in his hands and the occasional rumble of horse-drawn traffic from the street below. At last he had looked at me over his steel-rimmed spectacles and I remember that his faded, old eyes had been kind.

'I am sorry to tell you, my dear, that you will not be a wealthy woman, but then I don't suppose you ever expected to be?'

I nodded, not trusting myself to speak. Of course he was right, for what little money my father had to spare was spent in old bookshops on books I felt nobody else ever wanted and old maps of lost civilizations.

'His affairs are now in order and I can tell you that you will be the richer by seventy pounds – hardly a sum which will allow you to live a life of luxury.'

He was not to know that my heart leaped in my breast for

I had really expected to hear that my father had left debts behind, and debts which I would be expected to honour.

'My duty regarding your father's estate is done, Carlotta, but I am nevertheless anxious to know what you intend to do now. You realize that you will have to seek employment. I wonder if you have anything in mind?'

'I really have not thought about it yet, but I am limited as to what I can undertake. My education, as you know, has been spasmodic. I have lived and worked with learned men but only in the capacity as general helper and because I was my father's daughter. I am not equipped to become a governess, even if such a calling appealed to me, and I am not domesticated. Perhaps I shall try to get shop work in Medchester. My aunt has offered me a home with her in that city.'

He reached down into his drawer and pulled out a copy of the *Times* newspaper, turning the pages quickly until he found what he was looking for.

'This is yesterday's paper which I was reading at my club yesterday evening and I happened to stumble upon this advertisement. It is for a companion to a Mrs Lytton at Milverton House, near Feltham, on the outskirts of the village of Gleave – a village which you know something of as you spent much of your youth there. No academic qualifications are requested but they say they are looking for a presentable gentlewoman who is in need of a home. No domestic duties are required, only patience and consideration when dealing with a lady suffering from a nervous breakdown. The successful applicant will expect to live in the house but she will receive adequate time for leisure and holidays. The salary is to be agreed.'

I looked at him anxiously. 'Do you think I would be suitable for such a post? I know nothing about nursing besides what common sense suggests. I do not even know if I possess the sort of patience they will be looking for.'

'You have the patience, I feel sure. In many ways your father was a dear man, but he must also have been a trial to you. Now tell me, how much do you know of this family from your visits to Gleave as a girl?'

'I know the house and have seen most of the members of the family riding through the village. I remember Mrs

Lytton too, although she must be getting on in years now. I suppose there is no harm in writing to them.'

'I will approach Mr Lytton so that I can fully explain your circumstances. Perhaps you will arrange to stay on in London until I have had time to receive his reply? I cannot think that your father would have wished you to tramp around the shops of Medchester looking for employment.'

I thanked him most gratefully and for the rest of that week and most of the week after I heard no more about the matter. I packed my father's books together and offered them to the bookshops from which he had bought them. In the end I disposed of the lot for the princely sum of thirty shillings, keeping only two of them for myself. I kept them in his memory and also because they were the only two which my limited intelligence could fully understand and appreciate.

For no very good reason I revisited all the places I had ever been to with my father, and when I did so it seemed that he was with me still, making the past live again as only he could. As the days crept by and the lawyer did not send for me I thought that the news from the north must be bad and that the Lytton family considered me unsuitable.

At last, however, a boy messenger arrived at my lodgings to inform me that the lawyer required my presence once more in his office and, as I sat before him on the edge of my chair, my hands clenched tight in my lap, I felt some of my anxiety leave me. The letter before him ran into several pages and after he had read it through again his eyes twinkled at me over his spectacles.

'This is Mr Thorn Lytton's reply to my letter, my dear, and I fear I had mistakenly thought the poor lady requiring companionship was elderly. She is not; indeed, she is Mr Lytton's wife, not his mother, and is barely over thirty years of age.'

My eyes opened wide, registering the shocked surprise I felt, and he looked at me for a long moment without speaking, his eyes shrewd but kind.

'I see from your expression that you are shocked, and it is indeed sad that one so young should suffer from such a malady, but your anxiety tempts me to believe that you know this lady. Could that be so?'

'No, I do not know her, but I think I may have seen her. She was young and very beautiful – so lovely in fact that I have never forgotten her.'

'Then that makes it doubly sad,' he said, and his eyes returned to the letter before him.

Satisfied, he looked up again and, placing his hands together with his elbows on the desk before him, he said, 'Well, Mr Lytton has suggested that you go to them for a trial period of three months. When I wrote to him I gave him a full picture of what your life has been, but I also told him that you were a sensible and level-headed young woman. I said that although you had led a somewhat Bohemian existence with your father, your aunts had had a most steadying influence on your early life. The outcome is that he wishes you to travel to Gleave on Tuesday week on the afternoon train from Medchester, and he also says that the train will be met.'

'I wonder if he will find me suitable?'

'It may be that you will not be happy in such a post. You are a vital, intelligent person and the companionship of one who is mentally sick will not compensate for the learned talk to which you have become accustomed. Nevertheless, my dear, the seventy pounds your father has left you will not stretch into a fortune and, if this post proves to be unsuitable, another must be found.'

He was right, of course. I was not sure if Mr Lytton would expect to be confronted by a bluestocking or a gypsy, but one thing was sure: I needed this post. It was up to me to convince Mr Thorn Lytton that any trust he placed in me would not be misplaced.

I was brought back into the present by the change of the road surface under the carriage wheels, and the sudden lurch as the horse pulled the carriage to the left. I rubbed the windows with my gloves in an effort to see through them and was surprised to see that the moon was up. We were travelling along a driveway surrounded by parkland blanketed in snow, and I realized at once that the lurch I had experienced was caused by our entry through the iron gates leading towards Milverton.

At each side of the road grew rhododendron bushes, now

18

heavy with soft snow, but I remembered them well in their showy flowering of red and purple. The sight of them sent my mind hurrying back across the years again and I gave myself up to that summer long ago when I, a terrified young girl in a starched white apron, my heavy, fair pigtails flying, had run down this same driveway for dear life, pursued by the pounding hooves of two horses and the high, silvery laughter of the girl who rode one of them.

It seems to me now that I was always the ringleader when it came to boldness and daring during those summers of my childhood. To the other children of the village I was like a being from another world who descended upon them at varying intervals, leaving just as suddenly when my father took it into his head to remember me. My childhood playmates were usually the sons and daughters of farmers or tradesmen, although occasionally we were honoured by the company of the doctor's son and the vicar's two daughters. Even in this exalted company, however, I was the one who could talk to them of London, and of other cities in more exotic lands.

It had been the end of the summer and the men were out in the fields gathering in the harvest. Soon for some of us the little schoolroom would again open its doors, but all of us were intent on enjoying every golden day of what was left of the summer holidays. As long as the warm sun lingered we were out in the fields surrounding Gleave. We armed ourselves with water-filled jamjars held by impro-vised handles made out of string, butterfly nets and hampers packed by loving hands, and the fields rang with our laughter. To a few of us the end of the summer would herald the end of our childhood; to me, it brought nearer the time when I would join my father and travel with him to Persia in the autumn. Meanwhile, we fished in the streams and romped in the meadows separated from Milverton's parkland by a stone wall on which the ivy clung, and now that I am returning to Milverton as a grown woman the memory of one day stands out clear and sharp.

I sat with a line of village children upon that stone wall looking with unabashed curiosity at the house on its mound behind the trees. It seemed to me then that Milverton had not been built by human hands but had grown year by year as the trees grew, as much a part of the wild rugged landscape as the moors themselves and the stone crags from whose stone the house had been built. Its tall, narrow chimneys grew upwards against the sky and from where we sat the late afternoon sunlight shone through the mullioned windows so that the rooms behind them appeared to be on fire. We speculated amongst ourselves as to whether we should be seen if we ventured beyond the wall to hunt for conkers in the woodland or even to look at the swans paddling majestically in the shallows of the mere. That day, however, Elliot Cliffe, the doctor's son, was with us and, in his grave, studious fashion, he advised us against doing anything so foolish.

One of the boys, the blacksmith's son to be exact, tossed our ball over the wall so that it rolled down the driveway, gathering momentum as it careered downhill, then he dared me to chase after it.

If it had been any other boy I would have hesitated, but this boy was fond of calling me names, accusing me of inventing my adventures, imitating my non-country accent and when I fought with him, as I often did, he said my father was probably in some sort of trouble otherwise he would have me to live with him. Once I grew older I knew that the villagers talked. My two aunts were well respected in the community but they could not understand the strange child they had to live with them from time to time. Fathers worked on the land or were in trade, and they lived at home. To the people who would live and die in Gleave it was as simple as that. Anyway, to cut a long story short, I jumped down from the wall and ran swiftly along the drive in the direction of the errant ball. I was almost upon it when I heard the sound of pounding hoofbeats behind me and with quaking limbs and a wildly beating heart I took to my heels and ran, flinging myself after the ball, which had disappeared into the rhododendron bushes seconds before.

I peeped out through the branches, miserably aware of my soiled pinafore and the branches tangled in my hair. Standing guard outside my shelter were two enormous hunters and I was aware of laughter – the deep, amused laughter of a man and the light, gay laughter of a woman. I poked my head out through the branches and met the eyes of the man, eyes that were dark, laughing in a brown, handsome face and I knew that this was Mr Thorn Lytton, the eldest of the Milverton sons. He sat his horse with easy grace, and he was tall in the saddle and very slender. He wore a riding jacket but his head was bare and his dark hair shone like a raven's wing in the sunlight. I removed my gaze from him to the girl at his side and she too was dark, as dark as he, and I gazed in open admiration at her beauty. I knew that her name was Caprice, a strangely beautiful and exciting name.

She wore her hair loose so that it fell on to her shoulders with the look of a ripened plum against the rich, red velvet of her riding habit. Her eyes were merry as they met mine and they were the most beautiful, unusual eyes I have ever seen. They were violet, like the pansies in the flowerbeds in front of our cottage, or like the violets we gathered in the woodlands in the springtime, and her mouth laughed over small, even, white teeth.

I picked up the ball and dodged through the bush, scratching my arms and legs and tearing my dress. I dropped the ball and took to my heels, but the next moment I heard footsteps running after me and with a terrified sob I stumbled and fell upon the driveway. Bodily I was lifted to my feet and for the second time I looked into the man's eyes, this time anxious, concerned, as he held out the ball for me to take. I snatched it from him and ran sobbing through a small door let into the wall, and the light, silvery laughter of the girl followed me all the way back to my companions.

I was the heroine of the hour but my brief glory did not save me from a good spanking or being sent to bed early without supper. Now it appeared that I was to see this lady again, for I had no doubt that the beauty of the violet eyes was now Mrs Thorn Lytton.

2

I rubbed the windows again and peered through them. We were skirting the lake before taking the gently sloping incline which led to the house. It was dark in the carriage and I had no idea if I was presentable enough to appear before my new employer. I settled my felt hat at what I hoped was a decent angle and checked that my hair was tidy.

Old George gave a gutteral command to the horse, whose feet slithered to a halt on the wide drive outside the house, and after a few moments it dawned upon me that I could expect no assistance in opening the carriage door. I managed it with difficulty because the lock was stiff and hurt my fingers, but in the end the wind caught hold of the door and whipped it from my grasp so suddenly that I almost fell headlong on to the driveway. The coachman was struggling with my trunk so I joined him to render whatever assistance I was able. He waved me aside impatiently however, and my poor old trunk fell with a dismal thud on to the drive. He tugged and pulled it towards the door where he finally left it standing on its side beside my other case which had fallen out of the carriage with me. Hesitantly I asked how much I owed him for the journey.

'It's nowt,' he answered, 'Av'e bin paid.'

He turned on his heel abruptly and climbed back on to his driving seat; then, with a crack of the whip and a harsh word of command to the dejected old horse, they moved off into the night.

The snow had ceased and I looked curiously out across the terrace towards the gardens below. Giant, stone urns stood at regular intervals along the edge of the terrace, empty now but in the spring and summer no doubt gay with geraniums and other plants. The terrace steps led down to an Italian garden, the paths formal under their covering of light snow. Beyond, white-clad lawns and meadowland sloped down towards the tarn and the distant woodland, before the drive climbed upwards again towards the gates.

I stood for a few moments, hesitating to use the giant, brass knocker on the door; then, taking my courage in both hands, I raised it, bring it down so heavily that the noise seemed to echo with gloomy resonance through the whole of the great house beyond, and from the holly bushes which grew on either side of the door light powdery snow fell around my feet. I stepped back to look up at the windows of the house. The upper storeys were in total darkness but chinks of light showed through the heavy curtains drawn across the windows in a room to the left of the door.

I felt very nervous as I waited for what seemed an eternity before the sound of bolts being drawn back behind the heavy, oak door reached my ears. It swung back silently to reveal a tall, darkly-clad figure whose features I could not see because he stood against the light. He stepped aside, however, so that I might enter, and then I turned to look at him. As I have said, he was tall and rather portly. In his early fifties I judged but with scant hair and a long, somewhat gloomy, face.

I hurried to apologize for the lateness of my arrival, explaining with something of a rush that there had been snow on the line and the train had been delayed. He held up his hand to stop my flow of words but his voice was not unkind when he said, 'You are expected, miss. If you will leave your small case there I will have your trunk brought in and they will be taken to your room. Mr Lytton would like you to wait in the library for him.'

But, just as he was about to open a door on the left of the hall, another door across the hall was flung open and a man's voice called, 'Is that you Bamber? If the young lady has arrived bring her in here.'

The room into which he led me was brightly lit after the hall, and adding to the glow was a roaring log fire burning in the hearth. Despite the brightness, however, I was conscious that before my arrival heated words had been spoken in that room and an atmosphere of anger, elusive

23

and intangible, still lingered. I have always been sensitive to atmosphere and the atmosphere in this room was charged with perplexities.

A tall, slender man was standing on the hearthrug. He was in black evening dress with lace ruffles at his throat, but in an instant I knew him for the man who had retrieved my wretched ball with teasing banter years before. His hair was still black, but at his temples silver had appeared, lending a certain distinction to his air of handsome devilry. His dark, piercing eyes appraised me now, whereas on that day long ago they had been filled with laughter. He was bronzed, as though by suns other than those of the north country, and about his tall, whipcord figure there was an easy grace. I did not have time to look at the other people in the room because he addressed me immediately and, if his voice was uncompromising, I realized afterwards that it was not because of me, but because of whatever had happened before I arrived.

'I regret, Miss McAllister, that my own coachman was unable to meet you and that I had to rely upon the dubious qualities of old George. I am Mr Thorn Lytton. Allow me to introduce other members of my family.'

He held out his arm and I walked forward towards the two women sitting on the velvet couch on the left side of the fireplace.

They were both in evening dress, and both lovely in their own fashion. The younger one I recognized as the daughter of the house, for I had seen her many times riding through the village on her pony or with her mother in her carriage. Even in those days I had thought her spoiled and wilful but her promise of beauty to come had been fulfilled. She wore her mahogany-coloured hair taken back and then allowed to fall in heavy ringlets on to her shoulders, and her eyes were a deep, intense blue in her magnolia skin. The other woman was only slightly older but her flame-coloured hair was worn piled on her small, regal head, and the jade green satin of her gown complemented to perfection her pale delicate skin.

'This is my sister-in-law, Mrs Judith Lytton, my brother Stephen's wife, and my sister Rowena, Mrs Allington.'

I murmured a greeting and was in turn favoured with a

brief smile from Mrs Lytton and a cool nod of the head from Mrs Allington. Then Mr Lytton turned towards the two men standing behind a couch, identical to the one on which the two ladies sat but on the opposite side of the fireplace.

'My brother Stephen,' he said, 'and this is Mr Allington, my sister Rowena's husband.

Mr Stephen held out his hand and took mine in a brief but friendly grip. Mr Allington, however, stared coolly at me, and I decided at once that I did not like him. He was tall and thin, with a fair, insipid face and cold, blue eyes which, despite myself, reminded me of the eyes of a fish. Beside him the two Lytton brothers looked the picture of robust health and I wondered what had persuaded the gay and beautiful Rowena to take such a man for a husband.

Mr Thorn pulled a cord beside the fireplace and almost immediately the manservant returned.

'This is Bamber, my butler, and I must ask you now to go with him to the library where I will join you presently. We have almost concluded our family business, but there is a fire in the library and Bamber will see that a tray with some food is taken in to you.'

The library was a lofty room lined from floor to ceiling with books of all shapes and sizes. There were platforms and steps leading up to the shelves, but my eyes were immediately drawn to the log fire in the grate and the easy chair set before it. The butler pointed towards it but as I approached it I became aware that a huge dog had risen from his place on the hearthrug and stood menacingly with a growl in his throat.

'Down Laird,' the butler said sternly, whereupon the great creature sank on to his haunches but continued to eye me suspiciously.

'Do not be afraid of him, Miss, he will not harm you. He belongs to the master and no doubt he is tired of waiting for him.

I had never seen a dog like this one. The dogs of my experience were of small to average size, with merry eyes and wagging tails, not at all like this grey, gaunt creature with the long nose of a greyhound and the stature of a pony.

'What sort of a dog is he?' I asked in dismay.

'He's a Scottish deerhound, miss. I don't know of any other in these parts but when you get used to him you'll find he's not a bad old fellow.'

Laird and I sat eying each other and I volunteered a trembling, 'Hello doggie. Good boy.' I was rewarded by a small thump of his tail upon the rug. Encouraged I held out my hand and he stretched forward his huge head. After a few tentative sniffs at my fingers he put out his tongue and licked them. I called him to my side and he came willingly, allowing me to pat his head and stroke the coarse hair along his neck. He looked up eagerly when the door opened but when he saw that it was not his master he walked over towards the desk and flopped down upon the carpet again. A plump, matronly woman entered, bearing a tray, and I realized that I was extremely hungry, for I had not eaten since before noon. The huge, silver tray carried a silver tea service, a pile of thin, freshly cut sandwiches and a covered dish containing hot muffins dripping with butter. The woman smiled at me and I wondered if she might be the butler's wife. She placed the tray on a table beside the fire and left me to get on with my meal.

I needed no formal invitation, nor did I finish until every crumb was eaten. I had been brought up in the tradition that it was not ladylike to eat up every morsel, and I could almost hear Aunt Maud's genteel accents dictating that a small amount should always be left upon my plate so that I would in no way be thought of as a glutton. So much for Aunt Maud.

The dog was stretched out at full length upon the carpet, and curiously I looked round the lofty room, thinking how sombre the house seemed when compared with the last time I had seen it. It had not been snowing on that night, but the trees in the parkland had been white with frost and so, too, had the lawns which sloped down to the mere.

It was Christmas Eve, the last time I stayed with my aunts in Gleave. My father was in the Middle East and was not expected home until the New Year. I arrived to find that we had been invited to the vicar's house to take tea with them, and then we were all to attend the annual Christmas Eve party which took place in the village hall next to the church.

We played all the usual party games while the grown-ups sat around and talked, or drank fruit punch from a giant bowl near the door. I revelled in the games because I had always been a somewhat solitary child and had never stayed in any place long enough to meet other children apart from the times I spent with my father's sisters.

I was delighted when Elliot, the doctor's son, joined us. I liked Elliot the best of all the children I met in Gleave. I considered him more intelligent than the others which was not surprising when one considered his superior education. He informed me that his parents had been invited to attend the Christmas Eve Ball at Milverton. I do not know what devilry overcame me, but I persuaded him, against all his better judgement, to take me over to Milverton to spy on the festivities going on there. The village hall was crowded and I convinced him that we would not be missed. With glee I helped Elliot saddle his pony, which bore us both on the three-mile journey to Milverton.

We dared not ride the pony up the drive, for carriages were arriving all the time, so we had to ride him across the fields and approach Milverton from the back of the house. We found an old, dead tree to tie him to, then we crept along the stone wall until we found a place where the wall had crumbled and we could clamber over it. I am afraid I gave little thought to my scuffed shoes or to the state of my new, blue, velvet dress.

It was cold, but the exhilaration of our ride and our excitement had brought a sparkle to our eyes, and our rapid breathing hung like rainbow mist on the frosty air. We stood hiding in the shrubbery to watch the guests arrive. They came in handsome carriages pulled by fine, spirited horses, some of them from as far away as Feltham; and Elliot informed me that these people were gentry, county people, as well as professional men and magistrates. The men wore sombre evening dress but the women sparkled with jewels and wore beautiful dresses of satin and chiffon.

At last it seemed that all the guests had arrived and the great doors were shut. That was our signal to creep closer to the house and I, for one, caught my breath at the delights we could see through the downstairs windows. The rooms were a blaze of light from glass chandeliers and at the top of the first flight of shallow stairs which ran from the hall a giant Christmas tree glittered with candles and decorations. The women had discarded their cloaks and the light fell upon bare, creamy shoulders making the jewels they wore sparkle with a thousand lights. My eyes looked for the girl I had seen with Mr Lytton, whose violet eyes I had never forgotten and whose silvery laughter haunted my girlish dreams.

I was still a child in my emotions. I was too young to look upon men as anything other than father figures, or upon the younger ones as friends or playmates – nothing more – but the girl I had seen riding her horse along the driveway on that summer's afternoon two years before had captured my imagination as no other creature had ever done. To me she was the fairy princess of all my dreams. Her face had haunted my days and, standing outside the windows of Milverton with the sharp night frost sparkling on the branches of the trees surrounding us, I had no thoughts for the cold as my eyes scanned the throng for a sight of my idol.

At last I saw her and my heart lurched in my breast. She was running lightly down the stairs, surrounded by a crowd of laughing young men and, if I had thought her beautiful in her rich red riding habit, she was even more so now. Her blue-black hair was dressed so that its shining strands fell over one shoulder and she was wearing a white satin dress. It fell away from her shoulders and the narrow waist of the dress billowed out into a swirling skirt. There were violets at the waist of her gown and in her hands she carried her dancing card which the men were endeavouring to take from her. She twirled and danced in the hall as one after the other they tried to catch her; then Mr Thorn came down the staircase and in the midst of much laughter he spun her away from them into the waltz.

I looked at Elliot with dazzled eyes. It had been worth the ride over the moors, worth all the displeasure I would encounter if we had been missed at the village hall. Elliot was not looking at me, he was busy scanning the dancers as he searched for his mother and father amongst them. I wondered if he would know anything about the girl, who

28

she was, where she lived, or if one day soon she would marry Mr Thorn. I made up my mind that before long I would ask Elliot to tell me all that he knew about her.

I reached out to touch his arm, but just then he caught sight of his parents dancing together in the hall. He decided to climb upon the window ledge to see them better, but his shoes slipped on the icy surface and the next moment he fell with an almighty clatter against the window, pulling me down on the ground beside him. Almost immediately lights shone out into the night from the front door and we were surrounded by a crowd of astonished men.

We were escorted ignominiously into the hall and the next moment Elliot's father was there, eying us sternly, humourlessly. His mother was close to tears and I heard her whispered words to him, 'Don't be too hard on him, dear.' Then she said to another woman standing beside her, 'He has never done anything like this before. I can only think it is that strange child who put him up to it.'

My new dress was dirtied where I had fallen on to the soil outside the window, my hair ribbon had come awry so that my hair fell around my face in a tangled mess, and my light dancing shoes were scuffed and cut along the sides. Elliot was quiet, not daring to speak, but my eyes were filled with stormy tears. I longed to take a good hefty kick at whoever was holding me but, just as I decided to try to free myself from that firm hold, Mr Thorn arrived.

'Bring the children into the blue drawing room,' he said. 'They can have something to eat then they can be returned to the village hall.'

He was laughing good humouredly, and in the face of his laughter the others found something to laugh at also in our escapade.

We were taken into a small drawing room somewhere at the back of the house and they sat us in front of the fire. By this time we were both shivering, whether through fear or because at last the cold had overcome our excitement I do not know, but we were handed small glasses of punch, strong enough to make our eyes water.

Elliot was very quiet and there was a worried look on his face, but I looked around me with interest and met Mr Thorn's amused dark eyes twinkling at me from his great height. Then I had forgotten him, for she was there, and after one look at me she said, 'Why, it's you again! Thorn, you must remember this child, she's the little girl you caught running along the drive in search of her ball in the summer,' and she laughed gaily, her red lips curving enchantingly over her small, even, white teeth.

Mr Thorn, however, was looking at Elliot, who by this time was almost in tears. He leaned forward and patted his shoulder.

'Don't worry, Elliot,' he said kindly, 'I will speak to your father. I am sure that by this time your escapade has become the entertainment of the evening.' With that he left us, but the girl remained sitting opposite us, perched unceremoniously on the arm of a large velvet chair.

'Who are you?' she asked curiously. 'Are you staying with Elliot's parents?'

'No. I am staying with my aunts in Gleave.'

'Do I know them?'

'I don't think so. They are Aunt Maud and Aunt Beatrice McAllister. They live at the last stone cottage on the hill as you leave the village.'

'I know the cottage. It is a dear little cottage with chintz curtains at the windows and a bright green door. Have you no parents that you stay with your aunts at Christmas time?'

'My mother is dead, but I have a father. He is abroad and I shall not see him until the spring.'

'I, too, have a father who is abroad and I shall not see him for over a year. My father is in the Indian army and is stationed at Lahore. Do you know where that is?'

'Yes, it is in India.'

'Perhaps your father, too, is in the army? That is why you do not see him very often?'

'No. My father finds things. He digs for them.'

Her voice went off into peals of laughter and she called out to Mr Thorn who had just returned to the room, 'Darling, listen to this enchanting child. Her father finds things, he digs for them. Is he, then, a miner?'

I looked at her with some degree of scorn. 'No, he finds treasures in old cities. Things that have been lost for thousands and thousands of years. He is a professor of archaeology.'

Her face lost some of its merriment as she said, 'You must pardon my ignorance my dear, I had not realized he was so grand.

I felt suddenly contrite, feeling perhaps that I had hurt her in some way and I hurried to say, 'It is natural you should think he was a miner when I told you he dug for things. He doesn't make much money, no more than a miner or one who is in the army.'

Both she and Mr Thorn laughed heartily and he put his arm around her shoulders, looking down into her face with such an expression of love that my heart ached to see it.

'Come, my darling, I must return to my guests and there are at least twenty men impatient to dance with you. I have had words with your father, Elliot, and I don't think you need worry any more about it. As for you, young lady, the next time you come to Milverton I would be obliged if you would knock on the front door.'

Well, now I had knocked on the front door, but I was quite sure he had long since forgotten the incident which happened almost twelve years ago. He had changed little except for the wings of silver hair at his temples, but I had become a woman.

It was warm in the library and the food and drink I had consumed had made me drowsy. I must have fallen fast asleep because the clatter of a log falling on to the hearth woke me and I opened my eyes to find that Mr Lytton sitting opposite me eying me with an expression I found hard to read. I was embarrassed, and felt the warm blood rising into my cheeks as I struggled to sit up and retain some sort of dignity in the enormous chair.

'Oh, sir,' I said nervously, 'I am sorry you had to find me asleep. It must surely have been the warmth after the coldness of the night and the length of my journey.'

'I came in earlier, Miss McAllister, but when you were sleeping I left you to sleep on. It is now well after midnight so that might give you some indication of how long you have been here.'

Dear God, I thought, what a disastrous start to my new employment as a companion, to sleep so soundly that people could come and go without awakening me. I tried to find words to express my regret but he brushed them aside as of no consequence.

'Tell me,' he asked, 'why does a young woman like yourself wish to bury herself away in this great house in the middle of nowhere as companion to one who will know her no better on her departure than she will on her arrival?'

My eyes opened wide at this strange beginning to our interview, and I wondered if he was trying to discourage me from continuing with the appointment. I decided to be completely honest.

'I am alone in the world apart from my two elderly aunts and I am not their responsibility,' I said, in a voice which I hoped appeared grown-up and sensible. 'My father was a clever and well-educated man, but he cared little for money and certainly never made any. He has left me the sum of seventy pounds, which I must confess was a surprise to me. I had expected him to leave me in debt.'

I could not be sure, but I believe his mouth twitched at the corners to hide his laughter. He looked down quickly at a letter he was holding in his hands and when he looked up again his face was composed into its customary severity.

'I see from this letter that your father was a noted archaeologist. It is true such men do not amass great fortunes, yet they seem curiously content with what little they can salvage from the past. I fear your seventy pounds will not take you far, although it could bring you in a small income if properly invested. If you care to talk to me again about it, I could perhaps advise you on where to place it.'

'Oh, that would indeed be kind, sir. I know nothing about such matters and naturally I would like it to earn a little interest for me. I am little better than my father in money matters.'

'I see that you have travelled abroad with him. Do I take it that you also are interested in lost civilizations?'

'I am not a scholar as my father was but his enthusiasm was contagious and it is perhaps natural that I caught some of his passion for ancient lands and the people who lived in them. My education, as I think Mr Runson pointed out to you, took place here in the village school for a short time, and then at English schools run by nuns in whatever country we happened to be living in at the time. Mostly in Egypt and Persia.'

'You speak of such countries as other people speak of villages beyond the fells, Miss McAllister. One day, when we have more time, we might talk together again on the past which interests us both.'

I felt pleased with his words and he sat for a long time without speaking, the solicitor's letter lying in front of him, his fingers playing idly with the pen in his hand. I found myself studying his features. He was very handsome in a dark, saturnine way and I marvelled to myself that once I had only been aware of the beauty and glamour of the girl and had ignored the masculine appeal of the man. That, I supposed was because I was little more than a child. Now I was a woman who looked at the man with a new awareness.

At last he raised his head and, fixing me with his dark, piercing eyes, he said, 'No doubt you will wish to know something of the complexities of the task facing you? Your father's lawyer says you are a level-headed girl who has weathered the storm of your father's preoccupation with the past with commendable fortitude. He considered you an ideal person to undertake the duties of this post, but before you make up your mind I want you to give the matter a little thought. We are a long way from civilization. Gleave is only a small village, largely a farming community, and the nearest town is Feltham some twenty-five miles away. He tells me that you had connections in the village when you were a child but I can tell you, Miss McAllister, the simple pleasures of childhood are a long way removed from those of adult life. There are only two trains to Feltham each week from Gleave and one to Medchester. To amuse you on the other days there are only the few shops along the village street and the fells to wander upon. Do you ride at all?'

'I am not very good. I had a few riding lessons in Egypt because the site was a fair distance from the nearest village, but the horse I rode was old and docile and I preferred our old donkey or even one of the camels owned by the Arab overseer.'

'Well, if you wish to practise your horsemanship, there are horses in the stables, one no doubt with a temperament to match your skill. There is also the pony and trap for driving into the village. Companionship, I fear, will be limited, for the nurse who looks after my mother is unhappy in these parts and is anxious to return to a position nearer London, nor shall I expect you to look upon my wife as a fitting companion.'

'But I thought, Mr Lytton, that I was supposed to be a companion for your wife.'

'Yes. A companion for my wife, not the reverse.'

I thought he seemed strangely ill at ease for he seemed reluctant to continue the conversation. At last, more by way of breaking the silence than to satisfy my curiosity, I said, 'It seems strange, sir, that you ask me to think about the position offered when I understood from Mr Runson that the position was mine for a trial period and then we would both make up our minds.'

He smiled a little and I felt that I had perhaps been presumptuous in the way I had worded my supposition.

That was before I had seen you. You are young, vital and intelligent, a woman who has seen something of the world even though you have not been blessed with a great deal of money. My wife is not as you or I, or indeed as any other person in this household. She is upset by small things, and the loss of a companion she had come to rely upon could be a traumatic experience for her and might easily cancel out any small improvement in her condition.'

'I understand that, Mr Lytton, but I can only repeat that I have my living to earn and have no home to call my own. I am not a child, and if I make up my mind to care for your wife I shall do so to the very best of my ability.'

I felt that my words were stilted and slightly pompous, and he was looking at me very keenly out of those dark, sombre eyes of his. He seemed satisfied, however, either with my words or with the sincerity with which I spoke them. I was startled now as he reached out a hand and took hold of the amulet I was wearing around my neck.

'That is a strange ornament you are wearing. I noticed it earlier in the drawing room when you undid the buttons on your coat. It is Egyptian, is it not?'

He had risen from his chair and stood over me, holding the amulet lightly in the palm of his hand. I was very conscious of the faint smell of cigar smoke on his fingers and the elusive scent of good soap. There was also a strange magnetism about this man, a steely strength like the graceful unleashed power of a big cat.

'The God Horus,' he mused, 'fashioned in gold and lapis lazuli, with the body of a hawk and perfectly matched sapphires for his eyes. This is a valuable bauble, Miss McAllister, but I had thought all such finds were to be handed over to the authorities at the Cairo Museum.'

I was quick to take offence, for my father had always been scrupulously honest in handing over everything he found, whether paltry or of value. His eyes were watching me closely with a certain degree of amusement for I was conscious that my eyes flashed angrily and that there was heightened colour in my cheeks.

'I came by this bauble, as you call it most honestly, Mr Lytton. Pasha Ahmed Saheed, who financed the last expedition my father worked with, gave it to me. He said it was to be my reward for all the hot, dusty days and long, cold nights I had spent endeavouring to bring a little comfort into the lives of men who had largely forgotten my existence. Perhaps I have no right to the amulet, but he was a kind man; he also said the God Horus would protect me from the terrors of the night and the ills which could beset me by day.'

He smiled down at me, his slow cynical smile, a smile which I suddenly found to be singularly sweet.

'If old gods hold on to their powers it would appear you come to Milverton well protected and in need of no warnings from a mere mortal.'

'Warnings?'

He laughed a little. 'Well, as you have already seen, the moors are dismal and unwelcoming, and this old house is not without its tales of restless spirits.'

He laid the amulet back against my breast and the light touch of his hand against the thin material of my blouse brought the warm blood into my cheeks and into his eyes a sardonic look that I recoiled from it. He turned abruptly away and walked over to the long windows, pulling the curtains back so that I too could see outside from where I was sitting. It was still snowing.

'It will be thick in the morning if this keeps up,' he said. 'Come I will show you to your room. You will find that a fire has been lit. I have ordered that on your first morning breakfast is to be served in your room and perhaps later in the day we can talk again.'

'When may I meet your wife, sir?'

'First familiarize yourself with the house and grounds, then we will talk again about when you may meet my wife.'

He was standing beside the door, holding it open so that I might pass out into the hall before him. He then lit the candles in two identical candelabras. They were of silver, beautifully chased and very heavy, as I soon found out when he placed one of them in my hands.

The great dog had followed us out into the hall, but at a word from his master he lay down at the bottom of the steps, his massive head resting upon his paws, his long tail spread out behind him.

'You will find that your trunk and your case have been taken to your room. If there is anything else you want, ask one of the servants for it in the morning.'

'I may make requests of the servants?'

'Certainly. You are an employee, not a servant. There is a difference.'

Together we mounted the wide, shallow staircase which led up from the centre of the hall to the first landing where it branched off on either side. We held our candelabras aloft and the glow played on suits of armour and over the warm, rich red carpet on the stairs. At the top of the first flight I caught my breath at the portrait which covered the wall from the floor to the ceiling above and I paused, holding my candelabra on high so that I could see the portrait better. He, too, had paused on the first step of the next flight and was looking down at me gravely.

The portrait was of a woman, but a woman barely out of girlhood. She was sitting on a grassy knoll in a gown of pale green voile sprigged with embroidered sprays of white heather, and on her head was a large, white hat caught under the chin with streamers of pale green ribbon. The hat was decorated with a wreath of white daisies and she played with a daisy chain on her lap. Her face was a pale, perfect oval, her lips and cheeks coloured faintly in soft

36

rose. The tender wisps of hair which had escaped from under her hat showed that it was silver-fair, not dull-gold like my own hair, but pale, like the soft sand which the tide never reaches. It was a lovely face, like the face of a child, innocent and untouched. I looked at him with a question in my eyes.

'My wife, Elsa,' he said simply.

My astonishment was so profound that I was unable to disguise it and, as I looked into his haughty, uncompromising face, I became so confused that I tried to cover my embarrassment by making fatuous statements about the beauty of the portrait.

His voice was cold as he said, 'You are surprised, Miss McAllister. Yet surely you must know that an affliction of the mind need not be reflected upon the face? I can assure you the beauty of my wife's face remains unchanged.'

How could I tell him that hers was not the face I had expected to see, that the portrait had come as such a shock that it had left me with a score of questions unanswered? He was waiting for me to say something, however, and humbly I said, 'Please forgive me Mr Lytton, I have too much imagination and little experience in hiding it. I had formed a picture in my mind of Mrs Lytton and was surprised to find it totally unlike her, that is all.'

He acknowledged my explanation by the merest inclination of his head, then said, 'I try not to let my imagination run away with me, but even so your astonishment interests me. Tell me now how you had pictured my wife.'

Miserably I looked down upon the ground and mumbled my reply. 'I had thought she would be dark, dark and gay.'

For what seemed an eternity there was silence as I continued to look down upon the carpet, with the light from our candles flickering fitfully around us, then in a calm, flat voice he said, 'You should learn not to put too much faith in your imagination, Miss McAllister, if you are to avoid being astounded each time it lets you down.'

'Your wife is very beautiful. It makes it doubly sad that she is unwell.'

I looked into his eyes and was appalled at the stark misery I surprised there. Then in a voice made suddenly angry he said, 'Yes she is very beautiful, my lost unhappy wife. Curb your imagination Miss McAllister or you open your heart and your mind to the tricks this old house can play upon you.'

Swiftly he turned and walked up the stairs ahead of me; I had to hurry to keep pace with him.

The corridors of the house were long and dark, and the light from our candles played eerily over portraits of men and women long dead. Many of the men were in uniforms no longer worn and belonging to other times and old wars, but some of the women were beautiful in their silks and satins, their gowns cut low to reveal pink flesh made warm again by the candlelight. We turned at last into a smaller, narrower corridor and he stopped and opened the first door on our right. He stood to one side to allow me to pass in front of him and my eyes lit up at the firelight playing on rose-patterned chintz curtains and bedspread, and on the soft bloom of polished mahogany.

'Oh, but this is charming!' I exclaimed with delight. 'I had not expected anything like this.'

'You expected to be put away on the top floor in an attic, with bare boards on the floor and bars across the windows?'

He was teasing me, which I found strangely troubling.

'Sleep well, Miss McAllister,' he said, smiling. 'You have another name, I know, but at the moment I must confess I cannot remember it.'

'I was christened Carlotta after my grandmother, but with McAllister it is too much. My father's sisters call me Lottie, but my father always called me Carla. I preferred his abbreviation of my name.'

He smiled again but made no comment. Then he closed the door and left me alone.

I was delighted with my room and I could not resist spinning round on the soles of my feet with the same excitement I greeted my birthday mornings in the days of my childhood. I undressed before the fire, ecstatically curling up my toes in the thick, white, skin rug. The water in the tall pitcher was still warm and a new tablet of faintly perfumed soap had been provided as well as soft, white towels with which to dry myself.

I could not help but compare this room with the one I had left in London. It had been clean but spartanly furnished.

The wallpaper had been dreary and dark, the sun something only to be glimpsed across the rooftops. The linoleum upon the floor had been faded and was rotten from too much washing in hot water lavishly laced with disinfectant. I had thought I would never rid my clothes of the smell of mothballs from the large, cavernous wardrobe or my bones from the aches caused by the sinking springs on the narrow bed.

I opened up my small case and took out my nightgown. My dressing gown was still in the trunk and this I decided to leave until the morning. The room was deliciously warm and for a long moment I knelt on the rug before the fire, my arms extended luxuriously towards the coals. Then I placed my candelabra on the small table beside the bed. I felt very tired. It had been a long day and my eyes felt heavy and prickly with fatigue. I leaned over to blow out the candles. Only the dying embers in the firegrate glowed dully in the darkened room and wearily I gave myself up to sleep.

3

I do not know what aroused me but suddenly I was wide awake, my eyes staring into the thick darkness of the room, my ears straining to hear any slight sound, but the house was still. The room felt cold. Probably the fire had been out for hours and no chink of light from outside showed through the thick curtains drawn against the windows. I had no idea how long I had been sleeping but now that I was awake my dreams came back to me in a jumbled mass of improbabilities. Of one thing I was sure, no dream had been responsible for my racing heart and the cold chill of fear which lay over my body.

How is it possible, I wondered, to distinguish between dreams and reality? I was convinced I had heard voices, voices raised in anger and then light, silvery laughter. Of course it was nonsense. Such happenings came from a vivid imagination and a mind made anxious by too many perplexities. I lay back against my pillows with my eyes closed, langorously comfortable, drifting again into pleasant slumber when I heard it again, and this time I sat bolt upright in my bed.

This was not a dream, nor was it a figment of that imagination which would supposedly one day do me a mischief. I could not tell from which direction the laughter had come, but I had heard it, and then a tune hummed airily in a woman's voice in the dark hours of the morning while the rest of the household slept. I wanted to go out into the corridors beyond, but my robe was still in my trunk and I could not be seen wandering about in my nightgown, however well it covered me, besides I did not yet know the layout of the house and it would be easy to get lost within its vastness.

With trembling hands I fumbled on the bedside table for the matches, spilling several of them on to the table top before I was able to light the candles. The room looked nothing like as inviting as it had on the evening before, when the firelight played on the drapes and polished furniture. Now the empty grate loomed large and dark in the wall opposite my bed and the flickering light from the candles failed to penetrate into the dark corners of the ceiling.

The thick carpet felt cold under my bare feet but I was too impatient to hunt for the slippers I had carelessly kicked off the night before. I tiptoed over to the window, although there was no need for such caution. No footsteps of mine could possibly have been heard outside my room let alone in other rooms of the house. The curtains were of heavy, cotton chintz and I pulled them back to reveal a world of virginal whiteness and the sparkle of frost shimmering on the tendrils of virginia creeper which grew around my window.

My window overlooked a small garden and I could see now that this was not the end of the house. It appeared that my room was at the start of a short corridor. At the end of it the house moved on again at right angles joined by a corridor with tall windows in which the pale reflection of the moon gleamed weirdly. There were no lights in the windows of the old wing but I hastily blew out my candles in case some person stood behind those dark windows. I did not wish them to think that I was poking and prying into things which did not concern me.

Impatient with myself, I was about to turn away when I saw a light in one of the rooms of the darkened wing level with my own. It was moving slowly in my direction. Just for a moment I saw it, then it was gone. I waited with bated breath for it to return, my imagination running riot as usual, but when next the light appeared it was in the corridor with the lofty windows, its gleam sparkling and dancing on the small panes of glass and as I watched it it seemed to float and dance, twirling this way and that as though whoever carried it was waltzing through the corridor. Once again I was convinced I heard a woman's light laughter. Then the light went out, and I supposed that the night walker had reached the corridor outside my room. I waited for some sound that he or she was passing my door but heard nothing. Stumbling, I groped my way towards the bed, rubbing my thigh ruefully where it had caught the corner of the bedpost. No doubt there would be a purple bruise to show for it in the morning. I was wide awake now, watching the play of moonlight across the ceiling, shivering a little, for the bed I returned to felt cold.

I had thought that I would lie sleepless until the morning but I was wrong. Dreams invaded my slumber in a confused jumble and at one time I felt myself stumbling along a snow-covered railway track pursued by my companion of the train, then just as he reached out to snatch the amulet from around my throat the scene was replaced by another. Now I was dancing, whirling round and round to the music under chandeliers whose lights seemed to swirl and dance above me as I waltzed. Then a man stepped in front of me and took me into his arms. I could not see his face but I only knew that I was happy, happier than I have ever been in my entire life. As we neared the staircase I looked up and over his shoulder I saw that a girl stood watching us. She was leaning over the balustrade looking down upon us, a girl whose face was bright and beautiful as the morning, surrounded by dark, blue-black hair, and as we spun away from her her silvery laughter followed us down the length of the room and I woke up sharply to the cold light of a wintry dawn.

My next sleep was dreamless and I was brought back into the realms of reality by a soft knock upon the door of my room. I opened my eyes sleepily to see a maidservant entering the room carrying a fresh pitcher of water and I struggled to sit up so that she would know I was awake. She was young. A country girl, with dark hair and fresh, apple cheeks, and in answer to my smile she bobbed a little curtsey.

'I'll be bringing your breakfast, miss, now that you're awake,' she said.

'Oh, but I'll get up and dress, then perhaps you will show me where I am to take my meals.'

'I'm to serve breakfast in your room miss, Master's orders.'

She soon returned with my breakfast, and lit the fire. As I ate, the events of the night before came crowding back to me but in the cold light of day they no longer seemed sinister. Doubtless there was a logical explanation for the voices I had heard as well as for the light in the rooms opposite. I could think of no good reason why the candlelight should appear to be spinning and whirling along the corridor unless whoever was in there was dancing. That must have been an hallucination caused by fatigue.

Another knock upon the door interrupted my thoughts and this time the head which bobbed round the door wore a nurse's cap. Although the face was not pretty, it had a lively merry look.

'I heard you'd arrived,' she said. 'May I come in for a moment?'

'Please do.'

She turned and looked up and down the corridor before she came in, closing the door firmly behind her. She stood looking down at me until I said, 'I hope you won't mind if I finish my breakfast? Why don't you bring up a chair. I'm sorry there isn't another cup or you could have joined me in some tea.'

'Oh, that's all right, I had breakfast much earlier and I usually go down into the kitchens and have a cup of tea with cook mid-morning. My name is Westwell, Celia Westwell, I am Mrs Lytton's nurse – old Mrs Lytton, not the young one.'

'I am Carla McAllister,' I said, holding out my hand. I had hated it when my aunts called me Lottie and I was determined that from now on I would be Carla McAllister, the name my father had always used, a name which had somehow lent an enchantment to a singularly ordinary existence.

The girl raised her eyebrows and I laughed.

'My name is really Carlotta, but it is such a mouthful and although I was Lottie as a child I don't see why I should be saddled with it now.'

'I know how you feel,' she said sympathetically. 'I didn't know you had arrived until Nancy told me. It must have been quite late.'

'It was. The train was delayed because there was snow on the line. It looks as if it has stopped snowing now.'

'For the time being, but from the look of the sky out there I wouldn't be surprised if there is not more to come. Whatever made you come to a place like this to work?'

I looked at her in some surprise.

'I didn't have much choice.'

'Well, I hope you don't live to regret it,' she said with engaging candour. 'I handed in my notice on Monday so with a bit of luck I shall be leaving as soon as they find a replacement. I wouldn't like to leave them in the lurch, they've been very kind to me and the pay is good.'

'You don't come from these parts then?'

'No. I'm from the south. Mr Lytton's doctor got me through a private nursing home but I'm anxious to get back to London. I'm hoping to be married in the spring. Besides, I hate this desolate countryside; you will too when you've been here a bit longer.'

'Well, perhaps not. I spent a lot of time here as a child, so I am no stranger to it.'

By this time I had come to the conclusion that the nurse might prove to be a bit of a gossip, and I decided to take full advantage of her desire to talk.

'How is Mrs Lytton?' I asked. 'I remember seeing her in the village years ago, but of course she was quite well then.'

'She's getting on for seventy now and since her stroke keeps to her room all the time.'

'Can't she get about at all?'

'Oh yes, she can walk around her bedroom and into her sitting room next door. But she is unable to speak although she hears what is said to her.'

'Oh, poor lady. Will it ever come back do you think? Her speech, I mean?'

'It's doubtful after so long. At first the doctors thought there was a chance but I can't really see it myself. It's my view there should have been signs before now if she was ever going to speak again. Sometimes I get so frustrated I could go out into the gardens and scream my head off. I'm glad you've come, at least we can chat a little whenever we have the time.'

'Can you tell me a little about the young Mrs Lytton?'

'You mean Mr Thorn's wife?'

'Yes,' and I marvelled at the strange hint of fear in my

heart as I waited for her answer.

'Well, I've seen her, of course, although she doesn't often go into the downstairs rooms of the house.' I've seen her when Mr Thorn takes her out in the carriage and I helped to nurse her in the summer when she caught a virus and was ill for a time. She has her own maid, a girl she brought with her from her father's house. She is like a child, living in a child's world.'

'Are her rooms on the other side of the house?'

'Oh, no. They have a suite of rooms on the first floor on the front of the house. Beautiful rooms they are with every luxury, and her maid sleeps next door to her.'

'Is it possible to converse with her intelligently at all?'

'I shouldn't think so. I've nursed mental patients myself but she's unlike any other I have ever come across. She's sweet, so sweet it's like the sweetness of honey, but I once saw her pull the wings off a butterfly with an expression of such joy on her face I was sickened by it, but then poor lady she's not responsible for her actions any more.'

'How about the rest of the household? Do they visit her?'

'Oh, yes. Miss Rowena goes in to see her and Mrs Stephen. Mr Jeremy too when he's at home. He brings her presents, dolls and things, and you can hear them laughing all down the corridors. The old lady never sees her. She won't have her anywhere near her, but then no doubt it is her illness. People who have had strokes often suffer from strange fantasies.'

'Who sleeps in the other wing of the house? I had no idea it was so big.'

'Oh, that part of the house is shut off now, I think. I believe there is dry rot in some of the rooms and it is unsafe. The place is quite big enough without the extra wing – apparently it's not been used for years.'

The nurse rose to her feet as another knock sounded on the door, and a a tall, black-clad figure entered the room.

'I am Mrs Bamber, the housekeeper,' the newcomer informed me, 'I will send Nancy up to collect your breakfast things if you have finished with them. In the meantime I should get dressed, miss. Mr Thorn will see you in his study at eleven o'clock.'

She did not smile, but after a brief nod of her head went

out, closing the door firmly behind her. I had the distinct feeling that she disapproved of my talking to Celia.

The nurse's words about the young Mrs Lytton had left a nasty taste in my mouth and a feeling of foreboding in my heart. All of a sudden my earlier desire to stay at Milverton became less powerful. The sunlight had gone and it was snowing again with bigger flakes this time, and I looked out of my window upon a desolate landscape – a landscape which found a lonely echo in my private thoughts. I washed hurriedly in the water provided, now lukewarm, then I dressed quickly in front of the fire.

Squaring my shoulders, I marched out into the corridor and walked quickly towards the hall, not even pausing to look at the portraits which lined the walls. I did however pause at the head of the stairs which led down to the hall to look again at the portrait of Mrs Lytton, and now, without the glamour or the kindness of candlelight, I found that her face had a somewhat vapid look. The porcelain skin from which china-blue eyes stared out into the hall, the soft, silver-fair hair escaping from under the wide-brimmed hat, even the rosy lips with their gentle smile seemed to me to have a petulant air.

I heard brisk footsteps crossing the hall and I saw that Nancy was just about to enter the drawing room carrying a copper hod filled with coal. I called to her softly, 'Nancy, I am to go to the study. Where do I find it?'

She put the bucket down and came back to me wiping her soiled hands on her apron. 'The next door on the corridor, miss. Knock on the door and wait. I think the master already has a visitor.

I consulted my watch. It had been my mother's and I wore it round my neck on a heavy gold chain. Apart from the amulet I had worn the night before it was the only thing of value I possessed. It was five minutes to eleven, so I sauntered across the hall and down the corridor towards the study. A large log fire burned in the hall but through the long windows on each side of the front door I could see that the snow was coming down thick and fast and that the sky above was leaden. There were wet footprints in the hall as though some member of the household had already braved the elements.

As I approached the study door I heard voices, a woman's and a man's, and this time they spoke in anger. I was reluctant to stand outside the door in case I should be thought to be eavesdropping. On the other hand, where was I to go when the sound of their voices already echoed round the hall? Miserably, I stood back against the wall waiting for a lull in the proceedings so that I might knock on the door. There was exasperation in Mr Lytton's voice as he said, 'I will not have my arrangements disrupted again, Rowena, and I must ask you to make up your mind. Either you leave your husband and return to Gleave permanently, or you fulfil your wifely obligations and return to him. Your life could have been very different but it is now entirely what you have made it. You are no longer a child. You are a married woman and I am tired of your husband's arrivals and departures at times which inconvenience both myself and my servants. I have already had one scene with him this morning and I can assure you the sight of a man in tears is not a pretty one on an empty stomach.'

'I cannot go back to him permanently. He is weak and ineffectual. Besides, he is not interested in me as a wife, but merely to keep up appearances long enough to placate his uncle and make sure of the title and the family estates. I knew on my wedding night that our marriage was a sham, and if I took other lovers it was with his full approval.'

'Surely you had some indication of his peculiarities before you married him?'

'No, I had not. I was little more than a child and such peculiarities were not discussed by the girls at the finishing school you were careful to send me to.'

'With one broken engagement behind you, Rowena, and God knows how many discarded lovers, I cannot altogether believe you were ignorant about Allington's character. You desired the title which will one day be his and gave little thought to what your married life would be like, but you heard what he said. If his uncle has any inclination of what he is like, and that there is trouble between you because of it, he will disinherit him and name his younger brother in his place. If such a thing comes about, you will have wasted your life to no purpose. Think carefully, Rowena, you have the rest of the week to make up your mind. If you decide to leave him, then he does not come to this house again. If you decide to go back to him, then you must be ready to travel with him on Friday.'

There was silence and timidly I knocked on the door.

'Enter,' called Mr Lytton's voice, and I opened the door to find him sitting behind a large mahogany desk. Facing him was his sister, Mrs Allington. She turned round on my entry and threw me a look of the utmost disfavour.

'Come in, Miss McAllister, my sister is just leaving.'

At his words she tossed her head and flounced out of the room, slamming the door behind her. Her brother sighed and leaned back in his chair with his hands resting on the desk in front of him. He looked altogether different from the night before. Then, I had thought of him as a man of darkness in his sombre evening clothes, with his black hair and dark eyes. Now, he was attired in a riding jacket of brown and beige tweed with a green cravat around his neck. Even more pronounced than the evening before were the wings of silver at his temples, startling against the deep tan of his face. His clear-cut features reminded me of the profile of the hawk in my amulet.

'I have sent for you, Miss McAllister, so that I might embroider upon our conversation of last night,' he said. 'No doubt if you decide to stay here you will wish to know more about your duties. My wife does not require a nurse. She is not physically sick, but she does require someone who will take an interest in her. She lives in a world of make-believe. She likes to be read to. You will know the sort of books to choose, books more suitable for a child or a young girl than for a married woman of thirty-two. Your time, however, will not be spent exclusively in her company for I decided at an early stage in her illness that it would be wrong of me to expect another woman to devote her time entirely to one who is mentally sick. She has a maid who is devoted to her and who came with her from her father's home when we married. One thing you should know, Miss McAllister. My wife dislikes me. I visit her out of a sense of duty but I am fully aware that the visits are painful for us both.'

I raised my eyes to his in stunned surprise.

'I have heard it said, sir, that in such cases the person who has been most loved or who is closest by ties of kin is

48

always the one who is turned against first.'

'I too have been given that information, perhaps in the hope that it will bring me comfort. It does not. The fact that something happens in the lives of a thousand others is no consolation to oneself. The situation is one I have come to terms with and indeed it ceases to trouble me.

'But, sir, it is hard to know that a being one has loved, still loves, no longer cares, or indeed that love has been replaced by dislike.'

He laughed, but it was not the gay, open laughter of a man in good humour.

'Love, Miss McAllister, is a subject I do not dwell upon. Love is for children, for wide-eyed girls fresh from the school room yearning for a fairy prince, or country swains drooling over their first girl. I know about love, but it is a foolishness a man is wiser to live without. Now let us press on for I have a deputation of farmers to meet at twelve.'

I felt rebuked, and with my face burning with colour I raised my head proudly.

'You will be the third companion my wife has had since her illness began. I think you should have the rest of the week to think matters over. I shall not blame you if you decide that the position I am offering is not for you, and if you do not wish to stay here I will see that you are taken into Gleave to catch the noon train into Medchester on Saturday. Do not be afraid to decide against it simply because you have your living to earn. Other opportunities will present themselves.'

I rose from my chair but stood hesitatingly beside it, a troubled frown upon my face.

'Perhaps you have some questions you wish to ask me?' he said kindly.

'Only one, sir. Have you any idea what caused the illness Mrs Lytton suffers from, and is there no hope of her recovery?'

'As to the first part of your question I can only tell you what the specialists have told me. The dividing line between sanity and insanity is like a needlepoint balancing upon a hair and the slightest happening and uncertainty can cause the needle to slip and fall on the wrong side of the dividing line. There was a tragedy in my wife's family before we were married which may have had some bearing upon her illness, for it is true that some of us are better equipped to deal with life's disasters than others, but, as to the second part of your question, I do not know and no such hope has been given to me.'

He looked at me for a long moment before he pulled the papers on his desk towards him and, picking up his pen, he started to write. I was dismissed, and he did not look up again as I went towards the door, letting myself out and closing it quietly behind me.

I retraced my steps up the staircase with so preoccupied an air that I almost collided with Mrs Allington on her way down. She had changed her dress and now wore a dark green riding habit. I was struck afresh by the petulant beauty of her face under the small green hat she wore with its waving cock feathers. She favoured me with a haughty stare as she ran down the steps into the hall, and the sound of her riding boots echoed sharply on the polished floor. Just as she reached the door, I heard the study door open and the next moment Mr Lytton was striding urgently across the hall. By this time Mrs Allington had flung open the door and the snow flurried into the hall and settled in melting globules on the polished floor.

'Where do you think you are going?' he demanded, seizing the door from her grasp and closing it with the utmost difficulty against the driving wind.

She tossed her head angrily. 'I am riding over to Ringwood to see the Wentworths.'

'Not in this weather you are not. Are you out of your senses, Rowena? If this snow continues, by dusk the bridle paths will be completely obliterated. The Wentworths' house is several miles from the road. Return to your room and take off your riding habit, I want no more catastrophes in this house.'

Brother and sister glared at each other with such a degree of animosity that it seemed to hang like a tangible thing between them; then with a toss of her head and a swish of her skirts Rowena turned and flounced across the hall into the drawing room, slamming the door behind her. I waited on the stairs, not daring to move in case I was seen, but on his way back to the study the master of the house looked up and saw me there, and immediately the anger on his face was replaced by a polite mask.

How high-handed he was in his domination of others ! The fact that he had right on his side did nothing to quell my anger. This was no fit morning for a ride over the fells, but his blistering arrogance had whipped her up into a fury from which no doubt she was still smarting.

My room felt cold, for the fire had burned low. I knelt down on the rug and added more coal, leaving the poker under the coals for a few moments to encourage the blaze. It was a trick I had often seen Aunt Maud use and I must confess I had never seen it fail.

I took the keys out of my purse and decided to open my trunk. On top lay the books of my childhood as well as the one or two cherished volumes which had been my father's and which I had been loth to part with, and as I placed them in the shelves besides my bed I could not help wondering if those expensive volumes in the library downstairs had ever been read with greater pleasure. I took out my dark blue robe and held it in my arms for a few moments, comforted by its soft warmth, then I viewed the rest of my clothes with some dismay.

Whatever had possessed me to bring my one evening gown, I wondered? It had been a mistake, for when would I ever wear it in this house? It was deep rose-coloured velvet and, after shaking it free from the tissues I had used to pack it, I held it against me in front of the long mirror. Aunt Beatrice had had it made up for me by a dressmaker in Medchester so that I could accompany my father to the only function he ever attended – an archaeological dinner in London – and she had made it most beautifully and, I suspect, most expensively. It fell away from the shoulders and fitted into a small, pointed waist like a second skin, then the skirt billowed outwards in soft folds to the floor.

Tears sprang into my eyes as I remembered the first time I had worn it. My father was waiting for me in the foyer of the London hotel where the dinner was to be held, and I shall never forget the look of amazement on his face when he turned round to find me waiting for him at the foot of the stairs. He had walked towards me gladly, with a bemused expression on his face; then, gently stroking my hair, and with tears in his eyes, he murmured, 'You are so like your mother Carla, I had never really noticed before.' All that night we were gay together, and in the eyes of other men in that sober, learned crowd there was admiration.

Ruefully, I put the gown away at the back of the wardrobe, together with the black satin slippers with the diamante buckles, and resigned myself to a day of loneliness and boredom. Which indeed it was – punctuated only by meals brought to me in my room by Nancy and a brief visit from Agnes, young Mrs Lytton's maid.

At seven o'clock I could bear the inactivity no longer. I decided I would go down to the library and choose a book. I thought that the family would probably be at the dinner table and that I would be able to enter and leave the library unnoticed. I could not think that Mr Thorn would object to my borrowing one book from all the hundreds upon the library shelves.

Only one lamp had been left burning and the glow failed to reach into the dark shadows round the room, or upwards towards the ornate, plastered ceiling. The dog Laird lay in his customary position on the rug before the fire. He raised his great, shaggy head to look at me, but this time he did not growl. I spoke to him softly and, as though satisfied that my presence required no show of animosity from him, he lowered his head upon his paws to resume his slumber.

Where could I possibly find something which would not defeat my modest intelligence? A pile of magazines lay on the table and I thought that perhaps amongst these I might find something. They were in the main geographical and country life magazines and I took three of them at random. The dog lay with his eyes open watching me, but bravely I stepped forward and patted his head. Then, encouraged by the faint thump of his long stringy tail upon the rug, I spoke to him gently. I turned to leave, but with my fingers on the doorknob I felt it taken from my grasp and I found Mr Thorn looking down at me with an enquiring smile upon his lips.

I could feel my face blushing furiously but my stumbling words of explanation were stopped by an imperious wave of his hand.

'You need not apologize, Miss McAllister. Take all the

books you like if they help the evening to pass more quickly for you.'

I thanked him; then, with an impetuousness borne out of frustration, I said, 'When may I start my duties, sir? Or at least may I not be found other work until you decide when I might meet your wife?'

He looked down at me thoughtfully and again I was conscious of his dark eyes studying me intensely, almost as though he searched for some unknown flaw in my character. Much later, when I knew him better, I realized it was fear that had made him reluctant to accept me, fear that I would not stay and fear that I too would be afraid.

He was silent for what seemed like an eternity, his face grave, then suddenly he was speaking briskly, 'My wife breakfasts late and does not take luncheon. I think an appropriate time to meet her would be around noon.'

'I may meet her tomorrow then?'

'Come to my study just before twelve and I will take you to her,' he said, then with a brief nod he left me and entered the library.

All that night I was happy, sitting in my comfortable chair pulled up close beside the fire. I enjoyed reading the articles I found in the magazines concerned with functions attended by the gentry in the districts around Gleave, and I saw that Mr Thorn's name figured prominently as a patron of the local art an musical societies, as a former master of the local hunt, and as a magistrate.

Soon after nine I went to bed and, since nothing came to disturb my slumber, I awoke refreshed to the sight of a pale, wintry sun shining in through my window. The snow had stopped. Outside the frost sparkled on the ground and there were patches of blue in the sky.

My spirits were high when Nancy arrived with my breakfast.

'I am starting my duties today, Nancy,' I informed her, 'so I shall not be taking breakfast in bed after this morning. No doubt I shall take my meals with Mrs Lytton if that is what the previous companions have done.'

'Well, I don't know, miss,' Nancy answered doubtfully. Miss Osborne always ate in her own room and so did the young lady who was here before her, except when they dined with the family, that is.'

'They never took their meals with Mrs Lytton?'

'No, miss. Agnes sees to Miss Elsa's meals and the nurse serves Mrs Lytton in her room. You will soon get used to how things are run.'

She smiled at me and bobbed her quaint curtsey, then she left me to my breakfast. I was just about to pour a second cup of coffee when the door opened and Mrs Lytton's nurse came in.

Her eyes were sparkling as she sat down on the edge of my bed, and before I could ask what events had brought the colour into her cheeks she said, 'I've just been informed that my replacement will be here in three days. That means I shall be leaving at the weekend. Why don't you change your mind and leave with me? I'm sure you could find something in London if you looked around.'

'Don't think I haven't already looked and found nothing. Have you any idea who is to take your place?'

'Only that she is a qualified nurse whose patient has recently died and she is looking for a new place. Apparently she prefers a post in the country. She's welcome to it.'

'But you must be fond of your patient, surely? Doesn't it bother you leaving her?'

'A nurse can't afford to get too fond of her patients. After all, they die or get better as the case may be. Either way there comes a parting and, although I am fond of the old lady, we have no conversation unless she writes me a note, usually about her library book or her embroidery silks.'

'She can read and do embroidery?'

'Heavens yes! She has embroidered a tablecloth as a wedding present for me. It will probably be the most expensively beautiful thing we have. It's only her speech which has remained affected. She asked after you yesterday.'

'After me? How did she do that?'

'She keeps a pad of writing paper near her chair and all day long she writes out her questions and passes them to me. Sometimes I forget that she can hear perfectly well and I write down the answers and pass the writing pad back. She asked if you were young and pretty, and when I told her you were she didn't seem to like my answer. No doubt

54

she is thinking of the temptation placed before Mr Thorn, saddled as he is with a mentally sick wife, poor man.'

I knew that I looked extraordinarily self-conscious, which amused her greatly.

'You are blushing, Carla,' she said impudently, 'that means you do find him attractive. I know I do.'

'I can assure you I have given no thought to the matter. I am here as companion to his wife, nothing more.'

I was well aware that my words were pompous but I doubted if anything could have quelled her good humour.

'Oh well, it's just as well he doesn't appeal to you, for you won't get many opportunities to charm him if that designing young woman from Medchester has anything to do with it. She looks upon Mr Thorn as her personal property and when I have seen them together he doesn't seem averse to the idea.'

'What is she like this lady from Medchester?'

'Very dark, very beautiful, very gay, and a widow they tell me. You'll be seeing her for yourself one of these days, no doubt as soon as the snow clears. She spends a great deal of time in this house, either with Mr Thorn when she can get hold of him, or as a guest of Miss Rowena's.'

The nurse rose from the edge of my bed and stood looking down at me, a twinkle in her merry eyes.

'Mrs Lytton wants to see you some time today. When can you visit her?'

'I'm not sure; as I said, I am to meet Mr Thorn's wife this morning.'

'Oh well, you won't be with her all the time. My patient sleeps for a little while after lunch but if you are free round about four o'clock ask one of the maids to show you to her room.'

With a bright smile from the door she let herself out quickly and closed it behind her. Her departure, however, had taken my appetite with it.

I felt angry with myself. Once again my stupid imagination had led me down the paths of a suspected tragedy, only to find that Mr Thorn and his beautiful companion of the past were still together, even though he was now married to another. Would she remember me if ever we met, I wondered? The nurse had made her out to be a flirt, seeking to lure Thorn away from his sick, young wife, but the girl I had known had had no need to lure Thorn away from any. It had been all too obvious that he had adored her, so why then had he ever married another, and why had she? I was getting tired of the Lyttons and their mixed-up love stories. Mr Thorn had no right to quarrel with his sister Rowena if he was capable of such underhand dealings himself.

I took special care with my toilet and at shortly before eleven o'clock I made my way towards the study. The room behind the closed door was silent and there was no answer to my knock, so I turned the knob and pushed open the door. The room was empty and I stood hesitating on the threshold, wondering if I should sit down and wait for him or if I should return to my room until I was summoned. I walked over to the window behind his desk and looked out over the parkland shimmering in the pale sunlight and its light blanket of snow. The snow had been cleared from around the front door and it lay in heaped pyramids on the edges of the drive. From the distance I could hear the sound of men's voices and just then Mr Thorn came to the front of the house from the direction of the stables, talking most earnestly with a man I judged to be slightly younger than himself. The man was carrying a small, black leather bag and they entered the house together.

I decided to wait. I could still hear the sound of their voices from the direction of the hall, although I could not hear their words. Presently, I heard the hall door open and close, then I heard footsteps striding in my direction and the door of the study was flung open to admit my employer.

'I am sorry to keep you waiting, Miss McAllister, but I had to call the vet out to one of the horses. I am glad you decided to wait.'

'If it is not convenient Mr Lytton, I can come back later.'

'No, no, my business with the vet is finished,' he said. 'Come I have informed Agnes that we should be visiting my wife this morning, so they will be expecting us.'

Meekly I followed him out of the room and up the shallow staircase from the hall. I walked behind the tall, slender figure down a corridor wide enough to take pieces of furniture and carved tables bearing figures of bronze. The room we entered was large and airy, with long, tall windows looking out across the parkland and hung with rose-coloured velvet curtains. There was a thick carpet of the same colour upon the floor into which my feet sank. Delicate, shell-pink damask covered the walls against a white, ornate ceiling, and from two points in the room hung crystal chandeliers. It was a woman's room, the most beautiful room I had ever seen, but the beauty of its furniture and it's decor was marred by the enormous doll's house which occupied the centre of the floor. Agnes turned as we entered the room. She had been busily arranging a large bunch of white chrysanthemums in a bronze urn beside the window and, although I took all this in at the first glance, it was at the woman kneeling upon the floor that my eyes returned to.

Although she was kneeling I could tell that she was tall. Her blue gown of watered silk clung to her delicate waist and her pale, silver-fair hair fell loosely on to her shoulders, unrestrained by hair-slides or ribbons. She did not turn her head to look at us but sat poised over the open rooms of the doll's house, one hand raised as though we had disturbed her as she was about to place a small piece of furniture in one of the rooms.

Mr Thorn turned and, putting his arm lightly under my elbow, drew me towards her saying at the same time, 'Good morning Elsa. Look I have brought Miss Carla McAllister to see you.'

She remained kneeling as though he had not spoken, nor did she turn her head. I could see now that she held in her hand a small gilded chair which she placed calmly in a corner of the drawing room. I could see into the rooms of the doll's house plainly now as we stood behind her and never had I seen a child's toy or any other toy so beautifully perfect. It copied faithfully the proportions of Milverton. From the hall rose the sweeping staircase dividing at the first landing where a miniature of the large portrait covered the entire wall, exactly as Elsa's real portrait covered the wall at the head of the first flight of stairs. I recognized instantly the library with its array of books and the drawing room I had entered the night before. There was my own little room at the end of the first floor and the long carpeted corridors which took me there. After so short a time I was unable to identify much, but I immediately recognized this sitting room, and a quick look round assured me how faithfully the furniture had been copied, as well as the carpets and cushions, even the curtains at the windows.

She had returned to it now and was removing furniture from one room to the next, a cushion from here to there, an ornament from the top of the miniscule grand piano to the top of a small chest of drawers and I watched her fascinated, as her long, pointed, white fingers hovered over their task.

It was quiet in the room, apart from the light pattering of rain against the window. I was aware of Mr Thorn standing behind me, darkly silent, and Agnes sitting on the window seat watching us, her needlework idle in her lap. I was surprised to see that the old wing of the doll's house was missing. The toy ended at the windows of the rooms adjacent to mine and I wondered if only a copy of the newer part of the house had been made or if the old wing was stored away somewhere now that it was no longer in use.

She appeared to be having great difficulty in removing a small oak chest and her frustration was such that it brought the warm colour to her cheeks. Impulsively I knelt on the carpet beside her and she turned her head to look at me. She allowed me to remove the chest which I handed to her; then she sat back on her heels, inviting me to play with her toy. I felt her eyes upon me, watching every move I made and I became so nervous that when I withdrew my hand from the house I accidentally knocked over a small table which had been standing in the hall. Immediately she jumped to her feet with a cry of anger and slammed the doors of the house so sharply that she almost trapped my fingers in the process. I, too, gave a small cry and recoiled from the expression of hatred I saw in her face.

Agnes hurried to her side and stood with one arm encircling her shoulders, her face concerned, anxious, while I stood miserably looking down upon the ground, wishing I had never been born.

'She has been fretful all morning, sir,' Agnes was saying. 'Perhaps if you were to go now and let the young lady come later it would be best.'

'Come, Miss McAllister,' Mr Thorn said lightly, 'It would

seem this is not a good day for my wife to receive guests. Return with me to the study and we will recover our good spirits over a glass of sherry.'

I remember little of our walk back to the study because my eyes were swimming with tears. It was only when he placed a glass of sherry in my hands that I realized I was sitting in the chair he had drawn forward for me and that the firelight was warm upon my skirt. The dog Laird came to stare at me, his brown eyes filled with canine sympathy, and when he placed his huge shaggy head upon my lap I am ashamed to say I dissolved into tears again. The glass was taken from me and placed upon the desk so that the sherry would not be spilled.

I was only too aware of the woebegone picture I must present, with my eyes puffed up from weeping and the tears drying on my cheeks, but I was also ashamed and angry with myself. I was not fit for the position he had thought to offer me, not when I had been so abjectly defeated at the first hurdle. I looked up into his face and surprised a great kindness there, a kindness which suddenly warmed my heart and gave me hope.

'You have possibly today seen my wife at her worst, tomorrow you could be enchanted by her sweetness. At least allow me to apologize for her rudeness and do not think I shall hold it against you if you now decide not to accept the position I am offering.'

'You still want me to stay, even after I behaved so stupidly?'

'You were surprised and bewildered, you could have behaved in no other way unless you had been insensitive. Shall we strike a bargain, you and I? Let us say that for three months you accept the position as companion to my wife. If at the end of those three months you feel you are unable to stay longer, be sure that I shall understand. I only ask that you remain until a replacement can be found.'

'Do you think she will accept me?'

'I know she will accept you, just as I knew your first meeting would be a disaster. Elsa's behaviour always follows a pattern.'

'Always?'

'Since her illness. Before that Elsa could be enchanting –

as all who knew her then would agree. How do you propose to spend the rest of your day now that the snow has stopped?'

I was surprised at his question and at the speed with which he had changed the subject. I told him that his mother had asked me to visit her and he raised his eyebrows.

'By all means meet my mother if she requests it. Indeed it is perhaps a good idea that you should become acquainted with the darker aspects of this household in one day, so that whatever comes after can only be seen as an improvement.'

'It is sad that Mrs Lytton is unable to speak,' I ventured.

'Yes. My mother enjoyed good health until her stroke and she now becomes frustrated when she is unable to converse freely with those who visit her. She will write her questions on a writing pad but you may reply to her normally. She can hear perfectly well and, I should tell you, her intelligence is unimpaired.'

I rose from my chair feeling that I should make the first move to end our meeting. Indeed, I was halfway to the door when the gong sounded for luncheon.

I had no appetite for the lunch Nancy brought to my room and sent it back to the kitchens untouched. Nancy looked at me unhappily. I had little doubt that by this time the morning's events would have become common gossip in the kitchens. Outside in the garden the snow was melting a little, and already the leaves were shining wet where the night before they had glistened with frost. I decided that I would wrap up warmly and walk in the parkland, no doubt the fresh air would bring some colour into my cheeks and restore my flagging spirits.

The sharp, cold wind at first took my breath away but after a few moments I felt exhilarated by it, like a caged bird suddenly set free. I walked quickly, my feet crunching on the light snow, the wind blowing my skirts against my legs, freeing my hair from the scarf I had thrown over my head. I took the path which led down to the mere, surprised to find that the water sparkled and danced in the sunlight so that I had to screw up my eyes against the glare.

For the first time since my arrival at Milverton I felt

young and alive and free. I would not allow the unhappy events of the morning to defeat me. I would forge a bond of affection between Elsa Lytton and myself, make her see that I wished to be her friend as well as her companion. Agnes would help me I felt sure. Obviously, she was devoted to her mistress for she would have happy memories of her as a child in her father's house. If Agnes saw how desperately I wanted to befriend her, together we could accomplish much.

I would forget the dark-haired beauty who had haunted my imagination for so long. No doubt I had endowed her with a bewitching glamour entirely superficial, and what I had taken to be a deep love between Mr Thorn and herself had proved to have been nothing more or less than a light flirtation since they had looked for marriage elsewhere. My loyalty must be with Miss Elsa, poor unhappy lady; she was unable to help herself and had need of all the love and protection she could get.

All the way round the lakeside and back along the drive I lectured myself on my duty as I saw it, so that I returned to the house with squared shoulders and firm resolve in my heart.

The reflection which met my eyes in the mirror filled me with dismay. My long skirt was wet around the hem and my hair fell around my face in unruly curls. The wind had brought a sparkle to my eyes and colour to my cheeks, but all the same I hastened to brush my hair smooth and rid myself of my damp clothing. I decided to wear my cornflower blue serge, hoping at the same time that Mrs Lytton would not think it too decorative for my station.

A light knock on my door heralded the arrival of Mrs Lytton's nurse and the surprise on her face did nothing to reassure me that I had been wise to change.

'I have been walking in the park and the hem of my skirt was damp,' I hastened to explain. 'I could not appear before Mrs Lytton looking so dishevelled. Will she disapprove, do you think? I wouldn't like her to think me frivolous.'

'I was just thinking how pretty you look. That dress does far more for you than the blouse and skirt you wore this morning. It's a pity you didn't wear it then.'

'What do you mean?'

'So that Mr Thorn could have seen you looking less like a school marm and to confound that dotty wife of his.'

'Oh Celia, you talk as though the poor lady can help her condition. It is sad to find one who looks so beautiful, so ...so ...'

'Dotty,' she finished for me, disrespectfully. 'Miss Elsa's had one of her bad days today. Poor Nancy caught out for it and you too were seen leaving her room behind Mr Thorn in tears. It doesn't take much imagination to know how she received you. Surely, Carla, you can't intend to stay after that?'

'I must stay. It is essential that I do the best I can. Such employment is hard to find. Mr Thorn has assured me that tomorrow his wife will be completely different. I expect any kind of change unsettles her and I am just another change.'

'She's like no other mental patient I have ever come across. What did you think about the doll's house? It cost enough to keep twenty families in luxury for five years at least and that room was so beautiful before the house took over. It is a copy of Milverton you know, down to the carpets and the furniture. Even the portrait at the head of the stairs was done in the form of a miniature.'

'Was it copied locally?'

'Gracious no ! Nothing so simple as a local craftsman. No, some man came over from Florence and stayed here for months making sketches and taking patterns of carpets and curtains. Then months later he came back with the house in crates and it took another few months to assemble it. The furniture has been arriving periodically ever since, until now I believe it is complete.'

'Is it a copy of the entire house, the old wing as well?'

'Not the old wing, at least I don't think so. One day when Miss Elsa was out with Agnes, I went in with Mrs Bamber to have a look at it and I must have accidentally touched a piece of furniture, either I knocked it over or moved it; anyway, when she returned I heard she had hysterics and Mr Thorn gave instructions that none of us should go into her room again or touch the doll's house.'

I nodded unhappily, but I did not tell her that that had been my offence or that I could not forget the hatred I had seen in that lovely face.

She was looking at me kindly, albeit a little impatiently. 'Oh well,' she said at last, 'stay if you must, but rather you than me.' Then with a return to her bright good humour she went on, 'We are to be honoured by an invitation to take tea with the old lady, so come along and let her see how pretty you are, and don't forget to address her quite normally as though nothing ails her.'

After the morning's episode I couldn't help the feeling of nervousness that made me speechless as we walked from my room to Mrs Lytton's at the extreme end of the house. Only Celia, with her brash good humour, imparted a semblance of normality to this strange household. She jauntily hummed a little tune, one that was popular in the musical halls, and I wished with all my heart that she were not leaving so soon.

We came at last to a door upon which she knocked briefly before pushing it open and beckoning me to follow in her wake. The room we entered was a sitting room, large and comfortably furnished with a blue, velvet couch and chairs. The dark, mahogany furniture glowed red in the firelight and under our feet was spread a thick oriental carpet. My eyes, however, were drawn to the frail figure of an old lady sitting propped up amongst her cushions in a large chair which had been drawn up before the log fire burning on the hearth.

The memories I had of Mrs Lytton from my childhood seemed incongruous now when faced with her fragility. In those far-off days she had seemed to me a figure larger than life in her fashionable hats with their sweeping ostrich plumes, coats and capes liberally edged with fox fur. Her role had always been a leading one for she had been the gracious patron of innumerable church bazaars, the confident presenter of prizes at country shows, and the woman who had brought a sparkle into the eyes of a gathering of children by her charming condescension in awarding a half day's holiday after the visit of the governers to the school at which I was a short-term pupil.

In those days I had stood fascinated by the jewellery displayed upon her ample bosom, and the jostlings and pushings of Sunday-dressed villagers had sent Elliot and me into fits of laughter, laughter which had earned looks of extreme displeasure from my aunts as well as from Elliot's parents.

It was hard now to reconcile my memories of that Mrs Lytton with this diminutive old lady in her enormous chair. Even the warm rug which had been draped across her knees only emphasized their spindly thinness. In her hands she held a writing pad and pencil, but they were less like hands than yellowing pieces of old ivory, transparent and marled by dark blue veins. Her face had lost the healthy flesh of middle age but it had taken on the timeless beauty of good bone structure, and her snow-white hair had been carefully dressed, I assumed by her nurse. The changes her illness had wrought in her filled me with dismay, but there was no denying the intelligence in her faded, blue eyes.

'This is Carla McAllister, Mrs Lytton,' Celia was saying, 'come to be companion to Miss Elsa. I have been telling her how pretty she looks in her blue dress, worn specially for this occasion.'

Mrs Lytton smiled, and I smiled also because Celia had left me with little to say.

The old lady indicated that I should sit opposite her, and Celia went forward to assist Mrs Bamber who had just entered the room pushing a heavy, oak tea trolley before her. As Celia busied herself at the tea trolley Mrs Bamber came to speak to the old lady, enquiring after her health, patting her cushions and smiling briefly at me but, after she had left us and we helped ourselves to freshly baked scones and home-made strawberry jam and fruit cake, a silence descended upon us and I wondered how long I would be expected to stay.

At last the teacups were laid aside. Celia appeared to have run out of small talk and Mrs Lytton applied her pencil to the writing pad which she passed across to me.

She had written upon it the words, 'Are you going to stay?'

I looked up at her startled, not quite knowing what expression I might find on her face, whether it was one of hope, relief or caution, and after a little nod from Celia I said, 'Yes. I have promised Mr Thorn I will stay three months to see if Mrs Lytton and I are compatible. If we are not, then I shall have to seek other employment, and a replacement for me here will have to be found.'

After what seemed an age, she nodded her head, but the relief I had hoped to see on her face was absent. Again silence descended upon us and I found myself looking round the room, my eyes searching for some small thing which would provide me with a topic of conversation.

They found at last an embroidered firescreen standing against the wall, on which some work still needed to be done, and a cry of admiration rose to my lips.

'How beautiful it is! ' I said rising to my feet and walking towards it so that I could see it better.

I was conscious that the tension in the room had relaxed considerably and on closer inspection of the screen I saw that it was indeed a beautiful thing and I blessed the happy inspiration which had led my eyes towards it. The work was Jacobean, the pattern an improbability of fruit, flowers and exotic birds which could never have taken wing except in fantasy. Much of the screen still had to be completed and I wondered if she had suddenly grown tired of it. As I returned to my chair, however, I saw that she was writing, her thin fingers holding the pencil lightly, yet seeming to fly across the page. She handed me her pad and I read, 'I have run out of wool and until the weather improves I shall not be able to get any.'

'Can I get it for you Mrs Lytton? I have to go into the village as soon as the roads have cleared a little. Or does it have to come from Feltham?'

Again the writing pad was produced and this time she informed me that the wool was available in the village and that Miss Phipps got it specially for her in Medchester.

I promised I would call at the draper's in Gleave when I went into the village and Celia laughed saying, 'I'm glad you offered. I am quite colour-blind and the last time I got the wool I got a scolding because all the colours were wrong.'

The atmosphere in the room had by this time quite changed and for the next half-hour we talked happily together while occasionally Mrs Lytton applied pen to paper so that she too could join in our conversation. We watched the great, red ball of the sun sink slowly behind the western fells, tinting the snow a delicate pink, shining like a furnace in the windows of the house, and then the lamps were lit and the heavy, velvet curtains were drawn to shut out the night.

When at last it was time for me to leave, Celia excused herself also, saying I could easily get lost in the rambling corridors of the house if she did not walk back with me. I knew it was because she wanted my reactions to the afternoon I had just spent.

On the way back to my room, and well away from Mrs Lytton's room, she whistled in relief. 'Whew, but I thought at first your visit was going to be a disaster. I'm glad you spotted the firescreen, at least it found us something to talk about.'

'I think she has overcome her disability marvellously,' I replied.

She did not speak again until we were in the corridor leading to my room, then she said, 'Those are not the rooms the old lady used when first I came here. Her rooms were off the main hall near the room Miss Elsa has now, but when she had her stroke she was completely helpless and once or twice I found Miss Elsa standing at the bottom of her bed just looking at the old lady. You can imagine the scene: Mrs Lytton helpless and terrified and young Mrs Lytton nutty as a fruit cake. Then Mr Thorn decreed that his mother should move into the suite at the far end of the house and he moved into his mother's old rooms.'

'Does Miss Elsa never visit her now?'

'No, although I am always afraid that when I go out she will find some means of getting to the old lady.'

We walked the rest of the way in silence but the miseries of the beautiful, old house seemed all around us. I wondered what the companion of Mr Thorn's gay, young days thought when she visited this house now, but I said nothing of my thoughts to Celia.

I had only been back in my room a few minutes when a light tap sounded on the door and, in answer to my invitation to enter, Agnes came in. She stood in front of me, blushing a little, whether from walking too fast or for some other reason I could not tell, but she placed in my hands a small parcel wrapped in blue paper and tied most artistically with blue ribbons. Wonderingly, I took it from her and opened it. A small, leather jewel box lay in the palm of my hand and when I opened it I gasped in admiration at what it contained. Lying on a bed of cotton wool was a locket, the most beautiful locket I had ever seen, made of gold and inlaid with tiny, seed pearls and dark red garnets. I lifted it out and held it up so that Agnes too might see it, and I was surprised at the consternation on her homely face. I touched the little spring at the side of the locket and it opened wide to reveal a single lock of blue-black hair, curled round inside it like a sleeping dormouse. The elusive scent of honeysuckle rose to my nostrils.

I looked at Agnes sharply, aware of her distress.

'Oh miss, I had no idea what was in the parcel. She insisted on wrapping it herself and she said it was for you and no other but you.'

'But why me Agnes? Why should she send this locket and that lock of hair to me?'

'I can't think it is for any special reason, miss. She is aware that her tantrum this morning upset you, and no doubt Mr Thorn will show his displeasure by keeping away from her for a few days. I thought it was a peace offering sent in the hope that you will both forgive her.'

'If Miss Elsa is capable of such thoughts and actions how can she even be considered to be mad? This is the sort of behaviour any normal woman might adopt in order to restore herself to her husband's good graces.'

'But would any normal woman play with a doll's house miss, or work herself into a tantrum because of it?'

I was silent, holding the locket unhappily in my hand.

'I suppose the locket belongs to Miss Elsa?' I asked.

'I have seen it before, but a long time ago. It has never been with her other jewellery,' she answered me, and I felt she was very anxious not to give anything away.

Sadly I replaced the locket in the box and wrapped the blue paper around it. 'I cannot accept it Agnes, it is far too valuable. Besides, another day she could forget she has given it to me and demand its return. She may even accuse me of stealing it.'

'Yes miss, but I cannot give it back to her now. Perhaps you could hand it to Mr Thorn and explain to him how you came by it?'

'That is a good idea. I will give it to him this evening after he has left the dining room. The hair is not Miss Elsa's, whose is it?'

'I couldn't say, miss. As I said I have seen the locket before but never knew what was inside it.'

Her colour had heightened and, with a confused bob by way of farewell, she turned on her heels and left me holding the locket in my hand. What is more, I was convinced that Agnes knew well whose hair the lock had been cut from, although she had no intention of telling me.

I was absolutely certain that it had once graced the head of Mr Thorn's former love and wondered how it came to be in his wife's possession. What was the strange antipathy which made her send it to me? Was it a warning or a challenge, I wondered. I would watch his face closely when I returned the locket to him, but in the meantime I sat down on the side of my bed, looking down at the lock of hair much as a hynotized sparrow might look at a snake.

My opportunity to return the locket came that evening after dinner, as I stood on the landing below Miss Elsa's portrait listening to the murmur of conversation coming from the dining room. The dog Laird lay across the entrance to the room and, when I saw him jump to his feet, his head cocked expectantly, his thin, stringy tail thumping against the oak-panelled wall, I knew I would not have long to wait. Only Mr Lytton emerged from the room, closing the door behind him, and inside the room the voices continued their conversation.

I ran lightly down the steps and crossed the hall, returning Mr Bamber's raised eyebrows with a calm stare. Following my light knock I entered the room to find Mr Lytton standing on the hearthrug in the act of lighting his cigar. He seemed surprised to see me, but undaunted I marched towards him until I stood looking up at him, holding out the trinket in my hand and thinking all the time how much more unapproachable he appeared in formal dress.

Breathlessly, I explained what had happened. In some surprise he took the locket from my hand and stood looking down at it with a strangely bemused expression on his face.

'Obviously, I cannot accept it,' I was saying. 'It is far too valuable and no doubt in the morning she will either forget having sent it or will be demanding its return. Perhaps if you took charge of it you could give it back to her at some later date?'

'I was not aware she had this, it is years since I have seen it,' he said at last, looking at me strangely.

'I opened it Mr Lytton, and it contains a lock of hair. It is not Miss Elsa's hair but no doubt she knows the person to whom it belongs.'

'No doubt,' he agreed drily. 'By all means leave the trinket with me, Miss McAllister. I am only sorry you have been embarrassed by it. I expect my wife wishes to atone for her ungracious behaviour this morning and I hope you will accept her apology in the spirit in which she made it. I also hope you will try to forget the incident.'

'Shall I start my duties in the morning, sir?'

'No. I have decided to take her over to see some friends of mine in the morning. The snow has almost cleared from the roads and she enjoys driving. At least it will provide a change for her. The day after tomorrow will be a good time to reintroduce yourself and by that time she too may have forgotten the incident of the doll's house.'

'Very well, sir. I promised Mrs Lytton, your mother, that I would call for her embroidery wool from the village draper's and there are one or two other matters I need to see to myself. Would you have any objections if I went into the village tomorrow?'

'None at all. Can you drive the pony and trap?'

'I am not expert, but adequate I think, although I have no objections to walking into the village.'

'That is out of the question, for one thing it is too far and for another it is too bad underfoot. I will give instructions for the pony and trap to be made ready for you at ten o'clock and there will be no hurry for you to return. I wish you a pleasant day, Miss McAllister.'

I was dismissed but in the face of his quiet amusement I could feel the warm colour rising into my cheeks. However, I thanked him quietly and made for the door. I had my hand on the doorknob when I heard his voice again.

'Miss McAllister,' he said, 'in this household my mother is referred to as Mrs Lytton, my wife as Miss Elsa. I am Mr

Thorn and the rest of the family are addressed in a similar fashion. My brother is Mr Stephen and his wife is Miss Judith, my sister of course is Miss Rowena, although I expect there will be little need to address her in any way for some time.'

'She is leaving sir?'

'In the morning.'

Our eyes met for a few moments only, then he became absorbed in the work on his desk and I quietly let myself out of the room.

4

Oh, but it was exhilarating that drive into Gleave the next morning! The wintry sun sparkled on the snow heaped up on each side of the road and the vistas of the distant fells rose upwards in forbidding crags topped by frozen snow. Beside the gates and all along the lower drive grew the rhododendron bushes, their leaves shining darkly where the snow had melted. White clouds scudded across the blue sky. It was the sort of day I had always imagined whenever my thoughts had turned to home from hotter climes, and now I revelled in the sharp wind against my face, glad that my hair was safely contained under my woollen cap.

The pony was fresh and lively between the shafts and it took all my modest skill to handle him. I restrained him from cantering recklessly along the village street, and with something approaching decorum we finally came to a halt outside the little draper's shop owned by the Misses Phipps. Nothing about the shop window had changed. It was still overcrowded with ribbons and embroidery materials, as well as lengths of calico, gingham and sprigged muslins, and when the bell tinkled over the doorway the younger Miss Phipps came smiling to the counter.

When I said I had called for Mrs Lytton's tapestry wools, she produced them from under the counter with such an air of conspiracy I wanted to smile. It was obvious that she did not remember me and I was very conscious of her curiosity as she wrapped up my parcel. Neither of my aunts had numbered the Misses Phipps amongst their friends. The elder, Gertrude, was a noted busybody, and the younger, Emily, was given to hushed scandalmongering and high, twittering laughter which reminded one of a startled sparrow. She made several attempts to discover what connection I had with the Lytton family but I was careful to give nothing away. I left the shop feeling rather pleased with my diplomacy, but was well aware that two pairs of inquisitive eyes watched me march down the street in the direction of Mrs Merryweather's cottage.

My aunt's letters lay in my bag – one for Mrs Merryweather whose husband had recently died and one for Mr Fellows, the vicar. I decided that he should be my last port of call since I could now see Mrs Merryweather on her hands and knees outside her cottage, busily applying donkey-stone to the doorstep. I had always thought what a painstakingly laborious task north country people set themselves by applying donkey-stone to their doorsteps and window sills, but I had to admit that the small blocks of soft sandstone, ranging from palest cream to deepest tan, gave the long, straggling, village street an attractive look. The villagers obtained the sandstone from the tinkers, or rag-and-bone men as they preferred to call them, in exchange for old clothing or discarded household goods, and I could now see that Mrs Merryweather was so engrossed in her task she did not look up until my shadow fell across her path.

She knelt, blinking upwards into the bright sunlight, brushing back her hair from her forehead with sand-encrusted palms, then she hastily endeavoured to wipe her hands clean on the rough apron she wore. She was a plump, country woman with rosy cheeks and soft, brown hair lightly sprinkled with grey, and although she smiled at me in the usual way of country folk I knew she had not recognized me.

'Good morning, Mrs Merryweather. I don't think you remember me,' I began as she sat back on heels regarding me.

'No miss, I can't rightly say that I do.'

I reached into my bag and held out my aunt's letter. 'You will remember the Misses McAllister though. The letter is from Aunt Maud. They lived in the last cottage along the street yonder.'

'I do remember them, I remember them very well, particularly Maud. My, she had a sharp tongue in her head. But a good heart.'

She took the letter from me, then her eyes lit up. 'You must be little Lottie! Well, to be sure but I would never have thought to see you grow up into such a fine lady, a regular little tomboy you were and no mistake, always getting into mischief. I've finished out here now but the snow makes such a mess when it's melting. Come into the cottage, Lottie, and we'll have a cup of tea together, I want to know all about your aunts and how they like living in a big place.'

I followed her limping figure into the cottage and stood looking round with interest. It had not changed since I had last been in the room more than ten years before. The large, black fireplace still shone from constant black leading, and a dark red, velvet cloth was laid on the round table. Mr Merryweather's big horsehair chair was in its customary place before the firegrate but there was a new rug on the floor. I had often seen the villagers making them from old clothing which they cut up into narrow strips called 'lists'. They threaded these through oblong pieces of coarse canvas using a rug needle, and made up patterns according to the colours of the clothes they had available. In time, of course, the rugs became flattened and soiled, but when they were new they gave a cosy warmth to many a cottage hearth.

'Sit down, miss. That's Merryweather's chair but he won't mind you sitting in it, I'm sure. Regular little caution, he always called you.'

'I was very sorry to hear that he died during the summer, Mrs Merryweather. And will you please call me Lottie? You always did when I was a little girl.'

'Well, it was just with you looking so grown-up and stylish you know. Ay, it was sad at the end, Lottie, and I miss him something awful. Still, I wouldn't have him back to suffer and it comes to us all in time.'

She went into the kitchen still shaking her head, but soon came bustling back with a large tray laden with crockery and a home-made fruit loaf. The kettle sang merrily on the hob in front of the fire and she placed the teapot on the hearth to warm it. Then she settled down in the chair opposite to mine and regarded me inquisitively out of brown, twinkling eyes.

'Where are you staying Lottie now that your aunts don't live in these parts? Are you at the vicarage?'

'No, I am staying at Milverton.

Her eyes grew round and wide with surprise. 'Up at the

Hall, Lottie! Well now!'

'Oh, I am not a guest there. I applied for a situation as companion to Miss Elsa, Mr Thorn's wife, and I am there on three months' trial, to see if I am suitable and also to see if Mrs Lytton is comfortable with me.'

'Well now, would you ever! We were all sorry to hear about young Mrs Lytton. Nothing but tragedy seems to have happened to that family of recent years, what with those two young people dying on the moor and then Miss Elsa, followed by old Mrs Lytton.'

'Two young people dying on the moor, Mrs Merry-weather?' I asked quickly.

'Well, Lottie, there was a lot of talk at the time, but you know Merryweather. He didn't like gossip and I never heard the full story. It was a young army officer and Miss Elsa's sister. They found the young man – he'd fallen from the top of one of the crags and he was dead when the search party got to him – but they never did find the girl. It was soon after that when Miss Elsa started to go funny, if you know what I mean, but I think at the time of their wedding she was all right.'

'I suppose their wedding was a quiet affair because of the bereavement in Miss Elsa's family?'

'I expect so. Then there was poor Elliot Cliffe and Miss Rowena.'

'Elliot and Miss Rowena?'

'Well they were engaged, you know, getting married in the spring, and she ups and runs away with a young fellow who had been staying at the Hall and in no time they were married. There was talk that one day he would come in for his uncle's title and no doubt she had her eye on that.'

I looked at her in stunned silence for a long time. Then she leaned forward and patted my hand.

'You were always very friendly with Elliot, weren't you Lottie?'

'Yes, I liked him very much. Poor Elliot, I expect he was very upset.'

'Well, he would be, wouldn't he? I know his mother was, she had a nervous breakdown and soon afterwards the doctor sold his practice and they went to live away. They never come to these parts now, leastways I don't think so.'

My disappointment was so intense I could have cried. Elliot had been the boy who had listened to my childish romancing with never a hint of ridicule, the boy who had followed my adventurous lead in every forbidden excursion, and now I found myself disliking Rowena Lytton for callously abandoning him. She did not deserve to be happy, it was her punishment for what she had done to Elliot.

Suddenly I wanted to leave Mrs Merryweather's snug little parlour and go out into the sharp, wintry morning. All she had been able to tell me about Milverton was of death and broken faith, now I needed to get out into the frost-laden air so that I could think straight upon what I had heard. I offered to help her clear away the remains of our repast but she would not hear of it.

'It will give me something to do,' she said sadly. 'I miss Merryweather something awful now that I don't have him to cook for. He'd just about be arriving home for his meal now, not that he ever had much to say. A man of few words was Merryweather.'

I took her hand and squeezed it sympathetically, promising that I would call again when next I was in the village for any length of time.

As I walked up the main street and across the little park which stood in front of the village hall, I could not help thinking how Milverton dominated the lives of all those who lived in the village. The great house towered over Gleave as protectively or menacingly as did the rugged crags. Every farm and homestead was built on Milverton land, all paying their dues to the Lytton family. Every shop in the rambling high street served them, every animal that fed on the lush, green grass of the meadows owed its wellbeing to the Lyttons' care of their farmland, all the children in the little village school would be made aware over the years of the generosity of a family who would probably one day employ them. For me there was a darker side to the question. Would I suffer at the hands of the Lyttons as Elliot had suffered, or would I go from Milverton at the end of three months ashamed because I had been found inadequate?

I saw the vicar locking the door of the village hall behind him then he turned to walk through the little gate which led to the vicarage. I called to him and ran forward, my feet slithering and sliding on the melting snow. He turned to watch me and I knew that he did not at first recognize me, then just as I reached his side he held out his hand to stop my headlong flight, and I laughed into his surprised face.

'Why, Lottie my dear,' he said, 'what are you doing in Gleave now that your aunts have left the district?'

I repeated the tale I had told Mrs Merryweather and he tucked my hand under his arm and walked with me towards the vicarage.

'I was sorry to hear about your father, Lottie. Splendid chap, absolutely splendid. Highly intelligent, you know. I used to enjoy his visits to the vicarage. I've always been interested in the lands of the Bible without ever having any hopes of visiting them, not with the pittance they pay me, but your father could make the past come alive as no other could and until I met him I had always had to be content with reading about such matters.'

I was silent, hearing again my father's low, cultured tones as he talked about his beloved tombs and temples, and the ancient monarchs who had caused them to be built. I was impatient with the tears which rose to my eyes and hastily brushed them away with the back of my glove.

He squeezed my arm and looked down upon me kindly. 'Will you come to the vicarage to have lunch with us?'

'Not today, Vicar. I stayed so long with Mrs Merryweather, and Mrs Lytton will be waiting for the wools I collected for her. I have left the poor pony standing outside the draper's and I expect by this time he will feel the world has deserted him.'

'Well, one afternoon soon you must come down to the vicarage and take tea with me and Mrs Fellows. It will be a nice change from the arduous task you have set yourself.'

'Oh, Vicar, I am not really sure if I am up to it.'

'You will be, my dear. Pray to God to make it so, and I will pray for you also. It is some time since we have seen Mr Thorn in church but then no doubt he has much on his mind. Do you think you could give Mrs Stephen a message for me?'

'I will certainly try, although I have only met her once.'

'A nice lady, you will find. She has promised to talk to

my young mothers on her life in Provence as a young girl. Her grandmother is French and when she was a child she spent much of her time in the south of France, just as you spent much of your childhood in Gleave.'

'Gleave is a far cry from Provence, Mr Fellows.'

'Yes Lottie, but take my message to Miss Judith. She could be a good friend to you in that sombre household. Ask her if Tuesday week is convenient, in the village hall at seven o'clock, and try to accompany her if you are able.'

'Well I will try, Vicar, but I am not certain. As yet I do not know the extent of my duties and perhaps Miss Judith would prefer to come alone.'

'She would prefer, I am sure, to have you with her. I shall expect to see you both.'

I turned to walk away, then I hesitated and asked of him, 'Do you ever hear from Elliot Cliffe? I was so hoping to see him here in Gleave but perhaps you can tell me where he is living?'

'I had a letter from him from his father's house in Cornwall and I replied to him there. That, however, is almost three years ago. Presumably, he has taken a practice somewhere but I have no idea where.'

I thanked him and we bade each other farewell. I thought he stood and watched me as I walked away because, when I turned to look back as I reached the village street, he was only just entering the gates of the vicarage, holding up his hand by way of farewell.

I was pleased with the way I managed to turn the pony and trap in the narrow, village street, but was conscious that eyes watched me from behind many a cottage curtain, and that the Misses Phipps were busily engaged in turning out their shop window. Perhaps Mrs Merryweather had already seen fit to acquaint them of my identity, as well as my reason for being in the district. I didn't know. I did however drive a trifle recklessly on the return journey to Milverton and with an aplomb which outmatched my skill.

I left the pony and trap in the capable hands of one of the stable boys and let myself in the house by the side door.

Mr Bamber was making his stately way across the main hall, but he paused, eying me with some degree of superiority and no doubt disapproving of my wind-whipped complexion and sparkling eyes.

'I have a letter for Miss Judith, Mr Bamber. Can you tell me where I might find her?' I asked him.

'I will see that Miss Judith receives her letter, miss.'

His face was not inquisitive, it was the face of a well-bred servant who saw his duty clearly and was determined that a paid companion should not usurp it. I, on the other hand, began to think that there was a lot of Aunt Maud in me as I stood my ground.

'I was asked by the vicar to hand his letter to Miss Judith personally, Mr Bamber. I should like to do so.'

He looked down at me, much as one might look at a bothersome insect at a garden party.

'Very well miss, you will find her in the music room, through the drawing room. I must tell you, however, that Miss Judith does not like to be disturbed when she is playing the piano.'

I thanked him, but as I walked across the hall in the direction of the drawing room I could almost feel his eyes boring into my back. I could hear the piano now, played softly by skilful hands, and, because I had always loved music even though I had no talent of my own, I could recognize perfection when I heard it. I knocked lightly on the door of the music room but when there was no response I opened it and walked in.

It was large and beautiful. At one end and in front of the window a dais was raised to accommodate a grand piano. There were music stands laid back against the wall and I realized at once, and not so very long ago, an orchestra had played on that dais, and men and women had happily sat to listen. Now the late afternoon sunlight fell upon the flame-coloured hair of the woman seated at the piano and the music her fingers made, rippled round the room. I recognized the melody as that of a Chopin Étude and, entranced, I stood just within the door, afraid to move in case I broke the spell.

She seemed very different from the lady I had met on the night of my arrival. Then her bright hair had been piled on top of her head, giving her face a severity it did not possess in the light of day. Now it fell below her shoulders in large waves, caught back from the temples by a green velvet bow that matched her gown. There were ruffles of lace at her throat and wrists and she wore no rings on her long, white fingers.

As I listened to the magic of her playing, for the first time I found myself resenting my father who had always put me second to his profession. My education had never worried him, and in reply to my aunts' criticisms he would always say that I was pretty and would no doubt marry young. How I would have loved to have been taught to play the piano and how I would have practised! As her playing came to an end I found myself chiding myself for harbouring such disloyal thoughts against one I had thought of as little less than perfect.

Shyly, I moved forward and she looked up startled and without recognition.

'I am sorry to intrude Miss Judith, but I have a letter for you from Mr Fellows, the vicar. I promised I would hand it to you personally.'

Wonderingly, she took the letter from me, then her face cleared and she smiled. 'Of course, you are Miss McAllister. You must forgive me, I did not recognize you at once but then I have not seen you since that first evening.'

I made as though to leave her but she beckoned me back.

'Come, sit with me, or shall we go into the drawing room where it is warmer?'

She rose from her seat and led the way, and I noticed that she was taller than myself by almost a head.

She indicated that I should take the chair across from hers, then she excused herself whilst she opened the vicar's letter and read from it. The letter read, she looked up at me and smiled.

'My brother-in-law tells me you have decided to stay at Milverton, at least for a little while. I am so glad.'

My heart warmed to her. She was the first person who had shown any real pleasure in my presence at Milverton. I had not thought that Mr Thorn cared either one way or the other, and even old Mrs Lytton had seemed unsure. Now, for the first time, I felt I was face to face with a genuine friend and I responded wholeheartedly to the kindness I saw in her face.

'Mrs Lytton, may I ask you something? Do you think that in time Miss Elsa will come to accept me?'

I thought her eyes looked at me startled for a moment, then she smiled again and said, 'Please call me Miss Judith. That is how I am known here. Elsa accepted her other companions, why should she not accept you?'

'I don't know. She looked at me with such hatred the other morning and perhaps I am not the one to cope with an illness of this sort.'

'I can only advise you to take each day as it comes. Be yourself. If one day you find her insufferable, leave her alone. When she is good, give her your fondness and attention.'

'Oh, Miss Judith, I am afraid.'

The sympathy in her eyes was very real and she leaned forward to take my hand. 'Try not to be afraid. Remember that Mr Thorn is grateful to you, as we all are, and you must not be so isolated from the rest of the household. I think perhaps it might be a good idea if you were to dine with the family occasionally and concern yourself in the life of the village and the district.'

'I cannot intrude upon the life of the family – doubtless, there are many things you will need to discuss without the presence of a stranger.'

'Well, it is true you are almost a stranger now, but as the days and weeks pass you will be less a stranger and will have become one of us.'

I had no answer to such kindness, but she could see from my face that her words had warmed my heart.

'Tell me, Miss McAllister, or shall I call you Miss Carla, have you ever visited Provence?'

'No, never, although I have heard that it is very beautiful.'

'Some of my happiest years were spent there. At first, when I came to the north of England I hated it. I hated the wild, sweeping moors which seemed to change like the sea, and those cruel crags rising steeply towards the high fells. I missed the mellow stone and warm winds from the Mediterranean bringing the scent of oleanders and jasmine. I have learned to live in this rugged countryside, but now and again my heart turns to Provence and that is why the vicar has written to me.'

'You are to talk to the young mothers in the village about it.'

'Ah, I see that he told you. Did he also hope you would be there?'

'Yes, but I didn't promise. After all I may have other things to do.'

'You are not here to spend all your time in Miss Elsa's company, that would be an impossible situation. He expects to see me in the village hall at seven o'clock next Tuesday evening, which means I shall not be able to dine here since we do not dine until eight. I suggest that you and I have tea together about half past four and that will give us time to drive down to the village for seven o'clock.'

'Oh, Miss Judith, I should love it, but will Mr Thorn approve, do you think?'

'You can leave Mr Thorn to me. I shall expect to see you next Tuesday in here at four o'clock, indeed I shall need some moral support if I am to face the young mothers of Gleave.

How my feet danced up the stairs and along the thickly carpeted corridors, and not even Mr Bamber's disapproving stare was able to stifle the new found joy in my heart! The fire in my room welcomed me warmly and the chintz bedcovers and curtains had never seemed so bright. I now had something to look forward to and with my lighter spirits I even dared to hope that my meeting in the morning with Miss Elsa would be a happier one.

Promptly at ten o'clock Agnes appeared at my door wearing her outdoor clothes and when I stared at her in some surprise she said, 'Miss Elsa has decided she would like to walk in the park, miss. It is a raw morning so I should wrap up warmly if I were you.'

She waited whilst I put on a woolly hug-me-tight under my coat, lastly pulling on a soft, woollen cap over my hair and woollen gloves over my hands. I thought ruefully that this was no morning to go walking in the parkland but humouring the vagaries of Miss Elsa was destined to be part of my life.

As we neared her room I could feel my heart hammering in my breast and Agnes must have thought me nervous

81

because she touched my arm lightly and said, 'Don't worry, miss, she's looking forward to seeing you again.'

The first thing I noticed when we entered her room was that the doors of the doll's house were closed, although it stood as before in the midst of the carpet, a complete miniature of Milverton apart from the old south wing.

Miss Elsa was standing at the window looking out into the park but she turned as I entered and I felt that this morning she was different in a strange and subtle way. She watched me curiously as I crossed the floor to stand beside her, then she startled me by asking, 'What is your name?'

'I am Carla. I hope you will call me by that name and that we can be friends.'

She shrugged her shoulders carelessly. Then, just as my heart sank dismally, her face broke into an enchanting smile – beautiful, bright, but the most empty smile I had ever seen, for its enchantment never touched the coldness of her blue eyes.

Swifly she turned on her heel and ran towards the door calling, 'Come quickly or we shall be late.' We heard her running along the corridor towards the stairs leaving Agnes and me to follow her.

The damp chill of the late November morning hit me forceably as I stepped outside, and the heavy, grey skies did nothing to restore my spirits. The frozen snow under our shoes crunched as we hurried after Elsa's flying figure. I thought that any moment there would be a disaster and that her feet would slide from under her.

She turned round to look for us as she reached the steps which led down towards the Italian garden and there at last waited for us to catch up with her. She was flushed and obviously delighted with her escapade. Agnes caught hold of her arm with some degree of annoyance.

'You must wait for us, Miss Elsa,' she said firmly, 'It is slippery underfoot and we don't want any accidents do we?'

Elsa shrugged her arm away and I was more than surprised when she took my hand. 'I will walk with you,' she said firmly. 'You can go back, Agnes. I don't need you today.'

Agnes looked at me doubtfully and I stood there, unsure and not a little dumbfounded.

'I think you'll be all right, miss, but I'll be watching from the window in case you need me.'

'Oh go away, Agnes, you fuss too much,' Elsa said irritably, and I was surprised how normal her words sounded to my ears.

She tugged sharply on my hand and I could do nothing else but follow where she led. I turned once to see Agnes standing where we had left her, then we were walking quickly through the sunken garden then upwards towards the distant fells.

She was tall and her stride was longer than mine, so I had almost to run to keep pace with her. All the time, however, she clutched my hand in hers, and so running and walking we came at last to the grey, stone walls which marked the boundry of the park. She released my hand and, gasping for breath, I stood beside her looking out across the moorland, grey and dismal under the threatening skies.

She seemed to have forgotten my presence as she gazed in brooding silence towards the distant crags, and I was glad of the respite to calm my thudding heart. I leaned against the stone wall, racking my brains for something to say. Just then I looked up and was delighted with the sight of a flock of wild geese flying inland in the shape of an arrow, their necks outstretched, their wings beating against the wind, and I pointed upwards so that she might see them also. We both watched them disappear into the distance and then she turned and smiled at me, the gentle smile of a child.

'The moors look unfriendly today, Elsa,' I ventured. 'They can be beautiful under a summer sky but this grey sky only makes them forbidding.'

She pointed towards the distant fells. 'What are they?' she asked almost in a whisper.

'I don't know all their names, but the one nearest to us is Grant's Peak and the white one you can just see through the mist is Fender's Rake. There are higher ones behind but we can't see them through the mist. When the mist clears we must come here again.'

'She's out there,' she said, her voice expressionless, but her pointing finger led my eyes to where, behind the mist, Mower Gap raised its bleak summit towards the skies.

Compassion made me put my arm around her waist. Poor lady, confused and sick in mind, she associated those fells with the sister whose death had seen the start of her illness and I had no words of comfort to say to her.

I drew her away from the wall and slowly we made our way back across the damp grass towards the path.

She suddenly surprised me by taking both my arms in a grip which would surely leave them blue with bruises, and with eyes burning into mine, she said, 'She won't ever come back. They say she will, but she won't, I know.'

'No, Elsa, I don't think she will ever come back, but you must remember her with love and pray for her soul.'

'He came back, but not her. They'll never find her now.'

'Probably not. It is wiser not to wander over the moors, they can be very dangerous to those who do not know them.'

'She knew them, but she's still there on Mower Gap.'

'Do you remember her name, Elsa?'

She looked at me sharply. Then, like a petulant, sulky child, she said, 'Of course. It was Caprice.'

My face must have registered its shocked surprise because I clutched at her hands tightly for a long moment before I could answer her.

'Oh no, Elsa, it is not Caprice who lies up there. Caprice still comes to Milverton.'

All I could think of was that in her sick mind she wanted it to be Caprice who was lying up there on the dismal moorland because of what she had once been to Mr Thorn. But even as I thought it the expression on her face changed into one of fear and panic. Withdrawing her hands sharply from mine with a cry of horror, she turned to run headlong into the direction of Milverton, leaving me to follow as best I could.

I had no hope of overtaking her and could only run in her wake, my feet slipping and sliding on the snow which yesterday had melted and overnight had frozen into solid pieces of ice. I saw her flying figure leaping up the steps which led from the Italian garden and then her headlong flight into the house. When I reached the hall there was no sign of her but I was horrified to see Mr Thorn standing at the foot of the staircase with a look of the utmost displeasure on his face.

I was only too aware of my dishevelled appearance after my flight from the boundary and I stood before him gasping for breath, quivering and silent under his stern regard.

'You appear to have the unhappy and effortless knack of antagonizing my wife, Miss McAllister. I arrived here in time to see her entering the house in great distress because of something you appear to have said to her. Just what it was she would not say.'

I would not answer him. I was furious with the unfairness of his attitude, and for a long moment we stood looking at each other, antagonism and dislike like living things between us. Then coldly he said, 'Perhaps it would be as well if you did not see her again today. I have given instructions that she is to stay in her room tomorrow; it is far too cold for walking in the park anyway, and no doubt she will by that time have forgotten what passed between you today. Read something light to her, something not intended to scare her to death.'

For a few moments he stared at me coldly, then he left me to go to his study. With tears streaming down my face, I made my unsteady way towards my room, where I threw myself on my bed in a torrent of weeping, promising that in the morning I would leave Milverton. I would work in a shop, serve ale in a tavern or scrub floors in a workhouse, anything to take me away from this dreadful house and that insufferable man.

Nancy served my lunch, avoiding my eyes as she set the little table in front of the fire, but I had no doubt she would report my tear-stained face to anybody in the kitchens who cared to listen. I hoped Agnes would come to my room but, when she did not, I thought that she too obviously disapproved of my morning's work and had no desire to see me again that day. Soon after three, there was a light tap on my door and Celia entered bearing a tray on which rested a teapot, milk and sugar, and two cups and saucers. She placed them down on the table, then drew up the chair opposite to mine.

She came straight to the point, not mincing her words and using her most forthright nurse's voice to give added weight.

'I couldn't help hearing what he said to you in the hall this morning,' she said briskly. 'What you should do now is pack your bags and leave here. I get to hear of plenty of jobs which would suit you and you could stay at my sister's until something turns up.'

Oh, how I longed to say I would leave with her! But some innate independence would not allow me to admit defeat even when it stared me in the face. She lectured me severely for half an hour and although I listened to her in the end she knew I would stay. She swept the tea things together with the air of one who has washed her hands of me, and I sat miserably alone after her slim figure, bristling with annoyance, had swept from my room, carrying the tea things with her.

The long winter's night stretched endlessly before me but I sat in my chair, not even bothering to light the gaslamps and the fire burned low in the grate. Dinner was served to me at seven o'clock when Nancy lit the lamps for me and built up the fire, startled to find me sitting in the dark. I thanked her and this time she gave me a sympathetic look and pointed to the tray. At first my eyes only saw the covered dishes, and then as I reached out to unwrap my napkin I saw the pale-blue envelope propped up besides the salt-cellar. With a swiftly beating heart I reached out for it and, on opening it, found a single sheet of pale blue paper from which rose a delicate perfume. A woman's notepaper bearing a message written in a woman's hand.

I looked at the signature first, wondering who could be writing to me in this household, and my heart lifted to find it was from Miss Judith. She wrote:

Dear Carla,

I am sorry to hear of the unfortunate episode with Miss Elsa this morning and understand how much the incident must have distressed you. I ask God to help you in the task you have set yourself and ask you, dear Carla to bear with Mr Thorn who has many grievous problems on his mind, not the least of which is the care of his wife. I am looking forward to our meeting next Tuesday afternoon and to a pleasant evening.

Yours most sincerely, Judith Lytton

I sat back in my chair with the letter in my hands, and the salty tears rolled down my face blurring the words she had written. She was kind, Mrs Stephen Lytton, and my sad heart responded to her kindness at a time when I believed the world was starved of it.

For Miss Judith's sake, I would try again, because of the faith she placed in me and for no other reason, I told myself. I would not let myself fall into traps which seemed to have been specially placed for me. There would be no more talk of Elsa's sister who lay somewhere in the shadow of the distant fells, or of Caprice whose beauty had captivated the days of my childhood. We would walk no more where Mower Gap shed its formidable shadow across the coarse, blue grass of the moorland and where only the lonely curlew found pleasure in its rugged company.

5

Miss Elsa did not forgive me immediately. Next morning I sat miserably on the window seat in her room, shivering in the draught which came through the small, oblong panes and Elsa knelt before her doll's house changing and rechanging the furniture. Not once did she look in my direction and I poured over the book in my lap for over an hour without turning a single page.

Agnes brought coffee during the morning and although she looked at me strangely there was no smile in answer to mine. Thankfully, I escaped from the room at noon to take my lunch in my own room, saying that I would be back at two o'clock. Only Agnes nodded her head by way of reply.

When I returned to them I found Agnes sitting beside the fire with some sewing on her lap and Elsa was sitting disconsolately on the window seat I had occupied all morning. I was glad to see that the front of the doll's house was closed and deliberately I went over to the window to sit beside her. She did not look at me and after a while she began to draw a circle on the pane of glass which her breath had misted over. As her finger paused I bravely inserted two eyes and a mouth within the circle. For a moment I wondered if she would be angry, then suddenly she laughed, breathing upon another pane so that I could repeat the experiment. Agnes looked up from her sewing, and seeing that harmony had been restored she rose from her chair saying she had business with Mrs Bamber.

The game continued until every pane we could reach had been so ornamented, then when no panes were left Elsa walked over to the fireside and dropped down upon the hearthrug.

By this time I was feeling very cold and was more than glad that she had elected to sit near the fire. I took the chair Agnes had vacated and asked hopefully, 'Would you like me to read to you?'

She shook her head. Then, having second thoughts, said, 'What will you read?'

'Shall we try to find something together?' I suggested.

In one long, liquid movement she rose from her position on the rug and taking my hand she led me over to the small bookcase standing against the wall. It contained many new volumes and there were books filled with poetry as well as others illustrated with pictures of birds and animals. Many of the books might have been enjoyed by children of ten or twelve, but there were others written by Charles Dickens and even the novels of Jane Austen had a place on the shelves.

I watched as Elsa's long finger lightly ran along the volumes, pausing at last to take out a volume bound in dark red leather. I took it from her and was delighted to see that it was Jane Austen's *Emma*. I had read it twice already but Elsa opened the book at a page two-thirds through and halfway into a chapter. Even as I complied with her request I felt certain that the book had never been opened before.

I had always enjoyed reading and therefore read well. Because of the life I had led I had never had time to develop an accent, although once, many years before, my father had laughingly accused me of speaking with a north-country burr, a fault which he quickly remedied. He always said that English was the most beautiful language in the world when it was spoken properly, and that true English was classless. I wasn't very sure about my English but we duly settled down before the fire and I started to read where her finger pointed.

Agnes returned to the room and took the other chair and I was happy that she too listened whilst the afternoon passed pleasantly, although how well Miss Elsa understood the unfurling story I could not tell.

At five o'clock Nancy served Agnes and Elsa with tea and I was informed that mine waited for me in my room. Reluctantly, I put the book away and looked up to find Miss Elsa's eyes watching me so curiously that I wondered how much intelligence lingered still behind that disconcerting stare.

I promised I would return to her room at ten o'clock the

next morning but Agnes pointed out that I was not required to work during the weekends.

She walked to the door with me but before she closed it behind her I said, 'I feel so much happier this afternoon, Agnes. I cannot allow the weekend to interfere with even this small improvement.'

'Well, just as you wish, miss. I only mentioned it because neither of the other two ladies worked over the weekends. They said it gave them a chance to attend to other matters or even to go into Feltham if they wished.'

I hoped that I had not offended Agnes and I laid my hand gently upon her arm. 'You have known Miss Elsa a long time, Agnes, and I am new to all this. Please understand, I seem to have wasted so much time and made so many mistakes since I arrived. Now that there is an improvement I have to see that it continues.'

So the weekend came and went, happily enough, I think. I saw little of the family and the house seemed at times unnaturally quiet. On Sunday morning I watched Miss Judith and Mr Stephen depart for church, accompanied by Mr and Mrs Bamber, and later, from the window in Miss Elsa's room, I watched Mr Thorn ride out on horseback in the company of a younger man I had not seen before.

Monday morning saw the arrival of Mrs Lytton's new nurse, a middle-aged woman who marched through the front door looking entirely competent and, I thought, wholly unimaginative. Shortly after lunch I went downstairs to say good-bye to Celia. I had not thought she would be upset to be leaving Milverton but she stood in the hall surrounded by her luggage and numerous boxes containing gifts from the Lytton family with tears streaming down her face. She enveloped me in a hug which left me gasping for breath, but largely to disguise her woebegone face than from any real affection she had developed for me, I felt sure. Then she made me promise that I would write to her frequently, and promptly departed without leaving me a forwarding address.

It was only just over a week since I had arrived in old George's ramshackle carriage to take up my duties here. Yet

It seemed to me now that I had known no other scenery except the view I had from my window of the old wing of the house and the mournful vista of the distant fells. Milverton and the people who lived here seemed to have taken possession of me entirely, but I was no longer unhappy. I had made one friend, if it was not presumptuous of me to call Miss Judith a friend, and since the morning that I was trying to forget I had not encountered Mr Thorn. I was therefore disconcerted to find him leaving his wife's room just as I was about to enter it, and he stepped aside so that I might walk in front of him.

He looked down at me with that amused expression which I found both tantalizing and infuriating.

'Ah, Miss McAllister,' he said lightly, as though he found some surprise in seeing me embarked upon the duties for which he was paying me. 'I am pleased we have met, since it reminds me there is something I want to say to you.'

I paused, looking up at him expectantly, wondering with some degree of trepidation what I had done now to earn his displeasure.

'My sister-in-law tells me that she has invited you to take tea with her tomorrow afternoon and that later you are to accompany her to the village.'

'Yes, sir. But, if it does not have your approval and I am needed here, then of course I will explain to Miss Judith that I cannot go.

'You do not need to seek my approval for such a venture, Miss McAllister. I intend to take my wife with me tomorrow so it will not be necessary for you to see her. Allow me to wish you a pleasant evening.'

With the briefest of smiles he had gone, leaving me staring after him until his tall figure turned the corner at the end of the corridor. Oh, but he was incalculable, this man! One minute he was looking at me with the utmost distaste and the next he was showing a kindness of which I had not thought him capable. My hand was shaking as I closed the door behind me and all I could think of was the twisted, impersonal smile on his darkly handsome face.

The sitting room was empty and the front of the doll's house closed. From the bedroom beyond I heard laughter, so I walked forward, unsure what I should find there. The room was in a mess but Miss Elsa was in high good humour as she paraded before Agnes in a ball gown of emerald green satin, heavily encrusted with gold embroidery and tiny, seed pearls. Agnes looked at me warily but it was obvious what the pattern of our afternoon would be.

Every conceivable drawer, every wardrobe, every hat box was opened, and the bed strewn with furs and feathers, the property of a spoiled and adored wife. Once, under the sparkling chandeliers and in the fresh, fair beauty of her youth, Miss Elsa had waltzed in the arms of Mr Thorn in the rooms of this house, but now in the cold light of a November afternoon the dress looked garish, almost like the attire of a circus performer, and her silver-fair hair flopped untidily over her eyes in heavy curls on to her shoulders.

She was not interested in the tea gowns and outdoor apparel, only in the ball gowns, and there were so many of them – in velvets and watered silks, taffetas and heavy satins – and with them were the evening shoes and evening bags, the capes edged with fox fur and ermine, and ivory and ostrich-feather fans. She insisted that I too should try them on then dissolved into laughter when she found that they were far too long for me and trailed about my feet. As I took off one of the gowns and stood in my petticoat she stretched out her hand and clasped the Egyptian amulet I wore round my throat.

'What is this?' she asked curiously.

'An amulet. It came all the way from Egypt and is very old. Do you like it?'

'No. I would rather have the locket I gave to you. Why did you not wear it?'

Agnes gave me a warning look, then, much to my relief, she came to my rescue. 'The clasp got broken Miss Elsa and it has gone away to be repaired.'

'Who broke it? she enquired haughtily.

'I expect it broke with age, these things happen you know,' I said, trying to console her.

'You broke it didn't you Agnes?' she accused.

'No, Miss Elsa. As Miss Carla said, it was very old and the clasp needed replacing. You wouldn't like it to get lost would you?'

'What have you done with the hair? Bring back the hair,

that has not gone to be mended.'

'The hair is still in the locket. The jeweller said he would be careful not to lose it, and it belongs in the locket.'

'The locket belongs to me, it is her hair!'

I could feel myself trembling and my tongue felt dry and sore in my mouth as I listened to Agnes's attempts to placate her. Already I had come to dread her sudden tantrums. Now, in her bright green gown with its gold and pearls, her hair untidy from the taking on and off of innumerable dresses, her face flaming with anger, there was an obscenity about her.

'Go away, both of you,' she said flatly. 'I don't want you here again, not without the locket.'

I looked at Agnes helplessly as she walked towards the door. Then Elsa turned her eyes upon me – baleful eyes, filled with a fierce hatred which I had done nothing to deserve.

'Take your clothes and go,' she said contemptuously.

I struggled into my skirt and blouse in the sitting room with Agnes's assistance, and she whispered, 'Don't worry, miss, by tomorrow she will have forgotten, but it's better we go now.'

'But is it safe to leave her alone?'

'Safer than if we remain; she's likely to take the room apart if we don't do as she asks.'

'What can be done about the locket? Obviously, she remembers sending it to me and expects me to wear it.'

'I'll mention it to Mr Thorn, miss. No doubt he will know how to handle things.'

Looking at her quiet face I saw a great perplexity there and in a voice intended more for her own ears than mine she said, 'I can't think how she came by it.'

'But she said the locket was hers.'

She looked at me steadily for a few moments; then in a quiet flat voice she said, 'No, Miss Carla, it was never hers. The locket and the hair that is in it belonged to Miss Caprice.'

For a long time I stared after her in disbelief before I made my bemused way back to my own room. Questions chased each other endlessly through my head. If the locket belonged to Caprice why wasn't it in her possession? Surely

Agnes must know that Caprice still came to Milverton, that she and Thorn could possibly still be lovers, and what in heaven's name was Elsa doing with the locket?

Why after all this time should I be plagued by thoughts of Caprice? And, above all, what was it to me that she and Thorn could still be lovers?

The vicar had no cause to complain that his young mothers failed to turn out in force to hear Miss Judith's talk. Indeed, when we arrived at the village hall practically every seat was occupied.

On the platform chairs had been arranged for the vicar and his wife, as well as dignitaries of the church, and there were also two empty chairs – one for Miss Judith and one for myself. I asked the vicar if I might not sit in the body of the hall, preferably in the most inconspicuous place he could find, but as I took my seat at the end of a row about halfway down the hall I saw a number of heads turn to look at me, to be followed by whispered conversation. I was relieved when at last the lights were dimmed and the talk could begin.

The vicar spoke a few words by way of introduction, then he brought Miss Judith forward to stand alone under the only light left burning in the room. For the first few minutes she relied wholly upon the notes in her hand, but then her voice became more confident and she laid them aside, relying entirely upon her memory.

At first, I was not listening to her words, being more concerned with the pretty picture she made. She was wearing a jade green, watered silk tea gown, with cream lace at her throat and wrists, and from a narrow waist the skirt billowed out in unpressed pleats until it reached the floor. Her bright hair was caught back in the nape of her neck by a huge tortoiseshell slide and there were jewelled studs in her ears. I judged that in the early part of her talk the audience too were more concerned with her appearance, but then, as her voice took possession of us, I for one fell under the spell of Provence.

I gave myself up entirely to the visions she created in my mind of narrow, cobbled streets leading upwards from ancient harbours where the fishermen worked at their nets, singing the songs their kind had sung for centuries. I stood in sleepy village squares, watching the sunlight playing on faded plaster walls and lingering on red roof-tops and stately, dark cypresses, and I saw it shining on villas trailed in bougainvillaea in the villages which clustered untidily on pinnacles of rock overlooking the blue Mediterranean. In my nostrils was the scent of the pine trees and in my ears the sound of the surf breaking against the shore.

I stood with Miss Judith in the garden of her grandmother's villa, looking southwards towards Italy, watching the coastline as it curved this way and that and the distant haze over the Appenines.

I had forgotten the village hall and the villagers with their occasional coughs and sniffles, the floor which smelled strongly of carbolic and the earthy smell of these good people who lived close to the soil. All my heart and mind was concentrated on the soft, southern tones of her voice and the vistas of timeless beauty opened up by her words, so that when the lights were turned up at the interval I looked around me bemused, startled by the applause which broke out from all over the hall. Graciously she acknowledged it, then there was bustle and much activity as the long tables at the side of the room were set with home-made cakes and scones, and gigantic tea urns were brought in by the men and the older women while the young men handed round cups of tea and piled up platters.

I looked at the people nearest to me to see if I could find a familiar face but I was disappointed. It seemed to me that these faces had never been young but it was impossible to tell their ages. They were all of a pattern with ruddy cheeks and hair pulled back from their faces in shining buns. Most of them wore shawls about their shoulders but there was one or two in Sunday-best coats and hats, their stalwart legs warmly covered by dark, woollen stockings and ending in robust, sensible shoes to combat the slippery roads outside the hall.

The woman sitting next to me rose from her chair to assist at the tables and almost immediately her seat was taken by another, younger women who smiled at me brightly and said in a breathless whisper, 'I wouldn't 'ave known you, Lottie, but Mrs Merriweather told mi mither you were back up 'ere.'

I looked at her blankly, ashamed that I was not able to put a name immediately to her fresh, pert face.

'You've forgotten me, 'aven't you?' she laughed. 'Emily Peel that was, you know, the 'arrier's daughter.'

My face cleared. 'Oh, Emily, of course I remember you now, but it's been so long and everybody seems to have altered so much. I haven't seen a solitary face I can put a name to yet.'

'Well I 'ad to look twice at you, Lottie. You've altered and that's a fact, but then you were never really one of us, were you?'

'I don't know. I tried to be.'

She laughed. 'Well you never were, 'owever much you tried. Honestly if I'd met you in the street I'd never o' known you.'

'I didn't think I'd changed all that much Emily.'

'Well you talk different for one thing, more posh like, and you're prettier too, and fashionable, like a real lady.'

Now it was my turn to laugh.

'Emily, we must meet where we can talk properly. It won't be possible for me to invite you up to Milverton but perhaps I could call on you one day when I am in the village?'

'I'd like that Lottie. I'm married to Ned Fenton, you know, and we have a little cottage behind t' main street; it's only two up and two down but I've got a little parlour. Try to come in t' day time, there's no 'an much room at neet wi' Ned's long legs sprawled out across th'rug.'

'I will come, I promise, the very next time I come down to the village in the afternoon.'

'That'll be grand then. It'll be just like old times to 'ave you romancin' like in the old days.'

By this time people were returning to their seats and the woman who had previously sat next to me returned. However, she leaned over and whispered to Emily, 'If you want to stay there Emily, you can. I've got a friend a few rows further down.'

'I like the next bit best,' Emily confided in me.

'Oh, what happens now then?'

'Magic lantern slides. We often get these from the vicar

but I expect Mrs Lytton's are better'n 'is.'

So for the next half-hour we watched the scenery of Provence unfold before our eyes. The last slide showed us a picture of Miss Judith's grandmother's villa perched high upon a cliff-top overlooking the sea. Blossoms spilled over the terraces and along the walls of terracotta plaster, and the villa seemed to grow out of the hillside, as much a part of it as the tall cypress trees surrounding it. I watched her gracefully accepting the applause which followed her talk, then the vicar stepped forward with his speech of appreciation.

He ended his words by saying. 'I can see that you have all enjoyed Mrs Lytton's excellent lecture. Are you in the mood for more?'

There was instant stamping of feet and cheering so that he held up his hand for silence. 'Well,' he said, smiling down upon them with the air of a man who is quite sure he can follow up his words by his actions, 'we are fortunate enough to have another young lady in our midst whose father was a considerable scholar and who will no doubt have passed on much of his knowledge to his daughter. She has travelled with him extensively in the Middle East and of course I am referring to Miss Carlotta McAllister, a young lady who is known to a great many of you from childhood.'

I sat back in my chair petrified. How could the vicar do this to me? I had no magic lantern slides to show these people. I had never addressed a public meeting in my life and, if my romancings as they called them had amused them as children, they were not guaranteed to do so now that they were grown.

Emily sitting beside me beamed with pleasure. 'Well, did you ever!' she said. That'll be another night Ned'll 'ave to look to Sarah. Why, what's the matter, Lottie? You've gone quite pale.'

'I had no idea the vicar was going to do this, Emily. I can't talk to these people.'

'That you can, Lottie,' she said confidently. 'You talked to us long and often when we were little uns, it'll be no different now than it were then.'

I looked at her helplessly but by this time the vicar had come to stand at the end of the row and was holding out his hand to me with an encouraging smile. Like one in a dream I rose and went forward to meet him, following in his footsteps until we reached the platform. Then I saw Miss Judith looking at me, smiling her encouragement.

I stood beside him looking out over a sea of upturned faces, endeavouring to discover by their expressions exactly what they thought of his idea. No doubt there would be some of them who were open-hearted like Emily, but there would be others who would sniff with disdain, asking themselves, 'Who is this Lottie McAllister who gives herself airs and thinks herself such a fine lady that she believes she can copy Miss Judith without either her class or her education?'

My smile was stiff on my lips as I listened to the vicar bidding them attend in two weeks' time, then miserably I watched as they rose from their seats to troup out into the night, singly or in groups, morosely silent or chattering like magpies. Behind me Miss Judith was in conversation with a small group of church officials and I could only look at the vicar reproachfully saying, 'Vicar, how could you? I have never in my life addressed a meeting; how shall I know what will interest them?'

'You'll know, my dear. You were never at a loss in the old days. In fact, we always had the utmost difficulty in restraining you. You have a whole fortnight to prepare your notes and I have the utmost confidence in you. Don't worry, Lottie, you'll be splendid on the night, simply splendid.'

I had none of his confidence and when I continued to look unassured he placed an affectionate arm around my shoulders.

'You can have no idea what it is like finding something or somebody to interest these people, my dear. On the whole their lives are uneventful, revolving around seedtime and harvest, birth, marriage and death. I doubt if more than a handful of them have ever been further than Feltham. My few small adventures ran out years ago. Do this for me Lottie and I promise when you come here in two weeks' time I shall have some news for you.'

I looked up at him quickly.

'No, don't ask me anything now because I am not sure,

but in two weeks I shall hope to be very sure, then I will be able to tell you all that I have discovered about Elliot Cliffe.'

It was sweet and clever blackmail, I knew, but he knew that he had won. I looked at him helplessly asking, 'How do we know that they will come to listen to me?'

'They will come my dear. Out of friendship, out of curiosity, even out of spite, but they will come. I have not been in my profession so long that I do not know something about human nature.'

And so, despite my misgivings, I agreed to do it. Later, going home in the carriage with Miss Judith I pondered on the folly of my decision. Miss Judith assured me that the only necessity was to know one's subject well. What subject, I wondered! A smattering of Egyptology, the impressions I had gained of distant lands and foreign peoples; and almost against my will I recalled the last lonely journey I had taken, travelling home from Alexandria in a ship already crowded from the Far East and with the memory of my father sleeping his eternal sleep in the sandy soil of the English cemetery in Cairo. Was there anything in my life which would interest the villagers of Gleave, I wondered, but I agreed with what the vicar had said – curiosity would bring them to hear my words even though they might scoff at them later in the privacy of their homes.

6

The next two weeks passed all too quickly. I was with Miss Elsa every day and they were days which on the whole passed harmoniously enough. I read to her from all manner of books and we played childish games with cards. She did not refer to the locket again and I wondered if perhaps Mr Thorn had spoken to her on the matter. Yet I could not believe that Agnes had dared to raise the subject with him. Occasionally, when the weather was fine, we would wrap up warmly and venture out into the gardens. Never again, however, did our footsteps lead us to the point where we could look out across the moorland towards the distant fells.

In the evenings I worked on my notes, becoming more and more despondent as I struggled to find something to interest my country audience. Once I took tea with Miss Judith and read some of my notes to her. When I looked up to see what she thought of them, she said, 'You have made a good start, Carla. You will see how you can embroider upon all the things you have written down. The things you tell them will certainly be more exciting than the lives they lead here.'

No one had mentioned Christmas which was now only a little over two weeks away. I was expecting it to be a miserable affair. I could not think that time spent with Miss Elsa would be different just because it was the festive season. One day was much like another to her. I also felt increasingly that Agnes watched me, but whether it was benevolently or malevolently I was not sure. Whenever I saw Mr Thorn he favoured me with a polite greeting and an impersonal smile, but we had no other conversation. Then, on the day before I was to address the young mothers, Miss Judith sent me a note inviting me to take tea with her before the meeting so that we could travel into Gleave together.

From Miss Judith I learned that there was to be a larger

party than usual for Christmas. Miss Rowena and her husband, now Lord and Lady Wheeldon, with a close friend of theirs, were expected, as well as two other couples and a young widow from Medchester, a Mrs St Clare.

I lowered my eyes so that she would not see the tell-tale colour in my cheeks. So Caprice was coming again to Milverton, and I wondered if I would see her and find her very changed. They were arriving this very day and Mr Thorn was driving into Feltham to meet them. I was startled out of my reverie by Miss Judith asking, 'Have you any plans for Christmas, Carla?'

'I don't know Miss Judith. I do not know if I shall be expected to remain here or if I am entitled to take a few days' holiday. If I am, then I expect I shall go to Medchester to stay with one of my aunts, probably Aunt Maud.'

'No doubt Thorn has overlooked the matter but I will mention it to him. On no account should you be expected to carry on with your work here as though Christmas did not exist. Shall you like staying with Aunt Maud?'

'I think so. There will be friends to visit and things to do. Aunt Maud is a good cook and I have always enjoyed the Christmas fare.'

She laughed a little, 'And it will be a change from this sad, old house. That is what you are thinking, Carla, but you are too polite to say so. Once when first I came here this was a joyful place, but overnight it seemed to change. Mr Lytton's death, Mrs Lytton's stroke, then Elsa's illness. Even Jeremy left to go abroad and Rowena's unhappy marriage only added to the gloom.'

She sat silent, wrapped up in her thoughts and I, too, was remembering.

I remembered the Christmases I had spent with my father without the trappings of tinsel and holly, sitting out in the desert under a midnight blue sky ablaze with stars, and only the cheerful crackle from the camp fire lighting up our faces. Usually I was the only girl, listening to the talk of Old Kingdom, Middle Kingdom, New Kingdom, Ptolomaic or Graeco-Roman, and my mind would spin with talk of pharaohs and the names of their gods. Fascinated, I would watch how skilfully the men were able to read the hieroglyphics, tracing with sand-encrusted fingers the exquisite characters marching this way and that way across a sheet of papyrus, until in the end I would rise to my feet and wander away to where I could stand looking out across the valley below.

The workmen would be clustered round their camp fires a little way off and occasionally they would sing, a plaintive air as old as time, a melody some ancient pharoah himself might have heard as he sauntered with his love in the seclusion of his scented garden. Sometimes the men would dance to the music of drums and tambourines – music strange to western ears – writhing and whirling round the flickering flames in an ever-increasing crescendo until they fell, finally exhausted, on to the sand.

Looking back on those times now I could only think how biblical the scenery had been. The tall, feathery palms, graceful against the bright moonlight of a sky busy with stars, and men, huddled for warmth in their blankets against the cold of the desert night.

I had thought I might talk to the villagers about Christmas time in the lands of the Bible but in the end I decided against it. The villagers thought Christmas as much a part of winter as the snow itself. It belonged to long, dark, winter evenings and the companionable warmth around cottage hearths, carol singing on Christmas Eve and the opening of presents around the breakfast table on Christmas morning. I decided to leave talk of Christmas for the vicar, for how could I expect them to understand that in my travels I had seen how the first Christmas might have been? I became more and more dejected, wondering miserably if I had anything of value to tell my audience.

We were early, but the vicar was there before us, helping his flock to decorate the hall. Across one corner was a giant Christmas tree, given as usual by the Lytton family, decorated with baubles of all shapes and sizes as well as with streamers of silver tinsel. I did not flatter myself that the decorations were in my honour, but they would no doubt help to distract a critical public from my shortcomings.

My heart was hammering painfully in my breast as the vicar got to his feet to make his preliminary announcements; at the same time there was a stir at the back of the hall and a handful of people came in, standing with their backs to the wall. The lights were still turned on at full and with the utmost horror I recognized Mr Thorn and what appeared to be a small company of ladies and gentlemen. With my face burning I turned to Miss Judith while the vicar left the platform to go to them. He appeared to be inviting them to come forward, but I was thankful to see that they declined the invitation.

Aware of my miserably embarrassed face, Miss Judith leaned forward and whispered, 'I had no idea Thorn would bring his guests here, Carla. I knew he had gone into Feltham to meet them. I told him about our meeting and he must have remembered it as they passed through the village. You must not be afraid, they have not come to criticize, only to listen.'

The lights in the body of the hall were dimmed and now I stood alone on the platform under the only light left burning. I felt a kind of detachment, as though I stood outside myself seeing a slender, pale, young woman wearing a cornflower-blue dress, fingering nervously the amulet she wore around her neck. I was aware of the shuffling of feet and clearing of innumerable throats but apart from the first two or three rows the merciful darkness beyond gave me some sort of courage and resolutely I squared my shoulders in answer to the vicar's smile of encouragement.

At first my voice came to me as a whisper, and then, asking God to give me courage I repeated my greeting to those present. I was encouraged by their silence and soon it seemed that another being took possession of me. I found that I was able to talk as I had once talked to the village children, and to pretend that they clustered round me on the hillside above the village, with the scent of clover all around us and the lazy droning of bees on the warm, summer air. All at once I seemed to remember every word my father had ever said to me as I sat on my stool beside his chair, listening to his dear remembered voice filling my heart and my mind with the glories of the past.

I started my talk with a description of the liner which took us from Southampton to Alexandria, but I did not dwell too much upon the voyage. It was difficult to describe sensations or aromas, so I only touched lightly upon the scent of herbs wafting over the Mediterranean from the isles of Greece, or that first incredible, potent smell of the orient as the ship dropped anchor off Alexandria.

I had chosen Egypt as the country most suitable for my talk because, of all the countries I had visited, it was the one I had loved most. Launched into my lecture, I described to them the great and ancient river as it wound its majestic way through Egypt towards the first cataract at Aswan, sometimes through strips of emerald green pasture set before a backdrop of purple hills, at others through the desert stretching out on either side as far as the eye could see. The true charm of Egypt was its unvarying sameness as village succeeded village, each one composed of its quota of meagre huts clustered together on the river's banks – huts with whitewashed walls, their roofs covered by palm fronds to keep out the heat of the sun while in every village among the huts rose slender dovecotes and always a solitary minaret or the white dome of some saint's tomb. In the villages small, naked children played together in the dust, their eyes encrusted with flies while along the banks walked the daily procession of biblical figures as they must surely have walked from the beginning of time. Children pulling vast oxen or tall camels with supercilious expressions, enormous men riding small, fragile-looking donkeys, their feet almost touching the floor, and women, slender and graceful, carrying their pitchers on their heads as they came down to the river to draw their water.

All along the banks of the Nile, slim, brown-limbed men still drew the water to irrigate the fields as they had done in the time of Moses, and the songs sung by the fishermen casting their nets were the same songs the pharaohs must have heard sitting under the awnings of their opulent barges.

I told them how insignificent I had felt, and humbled, before their strange, stone gods, and before the pillars of the temples reaching upwards into the brassy blue of the sky, and I tried to describe that most desolate of valleys which the kings of ancient Egypt had chosen for the resting place of their earthly bodies in the hope that they could lie undisturbed for all enternity.

I desperately wanted these people to see that valley, so far removed from the lush countryside of England. In the Valley of the Kings no freshening breeze came to disturb the heat which bounced back from the limestone cliffs, no blade of grass ever blew between the giant boulders, and only the tiny, green lizards sheltered between the stones from the glare of the sun. Above the dusty road, great holes gaped on the cliff face. Once these had been stone doors, each one bearing its royal seal, behind which long, tortuous passages led down into the bowels of the earth to an underground palace which served as some pharaoh's tomb. Once, my father had pointed out to me the bare footprint of the last Egyptian to leave the tomb three thousand years before, and as I spoke of it I could feel his hand gripping my arm, unaware of the pain he was inflicting. I tried to tell them how I had felt about that footprint, the footprint of another human being divided from us by the centuries of the past, and how when I climbed upwards into the heat of the noonday sun, my eyes fell upon a hawk, symbol of the God Horus, circling lazily overhead as though he had come back to protect the dead from the living.

I had been afraid I would have nothing to say to the people sitting in this crowded hall and now I found I had too much to say and not enough time in which to say it. I hoped my imagination was able to do justice to my description of a Nile sunset, when the sky glowed with colours of red and coral, purple and tragic crimson, against the backdrop of the western hills, and how the dark came suddenly, almost before the afterglow had completely left the sky, then too quickly the sand cooled and in the bright moonlight somehow the pillars and pylons and obelisks became whole again.

I told them that between the end of October and the beginning of April in Egypt the days were warm like an English summer and the velvet nights were cool, and I described how, when the Nile flooded, the land where once there had been undulating sand dunes was covered now by pools of clear, blue water through which soon would sprout delicate shafts of green.

There was no stopping me now as I told them how in the wintertime Egypt became the playground for the rich and famous of the western world. Like an army of locusts, they descended on Egypt, armed with fly switches and sun shades, pith helmets and skin lotions, watercolours and sketching blocks, so that each day they could be seen toiling up the steep slope which led towards the plateau in an endless procession of donkeys, camels and carriages. At the summit they would stand in awestruck amazement gazing at the face of the Sphinx, insignificant and overpowered by those three giant cones they called the Pyramids. In Luxor, too, every morning as soon as breakfast was over, the hotels would disgorge their guests, similarly equipped and attired, chattering like magpies as they boarded the ferries which would take them to the other side of the river and that desolate journey into the royal valley. Then like an army of ants they would descend into the bowels of the earth to look at the tombs of the pharaohs.

My father and his group of archaeologists grumbled incessantly about the tourists, saying they disturbed their work and hindered their findings, and in turn the tourists looked upon my sand-encrusted face and burned complexion with horror, shaking their heads at my faded skirt and sand-soiled blouse. I never envied them, not even when I lay under my mosquito net at the end of the day listening to the sounds of music reaching my ears across the water from their hotel ballrooms.

I could not end my talk without telling them something of Cairo yet to me Cairo has never seemed part of my beloved Egypt, and by that I mean the Egypt of the pharaohs. Cairo is predominantly an Arab city, it is the city of the Caliphs, of Saladin, of the Mamelukes, a city of the thousand and one nights, not a place to speak to me of ancient things, but of the east, the orient. It is a city of white, high-stepping donkeys and blue-shirted Fellahin, of the tinkling of tiny, silver bells round the necks of proud Arab horses and the graceful, feathery palms in the Esbekiyeh Gardens.

In Cairo the tombs and temples, the Pyramids and the Sphinx are forgotten and along its avenues camel trains carrying gorgeous eastern carpets rub shoulders with swiftly pattering donkeys and heavy buffalo cows. In Cairo one must put away ancient things for one is now in the middle ages, in a city of mosques and minarets, of decorated domes and fairytale elegance with its mixture of desolation and beauty. Delicate stained-glass windows glow between the lacework of white stucco and behind brown meshrebiyeh windows the women of the harem look out into the gardens below, their dark brown eyes mysterious above their veils.

It seemed to me that as I talked I could smell again the potent perfumes of the east in this fabulous city of the Arabian Nights, and with the scents came a remembered poverty as well as a simplicity. I remembered with a shudder the cynical ugliness of the oriental mind, but on the other hand the Muslim's devotion to Allah, answering the cry of the muezzin to kneel and pray wherever he might be.

Oh, the mysterious darkness of those mosques only ever glimpsed by me, and the sad beauty of the eastern garden with the jasmin tumbling wildly along crumbling limestone walls!

I spoke to these village people of scenes and places I had loved and I was deaf to the silence around me so that when I did become aware of it I was acutely embarrassed. There was no shuffling of feet or intermittent coughing and the two rows of faces looking up at me showed rapt attention. Self-consciously I turned to the vicar who sat alone at the end of the stage, my hand outstretched in an attitude of suppliance.

'I fear I have talked too long,' I said, 'there seemed too much to say.'

He rose and took my hand in his, squeezing my fingers gently, then suddenly the lamps were turned up and I heard the applause. I stood there blinking stupidly in the light, blushing furiously as I acknowledged it. Anxiously my eyes looked towards the back of the hall and I caught Mr Thorn's eyes as he was about to leave the hall. Then Judith was at my side, her arm around my waist and she was saying, 'Carla, you were wonderful, you made my talk a fortnight ago seem most ordinary.'

I had no slides to show them after the interval when refreshments were handed round but the vicar threw the meeting open to questions and I was amazed to hear them – simply put, but proof that they had listened to me.

At last it was over and as we poured out into the clear, frosty night Emily came and squeezed my arm.

'Lottie, you were wonderful,' she said. Then she was running away across the road in the direction of her cottage.

Just as we were about to step into the carriage the vicar pulled me to one side. Miss Judith was busy speaking to his wife but all the same he spoke in a whisper.

'I promised you that one good turn deserved another, didn't I? Well, I'm not sure that my news can compare with your excellent lecture, Lottie, but I think you will be pleased. I have news of Elliot.'

My eyes lit up as I said, 'Oh, I am so pleased. Where is he?'

'I hear from my daughter Dora, who is married to a doctor in Medchester, that Elliot has gone into partnership in the city. Not near them, I fear, but on the Parkland Heights side. It is a new area with some very nice property so it would seem your old friend is prospering.'

'Did Dora say if he was married?'

'No, she didn't, but the next time you are visiting your aunts you should have no difficulty in locating him.'

I thanked him warmly and when Miss Judith rejoined us we were speaking of other matters.

I felt unreasonably happy with my lot as we drove back to Milverton, with the clear, frosty moonlight glistening on the branches of the trees and the winding road before us. I felt relaxed in Miss Judith's company and in no time at all we were turning in at the wide gates leading up to the house.

Miss Judith opened the door with her latchkey and we let ourselves quietly into the hall. The chandeliers were lit in the hall and over the wide staircase, showing up the perfection of Miss Elsa's portrait. From the drawing room on our left came sounds of laughter and the deep tones of men's voices. I bade Miss Judith goodnight quietly and I was half way up the stairs when the drawing room door was flung open. Mr Stephen came out to greet his wife, and, as he helped her off with her coat, I heard Thorn's voice from within the room call out. 'Ask Miss McAllister to join us, Judith, I feel congratulations are in order and my guests are anxious to meet the young lady who opened up such exotic vistas for us in the midst of this wintry night.'

I looked down at her from the first landing, standing under Miss Elsa's portrait, my hand resting lightly on the balustrade, every instinct urging me to run upstairs into the darkness of the corridors above.

Judith had paused and sympathetically she held out her hand, 'Come, Carla,' she said, 'we cannot disappoint my brother-in-law and his guests.'

Reluctantly I returned to the hall where Mr Stephen helped me off with my coat. The drawing room seemed crowded with people. The fire burned brightly in the grate and to this day I do not remember the names of all those people to whom I was introduced. I recognized Rowena, who only favoured me with a cursory glance, and I recognized her husband, standing with a pale, effeminate man some distance from the others. They were speaking together in quiet tones, but from the looks on their faces it was plain they did not wish to be interrupted, and as we turned away I saw Rowena's husband take the hand of the younger man, much as a man might take hold of the hand of a woman. Judith's face seemed confused although she said nothing; the next moment I was handed a glass of sherry and a chair was found for me by one of the men. Almost immediately the lady on my right said, 'I enjoyed your talk, my dear, but feel I must confess that I was one of those people who wintered in Egypt and now you have made me wonder if I saw any of its beauty separate from the luxury.

'I am sorry, I had not meant to be unkind.'

'But you were quite right, my dear. We did lap up culture like a cat laps up cream, and I shudder to think how little I for one remember about the more serious things we saw. I loved Egypt for the sunshine after our cold and rainy climate. I loved the ballrooms and the garden parties and now I feel abysmally ignorant when I realize how little culture we absorbed.'

I smiled. 'But you kept your rose pink complexions and social graces.'

She laughed. 'My name is Mary Eastman. That is my husband you see talking to Mrs Lytton now. It was a great pity that you had to hide your beauty under a tent in the western desert, my dear; the young gallants in the ballrooms of Luxor would have welcomed you with enthusiasm.'

Just then, Mr Thorn came to my side and as he looked down at me intently I saw how kind his eyes were.

'Are they looking after you, Miss McAllister?' he enquired. 'May I be allowed to congratulate you on the excellence of your lecture? I expect Lady Eastman has told you how much we all enjoyed it.'

'You are very kind, sir,' I murmured.

'Have you met all my guests?'

My eyes strayed towards the fireplace where a tall, slender, young woman stood in conversation with one of the men. I had seen her when first I entered the room, laughing up into Thorn's eyes as though no other person existed for her in the entire room. Her blue-black hair shone in the light of the chandeliers as it fell in shining coils on to her shoulders, shoulders which gleamed white against the dark-blue velvet of her dress.

Mr Thorn's eyes followed mine. 'Ah, I see you have not met Mrs St Clare. Well, come with me, and I will introduce you.'

She turned as we joined her and her eyes appraised me even as her full, red lips smiled their greeting. My own lips responded stiffly, my voice fading in my throat, and wide-eyed I looked up into Thorn's face to find him watching me curiously. Then I heard Miss Judith's voice saying, 'Carla, Sir John Eastman has asked to meet you. He wants to talk to you about your lecture.'

Like one in a dream I followed her to where Sir John waited for us, smiling and courteous, but although I answered his questions my mind was in a turmoil, and across the room I saw Mr Thorn eying me inscrutably.

It was hours later when I reached my room that I realized my coat still lay on the chair in the hall.

The curtains had been drawn in my room but it was in darkness apart from the firelight which danced upon the walls. I fumbled with the matches, spilling several of them on the floor before I could light the gas lamps; then I sank into my chair trembling for reasons I could not understand.

She was beautiful, Mrs St Clare, gay and beautiful and

obviously infatuated with Mr Thorn, but she did not have the beauty of Caprice, nor her fascination. She was not Caprice.

I could not understand myself – Carlotta McAllister, who had always been so level-headed in spite of an imagination she had never been able to control.

What did I know of Caprice except that she had been the beautiful woman who had captivated my lonely childhood, making me tongue-tied in her presence? I remembered her small, white teeth when she laughed and the way her violet eyes mocked me, dancing with suppressed amusement, but I was remembering, too, her kindness. The way she had looked at me as if she was my conspirator, and how she had plied us with gifts from the Christmas tree the night we disturbed the revelry of the adults. I wondered why I should care so much about her now. No doubt she had become a well-loved wife and mother in some great house and not in need of any concern on my part. I was tired but my brain would not let me sleep, not even when the moonlight filtered into my darkened room and I lay snug and warm in my bed. From somewhere inside the house I heard a clock striking every quarter, and for a long time after I retired I heard doors closing and footsteps and hushed voices in the corridors outside my room. I tossed and turned until I could bear it no longer, then I rose from my bed, pulled on my robe, thrust my feet into my slippers, and padded over to the window, where I drew back the curtains.

The parkland lay under a silver coating of frost, eerie beneath the moonlight, and the sightless windows of the old wing stared back at me like sinister hollows in an old skull. A door slammed somewhere above me and I drew back from the window, expecting at any moment to see the glow of candlelight in the old wing. My breath caught in my throat suddenly because footsteps were running in the corridor outside my room, then I heard a voice humming faintly the strains of a waltz tune. I pulled the curtain round me so that my face was hidden and I held my breath, only dimly aware of the knocking of my heart.

There was candlelight now in the long windows of the

room which led to the old wing and it was moving quickly as though whoever held the candelabra ran on swift feet and with a sense of purpose. For a short time only I saw the light reflected in one of the rooms, then there was darkness. I found myself trembling and realized suddenly that I was very cold. Slowly, I returned to my bed but that, too, was cold and I knew I could not remain in it to lie shivering until the morning.

I asked myself who ran along the corridors and danced into the old wing of the house. If I went to investigate, what could I say if I were caught? Suppose it was Miss Rowena who visited the old wing for reasons of her own, or even Mrs St Clair and Mr Thorn who conducted their love affair at a respectable distance from his wife's apartments? Then my heart lurched. Suppose it was Elsa, living in a world of her own making and putting herself in danger as she danced across the rotting floorboards?

Resolutely, I let myself out of my room and walked along the corridor towards the door which led into the old part of the house. The door was unlocked and the moonlight filtered fitfully through the tall windows of the wide corridor beyond. In reality it was hardly a corridor at all, but more like a hall with tall, small-paned windows on either side, and could quite easily have served as a ballroom. Pedestals stood along its length bearing busts of long-dead composers, and although chandeliers hung down from the tall ceiling there were no candles in them and they were covered with cobwebs. Dust, too, had settled heavily on the floor, but through it I could see the footprints of a woman's shoes and there were other marks, too, where the hem of a robe had scattered the dust. Even as I stood there uncertainly, I could hear the scurry from the skirting boards and then with squeaks of alarm two shadowy, grey rats ran along the side of the room and disappeared into the shadows where the light from my candles did not reach.

I am afraid of rats but even so I knew I had to go on or I would never find the peace to sleep in my room for what remained of the night. Every step I took along that room was accompanied by the patter of their tiny claws and I do not know which I feared the most, their presence or the silent rooms beyond. Cautiously I opened the door, lifting

112

my candles on high as I did so. The room I entered was devoid of furniture but it was large and had once been beautiful. It was hung with blue watered silk, now lined with dust and smelling musty, as all old disused rooms do. But the footsteps in the dust led on through the room and here also were small claw marks like tiny hands, which could only have been made by rats.

The dust and the musty smell of vermin caught at my throat so that I could hardly breathe, but I could not stop now. If Mr Thorn came upon me I would tell him that I feared lest it was Miss Elsa who invaded these rooms in the dead of night but, if the rooms were used for other more sinister purposes, or more immoral ones, then I did not know what I would do. I moved on through the empty room, surprised to find that the doors opened quietly on their hinges as though they had been recently oiled, but again all was darkness. My heart hammered so much that I felt all the world must hear it, but now I could feel carpets under my feet and I could see that curtains were draped at the windows. There was furniture also, covered with white dust sheets, but a noise behind me sent me hurrying towards the window where I stood protected by the drapes, their mustiness bringing a tickle into my throat and tears into my eyes, my candles extinguished in case of fire.

I stood for a while with my ears straining to hear other sounds beyond the closed door through which I had come, then I heard it open and I knew that some other person had entered the room as silently as myself and without a light for guidance. The next sound came from the rooms further on, the unmistakable sound of a woman's laughter – light, silvery laughter – and a woman's voice, speaking to herself or to another. I drew in my breath sharply and the new intruder came to stand beside me, sheltered by the folds of the curtains. I could hear the sound of breathing but I could not tell if it were man or woman who stood beside me in the dark. Then I became aware of a faint, elusive perfume, almost certainly lavender, and she stepped forward. I felt her hand brush mine and I opened my mouth to scream. Immediately I felt her hand firm and strong over my mouth and she was dragging me across the carpet towards the door.

I remember being pushed and pulled along the hall, with the rats squeaking with alarm in the shadows and her strong arms thrusting me out into the corridor leading to my room. I was propelled swiftly along that corridor, her hand like a vice around my arm and it was only when we reached the shelter of my room that she released me and I stood trembling against the wall. She went straight to the curtains, pulling them together to shut out the night, then after a moment's darkness I saw the flickering light from a match being applied to the gas jet. The room in the light from the one gas lamp looked cold and uninviting but for the first time I could see the face of my companion. I was astonished to find that it was Agnes's face looking into mine and in her eyes, too, was panic.

'Oh, miss,' she breathed, 'how you frightened me!'

'How you frightened me, Agnes,' I answered, my teeth chattering. 'How did you know it was me?'

'I didn't, not at first, but then I thought it must be you because only you could have seen the light in the old wing from the window of your room.'

'Someone is in there, Agnes. I've seen lights in the old wing before, but tonight I heard voices and laughter, you must have heard them too, or why did you go in there. Do you know who it is?'

She looked at me strangely, in no hurry to answer my questions, then at last she said, 'You didn't see who it was, miss? Only the candlelight?'

'That is all.'

'Then why did you go in?'

I could not tell if her eyes were accusing or not. Perhaps she thought I was merely a busybody looking for mysteries where none existed, a person who was overfond of prying into things which did not concern her.

'I thought perhaps it might be Miss Elsa,' I answered doubtfully.

She looked at me sharply, a frown on her plain homely face. 'Why should it be Miss Elsa, miss, when she's been sleeping in her bed these many hours?'

'I don't know, Agnes, but you know yourself she is fond of doing the inexplicable and I thought of those rotting floorboards and those dark, empty rooms. I thought that if it was Miss Elsa she could be hurt or terrified once she realized what she had done.'

I thought her face relaxed a little and I pressed home my advantage. 'I had no intention of spying, Agnes. If it had been someone other than Miss Elsa I would not have lingered in those rooms, I can assure you. I would have left as quietly as I entered.

'You must not go in there again, miss. Like you said, the floorboards are dangerous and you could easily get lost. Whoever is in there now is no stranger to the house.'

I shivered a little, drawing my robe closer about me.

'It is cold standing here,' Agnes said, 'and we are losing sleep. Goodnight, miss.'

Swiftly she let herself out of my room. After she had gone I walked over to the dressing table and took up my watch. It was just three o'clock. Why had Agnes gone into the old wing, I wondered. She could not have seen the lights from her room but she was devoted to Miss Elsa. Was she merely hoping to discover Mr Thorn in some act of infidelity, or even Miss Rowena? Agnes was only a servant in the house; what possible good would it do her to have knowledge of such things? I had heard a woman's laughter on the very first night I spent in this house. Now I tried to recall the laughter I had heard in the drawing room last night but my memory defeated me. Fearfully, I wondered if some other woman lived in that deserted wing, haunting the darkness with her laughter, gay and airy like the tinkling of silver bells.

My efforts to poke some semblance of life into the dead coals in the firegrate met no success but it was so cold in the room that I spent the next few minutes screwing up balls of writing paper which I placed between the coals to see if they would ignite. They came to life briefly, flickering for a time, but then the flames turned blue and all that remained were pieces of charred paper and dulled pieces of coal.

I dragged the eiderdown from the bed and, wrapping it around me, decided to spend the rest of the night in the chair. I did not expect to sleep but I was afraid to turn down the light and sit alone in the darkness, with my ears straining for every sound beyond the locked door of my room. I dozed fitfully for the rest of the night and it was only when the first pale fingers of light crept through the heavy curtains that I rose stiffly from my chair. With the eiderdown draped around my shoulders I pulled back the curtains to look out across the parkland. A fine mist hung low over the grass and the leaves of the holly bushes below my window were hoary with frost. The windows of the old wing stared back at me, empty and lifeless; I shuddered a little, as much at the thought of my night's adventures as at the vision of my bed with the sheets pulled back, cold and uninviting. It was just seven o'clock, and there was at least an hour to wait before Nancy brought my breakfast.

By now the early morning light would be creeping into those desolate rooms facing mine, and whoever the night visitor had been she must now surely be asleep in her bed. Brave in the pale light of a new day, I returned to the door at the end of the corridor. The cold morning light fell through the tall windows on to what had once been a highly polished floor. The rats had gone, though evidence of their presence still remained in the patterns of their tiny feet on the dusty floor and the musty smell of vermin which attacked my nose and throat.

Confident in my new found courage, I began to wonder if I had not imagined much of the previous night's events. Now the only sounds I could hear were the twittering of the birds from their nests high up under the eaves, and the room I had thought so sinister the night before only seemed pathetic now in its dilapidated state. I raised the corner of a dust sheet to see what lay underneath and found that it was a small wine table in marble and gilt. It was a beautiful thing, graceful enough to have earned a proud place in any room in the house; I wondered what other treasures might still remain in these deserted rooms.

I had ventured no further than this room the night before but now I opened the door which led on to another corridor, carpeted with a thick, ruby-red carpet. There were gas jets on each side of the corridor but no mantels had been fitted, and it was so dark that I left the door open behind me so that I could see where I was going. No doors led off the corridor; there was only one, ahead of me. I wondered why I should feel the need to walk on tiptoe as though I feared that someone waited for me in the room

116

behind that closed door. I reached out to turn the knob. My hand trembled visibly and I do not know which emotion was the most powerful – disappointment or relief – when I found that the door was locked.

What I had thought to find beyond that locked door I could not even begin to imagine, but one thing was certain. My mind had created a mystery surrounding Milverton and there was no person in this house who would tell me the truth.

I could not ask Mr Thorn about a woman he had once loved and whose name I had only heard on the lips of his wife's devoted maid. I could not ask Miss Judith because she had befriended me and I did not want her to think that I spent my nights listening and prying into matters which need not concern me. It seemed to me that there was a conspiracy of silence hidden behind a curtain of sorrow, and somehow the old wing held the secret.

I could not trust anybody in the village, not the vicar or Mrs Merriweather. Village folk gossip. If I as much as hinted only half of what I had seen to either Mrs Merriweather or Emily, in no time at all they would have those old rooms harbouring a monster and I could well imagine the disdain with which Mr Thorn would look at me. In this context there was only one person I could trust, and that was Elliot Cliffe. I had to go to Medchester to find Elliot, and that morning I resolved to ask Mr Thorn if I could go to my aunt's home for Christmas. I did not know how long I would have, but I was determined to seek him out and put to him the questions which vexed me so sorely.

I was well aware of my pale face and the smudges of fatigue around my eyes as I presented myself in Mr Thorn's study at promptly ten o'clock, and I was equally aware that none of the miseries in my face went unnoticed.

He looked at me keenly for several moments before he said, 'Come and sit beside the fire. I hope you are not sickening for a cold just before Christmas, or is it that your talk to the villagers took a greater toll than you had thought?'

'I didn't sleep very well, perhaps I was overtired.'

There was amusement in his dark eyes as he indicated

the chair placed before the fire. 'Such an excellent lecture would require a great deal of preparation,' he said. Then he smiled. 'As for myself, I sleep very soundly, but then I expect that comes from having a particularly clear conscience.'

'I am glad to hear it, Mr Thorn.'

He sat back in his chair, his fingers playing idly with his pen, his face suddenly serious, as though his thoughts were not connected with me at all, and yet I knew that they were.

'You know, Miss McAllister, you interest me strangely. Last night in the drawing room I had the feeling that you were surprised by something, more than surprised perhaps. Yes, astounded is a better word. Was it Mr Julian Chimes who surprised you, for I confess his relationship with my sister's husband never ceases to surprise me?'

'Mr Chimes, sir! No, I can assure you I was not surprised by him. Indeed never having met him before, how could I be?'

'If not Mr Chimes then, which of my guests brought that look of amazement into those wide, grey eyes of yours?'

I was totally embarrassed by his persistence. 'It was one of your guests, Mr Thorn, who reminded me of someone. I knew immediately that I was wrong and that we had not met before.'

'Well, which one? A man or a woman?'

'A woman.'

'Well don't leave me to ask all the questions. Which woman, for God's sake? Did you think she had been one of those tourists you spoke of who asked too many questions and listened to too much rubbish? Was it in Egypt where you thought you had met her? I know that Mary Eastman has been there several times.'

'The lady was Mrs St Clare and, as I said, I was wrong.'

'Lucy! Well she is a friend of Rowena's and to my knowledge has never set foot in Egypt. All the same I can well imagine her asking questions if there was a good-looking archaeologist about, and brave enough to invite him over to dance the night away at her hotel. I see you are amused.'

'Yes, sir. I could not help thinking of those serious, dedicated men and wondering where in the world any one

118

of them could have conjured up clothing presentable enough to grace the ballroom of any hotel in Egypt.'

He smiled, and I wondered why suddenly my heart felt lighter and happier than it had felt for days. I lowered my eyes in case he should see the sudden relief in them.

'Now, Miss McAllister, since you have cleared up the mystery, did you ask to see me this morning or did I ask to see you?'

'You asked to see me Mr Thorn, but if you had not done so I would have asked if you could spare me a little of your time.'

He raised his eyebrows. 'Then it is fortunate that we are met, is it not? Ah, I remember now. Miss Judith has reminded me that in two weeks' time it is Christmas and that you may wish to spend it with friends or relatives. Is that so?'

'I have relatives in Medchester, my father's two sisters, but if it is not convenient and you would rather I stayed on here I can quite easily do so.'

'I am not given to unkindnesses of that nature, and if indeed I had forgotten it was the festive season so soon, it was only because there are other things on my mind these days and this old house is not given to much joy. By all means you must visit your relatives and return to Milverton in the New Year. I shall pay your return fare. If you can be ready to travel the day after tomorrow I have business in Feltham and will drive you to the station myself.'

'Oh, sir, I would not dream of troubling you.'

'You do not trouble me, Miss McAllister. As I said, I have business in Feltham so we can kill two birds with one stone. I shall be ready to leave immediately after breakfast, so have your luggage waiting in the hall at about nine-thirty.'

He smiled briefly and silently resumed his paperwork. Assuming that I was dismissed I rose to my feet, offering him stumbling thanks which he waved aside. Outside his room, however, I could have danced with glee. I was to go to Medchester and I would find Elliot. If it took every minute of every day I would find Elliot.

7

The train puffed slowly into Medchester's central station. I was immediately plunged into the hustle and bustle of the crowds hurrying along the station platform and an atmosphere totally unlike that to which I had become accustomed during the last few months. It seemed at least a coat warmer than it had been a few hours earlier on the drive outside Milverton as I watched my small piece of luggage being handed into the carriage, and we waited for Mrs St Clare to join us. At the last moment the lady decided she would drive into Feltham with us; I had to content myself with sitting alone behind them, looking through the windows at the wintry landscape and a sun trying its best to dispel the morning mist.

She chattered happily to Mr Thorn throughout the entire journey but I could not tell if he was altogether enjoying her company or not. I was unable to join in their conversation since it concerned places and people unknown to me, and, because neither spoke to me directly, I had only my own thoughts for company. Once Mr Thorn turned his head to smile at me, an amused teasing smile, and all at once I ceased to feel an interloper. I told myself that it was loyalty to Miss Elsa which made me feel glad that for all her beauty Lucy St Clare would not capture his heart, but I could not be such a hypocrite. I decided that it was just as well I was going to stay with Aunt Maud. That most formidable lady would quickly dispel any romantic or imaginative notions I had about Mr Thorn Lytton.

The station was crowded with Christmas shoppers laden with parcels and bulky Christmas trees and I stood outside the barrier looking round for a familiar face. I hoped they had received my letter in time for them to meet me, otherwise I would have to find a cab to take me to the house. I started as I felt my arm taken, and the next moment was looking up into the smiling face of Aunt Beatrice's new husband, Mr Witty, now Uncle David. Behind him was a beaming Aunt Beatrice who quickly enveloped me in her motherly embrace.

'Let me look at you Lottie,' she was saying breathlessly. 'You are pale. Are you getting enough to eat? Have you had a cold? That great old house is far from cosy, I'm sure?'

We laughed at her questions and Uncle David said, 'Don't fuss, woman, the girl's right enough. You would look pale if you'd been travelling since early morning in the depths of winter.'

We picked up a cab outside the station; in no time at all we were in the narrow hall of Aunt Maud's house in a quiet, tree-lined road with Uncle David helping us off with our coats. As a child I had never known if Aunt Maud were pleased to see me or not. She had never taken me to her breast or kissed me, but had always looked at me critically to see if I had grown, if I appeared well fed and a good colour. Today was no exception.

After she had stared at me for what seemed like minutes she shrugged her narrow square shoulders and said, 'Humph'.

'Now, what's the matter?' Uncle David laughed. 'Let the poor child be, she's cold from travelling and needs a good meal inside her. Now Maud, which room is she to have so that I can take her luggage up?'

'I've had the small room at the front of the house decorated and there's a bed-warmer in the bed. You can put your things in the wardrobe, Lottie, you'll find it's undone.'

'Thank you, Aunt Maud. It's good to see you looking so well.'

'Well, it's more than can be said for you, my girl, you've lost weight. Are you getting enough to eat at Milverton?'

'Far too much, I'm afraid. There have been times when I've had to send food back because there has been so much of it.'

'It's good manners not to eat everything that's put in front of you, but not like you to leave any. You've got circles under your eyes through lack of sleep. I've always said that looking after that poor young lady is no fit place for you Lottie. You're too young and too light-hearted for that sort of work. It's an older, more sedate, woman they should be looking for.'

'Oh Aunt, by no stretch of imagination can it be called work. All I do is read to her and try to keep her amused. She has her own maid, and what else am I fitted for?'

'Your father should have seen to that instead of gadding about the world and dragging you with him.'

'Can we talk about it later Aunt Maud? I'd like to wash, and change my travelling clothes, then perhaps you will change your mind about how I look.'

I felt her disapproving eyes upon me all the way up the stairs and I heard Aunt Beatrice saying, 'Don't get on to the child so, Maud, she'll be telling us how things are up at the Hall as soon as she's unpacked and settled in. If you keep on at her in that fashion, she'll be wishing she'd never come home for Christmas.'

'She's thinner,' was all the reply Aunt Maud made and stomped away into the kitchen at the back of the house where I could hear her clattering the dishes.

I was delighted with my room. It had been decorated with a pale green wallpaper bearing springs of delicate, pink apple blossom, and the little dressing table and curtains were in rose-coloured taffeta to match the plain rose-coloured carpet on the floor. The room was small but it had a freshness and warmth which made me feel suddenly happy and cared for.

I don't think Aunt Maud had ever had any idea how much I loved both her and Aunt Beatrice. She thought I looked upon them both as a convenience – very much, I suspect, as my father had looked upon them – but it was not so. I had always longed for a conventional upbringing, for a settled home and stability in my life, but at the same time there was that other part of me which craved adventure, a restlessness which revelled in forgotten glories and foreign travel. I was two people: Lottie McAllister who did as she was told, who went to church on Sundays and obeyed the conventions she had sworn her life to; and Carla McAllister who sat wide-eyed listening to her father's tales of old loves, tormenting passions, the confusion of ancient wars and the sailing of galleys in the dawn of the civilized world. I could stand in the little village church singing the hymns that had been on my lips since childhood, but I could never forget that once I had stood in the halls of Karnak with the soft, desert wind blowing through my hair and my eyes filled with awe and a vague resentment for a past which had gone forever.

One side of the wardrobe was locked but the other side held all my clothes comfortably and the rest of my belongings fitted easily into the drawers of the dressing table. I washed my face and combed my hair, letting it fall softly about my face, then hurriedly I pinched my cheeks into some semblance of colour before running down the stairs to face the aunts.

A crackling fire burned halfway up the chimney in the small dining room and the table, laid for high tea, was groaning under plates piled high with scones and fruit cake, as well as large apple pies and plate custards. I was hungry, but the mere sight of so much food filled me with dismay and my appetite flagged long before my plate, piled high with meat and vegetables, was empty. I had no say about what was to follow. A large piece of apple tart smothered in cream was placed before me, followed by a cup of tea, and I must confess I was uncomfortably full although I did not dare admit it.

Afterwards, to my silent astonishment, it appeared that we were to be allowed to use the comfortable sitting room normally reserved for Sunday visitors. The room was warm and when the heavy curtains were pulled across the windows and the lamps were lit I sat back in my chair eying the three people I loved best in the world.

I listened to their news about the friends they had made in Medchester, about Aunt Beatrice's new home at the other side of the city, and Aunt Maud's involvement with the Church of St Luke where already it appeared she sat upon several committees and was a regular visitor at the vicarage. At last it was my turn and I talked and talked, about Milverton and Miss Elsa, about poor Mrs Lytton who could not speak and Mr Thorn who had so many sorrows on his shoulders. I told them about my friendship with Miss Judith, about the talk I had given to the villagers at the vicar's request. The vicar had given me the address of his daughter, Dora, another childhood friend, now married to a doctor and living in Medchester and I told them how I planned to visit her while I was here.

Aunt Maud's knitting needles clicked irritably. 'She lives not far from here but I'm surprised at Dora Fellows, considering she's a vicar's daughter; I've only seen her in church about five times in the last six months and I've not seen her husband at all. There isn't another church near here unless it's the Methodist Chapel and she's surely not going there.'

'I've found a new church, Lottie,' Aunt Beatrice made a valiant effort to change the subject. 'It's just round the corner from where we live, but it's a spiritualist church.'

I looked at her in some surprise because Aunt Beatrice had always been the more devout of the two sisters, but before she could say more Aunt Maud cut in with her most disapproving voice, 'I've told you before, Beatrice, that's no church you've been going to. It's tampering with the devil you've been doing, no good will come of it. If we were meant to talk to folks who have gone, the Lord would have found an easier way than through some heathen Red Indian.'

I looked from one to the other in amazement, and from his chair in the corner Uncle David chuckled quietly.

'What's all this about a Red Indian?' I asked.

'It's a lot of rubbish, Lottie, and I don't expect you've come all the way from Gleave to hear about Mrs Findlay and her Red Indian, Chief something-or-other.'

'Chief Summer Cloud,' Aunt Beatrice said quietly, 'and I wish you wouldn't be so dogmatic, Maud, just because you don't understand a thing doesn't mean it's rubbish.'

I was surprised to hear Aunt Beatrice stand up to her sister. Usually she sat back with a pink face, longing to speak but afraid to do so. Marriage had given her stature I was glad to see, and a new found confidence.

She turned to me, her eyes shining. 'It's a new movement, Lottie; Spiritualist Churches are sprouting up all over England. They do say the Royal Family have shown an interest in it, at least poor Queen Victoria did when she lost Prince Albert, and all over America there are groups of people dedicated to spiritualism.'

Aunt Maud sniffed derisively. 'Anybody can sell anything to the Americans.'

'But what is it all about?' I asked.

'We have a lovely church, Lottie. We have meetings during the week for faith healing and meditation, but on Sundays it's just like a normal service. We sing hymns and the medium gives us a talk and everybody gets a message.'

My mind was spinning with talk of mediums and messages, and I asked, 'What on earth is a medium and what sort of message?'

'Mrs Findlay is our medium, and a very good one. They come from all over the north to see her privately and they come for her to address public meetings in large halls before hundreds of people. I've seen her go into a trance myself, Lottie, and the voices of those who have been dead for years speak again through her lips. Then afterwards when she is herself again she cannot remember anything that has happened to her.'

'But how can this be?'

'Mrs Findlay has a gift, Lottie, which she uses to help people who have lost someone close to them. She gives them comfort and assurances that this little life we have on earth is only a preliminary to a happier life in the hereafter. I have heard people say they have had more comfort from our church than from the more conventional religions.'

Again Aunt Maud snorted and the needles clicked faster with disapproval. 'It's playing with things you shouldn't be playing with, Beatrice. I'm surprised at David allowing you to go.'

Uncle David laughed. 'Going makes her happy, Maud. Why should I object?'

'People believe what they want to believe. As I said before, if we had been meant to speak to the dead, God would have found a better way than through this Mrs Findlay, who is no doubt making a fair bit of money out of it. It's tampering with the devil, nothing more, nothing less.'

'Well, why doesn't lottie come with me and see for herself?' said Aunt Beatrice.

'Lottie will do no such thing. She will come with me to St Luke's in the way she's been brought up. All these new-fangled ideas seem to be coming from America, but you don't go to Beatrice's church with my permission, Lottie McAllister!'

Aunt Beatrice gave me a small, tight, little smile which promised that we should talk more about the matter, so I quickly changed the subject by speaking about my visit to Mrs Merriweather and telling them that I had spoken to the Misses Phipps and had not found them changed.'

'I suppose they asked a lot of questions as usual?' Aunt Beatrice said.

'They would have liked to have done so, I know, but I didn't give them the opportunity. How curiously spinsterish they both are,' I remarked and then could have cut out my tongue.

'Being unmarried is no sin that I can see,' said Aunt Maud.

'Well, of course it isn't Aunt Maud. I'll probably remain unmarried myself since I'm never likely to meet any unattached men in the life I lead, but all unmarried women are not like the Misses Phipps.'

'I had every chance to get married,' she went on, fixing me with a stern eye. 'Indeed when I was your age I had been engaged twice and was walking out with Clement Hill from the big stationers in Feltham. Isn't that so Beatrice?'

'Yes, dear. I can't think why you never married him.'

'No, Aunt, why did you never marry him?' I enquired, for many was the time I had heard of Aunt Maud's two engagements and the eligible Mr Hill.

'Because he was unreliable. I had an unreliable brother, I couldn't be expected to put up with an unreliable husband as well.'

'But Clement wasn't really unreliable Maud. It's true he liked his nights at his club but he always came for you when he said he would.'

'He was too fond of his nights at his club. I didn't see him for a whole week once and when he eventually did come I gave him his ring back and told him he could have that bit of time to himself.'

'You were hard, Maud. He would probably have made you a good husband.'

'Well, that was a chance I wasn't prepared to take. I don't want Lottie here thinking any sort of marriage is better than no marriage at all.'

'I can assure you I don't, Aunt Maud,' I retorted. Silence fell, but it was the warm family silence of four people who knew each other well and had little need for small talk.

'Aunt,' I said at last, 'did you know that Elliot Cliffe had been engaged to Rowena Lytton and that their engagement was broken off?'

'Better before than after.'

'Perhaps, but did you know?'

'Well, of course I knew, all the village knew.'

'Poor Elliot, I expect he was most unhappy.'

'He should have had more sense than get himself engaged to that young woman,' Aunt Maud said sternly. 'She was a spoiled wilful young girl and a doctor wants more than a pretty face for a wife. Her twin brother Jeremy was no better, wild he was, with a bad reputation with the village girls and others further afield, if you can believe the talk that was going at the time. I did hear that he'd had a quarrel with his older brother and been sent abroad out of the way.'

'But what about Elliot?'

'What about Elliot? The engagement was broken off, but I blame that silly mother of his, always fancying herself part of the gentry. I expect she was more cut up about it than Elliot himself. Anyway, old Doctor Cliffe sold his practice and they went to live away. It was only a nine-day wonder, people soon forget.'

'I have heard he's back in Medchester now in a practice of his own Aunt Maud. Have you ever seen him?'

'No. It's not in this part of the city. There's only old Doctor Kirk and Dora Fellows's husband. Still it's a big place is Medchester, he could be in one of the new fancy areas on the outskirts of the city. I expect Dora Fellows will know if he's back up north.'

'Yes, I expect she will,' I said thoughtfully.

Aunt Maud looked at me sharply. 'I hope you're not intending to find Elliot, Lottie. That would be most unseemly and, although you were friends once, you're both grown up now and things are different.'

The needles clicked faster and Aunt Beatrice gave me a

warning look, fearing as always the antagonism which sparked between Aunt Maud and myself.

'Elliot Cliffe was thought fit to be engaged to Rowena Lytton,' Aunt Maud said in her most caustic tone, 'you, Lottie, are a servant in the Lytton household. You are a respectable, hard-working girl, but Elliot's family considered themselves level with the gentry. Remember that and it might stop you from making a fool of yourself.'

I could feel my face burning with resentment and I clenched my hands in the folds of my skirt. I was angry with myself that I had had no more sense than speak of Elliot, but more angry with Aunt Maud who had always had this power to hurt me and make me feel of no importance.

Uncle David spoke quietly from his armchair. 'Your brother was a greater scholar than either George Cliffe, Elliot's father, or old Mr Lytton, who thought more of his prowess on the hunting field than the books in his library. Lottie's father had little money but he had learning and culture. All that some of these so-called gentry can lay claim to is arrogance.'

I threw him a grateful look, but Aunt Maud's lips were compressed into a thin line as she said, 'I don't want Lottie to get hurt or give Elliot Cliffe cause to think she is chasing him.'

'Oh Aunt, how can he possibly think that when I simply hope to see him and wish an old friend well?' I protested.

Silence once more descended upon us and suddenly I felt very tired, and anxious to seek my warm bed and the solitude of my bedroom. I rose to my feet saying, 'Would you mind very much if I went to bed? I was up very early this morning.'

'You can't go to bed without supper,' Aunt Maud said sharply.

'Honestly, Aunt, I couldn't eat another morsel. I'd much rather go to bed and eat a hearty breakfast in the morning.'

I bent down to kiss her lined, old cheek then Aunt Beatrice's, and with a smile at Uncle David I escaped into the hall and groped my way up the stairs.

The room felt cold but I undressed quickly and slipped between the sheets. It was blissfully warm where the heated oven plates had been slipped into the bed, wrapped inside old blankets, and I lay on my back watching the shadows cast by the bare branches of the beech trees from the road outside across the ceiling.

It was much later when Aunt Beatrice woke me with a little knock on my door and she entered carrying a mug of hot milk in which Uncle David had added a fair measure of whisky.

'Drink this, dear, it will warm you,' she said softly. 'I'll come and sit on your bed until you've finished it but we must talk quietly or Maud will hear us.'

'Has she gone to bed?'

'Yes, about an hour ago. 'Don't mind her, Lottie, you know she always had a sharp tongue but she means well and is really very fond of you.'

'She always makes me feel inadequate. She demoralizes my initiative, hurts my pride.'

'I know dear, she's done it with me all my life but she's too old to change now. One day before you return to Gleave, you and I will go to see Mrs Findlay without Maud knowing anything about it.' She bent down and kissed me, then smiling at me gently she let herself out of the room.

Aunt Maud was often absent during the next few days so that Aunt Beatrice and I could roam at will around the busy streets of the city. The shops were bright with tinsel and holly, and on the streets people were rushing about in all directions in an effort to finish their last minute shopping. There were times when I wondered what sort of Christmas they would be looking forward to at Milverton, and visions of the great house at one with the impressive crags above it intruded on my joy at being home.

I bought my Christmas presents with the first salary I had ever earned, but I was glad of the extra gift of money Mr Thorn had pressed into my hands as he left me. With it I could afford the little luxuries I wanted to give my family – a bottle of whisky for Uncle David, a bottle of perfume for Aunt Beatrice, and warm bedroom slippers for Aunt Maud. I decided if I was going to see Dora I should take her a small gift and strangely enough this took longer to choose. At last I settled on a small plant, gay with red berries, wrapped in bright, silver wrapping paper and tied with a shining bow of scarlet ribbon.

During the afternoon of Christmas Eve I walked the short distance to her home only to find that she was out shopping. I was naturally disappointed because as the days passed by it seemed more imperative than ever that I find Elliot. I left the plant and scribbled a short note to say I would call again between Christmas and the New Year.

Christmas Eve was a quiet affair. We walked through a light powdering of snow to attend the service at Aunt Maud's church. It was a tall, imposing church of Gothic proportions, and inside a giant Christmas tree stood ablaze with candles near the choir stalls, and round it were placed parcels for the children as well as the poor of the parish.

The church was crowded and all along the length of the red-carpeted aisle my aunts greeted friends on their way out. In the churchyard the snow flurried in the freshening wind and the bells rang out their message of goodwill. When we returned home we drank hot soup and ate mince pies before opening our gifts. My own were surprisingly small things. A new hairbrush and a bottle of lavender water, a handkerchief sachet smelling of pot-pourri, a pair of pure silk stockings and an illustrated book of verse. My presents to them were received with pleasure and I was instantly assured that I had chosen aright. I gathered mine together in a box saying I would take them upstairs to my bedroom, but just as I was about to mount the stairs Aunt Maud took my hand and placed a key in the palm of it.

'This will unlock the side of the wardrobe you have not been able to open Lottie,' she said. 'What you find inside is from all of us and, although it wasn't my choice, I hope you like it.'

Filled with amazement I hurriedly dropped my gifts on my bed and hastened to unlock the wardrobe door, then with an exclamation of delight I took out the gown I saw hanging there. It was velvet, a rich, glowing, ruby-red velvet, unadorned but beautifully cut, with a small bodice and long sleeves. The neckline was wide but the skirt billowed out into rich folds and I hugged it against me, loving the feel of it. I rushed to throw my arms around them in turn, my words tumbling over one another as I thanked them.

Aunt Maud looked at it dubiously. 'It was your Aunt Beatrice's idea,' she said, 'not mine. When will you ever get the chance to wear such a dress?'

'I shall make such a chance, Aunt Maud. It is too beautiful to keep hidden away.'

'I'm not sure about the colour, pastels suit you better, these colours are for dark women.'

In my heart I agreed with her. This rich, vibrant ruby was for women with the beauty and the colouring of Caprice, what would it do for my dull-gold hair and grey eyes? All my life I had wished for hair with the bloom upon it like a raven's wing and eyes that were velvety dark, but as I ran my hand lightly along the folds of the skirt I assured myself that it would give my Englishness the glamour it lacked. I did not know when I would wear it, I only knew that I would.

Christmas Day and Boxing Day passed peacefully. On Boxing Day Aunt Maud sallied forth to help with the catering for the children's concert and Aunt Beatrice dozed in her chair before the fire. Uncle David and I passed the time away playing cribbage, a game my father had taught me to play, and so successfully I had little difficulty in beating him. The day after Boxing Day it rained – cold icy sleet which made the footpaths slippery – and the cold, north wind blowing the sodden leaves of autumn along the road seemed to chill me to the very marrow. I decided I would walk the short distance to Dora's house despite Aunt Maud's disapproval.

Dora was at home and received me with open arms, pressing me at once to stay and take lunch with them. The house was untidy, with an untidiness that was entirely clean and completely homely. Magazines littered the chairs and opened boxes of sweets and chocolates were on every table and on some of the chairs. She swept them all into a pile on the carpet and then as I took off my coat she heaped coals upon the fire, ignoring the cinders which had already fallen upon the hearth.

I looked at her more closely as she came to sit besides me on the big comfortable couch in front of the fire. She was plumper, and prettier, and there was a contentment about her that caused me a momentary twinge of envy. Dora was not clever, she was not particularly beautiful, but she had a sweet nature and I felt that a happy marriage should be her reward.

As we sat before the fire she questioned me about my job at Milverton and we reminisced about our childhoods, until at last I thought I could safely ask my most important question.

'Dora, do you ever see Elliot?'

She looked at me intently for a few moments before she said, 'Father told us you had only just heard about Elliot and we were able to tell him that he was living in Medchester. Peter says that he has recently gone into a practice at the other side of the city. A group of the city's professional men dine together at the Rotary Club meeting on Thursday afternoons.'

'You haven't seen Elliot yourself?'

'No. Peter is supposed to be asking him round for dinner one evening but he hasn't done so yet.'

'Has he married?'

'I don't think so. No, I'm pretty sure he hasn't.'

'I would like to see him, Dora. In fact I must see him during my visit because I don't really know when I shall be in Medchester again. No, please don't raise your eyebrows like that, there is nothing romantic in my desire to see Elliot but there are so many things at Milverton I don't understand and Elliot may be able to set my mind at rest.'

'What sort of things? You know how I love mysteries, Lottie. Now that I've told you what you want to know you must tell me why it is so important to see Elliot.'

'Dora, do you remember the girl Mr Thorn was often with years ago? You must remember her, she was so very beautiful. Don't you remember the day I ran into their drive looking for the ball we threw over and they caught me in the rhododendron bushes? I told you at the time, she was so lovely and yet he didn't marry her.'

'There were always so many of them at Milverton in the summertime, and they all looked beautiful to me in their fine clothes and feathered hats. Besides, I never looked at the women particularly, not when Mr Thorn was about.'

'Her name was Caprice, Dora, does that name not mean

anything to you?'

She wrinkled up her brow in thought and I longed to say, 'Oh Dora, you never could remember things that happened yesterday. How can I expect you to remember something which happened years ago?'

Hesitantly she said, 'I vaguely remember something.' Then she shrugged her shoulders, 'Sorry Lottie, you'll have to forgive me.'

At that moment the door opened and two dogs bounded into the room, a small terrier who immediately leaped into my lap and a larger dog of dubious ancestry who tried to follow him. A large young man stood looking down at me, a young man with a shock of bright red hair and a rugged, though decidedly attractive, face. He was smiling, the kind of smile which brought an instant response from my own lips.

'Lottie McAllister,' he said, 'I've heard about you. The girl who descended upon the sleepy village of Gleave like a brave wind from the outside world. Dora didn't tell me you were a beauty.'

I laughed. 'Nobody ever thought it, and I'm sure not many people think it now.'

Luncheon was a happy meal, with much laughter round the table and the dogs darting to each one of us in turn in their search for titbits. I stayed until late afternoon when Peter promised he would drive round to Aunt Maud's house on his way to visit some of his patients.

I let myself into the house with my latchkey and Aunt Beatrice called out to me from the kitchen.

'Is that you Lottie? There are some parcels in the parlour, they came just after you left and have probably been delayed.'

She came into the hall, wiping her hands on her apron and followed me into the sitting room.

'They are all from Gleave, Lottie. The man who brought them said the weather on the moors was so bad the roads had been closed and only re-opened yesterday.'

There were three parcels, a large one and two smaller ones, and my mind filled with wonder as I knelt down on the rug before the fire, my hands busy with the knots.

'Wait Lottie, I'll get the scissors, you will break your nails if you try to undo them with your fingers,' Aunt Beatrice said.

She hurried away and I waited impatiently for her to return with the scissors. After that it was an easy task to cut the string and open the heavy folds of brown paper. I had chosen the largest of the parcels to open first and I gave a sharp cry when I saw what it contained. Lying in a final fold of tissue was the firescreen I had first seen in Mrs Lytton's room, now completed in all its warm, soft colours and quite the most charming thing I had ever owned. With it was a card written in her neat familiar handwriting saying simply, 'Christmas Greetings', and signed, 'Clarissa Lytton'.

'But, how beautiful!' exclaimed Aunt Beatrice, 'What a lovely thing for Mrs Lytton to have done.'

I picked up the other two parcels and, sitting on the edge of the sofa, I opened the larger of the two, handing the small one to Aunt Beatrice saying, 'You open this one, Aunt, my fingers are all thumbs.'

Inside the box I opened, lying in a mass of pale pink tissues, lay a shawl, as delicate as gossamer, as fragile as a butterfly's wing. It was white, of the softest wool, with an exquisite lacy pattern like tiny shells. I could never have afforded such a shawl, but I had seen shawls like it in London's most expensive shops. A small card lay on top and through a mist of tears I read, 'To Carla, with all good wishes for your happiness at Christmas time, from Mr and Mrs Stephen Lytton'.

I looked up at Aunt Beatrice wordlessly and she held out to me the remaing parcel. She had undone the string but left me to take away the wrapping paper. It contained a small, leather box and before I opened it I brushed away my tears so that I might read the card resting on top of the box. I recognized Thorn's flowing masculine hand as I read, 'from Mr and Mrs Thorn Lytton, with gratitude', and again the tears blurred my eyes so that I had great difficulty in seeing the brooch which lay on its satin bed inside the box.

The brooch was silver filigree in the form of a full-blown rose. The edges of the petals and the veins in the leaves were picked out in gold and I, who owned little jewellery, could only look at it with tremulous delight. I raised my eyes to Aunt Beatrice's face and saw that there were tears on her cheeks. The next moment she gathered me to her and together we wept a little.

Such rare kindness had always had the power to touch me emotionally. All the same I was glad that my aunt and I had the house to ourselves for a little while so that our lack of discipline would not be scoffed at.

8

On Thursday morning the pavements were slippery and wet from melting snow and over breakfast I viewed the darkening sky and lowering clouds with dismay. I knew I would have difficulty with Aunt Maud if I suggested going out on such a morning. She would demand to know where I was going, but I was determined that no words of hers would stop me fulfilling the purpose for which I had specially come to Medchester. She watched me pulling on my galoshes over my shoes and her grim face stiffened with disapproval.

'Might I ask where you are going, miss, on such a morning?' she asked eventually.

I lied, and I hated myself for lying, but how else could I have escaped from the house? 'I have promised to meet Dora and I can't have her waiting about for me on such a morning.'

'She will surely have the sense not to expect you on a day like this.'

'I don't know how long it will be before I can see her again, Aunt. I will take a cab and I promise I won't be late back.'

'The shops are full of rubbish after Christmas. Where are you going?'

'To lunch at the Fairlands Hotel.'

'An hotel is no place for women, at lunchtime or any other time. The dining room will be full of men, businessmen.'

'I know, Aunt, but times have changed since you were a girl, women lunch in hotel dining rooms all the time now.'

'Not without an escort, they don't.'

'But her husband will be there.'

The last retort was not a lie. Peter would be there, but not with me. He would be at his Rotary lunch, I hoped in the company of Elliot. As I walked and slithered towards the end of the road I felt more and more like a wayward child. The wind tore at my umbrella and the bitter, driving rain found its way underneath it, wetting my hair and making my face shiny.

I stood outside the hotel for at least ten minutes, wretchedly cold, my toes and fingers numb as if they no longer belonged to me. At last, driven by sheer desperation, I sought the warmth of the hotel foyer; then faced with the sight of several elegant women and their immaculate escorts, I retreated to the ladies' room to repair the damages to my appearance the wind had wrought.

The results were not impressive, but at least my hair under its little fur hat was smooth and the wind had whipped up a colour into my face that was not unbecoming. I walked over to the bookstall and stood fingering the magazines for a few moments until the assistant came over and looked at me expectantly. I smiled at him and for the second time that morning I lied, easily and naturally, though inwardly ashamed.

'I am waiting for my husband. I don't suppose you know if the Rotarians are still taking luncheon?'

'Oh yes, madam,' he answered me. 'Most of the gentlemen call here for tobacco or papers on their way out and I haven't seen any of them yet. There is a seat over there near the lifts. If you sit there you will be able to see him when the luncheon is over.'

I thanked him. Then, sauntering over to the vacant chair with all the aplomb I could muster, I began to enjoy myself. A big Christmas tree, lavishly decorated, still occupied a proud place in one corner of the foyer and two large urns filled with spring flowers stood in the centre of the room. The miserable day outside faded into insignificance in the scented warmth of the foyer. Each time the lift stopped, five or six people would emerge from it, but it was only when a crowd of six men left it that I realized somewhere upstairs a luncheon party was breaking up. They were all elderly gentlemen in the first group, but in the second group I saw Peter. I raised my book to cover my face in case he looked my way but he was in a hurry, and bade his friends a hasty good-bye before he rushed out into the street. Where was

Elliot, I wondered. I prayed that nothing had occurred to prevent him attending the luncheon.

Would I still be able to recognize him after all these years? I tried to remember his thin, sensitive face and his tall, gangling, boy's body, only to find that the memory was elusive. I was so busy watching the lift that I almost missed the group of young men who came running down the stairs. Then my heart lurched painfully, for there, sure enough, was Elliot. He was still tall and thin, and although his faced had filled out with maturity it was unmistakably sensitive. I rose to my feet as though unseen hands pulled me. They stood in a small group near the door and Elliot was the first to walk away. I hurried after him and just as they reached the swing doors I said in a breathless voice, 'Dr Cliffe, Elliot.'

He turned and looked at me in some surprise, then recognition dawned in his eyes and he stepped forward delightedly to take my hands. 'Good heavens, is it really you, Lottie? What on earth are you doing here, I thought you were in Greece or Egypt, or some other godforsaken place? Are you here alone?'

'Yes, quite alone. I have been waiting for you.'

'But how did you know I was to be here?'

'Dora Fellows told me you lunched here with her husband every Thursday. Is there somewhere we can talk?'

'Have you had lunch, Lottie?'

'No, and I'm not in the least hungry. Besides, I know you have had a large lunch and will certainly not want another. A pot of tea would be lovely.'

'Right. We'll go into the lounge and have tea, then we can talk all we want to.'

'Don't you have patients to see this afternoon?'

'It's my afternoon off, fortunately. Jack and I were on our way to the club for a game of snooker. We might have to fight for a table, Lottie, see if you can spot an empty one.'

We found one almost immediately, next to the wall and not too near the dais where a four-piece orchestra was playing excerpts from 'The Bohemian Girl'. It was only when I had poured the tea that had been placed before us that we looked at each other properly across the table.

'I would have known you anywhere, Elliot, you have

hardly changed at all,' I told him.

'And you have changed enormously,' he replied. 'The last time I saw you was at that Christmas party years ago, in your new party dress and with your shoes and stockings all muddied up from the soil outside the windows at Milverton and your hair in a mess from the brambles we had to scramble through to get into the garden. Look at you now, blonde and beautiful, like a piece of Dresden china.'

'Oh, Elliot, you musn't tease me like that. I have walked through the rain, the hem of my gown is decidedly damp and so is the hair which my umbrella did nothing to protect. Can we be serious for a while, do you think?'

'Oh yes, if seriousness is what you want. Where are you living?'

'Over Christmas and the New Year with Aunt Maud.'

'Is your father with you or is he still abroad?'

'My father is dead, he died in Egypt almost twelve months ago.'

'I'm sorry to hear that Lottie, I know how fond of him you were.'

'Yes, I loved him very much and his death has left my life completely changed. Do you know where I am living most of the time now and what I am doing?'

'I have no idea, Lottie.'

'I am living at Milverton as companion to Mr Thorn's wife.'

He raised his eyebrows in surprise. 'At Milverton, you!' He sat back in his chair, the amazement on his face very real.

'I cannot see you as anybody's companion, Lottie. You were always such an independent soul. Companion to one who has suffered a nervous breakdown which has left her strange, to say the least, is not a situation I would have thought you suited for.'

'I have little money and the job was found for me. I am there for three months to see how things work out, but I haven't met you to talk about me, Elliot. I need to ask you so many things.'

For a brief moment only I felt his eyes upon mine, tense and wary, but the next moment they cleared and he leaned forward inviting my questions.

'I heard in the village about you and Miss Rowena Elliot, I am very sorry.'

He nodded. 'Thanks, Lottie. It happened a long time ago, you know. I was only twenty, she was eighteen, and we were too young really to know our own minds. I don't think about it now, or hardly at all.'

'I'm glad. Is there someone else?'

'No, nothing like that. I was very hurt at the time, Rowena was so beautiful, so gay and full of life I could hardly believe my good fortune when she said she would marry me. Then, out of the blue comes this fellow from London with his posh accent and his uncle's title to be dangled over her head. Perhaps if she'd been older we could have put our heads together like civilized people. As it was, one day she was there, happy and loving, the next she had gone off with this fellow and before anybody really knew what was happening they were married. The wretched business made my mother ill and drove my parents away from the village. Mother had set her heart on that marriage.'

I didn't say anything immediately. Aunt Maud had been right about Elliot's mother. She should have been like a bulwark behind him instead of fussing and fretting because her big society wedding was not to be. At last I said gently, 'Perhaps it's a good thing you didn't marry Rowena Elliot, you deserve somebody sweeter and kinder, I'm sure.'

'Loyal as always, Lottie.'

'Well yes, I am loyal to my friends and you were my particular friend in Gleave. All the others thought me something of a curio but you were kind, you never laughed at my fantasies. I hope you are not going to laugh at them now.'

'More fantasies, Lottie. What are they this time?'

'Elliot, you remember that Christmas Eve and my mud-died shoes and messed up hair, so you must remember the girl Mr Thorn was with?'

'Yes, of course I remember her. Why do you ask?'

'What was her name?'

'Caprice. Caprice Langham.'

So, for the first time Caprice became a real person instead of simply a name with a fairytale quality. I knew her last name.

'Elliot, will you tell me about Caprice?' I asked quietly.

'You mean you don't know?'

'What don't I know? Elliot, why should there be all this secrecy surrounding Caprice? Why is her name never mentioned at Gleave when Thorn was so desperately in love with her? Why did he marry Elsa? Was Caprice another Rowena Elliot, did she jilt him and run away with somebody else?'

'You really don't know, do you Lottie, any of the events of that summer?'

'I don't know anything Elliot, but I hear her laughter in rooms that are shut away, I fancy I hear her step upon the stair and I dream about her so that at times she seems more a part of Milverton than the women of flesh and blood who live there.'

'Good heavens, Lottie! You mustn't let your imagination run riot in this fashion. Caprice is as much old history at Milverton as Rowena and me.'

'Elliot, I want to know. Where is Caprice now?'

'Caprice is dead, Lottie.'

It was as though somebody had hit my heart with a sledge-hammer so that for a moment it seemed to stop beating, then it raced making me breathless and in a whisper I asked, 'Dead, Elliot, but when?'

'Two years after the Christmas Eve we spoke of. Caprice and Thorn were to have been married in the autumn, her parents had come home from India for the wedding; in fact, it was at their engagement party that I really got to know Rowena but of course we were little more than children then.'

I wasn't interested in Elliot's romance with Rowena, and somewhat impatiently I prompted him, 'And they were in love Elliot, really in love?'

'Heavens yes. He adored her and she him, that's what nobody could understand afterwards.'

'What happened afterwards?'

'Well, like I said, they were to have been married in the autumn over at Sutton. Her bridesmaids were chosen, her wedding gown ordered from London and there was a big party at Sutton to welcome her parents home. . . .'

Sutton? Sutton? Where had I heard about Sutton? Then my mind cleared. Of course Sutton was also the village where Miss Elsa had come from. I had no hesitation in interrupting him, 'But doesn't Miss Elsa also come from Sutton?'

He looked at me in some surprise. 'Of course. Caprice and Elsa were sisters.'

Stupidly I sat back in my chair. 'I didn't know,' I murmured, 'but they are so different.'

'Yes, well Caprice was dark and Elsa is fair, but their mothers were different. Caprice's father married twice and because Elsa was delicate as a child she spent most of her time being privately educated in India, a school for English children in the hill country.'

'I see,' I said, and I did see because it seemed like a giant jigsaw puzzle suddenly falling into place. 'How did Caprice die?'

For a moment he looked uncomfortable but in the face of my ruthless questioning he had to go on.

'Well, here comes the scandal, Lottie. Elsa was engaged to a young army officer who returned with them to England on three months' leave. Elsa was very pretty, and all that summer there were parties and summer balls for the two sisters; they were both so lovely and so popular they were fêted wherever they went. You remember how gay Caprice was, and she seemed to sweep Elsa along in her wake but none of us dreamed of the tragedy to follow.'

'It was Elsa's young subaltern wasn't it?'

'I can see you've already heard something of the story. I'm not surprised. The county was agog with it for months.'

'But what about Thorn, didn't he know what was going on?'

'How could he? To see Thorn and Caprice together was like watching two people who had been created for each other since the beginning of time. Caprice was gay, elusive as gossamer. She flirted with them all, she even flirted with me, putting her arm round me and calling me her sweet Elliot. It never meant anything. She was only serious with Thorn, but by the end of the summer Elsa's fiancé too was under her spell. Everybody said he had obviously transferred his affections from one sister to the other.'

'Nobody actually saw them ride off together that afternoon. It was one of those warm, golden days in the late summer and afterwards the servants at Gleave remembered seeing Caprice's horse already saddled and waiting for her in the stable yard and they naturally assumed she had ridden out on to the fells. Both sisters and Elsa's fiancé were staying at Milverton, but Caprice liked to ride on the moors while Elsa seemed to prefer the gardens. When they had not returned at dusk and they had waited dinner for them for over an hour, Thorn decided something was obviously wrong. Elsa said her fiancé and Caprice had ridden out together and although they had not asked her to ride with them she was not surprised because they both knew she preferred to laze in the garden. I remember that night, I remember watching the search parties going out across the fells with their lanterns and torches, but it was the following day that the boy was found.

'They never found Caprice. Perry's horse came back to the stable the next day and two days later they found Caprice's horse with a bullet through his head. It was said at the time that they found his body lying at the edge of the swamp and that already it had been gnawed at by rats or foxes.'

I shuddered with horror, and in a hoarse whisper said, 'Have they searched for her since?'

'Yes, they searched on and off for the rest of that summer but without success. The village was full of reporters and lawyers. At the inquest on the man they brought in a verdict of accidental death but many people seem to think that he shot Caprice and buried her somewhere on the moor, then shot her horse. Afterwards he threw himself from the top of the crag and broke his neck. Personally I think Caprice's body is in the tarn, it was never dragged successfully and it is very deep.'

I shuddered, 'But why should he kill her if he loved her?'

'Possibly because her wedding arrangements had gone too far and she refused to break off her engagement to Thorn. I remember at the time that many people believed they had a suicide pact, but suicide and Caprice don't go together somehow.'

'Oh Elliot, that is a terrible story. How did Mr Thorn take it?'

'Badly, I'm afraid. He went abroad for a time, in fact he only came back when his father died. He is very different now from the man he used to be.'

'Yes, I feel that too, but he fell in love with Elsa and married her.'

'Well, we don't really know that he fell in love with her. He certainly married her, but whether it was because they fell in love or because their common suffering shut out everybody else I don't know. For a long time things seemed to be normal after they married, but then Elsa had this nervous thing and you know the rest, I think.'

We were both silent for so long people at nearby tables began to look at us curiously, possibly because of our thoughtful faces and air of abstraction. At last Elliot leaned towards me, placing his hands over mine. 'Let the past be, Lottie, none of it is our concern.'

'But I liked her, Elliot. I loved her in a way. She was the most completely beautiful, exciting creature I had ever seen, and she was kind. I felt that she was kind.'

'She was not kind to Thorn, or to her sister. People like Caprice are always the ones who are loved and made much of. It has been so down the years – you have only to look at women like Cleopatra and Delilah. It's not the beautiful, good women but the beautiful, bad ones history remembers.'

'Will you ever go to Milverton again, Elliot?'

'Yes, I shall go there. I have a standing invitation from the Lyttons to visit them, but I shall not go when Rowena is there. Old wounds are best left alone I think.'

'There are so many things I could tell you about Milverton, Elliot. Did anybody ever sleep in the old wing of the house?'

He raised his eyebrows in surprise. 'Well it was to be opened up and decorated in time for Thorn's wedding. Caprice always liked the views from the windows of the old wing and I did hear that she had asked for workmen to come in to do some work on some of the rooms. Why do you ask?'

In my efforts to describe my experiences my words tumbled over each other and one look at his incredulous face made me regret taking him into my confidence.

'You always had too much imagination, Lottie,' he said firmly. 'It led you into mischief when you were young, and me also if I remember correctly. Forget Milverton for a while, I have already laid one ghost for you, so why not stay here and let me entertain you to dinner?'

'Elliot, I am not romancing. Somebody did go into the old wing, I saw the lights from the candles in the long windows, I heard a woman's laughter in the middle of the night, I have heard her singing to herself.'

'And already you are thinking that Thorn keeps Caprice locked up in those empty rooms, chained to the bedposts perhaps and waiting for his nightly visit.'

'I think nothing of the kind,' I said crossly, 'but you must admit it is odd.'

'No doubt there is a logical explanation which is no concern of yours, Lottie. Look, my dear, all this happened a long time ago and by this time much of it is forgotten by those who were concerned with it then. I do not think of Rowena these days although at one time she was always in my thoughts. Thorn too will have forgotten, or at least he will have filled his life with so many other important matters that he will give himself little time for remembering.'

'Thorn isn't like you Elliot. He is cynical, harder somehow, but underneath his cynicism he could still be vulnerable.'

He looked at me so intently that I could feel my cheeks blushing.

'I hope you are not falling in love with him.'

My lips tightened angrily as I said firmly, 'I'm not in the least in love with him, indeed there are times when I find him insufferable and . . .' words failed me for a few moments, then I went on to say, 'besides he already has a lady friend, a Mrs St Clare who lives in Medchester.'

'I know Lucy very well, she is a patient with my senior partner.'

'Well then.'

'Well then nothing, Lottie. Lucy has the same colouring as Caprice, she is as vivacious as Caprice was, but in every other respect Lucy St Clare and Caprice Langham are poles apart. If Elsa died tomorrow I doubt if Lucy would ever succeed in capturing Thorn.'

'Elliot, I want to go back to Milverton but I am also afraid. I am afraid of Miss Elsa and her moods, I hate to see Mrs Lytton sitting in her chair day after day without speaking, her eyes filled with questions she cannot put into words. I hate the sound of laughter in the night when the rest of the house is asleep, and candlelight in the windows of rooms that nobody ever goes into, but most of all I hate to see Mr Thorn with that half smile on his lips, the coldest, most impersonal, smile you have ever seen.'

'In fact Lottie, you hate him for his God-damned indifference. Now be honest, it is so isn't it?'

'No, it is not. If you're going to be beastly Elliot I shall wish I hadn't told you any of this. I know I have to go back there, Elliot, but I dread it.'

'Well, forget about it for this evening at any rate. Stay and have dinner with me.'

'I would like to Elliot, but I must get back. Aunt Maud is already displeased with me and heaven knows I don't want to antagonize her further.'

He walked with me to the entrance doors and asked the commissionaire to find me a cab. Then, after he had handed me into it he leaned forward, his eyes kind. 'Good-bye Lottie, I shall come over to Milverton to see you as soon as I can.'

'Not to see me, Elliot.'

'To see both you and the family. If Thorn sees us together it might jerk his memory and he will remember when and where he last saw us together.'

'He will think that I have been secretive and devious.'

'No doubt, but he will be amused, as he was on that night.'

He stood on the steps of the hotel until my cab turned the corner and I sat back against the cushions to think on the things he had been able to tell me. Much of what I had heard at Milverton now fell into place and I shuddered a little, thinking of Caprice still lying somewhere under a carpet of snow where Mower Gap lifted its rugged splendour towards the wintry sky.

I was sad that the idol of my childhood had had feet of clay but when I remembered her beauty and how, like a flame, she gathered everything and everybody towards her, I was not ashamed that I too, like the rest of them, had been consumed in the fire.

I have always been sensitive to atmosphere and I was painfully aware of it in the small hall before I had even opened the sitting room door. Aunt Maud sat in her favourite chair, her knitting needles clicking their antagonism at every stitch, and Uncle David sat opposite with his eyes firmly fixed upon his evening paper. Neither of them looked at me. The mere turning of a page seemed to command his full attention and from the regions of the kitchen I could hear Aunt Beatrice rattling crockery. The smile died on my lips at the same time as the greeting in my throat. Aunt Maud's back was ramrod straight in her high-backed chair and I hurried back into the hall to leave my outdoor clothes.

I went along the passage into the kitchen and in answer to my unspoken question Aunt Beatrice put her finger to her lips motioning me to keep silent and close the door behind me.

'Don't tell me she's still sulking,' I whispered.

'Oh Lottie, wherever have you been? She's been to a function at the church and Dora was there. Neither David nor I have been able to speak to her since she came back.'

I could feel my cheeks burning. I had been found out in a lie and I did not know which angered me most, that I had been found out or that I had been afraid to tell her the truth.

I suppose she spoke to Dora?'

'I'm afraid so, Lottie, and was told Dora hadn't seen you all day.'

Just then the kitchen door was flung open and Aunt Maud stood there, accusation in every line of her figure.

'You can cease your whispering the pair of you. She's been found out and I'm waiting now to hear what she has to say for herself.'

She marched back down the passage and Aunt Beatrice and I followed miserably in her wake. I would tell her the truth and if she did not make me feel like a harlot she would make me feel a cheat.

She listened in stony silence as I recounted my little tale, and I left nothing out, from my determination to find Elliot to my vigil in the foyer of the hotel that very morning. Aunt Maud sat facing me in the role of Chief Inquisitor. Uncle David appeared to have found something entirely absorbing in the corner of the room immediately above my head and poor Aunt Beatrice hovered behind me like a frightened sparrow. Nobody spoke. I stood before them like a naughty child who has been discovered raiding the pantry, furiously aware of the rigid lines of Aunt Maud's face, waiting for the words of condemnation which would surely come.

At last she said, 'We could have told you what you wanted to know about Milverton without you pestering Elliot Cliffe for explanations. I don't know what he will think about you, I'm sure.'

'I think Elliot understands, Aunt, that there are things I need to know about Milverton if I am ever to be happy there.'

'You are at Milverton as companion to Mr Thorn's wife, not as a family friend, Lottie. It has nothing to do with you that poor Miss Elsa was sent off her mind by all that trouble, and does you no good to know of it now. You always had too much imagination for your own good, making up stories about people, inventing experiences where none existed. It was like you to turn that girl into somebody special simply because she was beautiful, regardless of the fact that she was quite wicked, taking her sister's young man away from her and carrying on a clandestine affair with him under the roof of the man she was engaged to marry. I'm not surprised there was a tragic end to the affair, but you, Lottie, would do well to forget about her and concentrate on your duty to Miss Elsa. That is what you are being paid for. I expect Elliot Cliffe thought the same thing but would be too polite to say so.'

I was miserably aware of my flaming cheeks and my hands clenched angrily in the folds of my skirt. This was how she had talked to me all my life. Not because I had ever given her any real cause to doubt me until today, but because of the antagonism my father had always aroused in her by his quiet, learned teasing.

With tears in my eyes I ran upstairs to my room and, lying on my bed, I gave myself up at last to the luxury of weeping. Outside on the wet pavements I could hear the pattering feet of pedestrians going home to their evening meal, and occasionally the wheels of a cab and the steady clip-clop of horses' hooves. It was cold in my bedroom but I was so eaten up with misery that I did not notice until the door opened and Aunt Beatrice came in bearing a tray.

She pulled the curtains, shutting out the dreary night, and applied a match to the gas lamps on either side of the fireplace.

'Get undressed, dear,' she advised me, 'and get into bed. I've brought you some hot soup and I'm going to put a match to the fire.'

'But Aunt Maud hates fires lit in the bedrooms unless there is sickness,' I cried in alarm.

'She knows what I'm about to do.'

'But you and Uncle David have to live with her when I'm gone. Please, Aunt, don't antagonize her further on my account.'

'After the New Year and as soon as you have gone back to Gleave, we shall go back to our own home. We don't see a lot of Maud, she has her friends and we have ours, it's only at pastimes when we really meet at all these days. Come on, dear, drink up your soup whilst it's hot and I'll wait until the fire takes.'

I found a handkerchief under my pillow and dabbed at my eyes but the soup was warming, and misery and I have never been compatible for long.

I know I slept because it was much later when Aunt Beatrice came into my room again, this time carrying a cup of hot milk which had been generously laced with whisky. She sat on the edge of my bed whilst I drank it, and it was only when the last dregs had been drained that she said, 'Maud went to bed at nine o'clock and we were glad to see the back of her. Don't worry, Lottie, she'll be better in the morning when she's slept on it.'

'I wish it was next Wednesday and I was on my way back to Gleave,' I said with feeling.

'Well, it'll soon come round, but next Tuesday you and I are going to see Mrs Findlay. I shall make an appointment to see her during the early evening and since I always go to the church on that day Maud will no doubt be sarcastic but she won't try to stop us.'

'She calls it tampering with the devil, Aunt. Don't you think I have tampered with enough devils for one visit?'

'We are going, Lottie, whether she likes it or not. I have Uncle David behind me now and although she will disapprove she can't stop me going or taking you with me.'

Dear Aunt Beatrice had always played the role of Greek chorus to Aunt Maud's solo, but I could see what a difference it made to have a man in one's life. I went to sleep wondering if the day would ever come when I would have such a bulwark behind me.

9

During the next few days it became increasingly apparent that I was not to be forgiven lightly. I busied myself around the house and went out to the shops, but on each occasion I did what I had to do quickly and scurried back in case they might think I had planned another assignation with Elliot. Aunt Beatrice informed me she had made an appointment for us to see Mrs Findlay the following Tuesday, the day before I returned to Milverton, and although I had mixed feelings about it at least it would get us away from Aunt Maud's caustic tongue.

New Year's Eve dawned with a pale, watery sun shining on the wet pavement and, as I went down to the kitchen to make breakfast, I could not help but wonder what possible jollity could be in store for us. New Year cards arrived from several friends and acquaintances but there was nothing for me. I felt a vague air of disappointment thinking that Elliot might have remembered, but then why should he? We had never kept up a correspondence.

Shortly after lunch Aunt Beatrice and I were busy in the kitchen clearing away the dishes we had washed when I heard the knocker on the front door, then Aunt Maud's voice bidding whoever stood there to enter.

I hoped it was somebody who could restore her good humour but I said nothing and after a few minutes we heard her light, brisk footsteps coming down the passage towards the kitchen.

'You have a visitor, Lottie, I've put him in the parlour,' she said, but amazingly she was smiling. I quickly took off my apron, smoothed my hair, and with a dismayed look at both of them, went towards the sitting room. Elliot stood there with his back towards the fire and I saw that on a chair was a large bunch of flowers tied with a pale pink, satin ribbon and two enormous boxes of chocolates. I took

151

his outstretched hands, and behind me I heard Aunt Beatrice's welcoming voice. He took the chocolates and gave a box to each of the aunts, then he placed the flowers in my arms.

Harmony had been miraculously restored and the afternoon passed most pleasantly. Aunt Maud left us in order to decorate the church for the midnight service and Elliot took tea with Aunt Beatrice and me. It was only when Elliot said, 'There is a New Year's Eve Ball at the Fairlands Hotel, Lottie, and I have booked a table for two. Will you come with me?' that Aunt Beatrice looked unsure.

'Oh Elliot, I would love to come. I can go can't I Aunt?'

'Well dear, I'm sure it will be very nice, but what about Aunt Maud?'

'Leave Aunt Maud to me, Mrs Witty,' Elliot said, 'I'll call for you at eight o'clock, Lottie. I can talk to Miss McAllister then.'

I was a little afraid of breaking the news to her, knowing full well that she was expecting us to accompany her to church that evening, but she received the news of my invitation without much surprise, only wamting to know what time I would be home.

'I'm not sure, but it will be after midnight of course.'

'Well, don't be out until all hours. You know you go back to Gleave on Wednesday.'

I was happy as I got ready for the ball. I put on my new gown, revelling in the graceful folds of the full skirt and tiny, draped bodice. I took three pure white carnations from the flowers Elliot had given me and fastened them at the back of my hair, then I danced and twirled into the sitting room so that they could see how beautifully the gown fitted and how my dull-gold hair complemented the rich red velvet. The only jewellery I wore was the filigree rose Mr Lytton had sent me and the white, lacy shawl which felt soft and luxurious around my shoulders.

Elliot called for me promptly at eight o'clock and I was instantly reassured about my appearance by the gleam of admiration in his eyes. He looked tall and distinguished in his evening clothes, his nice, clever face smiling as he handed me into the carriage. I felt cushioned by the warmth of an approval that had been sadly lacking over the last few days.

The foyer of the hotel was crowded and lights from the chandeliers fell on the jewellery worn by the women gathered there, while all around us was the scented warmth of furs and expensive perfumes. Candles burned on every table and I reflected that nothing became a woman so much as the glow of candlelight falling on creamy shoulders and shining hair. We talked, we danced, and all the time I was aware of the happy air of propriety with which Elliot held me. At twelve o'clock the pipers marched into the ballroom to proclaim the ending of the old year and the start of the new. Elliot drew me into his arms and kissed my lips. It was not a kiss of passion, but it was tender and longer than strictly necessary, so tender that I knew my cheeks were blushing under the warm regard in his blue eyes.

'Happy New Year, Lottie,' he said, his eyes laughing into mine.

'Happy New Year, Elliot,' I answered, then with a sudden rush of confidence, 'Elliot, will you please call me Carla? I would prefer it.'

He threw back his head and laughed. 'I'll bet you'll never get your Aunt Maud to call you Carla.'

'I know, but then it was my father's name for me and they never did see eye to eye. I've hated "Lottie" all my life – it went with gingham pinafores and hair ribbons, and those horrid thick-ribbed stockings and laced-up boots I used to wear. Tonight in this dress and in your company I feel like a Carla.'

'It'll take a bit of getting used to but I'll certainly try. Carla, when am I going to see you again?'

'I don't know. I am returning to Gleave next Wednesday so we may not meet again for a considerable time.'

'Oh yes we shall. I intend to visit Milverton in the New Year, as soon as the practice will allow it. I shall write to Thorn and invite myself over as soon as I am sure that Rowena has returned to London.'

'You are afraid of meeting her?'

'No, it isn't that, but old ties are better left alone and I wouldn't want to embarrass either Rowena or her family.'

I didn't speak. I had always assumed that when love was over it would not matter how often one met. My father had once told me that there was nothing in the world quite so dead as a dead love and when I did not answer him Elliot looked at me, smiling a little sadly.

'You find that strange, Carla?'

'Yes, but then I know so little about love. I have never been in love and no man has ever been in love with me.'

'I don't believe it,' he said gallantly. 'You have spent some of your life in the most romantic countries in the world and you say no man has ever loved you. What on earth were those young archaeologists thinking about?'

I laughed. 'Oh Elliot, if you had only seen those young archaeologists. None of them was in first youth, and all of them had wives and children and school fees. The only young ones I met would have shown more interest in me if I had been dead for three thousand years. I was simply someone who mended their clothes, cooked their meals, fetched and carried for them and was invariably referred to as "Carla, old thing".'

'Dear me! Then how about those journeys by boat and a full moon shining on the top deck? You're a beautiful girl, Carla. I can't honestly believe it when you say romance has passed you by.'

'Then you had better believe it because it is true.'

For a few moments it seemed that the ballroom faded from my sight and I was back once more in the vast silence of the western desert with the sand dunes stretching endlessly towards the horizon before a backdrop of stars. Somehow the music from the ballroom receded and instead I heard other sounds, the rustle of palm fronds, stirring in the breeze, the sad eerie cry of a jackal from across the shifting sands and the piercingly sweet notes of a reed pipe played by one of the workmen who sat apart. I had dreamed of romance in that most romantic of lands where history pressed down upon me like a tangible thing. How could I have helped it? From the temple walls, calm, lovely faces looked out into eternity – remote, always in profile, the faces of men and women who had loved in that land centuries before our own little island emerged from its primeval obscurity. I was suddenly conscious that Elliot was watching me across the table with curious intensity and my cheeks grew warm with my blushes as I hastened to disclaim all knowledge of love.

'You were so far away that I was reluctant to break the spell. Seeing you tonight looking so enchanting I find it hard to believe your denials but you must be doubly careful not to fall in love with Thorn if your experience has been so limited. Women find him romantic and something of a challenge. They long to bring the smiles back to his face, to compensate him for all that he has lost.'

Mention of Thorn Lytton seemed to cast a shadow over the evening. Instead of Elliot's thin, sensitive face with the lock of fair hair falling across his forehead and his blue eyes teasing but kind, I saw Thorn's face with the wings of silver at his temples; I saw his dark, cynical eyes and stern mouth.

Elliot was watching me so closely that I became confused and strangely angry. When he saw it he laughed a little, and said lightly, 'I am only teasing you, pet, come and dance.'

In silence we danced, then caught in the spell of the music, I became happy again, determined that I would not spoil a perfect evening by thoughts of Thorn.

The pavements were dry when we left the hotel to find a cab to take us home and a full moon shone in a clear sky. There were late revellers on the streets shouting New Year greetings to each other and we too came in for much good-natured banter. It felt warmer, but I suspected I was still living under the spell of the music in a world where the cold winds of winter never blew. We drove back in the dark warmth of the carriage, with Elliot's arm around my shoulders, listening to the steady sound of the horses' hooves on the cobblestones and the good-humoured whistling of the driver.

Elliot asked him to wait until he had put my latchkey in the lock and seen me safely into the hall.

'Have you enjoyed the evening?' he asked anxiously.

'Oh yes, Elliot, I have. It has been the most beautiful perfect evening of my whole life. I am so grateful to you.'

He laughed boyishly. 'You know, Lottie,' he said, and the use of my old name did not trouble me. 'You were always the most exciting person to be with. When you enjoyed yourself you let us all know it, there were no half measures, no withdrawals, did you know that?'

'Gracious no. I always thought you all thought me a bit of a charlatan.'

I knew he was going to kiss me and I was not sure if I wanted him to do so. However, it was not an unpleasant experience because I truly liked Elliot, and his kiss was gentle, not burdened with passion. It was the kiss of a man for a girl he admired, nothing more, but it did not exactly match the expression in his eyes, which left me confused and uncertain.

As I took off my evening finery in my bedroom, listening to the sound of Elliot's cab dying away into the night, I asked myself if love came slowly like the opening of a flower to the sun, or did it come swiftly, troubled by conflicting emotions. I loved Elliot now as I had loved him as a young girl. He was kind and sensitive. He understood me and we could laugh together about things which amused us simply because we saw life in very much the same sort of pattern. I did not know if I could ever come to care for him with that deeper passion which is not always logical but which is all consuming and when I tried to think of Elliot in the role of husband or lover all I could see was Thorn's face, his eyes suddenly tender.

Miserably, I clenched my hands together in an agony of pleading. I did not want to love him, only misery and frustration lay in loving him, and I prayed that my foolish, impressionable heart would recover its sanity and find some other on whom it could lavish its devotion.

Aunt Beatrice helped me pack my case on Tuesday morning and when she came to my velvet dress, she said, 'What about this dear, are you taking it back with you?'

'I don't think so, when will I ever wear it? I already have my rose-coloured velvet hanging in the wardrobe.'

'Well, that is different, the rose colour is a ball gown, this is a dinner gown and you never know, Lottie. You may be asked to take dinner with the Lyttons when you get to know them better, particularly if Elliot pays them a visit and informs them that you and he are old friends.'

I had not the heart to argue with her and watched as she folded my dress in masses of tissue before closing the lid on my case.

'We must go to Mrs Findlay's directly after lunch, Lottie. If we are late she won't have much time to spend with us,' she said.

Aunt Maud saw us depart with a frown of displeasure and an admonishment to me that I should not take anything I saw or heard seriously. We boarded a horse tram at the end of the road which took us across the city towards the district where Aunt Beatrice lived. We passed the Spiritualist Church on the way, a new modern building, unlike any church I had ever seen.

Mrs Findlay lived in a district of tall, imposing early Victorian houses, built from Pennine stone, double-fronted with short, curving drives lined with dusty rhododendron bushes. Although it was only early afternoon lamps had been lit in the room to the right of the bright green door, which was the drawing room where Mrs Findlay would see us. The door was opened to us by a tall man who was introduced to me as Mr Findlay. He helped us off with our coats and asked us to sit in the drawing room until his wife joined us. A bright fire burned in the grate and a small table was pulled up towards the couch on which we both sat. It was a warm, comfortable lived-in room, quite unlike what I had expected. On the walls hung several oil-painted portraits of people I assumed were related to the Findlays and over the mantelpiece was a rather sombre painting of a Scottish loch surrounded by forests of evergreens. I must confess to feeling a little nervous but Aunt Beatrice sat beside me looking quite unconcerned with her hands in her lap.

After about five minutes the door opened to admit Mrs Findlay and I felt at once that I liked her. She was tall, with a beautiful, serene face. Her silver hair was elaborately dressed and held in place by a large tortoiseshell comb. She was wearing a black tea-gown, plain and unadorned, but round her shoulders was draped an exquisitely embroidered Spanish shawl, with a heavy silk fringe.

Aunt Beatrice rose to her feet and the two women embraced each other in the way of old friends, then I was led forward to be introduced.

'I am glad to meet you, my dear,' she said. 'Would you prefer to have tea now or would you rather wait until I have given you your message?'

I looked at Aunt Beatrice for guidance and she said, 'I think we should have tea afterwards, Mrs Findlay. Everything is very new to Lottie and I'm afraid she is a little nervous.'

'There's no need to be nervous,' said Mrs Findlay briskly, 'I have a gift and I use it to help people. Once, when I was very much younger than I am now, I was frightened by it. Because I saw things others did not see I was thought of as strange, but now I value my gift. Is there something of yours which I can hold, something worn only by you and nobody else?'

I looked at Aunt Beatrice again and she said, 'Let Mrs Findlay have your amulet, dear. It is yours and worn by you since you were quite a young girl.'

I handed Mrs Findlay the amulet and for a few moments she twirled it through her fingers before looking up at me sharply to ask, 'It is Egyptian, ancient Egyptian, I think?'

'Yes. If you would rather have something else I could give you one of my gloves or my purse.'

'No, no, this will do splendidly, but don't be surprised if I get some of its history as well as yours, my dear.'

Aunt Beatrice and I took the chairs before the fire but Mrs Findlay pulled up another chair – a large, velvet chair with wings and deep cushions at the back. She leaned back with her head in the corner, all the time twirling the amulet in and out of her fingers. The silence was complete except for the crackling of the coals in the fire. The reflection of the flames leaped upon the ceiling, for now only one lamp burned in the room and that stood upon a small table beside her chair.

Quite suddenly she leaned forward, her eyes open wide, holding mine with such an hypnotic stare I struggled to look away but found I could not. Her voice was harsh and had a breathless quality. It was totally unlike the voice she had used to greet us only moments before.

Her hands were gripping mine so tightly that they hurt as she said, 'The amulet is a protector against evil but it will take all its ancient power and more if it is to protect you from the evil which surrounds you. Wear it constantly, call upon the forces of love and goodness wherever they are to be found.'

I heard Aunt Beatrice's gasp of astonishment and it seemed that the room turned cold as I listened to Mrs Findlay's sonorous voice speaking those words of dread. Slowly she released her grip on my hands leaving red marks where her fingers had held mine. She was breathing normally now, leaning back comfortably in her chair and when next she spoke her voice was lighter, more like her own voice.

'There is a lady here whose name is Catherine, she comes bringing flowers which are a sign of joy and she places them in your arms. I think this is an omen that in spite of the evil there can still be joy. Yes, I feel it. I feel in the end that all will be well.

'You have been called to a task for which you have little liking and which in the end will defeat you. But from one who is in spirit I have to say that the truth must be told. That is why you were chosen; because you are open and brave in spirit you will discover the truth. Do you know what I am trying to say to you?'

'I am not sure,' I said falteringly.

'As far as she is able she will protect you, but she tells me that you must be wary about placing your trust. Now she is showing me a tree, I cannot tell whether it is a flowering shrub or some other kind of tree . . . no, wait, she is handing me a rose.' She gave a little cry and held her finger.

'Oh, but the thorns are large on this rose and there are so many of them, but now she is handing me another rose and this time the thorns have gone and the stems are clean and shining. It seems to me that perhaps there are two men, one who will hurt you and one who will cherish you. No?' She seemed to be asking a question of one she could see and I could not. 'No, she tells me I am wrong in this. She tells me the man who could hurt you could yet become the man he once was, kind and gentle where he loves. Now do you understand me?'

I shook my head. I did not want to understand her, for how could I delude myself that Thorn Lytton could ever be kind and gentle with me because he loved me?

'Are there any questions you wish to ask me, my dear?'

'How am I to overcome the evil you speak of if I do not know where to look for it?'

Again she looked beyond us saying, 'You heard the question.'

She was silent, as though listening, then she said, 'I am told that the evil is there now but in the weeks and months to come it will intensify and you must be very careful. I can hardly hear you; you are so faint. Ah, she has gone.'

She sat back in her chair twirling the amulet in her fingers, then in a soft, far-away voice she said, 'It is like a tunnel of time with clouds swirling towards me and there is chanting of many voices in a strange tongue. The light is so bright – clear, golden sunlight like no light I have ever seen – and it shines on pillars of stone and painted with colours of great beauty. There are people, men and women in white garments, and the women carry sheaths of lilies and the men wear the skins of leopards around their shoulders.'

Suddenly she stopped speaking and her head fell forward on to her breast as if in a faint. I sprang to my feet as though to go to her but Aunt Beatrice held out her hand to restrain me, saying in a whisper, 'Don't touch her, Lottie, it always ends like this. In a few moments she will come round and will probably not remember anything she has said to you.'

So we waited and, sure enough, in a few moments Mrs Findlay's eyelids flickered open. She looked at us as though she had come out of a long sleep, then straightened her shoulders and said, 'Ah, here we are then. Have I been any help to you?'

Aunt Beatrice answered for me. 'You have given her some disquieting news, Mrs Findlay, I hope nothing harmful is going to happen to her.'

Mrs Findlay looked concerned. 'I'm sorry, my dear, but I can never remember afterwards what I say to people. Did I not tell you that in the end all would be well? I do hope so.'

'Yes, you did say that, but I am still afraid.'

'Did you recognize any of the people who came through to me?'

'I'm not sure. You mentioned a Catherine, but I cannot think who she can be.'

'I can, Lottie,' said Aunt Beatrice. 'Your great

grandmother was called Catherine, although you never knew her.'

'Then how can she concern herself with me now?'

'I know it is strange,' Mrs Findlay said. 'Perhaps in this life we shall never know why these things are. Did I tell you anything else which was relevant?'

'I'm not sure.' I answered. I did not mention her vision of ancient Egypt. I felt that because she knew the amulet was Egyptian this bit of knowledge could have been drawn from her imagination, although when I looked into her candid, blue eyes and serene, lovely face she did not seem like a fraud.

Mrs Findlay smiled at us both. 'Well now, let us have tea, I'm sure you are both feeling ready for that.'

She tinkled a little bell on the table at her side and almost immediately the door opened to admit a young maid carrying a loaded tea tray. There was China tea and a trayful of thinly cut sandwiches and plates filled with scones and small, home-made cakes. We ate, drank and talked until the shadows in the room caused our hostess to rise and light the gas lamps over the fireplace. With some dismay I looked out of the window to see that already it was dusk. Hurriedly we made our excuses and she walked with us to the front door. After she had embraced Aunt Beatrice she took my hand, holding it for a long moment so that I felt again the spell of those wide, blue eyes.

'I shall pray for you Lottie,' she said. 'If I warned you of evil, then be very sure that there *is* evil for I am never wrong in these things. Such warnings do not come from me but from spirits outside time and space, but I shall ask the good Lord to protect you and give you strength. You are young, and God will give you courage to face whatever may befall.'

We were silent on the journey home but I was aware that Aunt Beatrice looked at me from time to time with a worried, unspoken question in her eyes.

'Lottie dear,' she said eventually, 'I hope Mrs Findlay hasn't frightened you with her talk of evil, I am beginning to wish I hadn't taken you to see her.'

'I'm not afraid, Aunt. Whatever evil there is at Milverton is over now. In any case I am only a paid companion, not one of the family, so how could I possibly be affected by it?'

'I don't know,' she said doubtfully, 'but I wish you didn't have to go back to that great, lonely house.'

'Well, I must go back. I don't intend tramping round Medchester looking for work when I have a perfectly good post waiting for me at Milverton. Besides, the Lyttons have been very good to me, it would be unthinkable of me not to return there.'

'But you will take care Lottie. Don't trust people too readily and. . . .'

'What are you trying to say Aunt Beatrice?'

'Mr Thorn, Lottie. Don't care too much for Mr Thorn. He is married and not for you. Why don't you write to Elliot and perhaps in the spring he will come over to Gleave to see you?'

She put her arms round me and held me against her for a moment and I could see there were tears in her eyes.

That night I lay for a long time in my bed looking up at the ceiling, my thoughts busy with all I had heard that afternoon, and when I did eventually sleep I was plagued by dreams of Milverton, with the mist swirling through the woods behind the house, and of laughter, wild and sinister, and lights burning in the empty windows of the old wing.

I caught the nine o'clock train out of Medchester. The train was crowded with people travelling to the market at Feltham, but it stopped at every station to take in more passengers so that by the time it reached Gleave they were standing in the corridors. I was the only person to alight at the little country station, although there were quite a few people waiting to board the train and I recognized a number of familiar faces amongst them. I wandered along the platform in the direction of the waiting room hoping to find the station master to ask if there were any chance of persuading his friend George to take me up to the house. When I reached the waiting room however, I could see George standing near the gate, quite obviously awaiting me.

He looked no more prepossessing in the light of day than he had looked on our first acquaintance and, although I bade him a friendly good afternoon, he merely grunted in reply, and indicated that I should step into the cab.

The sun was shining – a pale wintry sun without any real warmth in it, but it enlivened the straggling village street with light and shadows. High over the village the moorland seemed to shimmer with shades of blue and purple, and the faded brown and gold of old bracken mingled with the dark shadows cast by the towering crags. The sky was blue, the cold wintry blue which complemented so well the snow on the high fells, and was reflected brilliantly in the waters of the mere.

I enjoyed the journey to Milverton. The old horse trotted with his head up and, although there were blue puddles in the roadway after the recent storms, I looked on the stately grandeur of the house with renewed pleasure. The sun was reflected in the tall windows set in the mellowed stone and smoke curled upwards from the chimneys. It was only when we rounded the curve in the drive and I could see the dark mass of the old wing that my fears returned and I shuddered despite myself.

George unloaded my one case at the front door and I asked him how much I owed him for the journey.

'I've bin paid, miss. Good day to thee.' After that, and with a laconic nod of his head, he climbed on to his perch on the driving seat and with a brisk word to his horse they trundled away down the drive.

I lifted the heavy knocker on the door, listening to the sound of it echoing dismally in the lofty hall behind. It seemed only moments before the door swung open and Nancy's smiling face greeted me; then she took the case from my hands.

It was very quiet in the house and I wondered if Miss Judith was in the music room, although I could not hear her piano. Nancy kept up a constant flow of chatter all the way up the stairs, telling me that there had been serious floods on some of the farmlands and that Mr Thorn and Mr Stephen were over at Stand Edge that very morning where the most serious flooding had occurred. She enquired about my holiday, telling me that the Christmas guests had now gone to their homes and Milverton, thank goodness, was once more back to normal. As I followed her along the familiar corridor towards my room I could not help feeling that I had come home.

10

Spring came late to Milverton, but it was present in the sparkling air which came through the windows from the moors beyond. Among the glossy leaves of the rhododendron bushes, fat, pink buds were ready to burst into great, showy flowers and the lilacs and azaleas vied with each other to see which should open their blossoms first. The meadows beyond the walls rippled fresh and green in the sunlight, and on the tarn the swans were raising their first brood of cygnets, as were the bossy, bustling mallards escorting their ducklings in precise formation across the water. Bluebells carpeted the woods behind the house and in the evening the scent of clover was powerfully sweet in the scented dark. The swallows had returned, busily building their nests high up under the eaves and the rooks too were nesting high – an omen, I was told, that the summer would be one to remember.

I was happy. Mrs Findlay had warned me of dark intrigue and evil but in my new-found contentment I forgot her warnings, or at least told myself that I should have had more sense than to listen to her tales of foreboding. My friendship with Miss Judith continued and strengthened and when I was not busy with my own duties we took walks together or rode in the little pony and trap around the country lanes. I saw little of Mr Thorn, but when we did meet he was always courteous and I believed he was pleased that Miss Elsa and I were getting along well together.

I had learned to cope with her tantrums which surprisingly had become fewer in the last few months. I was also getting to know Agnes better, now that the three of us took long walks in the parkland, when she and I watched Elsa happily picking wild flowers which she insisted should be put in my room. Sometimes when we sat together on the lawns leading down to the tarn I would find myself watching Elsa for any sign of her relationship with Caprice, but I could find none. She had none of Caprice's vivid colouring and her silver fairness bore no comparison to Caprice's remembered glow.

Now that I knew something of the tragedy of her past I felt a strange tenderness towards her. I could imagine her returning from India with her parents during that fateful summer, bringing with her the young subaltern she intended to marry. She would be happy, gay, very much in love and looking forward with joy to their future together. No doubt she had been spoiled a little in the ballrooms of Lahore and Delhi where her father held high rank and where there was an abundance of young officers all anxious to flirt with her and flatter her. She was young and lovely, and I could imagine the dismay and hurt she felt when the man she loved succumbed to Caprice's charm. I could envisage her agony as she watched them carry his lifeless body down from the fells, knowing that somewhere out there they had left Caprice.

Was that how Elsa and Thorn had come together, I wondered. A marriage born out of a common hurt, a hurt which in her case had tipped the scales on the wrong side of sanity, and which had filled Thorn with such cynical bitterness that there could never have been any hope of happiness for either of them. Caprice had been unworthy of the admiration I had felt for her. In my usual idealistic fashion I had made a beautiful garment which I intended Caprice should wear and she had been unequal to its perfection. I had been foolish and impulsive and I felt that it would take a long time and much heartsearching before I could give my love and admiration to either man or woman again.

It was early June before Elliot came. I heard his voice as I crossed the hall to pick up the afternoon mail. As I turned to mount the stairs the library door opened and he came out with Mr Thorn.

His eyes lit up when he saw me and he came forward to greet me with outstretched hands.

'Lottie. . . .' he began. Then, laughing a little, 'I beg your pardon, *Carla*, how are you? Didn't I say I would come to Milverton to see you at the first opportunity?'

'You look well, Elliot,' I said, smiling up at him. Then I was conscious that Mr Thorn was looking at us, a frown of puzzlement on his face, and he said, 'I see that you two know each other.'

Elliot laughed. 'We knew each other years ago in Gleave. Surely you haven't forgotten that Christmas Eve when we all but fell through the window yonder and had to be sent back to the village hall in your carriage?'

I watched Thorn's face, his eyes opened wide with the memory of that night. Then he looked at me, 'That was you – that child who was forever peering over the wall, or caught running along our drive, or trying to look through the windows? Why didn't you tell me?'

'How could I, Mr Thorn, when I so dreadfully wanted to forget that child and hoped that you had also?'

'And have you seen each other often since that particular Christmas Eve?' he asked.

'Not often enough, I'm afraid,' Elliot answered him. 'Carla, as she prefers to be called now, went abroad with her father and only came to visit her aunts when he could not take her with him. Most of the time I was away at school and we only met during the holidays, but we have renewed our acquaintance and only this year spent a very happy New Year's Eve together.'

'Indeed. Well, Miss McAllister, since Elliot is a guest with us for several days I must ask you to dine with us one evening and you can talk over your youthful indiscretions at greater length.'

With the briefest of smiles he left us together and Elliot grinned at me. 'He becomes more caustic each time we meet, but I suspect that underneath the veneer of remoteness he is the same old Thorn.'

'I doubt it,' I said stiffly, and he laughed.

'I shall see you when you are off duty, I hope. I have come to Milverton to see the family but I have also come to see you.'

'You have been long in coming Elliot. Did you have to pluck up a great deal of courage before you could make the journey?'

He flushed, and I regretted my hasty words. Why should I question him, what would I have done if he had come rushing over to Milverton early in the New Year? I cared for Elliot like a brother, and, as I mounted the stairs, I wondered sadly why life always had to be so complicated. Why men and women had to love where there was no hope of its being returned and how much more simple life would be if we could always love those who loved us!

Mrs Lytton's nurse passed me on the stairs and favoured me with a bright, brief smile. She was wearing her outdoor clothes so I imagined she was either going out for a walk or going into the village on some errand or other. Impulsively, I decided to call in on Mrs Lytton whom I hadn't seen for several days. I had not made a friend of her nurse although we were always polite to each other. She and Mrs Bamber were friends and no doubt she considered me too young and foolish – as members of older generations often do.

I found Mrs Lytton sitting in her chair which had been placed besides the window and reading. She looked up as I entered and pointed to a chair which I drew up beside her. She put down her book immediately and picked up the writing pad and pencil from the table beside her chair.

The speed with which she wrote never failed to astonish me. 'My son has a visitor?' she wrote.

'Yes, Mrs Lytton. It is Elliot Cliffe. He is here for a few days.'

'Do you know him?'

'Yes, since we were children.'

'He was engaged to my daughter.'

'I know Mrs Lytton. I am sorry.'

Our conversation was always like this. She could not be expected to write down long sentences and my replies were therefore unnaturally short.

'Does Thorn know that you know Elliot?'

'Yes, we have just told him so.'

In silence we looked out across the gardens towards the lake. Below us in the rose gardens the bushes were heavy with blooms and through the open window the scents of summer drifted into the room. She reached out again for her pad and wrote, 'This is no life for you, Carla, you should be with young people of your own age.'

'But I am constantly with people only a little older than myself and I am very happy here.'

She looked at me sadly. 'That is not what I meant my dear. You should be with young, healthy people, people with whom you could plan your future.'

I could not answer her, there was nothing to say. The next moment she pointed to a chocolate box lying on the table beside her chair. I handed it to her, but instead of chocolates there was a pile of the finest lawn handkerchiefs inside, which she took out and handed to me, then picking up her notepad again she wrote, 'Chose two, Carla, I have embroidered them myself.'

I took the two which lay on top, exclaiming delightedly over the fine petit point stitching and delicate appliqué work.

They were all so kind to me. Only the week before Miss Judith had given me an evening bag saying that she had too many already.

The library at Milverton had also become a source of great joy to me – a voyage of discovery, I called it, for I had been given free rein to choose books from it any time I pleased.

There were times when I wondered what it would be like to live and grow old at Milverton and to watch those around me growing old also. Miss Elsa did not look strong but I had no reason to think that she was less robust physically than myself. Would her mind deteriorate or improve with age, I wondered, and would my adventurous spirit be able to cope with a future which promised little in the way of change? I could not see myself as an old retainer, pensioned off into a small cottage on the estate; on the other hand, where would I go if I left Milverton? I wondered how Mr Thorn would change with the passing years. Would his tall slimness begin to stoop a little and his black hair become silver like the hair at his temples? He would be handsome still, I thought. Age could not destroy that firm, hawklike profile or that steely, upright figure.

Next morning Agnes came to tell me that Miss Elsa was unwell and that the doctor had been sent for, so I decided I would ask if I might go down into the village to see the vicar. I was surprised, however, to find a note on my breakfast tray from Elliot, inviting me to go riding with him later in the morning. I was pleased with his invitation but dismayed when I looked at my riding apparel. On the spur of the moment I had pushed my old riding skirt into my case, thinking that perhaps Mr Thorn would be true to his promise and have his groom find me a docile mare on which I could follow the bridle paths around Milverton unaccompanied when the weather was clement. The skirt was an unremarkable, grey flannel affair, and with it went a grey jacket of indeterminate cut over which I wore a bright scarf. The last time I had worn it had been in Luxor, mounted on a mule who was both indolent and incredibly peevish, and the mule and my riding habit had suited each other admirably. How could I possibly go riding with Elliot looking like a fugitive from a company of tinkers?

I was no horsewoman compared with either Rowena or Miss Judith. I had never seen Miss Elsa show the slightest interest in horses although Miss Judith told me she was no mean horsewoman. I stood irresolutely looking through the window wondering what I should do about Elliot's invitation and in the end I wrote him a note, explaining that I was not equipped for riding but that if he cared to walk with me in the country I would be delighted. Back came his reply that Miss Judith would be only too happy to lend me a riding habit.

In no time at all there was a knock on my door, and when I opened it Miss Judith was standing there. She was smiling, and over her arm she carried riding clothes. There was a long black skirt, but of such exquisite material that I withdrew my hand from it reluctantly. There was a black, velvet riding coat and a fine, white shirt with ruffles of lace at the neck and the wrists. A pair of black leather riding boots complemented the habit as well as a black, velvet hat in the shape of a tricorn.

'Oh, but these are beautiful, Miss Judith!' I exclaimed. 'Are you sure you do not mind lending them to me?'

'I propose to give them to you. I have not worn them for several years because I ride so little these days and have other habits, besides these things may never fit me again.'

'But you are so slender, as slender as I am.'

'But not, alas, for very long. I am expecting a child next February, Carla.'

I looked at her with delighted eyes and took both her hands in mine.

'Oh, Miss Judith, I am so very glad for you. It will be lovely to have a child running about the corridors of this lonely, old house.'

A shadow seemed to cross her face as I spoke and I looked at her closely, wondering what had put it there.

'You are happy about the baby?' I asked her.

'Oh yes, we are delighted, but not that it is to be born here. Stephen and I have our own home which we love and I would naturally like my child to be born in it and grow up there. This house is Thorn's house. If Elsa had been well no doubt she would have had children and life in this house would have been very different, but as things are how can we leave Milverton to make our own life?'

'But Mrs Lytton has a nurse, and Miss Elsa has both Agnes and myself. Is your house far from here?'

'About ten miles. It is beautiful, Carla, we fell in love with it the first time we saw it and furnished it so lovingly, taking time to choose the things we wanted. Occasionally we go over to look at it and come away distressed, knowing we may never be able to return to it.'

'The house is empty?'

'There is a housekeeper there and two village women go in to help her with the cleaning. It is our home, Carla, we should be there, but Thorn needs us here, or at least that is what Stephen tells me.'

'If your husband knows how sad you feel about it, could he not talk to Mr Thorn and ask for other arrangements to be made?'

'I don't know. The Lyttons are a close-knit family and so much has happened to them in such a short space of time – even Stephen is still dismayed by it.'

'But you are his wife, you should come first.'

She smiled, rather sadly, I thought, then she said, 'I often wonder who does come first with my husband's family, the human beings who are closest to them or this pile of old stones they call home. Stephen still calls Milverton home, but Jeremy should be here to help run the estate – he would be here quickly enough to pick up the pieces if anything should happen to Thorn.'

I did not know what to say now that she had unburdened herself to me and as she moved sadly towards the door I knew she was on the verge of tears. She pointed to the things on the bed.

'Wear them, Carla, they will suit you. You really are becoming something of a beauty you know.'

I laughed a little self-consciously, then she said, 'Elliot is a nice man. I would like to think he has forgotten Rowena, or at least that he is no longer fond of her. Enjoy your day with him.'

After she had gone I began to think about all she had said to me and perversely I blamed Thorn, believing him to be selfish, for surely he must see that his sick wife was his problem and nobody else's. Mrs Lytton was hardly any trouble, certainly she did not require two of her sons to remain in attendance. Judith was right. Milverton was no fit home to bring up a child, for how would a child understand an old lady who was unable to speak and a young lady who was unpredictable, to say the least?

I walked over to the bed and picked up the little, velvet hat with its ridiculous bunch of feathers, then I tried it on in front of the mirror. My hair wasn't right for it, but it would be when I had had time to fiddle with it. Some of my good spirits revived as I changed into the riding habit and I purposely did not look in the mirror again until I could see the finished result. I fastened the skirt easily and I knew at once that the rest of the habit would fit me just as well, even the riding boots. Finally I tied my hair back with a large, black bow, putting on the hat for the second time. I approached the cheval mirror cautiously but what I saw there brought the warm colour to my cheeks and I knew that I was beautiful. It was a cool, English beauty that looked back at me from the mirror. The rich velvet of the riding habit complemented my clear, grey eyes and pink and white complexion. The cut of the jacket emphasized my slender waist and against the sheen of the cock feathers my dull-gold hair took on a different glow.

I picked up the riding crop Miss Judith had left on the bed and with something of a swagger, made possible by the jauntiness of the outfit, I made my way to the hall below.

Elliot was waiting for me and I could not but be aware of

the sparkle of admiration in his eyes. Together we walked across the hall but just as we were about to go out through the door it opened to admit Mr Thorn. He looked at us with raised eyebrows, and eyes that contained a degree of ironic amusement.

'May I say Miss McAllister that you are looking particularly charming in that habit,' he said smiling, 'and most professional.'

'I fear I am anything but that, Mr Thorn, so I am hoping that a docile and patient mount can be found for me.'

'Ask the groom to saddle old Betsy, Elliot. She will give Miss McAllister no trouble and she knows her way across these moors blindfold.'

'Thank you, sir.' I said demurely.

I could not be sure if there was a twinkle in his eyes or not, but after a distant impersonal smile he walked away in the direction of the library.

'Come on,' said Elliot, 'let us get out on to the moors so that we can enjoy the best of this lovely day. I've had sandwiches put in the saddlebags as well as some fruit, so we can ride towards the fells and picnic there.'

Betsy proved to be as gentle and docile as Mr Thorn had predicted. Elliot was riding a big, bay gelding, but once outside the parkland of Milverton, with the wind fresh on our faces and the horses moving at a steady trot, I felt so invigorated that I became rash, urging Betsy to go faster, delighted by her response. We followed the old, winding tracks across the moors, picking our way over stones washed down from the fells, wading through shallow, bubbling streams, trotting along lanes scored by the wheels of farm carts over the years. Over our heads white clouds scudded in a clear, blue sky and the sun felt warm on our shoulders. The high fells in the distance looked nothing like as fearsome as they had looked under snow-filled skies and even the rugged crags seemed to have lost some of their starkness.

At first we chatted amicably about all manner of things, then as though our silence could only add enjoyment to our ride we concentrated on the views. White, silvery waterfalls ran down the crags and hillsides, swelling the bubbling streams below and at one time only the mournful cries of the curlews disturbed the silence. We were climbing now and the scenery became wilder with the trees left far behind. The wide, rolling fells were all around us and we could see Mower Gap now, taller than the others and more lonely. We dismounted from our horses near a low, stone wall, allowing them to crop the short, green grass, and by mutual consent we sat together on the wall looking upwards towards the fells. I was silent for so long Elliot finally asked, 'Is it the view which keeps you so silent or are we such old friends we do not need to talk?'

'I was wondering if they will ever find her.'

'You are not still thinking of Caprice?'

'I can't help it. It is horrible to think that somewhere up there she is lying all alone without a proper grave or even a headstone to say her name.'

'There are some who might say that is all she deserves.'

'Then they would be cruel. Oh Elliot, isn't it enough to die young and beautiful and full of life? How does anybody really know what happened up there that afternoon? Caprice and that boy cannot tell us and all the rest has been supposition on the part of magistrates and lawyers.'

'Well, we know that they rode off together and we know that only the boy came back dead, lying on a wooden gate. People at Milverton do not speak of Caprice. Why does it bother you so?'

'I don't know, I only wish I did. For a few weeks I forget her and then she comes back to me and oh, so much stronger than before. There are times when I have the strangest feeling that I have been brought here to find out the truth and then I am ashamed of appearing so fanciful.'

'But why you, Carla? You barely knew Caprice. Don't tell me you have had more of your nightmares about the old wing being haunted.'

'No, I haven't,' I replied somewhat crossly, 'nor did I dream it was haunted when I stood looking out of my window with my feet frozen solid and my bed getting icier by the minute.'

Abruptly I turned away and walked over to where Betsy stood champing the coarse moorland grass. Elliot came over to help me mount her.

'You could always convince me that black was white,' he

said ruefully, 'but not in this case, Carla. Caprice is dead. She is not waltzing about the rooms of the old wing in the dead of night and I can assure you her sad ghost would have little cause for singing.'

We rode back in silence, our picnic forgotten, and I was sorry that the happy camaraderie of the day had gone. As we rode across the ridge of the hill behind the house with the parkland spread out before us I heard Elliot catch his breath sharply, and following his gaze I saw a woman riding a spirited, black horse down the hillside towards the mere. She was wearing a red riding habit and her hair flew back from her face in the freshening wind. We halted our horses so that we could watch her and I felt the hairs rise at the back of my neck as she galloped recklessly towards the tarn, jumping the stone walls with graceful abandon. It seemed to me then that by speaking of her we had summoned Caprice's spirit back from the dark void of eternity and she was here to taunt us, riding her black stallion with easy grace as I had seen her ride him so many times before, as though they were one instead of two separate beings. She rode along the shores of the mere, then she turned to ride upwards towards the hill where we waited and I looked up at Elliot's face. He was pale, as though he too had seen a ghost, and underneath me my horse shied nervously, sensitive to my fears.

She came upon us suddenly, reining in her horse so that she sat looking at us across the wall, but her hair was not black, it was dark red and there was hostility in her dark eyes. I heard Elliot's whisper 'Rowena', and suddenly she whipped her horse before careering down the hill at full gallop in the direction of the stables.

In that one brief moment I knew that Elliot had not forgotten Rowena and I wondered how two people who could still look at each other as they had looked at each other could ever have been parted. In that look had been hurt and a strange kind of frustration that one of them had spoiled both their lives for something which had grown sour and dead in her hands.

'When did she arrive, I wonder?' he asked quietly. 'She was not expected or Thorn would have told me.'

'She comes whenever the spirit moves her,' I answered

him, 'whenever she is tired of the life she is living and the people around her.'

Without another word we turned our horses and walked them slowly after the flying figure of the girl on her black horse, but by the time we reached the stables her steaming horse was unsaddled and being led away. Elliot told me to go inside and said that he would see to the horses. I was sure he needed time to compose himself before meeting Rowena again.

I went into the house by the conservatory, more or less on tiptoe and hoping to cross the hall without being seen. As I passed the drawing room door I heard Rowena's voice raised in anger and I am ashamed to say that I paused to listen.

'What is Elliot doing here?' she asked.

'He is here as my guest.' It was Thorn's voice, curt, uncompromising.

'It is disloyal,' she replied petulantly.

'Do not speak to me of disloyalty, Rowena, or the lack of it. I like Elliot, that is why he is here, and while you are here I suggest you remember that he is my guest and treat him accordingly.'

'I do not intend to speak to him. I shall dine in my room.'

'That is as you wish, of course.'

The words he spoke were said as though he did not greatly care where his sister dined, and in a childishly sullen voice she asked, 'Does he know Miss McAllister so well that he saw fit to ride with her on the moor?'

'He knows her very well. I am told they were friends as children and since I had business which prevented me riding with Elliot myself I suggested he invite Miss McAllister.'

'Since when have you thought it a good idea for your guests to mingle with your servants?' she asked, and standing half way up the stairs I could feel my heart pounding with resentment, my hand clenched tightly upon the bannister rail. Inside the drawing room there was what seemed like a yawning silence before I heard his voice again, cold, clipped, dismissing her.

'Your question does not require an answer, and I prefer to think that it was never asked. Return to your room and endeavour to recover some of your good humour. Dinner is at eight o'clock, unless you are serious about dining in your room, in which case I suggest you inform one of the servants.'

I ran up the stairs as fast as my legs could carry me, but I heard the sound of the drawing room door being closed with something approaching a slam, and then Rowena's feet running swiftly up the stairs behind me.

I was trembling as I changed my riding habit for my robe, wondering if I should wear it for the rest of the evening or change back into my skirt and blouse. I felt hurt and angry, but logic told me I had no right to be. I was a servant in this house, but her words were particularly cruel when I remembered how I had known Elliot in days when I had never thought to be anybody's servant.

11

I did not know how long Elliot intended to remain at Milverton but I did not think I would see him again before he left. I was glad therefore next morning when Agnes told me Miss Elsa was much better and asking to see me. With work to occupy my hours the time passed swiftly and I had little time to think of Elliot or Rowena. Agnes and I had been busy making new curtains for some of the rooms in the doll's house and, although she did not normally allow me to handle any of the furniture or the dolls themselves, she watched with childish delight as I hung the new curtains at the windows.

Although it was a warm summer's day, the doctor had advised Agnes to keep Miss Elsa indoors for another day at least, and we sat in the window seat looking out across the park while I read to her from *Wuthering Heights*. I was not sure how much of the book she really understood, but she listened without interrupting me and when I looked up I found her eyes fixed intently on the parkland. I followed her gaze and saw that she watched two people, a man and a woman walking down the slope towards the mere.

Her normally pale cheeks were flushed with anger and she spoke sharply.

'How dare she come back to walk with Thorn in the park?'

I followed her gaze with startled surprise, realizing that she believed it was Caprice out there walking with her husband.

'It is Miss Rowena walking with Mr Cliffe.' I said gently.

She looked at me for a moment as though she did not see me, then as if addressing a backward child she said, 'Rowena does not live here anymore.'

'No, but she is visiting for a few days, so is Mr Cliffe.'

She frowned and I could see her hands clenched in her

lap so that the knuckles showed white.

'She's bad you know, like Caprice was bad. Somebody should kill her like they killed Caprice.'

For a moment I looked at her in shocked surprise. Her small face was vindictive, her china-blue eyes like flecks of ice, then I said, 'Oh no, Miss Elsa, I don't think Rowena is bad – headstrong perhaps, but not bad.'

'My sister was bad, everybody said so, but I've forgotten why she was bad. Do you know why she was bad?'

'I never really knew her. Shall we go on with the book?'

I continued to read, but when I lifted my head at the end of the chapter I found her looking at me so strangely and intently that I became flustered and dropped the book on the window seat, losing the bookmark and my page.

Agnes came in with the tea tray and I excused myself to go across the room to help her. As we sorted out the cups and saucers and poured the tea she whispered to me, 'Please, Miss Carla, don't speak to her of Caprice. It only upsets her.'

'But Agnes, I didn't. She spoke of Caprice to me.'

'I'm sorry, miss, I did not hear the whole conversation but talk of Miss Caprice can upset her for days on end.'

She called upon Elsa to join us for tea but Elsa merely tossed her head petulantly, saying, 'I shall go to my room, I am tired.' Then without looking at either of us again she walked into her bedroom and slammed the door behind her.

Agnes gave me a sad, resigned look and after picking up the tea tray she followed Elsa into her bedroom. I began to tidy up the room, plumping up the cushions and putting the books away in the bookcase. I was so preoccupied with my task that I did not hear the door open. When Mr Thorn's voice broke into my reverie I fear I must have jumped several feet into the air.

'Where is my wife?' he asked, but I had to ask him to repeat his question and my reply brought a small frown to his brow. 'She is better I trust?'

'Oh yes, I think so, but she said she was tired. Perhaps if the weather continues warm we could venture out into the park tomorrow, I think the fresh air would be good for her.'

'You must do as you think fit, Miss McAllister. I have

every confidence in your judgement.'

His face was perfectly serious but as always I looked at him sharply for the humour I was always so sure lurked in his eyes.

He strolled over to the window and stood looking out for several minutes before he spoke to me again. 'Since you are here, Miss McAllister, I should tell you that your friend Elliot proposes to leave us in the morning but I think he will want to see you before he returns to Medchester. I gather you have not met since your ride together?'

'No Mr Thorn. I have my duties to attend to and, although it was kind of you to allow me to ride with your guest, I had not expected to see him again.'

How stilted and pompous my words sounded even to my own ears! But I was still smarting from Miss Rowena's words of the day before and he was watching me with such a searching gaze that I had to drop my eyes before his. When next he spoke his tone was light and bantering, so unusual that I looked up at him surprised.

'How right and proper is your demeanour, Miss McAllister,' he said. 'It is difficult to remember that you were the child I once rescued from the midst of our rhododendron bushes, the same child who almost fell through the windows in a shower of glass dragging young Elliot with you.'

I could feel the warm colour flooding my face but I lowered my eyes and he went on in a more conversational tone.

'However, meeting you this morning has spared me the task of putting pen to paper. Since this is Elliot's last evening here, perhaps you would care to join us for dinner? We dine promptly at eight o'clock and, as you will have already observed, it is our custom to dress for dinner.'

I looked up at him, my eyes wide with surprise, and he was looking down at me, smiling a little, but with such self-assurance that I knew he was not expecting a refusal.

I bowed my head a little and mumbled, 'Thank you, sir, you are very kind.'

'What did you say, Carla? You really must learn to speak up or my poor wife will never understand the books you read to her.'

I lifted my head sharply. His mouth was set in its customary stern lines but there was no denying the merriment in his dark eyes.

'Thank you, sir,' I said clearly, 'I shall be pleased to accept your invitation.'

If anything the merriment increased, but after a brief smile he turned on his heels and left me staring after him. The door closed behind him with a slight click, but still I stared until a small sound behind me made me turn quickly.

Elsa stood at her bedroom door. She was watching me with the strangest expression on her face. I racked my brains for something to say to her but those bright, unblinking eyes staring into mine stunned me into silence. Agnes appeared to lead her away and the relief I felt was indescribable. At the same time, when she turned to look back at me, I sensed a threat on that childlike, lovely face and I shivered with an unknown fear.

Dejectedly I made my way back to my room, my thoughts busy with Mr Thorn's invitation to what I could only look upon as an ordeal for me. Then, incredibly, my anxieties about the dinner party and Miss Elsa vanished when I remembered that during our conversation he had called me Carla.

I had seen how beautifully the women dressed for dinner at Milverton and I hesitated between my ruby-red, velvet dress and my black, velvet skirt with the cream, lace blouse. I did not want Rowena to think that I was giving myself airs by appearing in too flamboyant a gown, at the same time I did not want Mr Thorn to think I was obstinately maintaining a servile attitude. In the end I decided to wear the red velvet.

I brushed my hair, tying it back from my face with a large velvet bow, but the only jewellery I adorned myself with was the filigree rose which I fastened at my left shoulder. I was very conscious of the heavy, rich folds of the skirt as I walked down the corridor. In the lights from the chandeliers the velvet took on a bloom like the sun-ripened skin of a freshly picked peach. Halfway down the stairs I paused, one hand resting lightly on the balustrade, and Mr Thorn, who had been crossing the hall, looked up and saw me there. For what seemed an eternity we looked at each other and, although the expression on his face did not change, he waited at the foot of the stairs for me to join him.

I had surprised a strange wariness in his eyes and I wondered why it should be so. This man had loved two women as different from each other as night and day – one gay and brilliant as a bufferfly, the other ethereal and silver fair as an ice maiden – but I had seen my own reflection in the tall mirror across the hall and I was not unhappy with it. The rich colour lit up my face, lending a rare clarity to my eyes, and the long, graceful skirt fell away from my waist in sweeping folds complementing my slender figure and small breasts.

We were the last to enter the drawing room and I was pleased to see that apart from Elliot I was the only guest. Miss Judith and her husband were sitting together on the couch before the fire but Rowena stood at the window looking broodingly across the parkland. Both Elliot and Stephen rose as we entered the room and Elliot came forward to meet me. I felt nervous despite Miss Judith's smile of welcome, and even the glass of sherry Mr Thorn handed to me failed to restore my poise in the face of Rowena's uncompromising, ramrod-straight back.

Thorn's gaze followed mine, and in a voice only slightly raised he said, 'Rowena, we have a guest.'

She turned slowly, sauntering towards us, but there was an insolence in her walk and I could not be sure if it was directed against me or against her brother. She, too, was in red, but a red as clear and vibrant as a poppy and I knew that if I had been the owner of dark red hair I would never have had the courage to wear such a colour. She inclined her head the merest fraction of an inch. Beside me Elliot stood looking miserably down upon the floor, fully aware of her condescending attitude. I looked up at Thorn and found him watching me curiously, reading my expression, and I was glad to turn away and join Miss Judith on the couch before the fire.

During dinner I was placed between Elliot and Thorn, with Rowena sitting on her brother's right. The meal was beautifully served and cooked but in my confused state it tasted of nothing and between the courses my face ached with the effort I was making to maintain a pleasant expression. My thoughts were entirely unreasonable. I was angry with Elliot for thinking that I might be flattered by his visit to Milverton – supposedly to see me – when at the first toss of Rowena's head he was prepared to be hers for the asking; and Thorn, what right had he to think that I would enjoy eating dinner with them when his sister had described me so scathingly as a servant, and treated me with less courtesy than she would afford any of the servants? What diabolical pleasure was my too-bright face and smarting pride giving him now?

Coffee was served to us in the drawing room while Mr Thorn dispensed the brandy and cigars. As I looked round I could only liken our faces to a company of waxwork figures. Elliot sat alone, aware of Rowena sitting on the couch beside me, her face sulky. Their eyes never met, and Judith and Stephen were ill-at-ease because of the atmosphere Rowena created in that charming, luxurious room. Only Thorn seemed not to care as he kept up a conversation designed to include us all.

When I finally rose to my feet with the excuse that it was late, I held out my hand to Elliot in a gesture of farewell.

'Good-bye, Elliot,' I said. 'It has been nice meeting you again. I hope you have a pleasant journey home.'

Then I thanked them all for inviting me to join them and bade them goodnight. It was Mr Thorn who opened the door and walked with me to the bottom of the stairs.

He looked down at me and the new awareness between us brought the warm colour into my cheeks and something of the old cynicism into his eyes.

'My wife's father, General Langham, is coming here tomorrow to spend one or two days with us. I would like him to meet you Miss McAllister.'

'I should like that Mr Thorn.'

'I will let you know when it is convenient to speak with him,' he said, then to my utmost surprise he bent his head over my hand and kissed it.

I lay awake for hours listening to the closing doors throughout the house; then, just as I felt myself drifting off to sleep, there was a knock on my door. I was immediately awake, my heart pounding in my breast, but I hurried on with my robe, thrusting my feet into my slippers at the same time. I fumbled with the doorknob impatiently, the catch had always been difficult, but when the door opened I was amazed to see Rowena standing there, a pale pink negligee over her night attire, her dark red hair hanging loose around her shoulders. My surprise was very obvious but I stood on one side so that she might enter my room. It was cold and the empty grate stared back at us dismally. I hurried to light the gas lamps from the candle I had lit, then I pointed to a chair inviting her to sit in it.

She shook her head, biting her lip a little; then raising her chin she spoke almost defiantly as though she had to force herself to do so.

'I have come to apologize, Miss McAllister, for my rudeness to you, but I ....' her voice faltered and I realized how much courage it had taken this proud girl to lower herself to one she regarded as a servant in her brother's house. She went on more steadily.

'I was distressed to find Elliot here. I can say this to you because you and Elliot are old friends so you must know that once he and I were engaged. I should not have behaved badly towards you. We are all very grateful for what you are doing for Elsa.'

'It was kind of you to come.'

'My brother was furious with me and I cannot afford to fall out with Thorn. Besides, he had every right to be angry with me, my behaviour towards you was unforgivable. Heavens, but it is cold in here! Have you no fire?'

'It is one o'clock in the morning, Miss Rowena.' I went over to my bed and took the eiderdown from it, offering it to her because the robe she wore was flimsy and held no warmth in it.

She sat down in my easy chair, tucking the eiderdown around her. I took the chair opposite her.

'I shall call you Carla,' she said promptly. 'Once, years ago, I sat on the landing upstairs and saw you and Elliot brought into the hall out of the frost. I remembered you the first night you came here but I knew my brother didn't remember you. You have been friends with Elliot a long time.'

'Yes, although we did not see each other often – only when I came to stay in the village.'

'Then how did you manage to meet again. Did Elliot look you up?'

'No, I found him.'

She raised her eyebrows at this admission of unmaidenly behaviour, and asked bluntly, 'Why should you do that?'

'I needed to ask him some questions. He was the only person I could think of who would be able to help me.'

'What sort of questions?'

I was silent and she had the grace to blush.

'I shouldn't have asked, no doubt it has nothing to do with me.'

How much could I confide in Rowena? She had been ungracious towards me it was true but, seeing her sitting in my big armchair, without the trappings of sophisticated apparel, and all the make-up removed from her face, huddled into the folds of my eiderdown, she looked such a child. The mere fact that she had sought me out in the middle of the night to ask my forgiveness prompted me to think that perhaps after all she was merely searching for a shoulder to cry on.

'Miss Rowena,' I said gently, 'ought you to mind now who Elliot numbers among his friends? You yourself broke the tie which bound you, you cannot hope to find him unchanged. Elliot should be allowed to go his own way and search for his happiness. You have your husband to think about.'

At first I thought she was angry with my words, but then to my extreme consternation, she raised her hands to her face and sobbed so that the hot, salty tears trickled through her fingers and on to her robe. I sat uncomfortably on the edge of my chair, appalled that my words had brought on such a storm of weeping, waiting for her to regain her lost composure.

At last she looked at me out of eyes swimming with tears, and with her voice shaking she said, 'How long must I pay for my mistake?'

I said nothing. Tomorrow this headstrong, proud girl might regret that she had confided in her sister-in-law's companion. If she wanted to talk to me I would listen but I could not intrude into the misery she was suffering.

'I was so young and foolish when I ran away from home to marry my husband. I was in love with the whole idea of being in love, and when James came, flaunting his wealth and the title that would one day be his, I believed I could be happier in the life he offered me than I ever could be as the wife of a young doctor in a provincial city. I knew my family would do all in their power to dissuade me – there seemed no other way than to elope with him.'

'Have you ever been happy with him?'

'Never. Not for one single night. I knew on our wedding night that I had made a mistake. I was so young, but Elliot had adored me and other men had told me I was beautiful, yet my own husband could not bear to touch me. He found me distasteful and left me alone to sleep in his dressing room. Next day I was so distraught that I accused him of all sorts of things, and he told me then that he already had a lover – another man. He had married me to appease his uncle, who despised him. It was to be proof that he was normal, worthy of the title and the fortune that would one day be his.'

'His uncle never knew that you were unhappy?'

'Never. His uncle thought that I was a bit wild because I did not spend more time at home and because I did not have a child. I never told him the truth and he died believing that James had made a mistake in his marriage. Now that Lord Wheeldon is dead our life together is unimportant. We go our separate ways. If I took a hundred lovers, he would not care.'

'But you cannot live the rest of your life like that?'

'I have money, I can have anything I want as long as I do not trouble him. What else is there for me?'

'Money is no substitute for happiness and, as for position, what position has a wife married to a man other men despise and whom other women only pity?'

'You are hard, Carla.'

'I do not mean to be. I only know that I could not live that sort of life. I could not stay with him, title or no title.'

'Then you are stronger than I. Now that I have told you why seeing Elliot again has so unnerved me, cannot you tell me why you needed to find him so desperately?'

'I wanted to know about Caprice, and I thought Elliot would be able to tell me what I wanted to know.'

'Caprice!'

'Yes. All those years ago when I came to Gleave it was Caprice I saw riding with your brother, walking with him over the fells, dancing in his arms, yet here he was married to Elsa. I needed to understand if I was to do my duty by Miss Elsa and also for my own peace of mind.'

'But Caprice is dead.'

'I know that now, and I know that she died somewhere out on the fells but, when I remember how gay she was and how lovely, I cannot believe she was ever as evil as people say.'

'Did Elliot say she was evil?'

'Not in so many words, but he implied that she did a wicked thing. At least, how can it be good to steal your sister's lover and desert the man who loves you?'

'If Elliot thinks Caprice was evil because she deserted Thorn, then he must think it of me also.'

'Did you think her evil, or was she simply young and thoughtless?'

Rowena sat back in her chair looking down into her lap, and I watched her, willing her to tell me her version of that old story. I was impatient, waiting for her to reply, but I knew she was weighing her words carefully before she spoke them. At last she looked up straight into my eyes.

'How could I think Caprice was evil?' she said simply. 'I adored her.'

'You adored her?'

'It wasn't difficult to love Caprice. My parents had Jeremy and me late in life. Thorn often says, when he wants to annoy me, that they had us when they should have had more sense, but we were children when Stephen and Thorn were already young men. We were terribly spoiled but we missed so much too – all those garden parties and winter balls when we used to sit on the landings watching the goings-on below. But it was always Caprice who came to kneel beside us, bringing anything she could smuggle upstairs from the dining hall. Caprice never gave me dolls at Christmas time, she always gave me jewellery or exquisite underwear, grown-up things instead of childish things, and Thorn was nicer then. He used to laugh a great deal. They were so much in love, I can never believe she fell out of love with him for that boy Elsa brought here.'

She spoke with such fervour that when she finished I knew silence was the only adequate response. After a little while, I asked, 'Does Miss Judith feel about Caprice as you do?'

'Her name is never mentioned in this house but I wouldn't think so. Judith blames Caprice for the fact that she had to leave her own home to live here, but it was not at Thorn's suggestion. Stephen himself insisted. Stephen was always my mother's boy.'

It seemed to me that once more I had been wrong about Thorn. I had accused him in my heart of selfishness when there had been none on his part. Now there were so many more things I needed to ask her but she surprised me by saying, 'Are you wondering why Thorn married Elsa?'

'I have wondered that, yes.'

'Well I have wondered about it too. Perhaps he was sorry for her because they had both suffered in the same tragedy, I don't know. Probably I shall never understand it. Elsa was very lovely, you know, although she was not like Caprice, but then they were only half sisters. Perhaps my brother thought he would never be hurt by Elsa as he was hurt by Caprice.'

'She has hurt him though, she has hurt him cruelly,' I said bitterly.

'Yes, that is true. Thorn is not like me. He always honours his obligations and he will never leave Elsa. She will be his wife for as long as she lives.'

She leaned forward to stare into my face, her big, dark eyes mournful, full of questions. 'Carla, do you suppose there is some curse on the Lyttons that we are made to suffer as we do? Only Stephen has found some measure of contentment. I have a marriage which is no marriage at all and so too has Thorn. My brother should not be made to live like a monk or stay chained to an idiot wife. He should love and be loved as he was when Caprice was alive. He admires you, Carla, I saw him looking at you in the drawing room tonight.'

I jumped to my feet, my face flaming and with a denial

instantly upon my lips. 'Oh no, Miss Rowena, you are wrong! Mr Thorn looks upon me as his wife's companion, nothing more. If I thought it any different I could not stay here.'

She tossed her head. 'Why ever not, for heaven's sake? I can't believe after all Elliot told me about you that you could be so prudish. Isn't life for living after all?'

'I am not prudish but I hope I am sensible,' I retorted, and then could not resist asking, 'What exactly did Elliot tell you about me?'

She laughed, showing her small, even, white teeth, but there was a malicious gleam in her eyes as she answered me. 'He said you were a tomboy, a child who thought the other village children unimaginative dolts, but he also said you were unafraid of what other people thought and had fine courage. With such qualities, why should you be afraid of what the world might say if ever my brother fell in love with you?'

'You have too much imagination, Miss Rowena. Your brother will not fall in love with me, so the qualities Elliot described will never need to be put to the test. It is late and you have a long journey tomorrow, hadn't you better go?'

'Now you are angry, and I only came so that we could be friends. We can be friends, Carla. Particularly now, when I know that there is nothing between you and Elliot.'

We looked at each other without speaking for several minutes and then like a piece of quicksilver she left me, letting herself quietly out through the door, leaving my eiderdown on the floor in a crumpled heap near her chair. After she had gone I lay in my bed staring upwards into the darkness. Over and over again I thought about the things she had told me and I discovered that I had no illusions about Rowena. I did not think that we would ever be friends, despite the olive branch she had proffered. She had admitted she dare not quarrel with Thorn. She needed Milverton and her family as a solid background to her restless, mercurial world. She had also wanted to reassure herself that I did not love Elliot. Rowena had told me that she had adored Caprice, but was it because Caprice's wild reputation matched Rowena's own? With these thoughts still buzzing in my head I must have fallen asleep because I was

still sleeping when Nancy came to draw back my curtains,
letting in the bright sunlight of early morning.

12

As I ate my breakfast I heard the sound of voices coming from the front of the house, then farewells being called as Elliot and Rowena climbed into the carriage.

When I went to Miss Elsa's rooms I was surprised to find her already dressed and sitting on the window seat with her eyes glued to the driveway. She was attired in a pale lilac dress whose only trimming was a large bunch of deep parma violets at the waist. It was a dress which accentuated her fairness and her fragility. Her hair had been brushed into a shining knot in the nape of her neck and a large, violet, velvet bow kept it in place. She did not look up as I entered but I had grown accustomed to this treatment now and it no longer worried me. I could hear Agnes bustling about in the bedroom so I joined Elsa on the window seat. There was an air of restrained excitement about her and I wondered how much real pleasure the view from her window gave her.

Agnes came out of the bedroom and bade me good morning. What happened next was so sudden that I was caught unawares by it. The door of the doll's house could not have been properly closed because I heard the click of the latch as Agnes shut it. The next moment Elsa had jumped to her feet and stood with heightened colour glaring across the room at Agnes. There was such menace in her eyes I recoiled from it.

'What did you take from the house?' she demanded.

'Nothing, Miss Elsa. The door was slighly open, I simply closed it.'

'You are lying!' she rushed over to Agnes and grappled with her, trying to unclench her hands to see what she held there. Agnes held out her empty palms so that we could see they contained nothing, but Elsa was still unconvinced. She dropped on her knees and began groping with her hands across the carpet, her hair dishevelled now where it had escaped from the ribbon, her face flushed, her voice mumbling incoherencies.

Agnes looked at me in despair. She had obviously been up since early morning and had gone to great pains to prepare Elsa for her father's visit. Now she watched as Elsa groped about the floor, her dress creased and soiled, her face dark with anger. I went to kneel beside her.

'Tell me what you are looking for and I will help you.'

'Go away, I will find it on my own,' she screamed. 'You are both as bad as one another. I saw Agnes take it, now she will put it back where my father will find it.'

'But what?' I asked helplessly.

'She knows what she has taken,' she spat venomously.

Just then I heard sounds of carriage wheels upon the drive, and I ran over to the window in time to see Mr Thorn walk down the steps in front of the house to greet a tall, soldierly figure who was being assisted down from the carriage by its driver.

He walked with a slight stoop, leaning heavily on the cane he carried and as I watched I saw that for longer than was strictly necessary the two men shook hands. Then they turned and entered the house.

'Elsa', I said urgently, 'your father is here. Surely you don't want him to see you crawling about the floor like a baby with your hair in disarray?'

'It is here somewhere,' she was mumbling, 'I know it is here'. Then, raising her eyes to look at me balefully, she said, 'Why don't you go away? I shall stay on the floor until I have found it.'

'What shall we do when her father comes?' I whispered to Agnes.

'There is nothing we can do. We are better to stay here than drag her to her feet by force – that way she would scream blue murder and it would look as though we were ill-treating her.'

When the door opened half an hour later to admit her father and her husband Elsa was still crawling on her knees around the floor, and they stopped in their tracks.

'Has my wife lost something, Miss McAllister?' Mr Thorn asked after a few moments.

'She thought something fell from the doll's house,' I ventured.

'I did not!' screamed Elsa. 'I said Agnes had taken it from the doll's house. She dropped it on the floor when I asked for it.'

'What are you searching for, Elsa?' Thorn asked her quietly.

She sat back on her heels, looking straight into his eyes; then after a brief look at her father she started her search again, mumbling, 'I am looking for her.'

'Her?' her father asked nonplussed.

'Yes, her,' said Elsa, 'Caprice.' This time her voice was clear so that we heard it across the room and Agnes drew in her breath sharply.

The old man's face was pale and I could see that his hands were trembling. Mr Thorn's face on the other hand showed no emotion whatsoever, and calmly he said, 'Come, sir, let us go down to the study and drink a glass of brandy together. You have been travelling since dawn, there will be a better time to see your daughter, when she has found what she is looking for and recovered some of her composure. Perhaps you will come to the library a little later, Miss McAllister, so that you can meet General Langham.'

For a few moments after they had gone Elsa crouched on the floor staring at the closed door, then with a little cry and tears streaming down her face she jumped to her feet and ran into her bedroom.

Helplessly, Agnes and I looked at each other, then Agnes said in a calm, resigned voice, 'I took nothing from the doll's house, miss, and well she knows it. I expected something like this when I knew her father was coming. He will be upset by it, as will Mr Thorn.'

'Mr Thorn is accustomed to her moods.'

'He is clever at hiding his feelings, miss. There are those who show they are upset and others who don't show it. I had better go to her.'

I listened but could hear nothing after Agnes had gone into Elsa's bedroom, closing the door after her. I walked over to the doll's house and knelt before it, holding my breath, praying that no sound of what I was about to do would be heard in the bedroom beyond. Slowly, hardly daring to breath, I opened the front of the house. Everything was in its place. The dolls were in the various rooms of the house – Mr Thorn in the library with his dog at his feet, Miss Judith at her piano, her husband in his chair, Mrs Lytton at the window of her sitting room, and guests in their bedrooms, servants in the kitchens – but nowhere could I see the doll she called Caprice.

With a puzzled air I closed the front of the house and got to my feet. Agnes would not deliberately have lied about the doll. Perhaps Elsa herself had removed it hoping later to create a disturbance. Irritably I shrugged my shoulders. It was after all only a doll. Even Elsa, with her fantasies and obsessions could not breathe life into a doll and resurrect Caprice.

Mr Thorn and General Langham sat chatting in the study, and I was surprised to see that a small fire burned in the grate although it was summer. Laird lay on the rug between them, as close to the fire as he could get, but he raised his head when I opened the door and thumped his ridiculous tail in greeting. The two men rose to their feet but only the General held out his hand in greeting.

'Sit down here, my dear,' he said, indicating a chair which had been drawn up in readiness for my arrival, or so I thought.

Mr Thorn left us, excusing himself on the grounds that two of his tenants were waiting for him at the stables and the General and I were left alone. His eyes were kind in a face which had been bronzed by a stronger sun than that which shone over the English countryside. It was a handsome face still under its fine, silver hair, but it was also a face which registered sadness as no other man's face I had ever seen. His thin, brown hands rested lightly on his cane but as he took his seat he explained, 'I do not walk or stand well these days, Miss McAllister. I have been accustomed to a hot, dry climate for most of my life, now I fear my old bones have learned to creak in the damp of our English climate. My son-in-law tells me that you, too, have spent some time abroad. Egypt and Persia were mentioned.'

'Yes, that is so, and like you, sir, I am none too happy in

England in the wintertime.'

'I was in Egypt as a subaltern, but later all my soldiering was done in India. Still, we are not here to talk of my travels. Tell me something about yourself, you don't want to know the history of an old man like me.'

He was easy to talk to, charming and with a wry sense of humour. I found myself telling him all manner of things – about my childhood, about my father and the aunts, about Gleave – and he listened to me kindly so that I warmed to him more and more.

He laughed at some of my stories, capping them with his own, and in the end we were laughing together like old friends who had been affectionate for a long time.

'Do you see any signs of improvement in my daughter's condition since you have been here?' he asked at last.

'I can't honestly tell. She was awkward with me when I came here, but then I was strange to her at first. Now that she knows me better she is easier to handle and Agnes is a tower of strength.'

'Ah yes, Agnes. Elsa was always delicate, even as a child. She was highly strung and needed so much love and attention that she was demoralized if she didn't get it. It grieves me to see her like this, yet I make the effort to come here as often as I can for Thorn's sake. Elsa's mother is not well so I do not burden her by bringing her with me, I am only sad that I have no good news to give to her when I return home.'

'I do not think your daughter is unhappy, General. Indeed there are whole days when the three of us have much to laugh at and then she seems almost normal. As I said, Agnes is marvellous with her, but there are odd days like this morning when she accuses us of all manner of things and we simply have to suffer her tantrums until she forgets. Fortunately for us, she always does.'

'I am glad she has somebody like you with her. I know Agnes has been a tower of strength but. . . .' The doubt in his voice made me look at him with wide, questioning eyes. He went on, 'Agnes was born on the estate at Sutton. She is the daughter of my batman and spent her young life on the estate with her mother while her father served with me in India. She was my other daughter's maid and would have come with her to Milverton in the event of her marriage. However, it was not to be. She worshipped Caprice.'

'She is equally devoted to Miss Elsa, sir, I can assure you.'

'I am glad. I must confess to being surprised when she asked if she could come to Milverton with Elsa. I had thought that would be the last thing she would want after Caprice died.'

I was silent, watching the shadows of memory cross the old man's face. Then he asked, 'Do you know anything of the tragedy which happened here, Miss McAllister?'

'Very little, sir, but I do remember Miss Caprice when she was engaged to Mr Thorn and that she died on the moor.'

'My daughter's body was never found but I saw them bring the boy down with my own eyes. He was one of my young officers and returned to England with us, engaged to my daughter Elsa.'

There was a hardness in his voice, as though in some inexplicable way he blamed only the boy for the disruption of his family life and the tragedy that followed. I saw him raise his hand to brush away a tear which trickled down his cheek. He did not speak for several minutes and I knew he was struggling to regain his composure and control over his voice.

At last he said, 'I have been married twice. Caprice was the daughter of my first wife but her mother died when she was only two years old. My cousin Anne came to keep house for us and eventually I married her. She is Elsa's mother but we have often reproached ourselves for taking that step. We were first cousins, you see.'

'Your daughters were very different, sir. When I was a child growing up in strange places and I thought about beauty, it was always Caprice's beauty I thought about. I wanted so much to be like her but I knew of course that I never could be.'

He smiled and, although Caprice's name was not one to be mentioned at Milverton, I knew that my words had pleased her father.

'She came out to India to stay with us several times and all my young officers vied with each other for her favours. Elsa was away at school then and only came home for holidays. We sent her to a school for English children in the hill country where it was cool. My wife always maintained that she was delicate and by educating her in India we could keep her near us. Caprice was never delicate, she was always so alive, so vibrant.'

'It is a most unusual, lovely name.'

'Yes, her mother chose it. My first wife was a gay, effervescent creature, but she had never been particularly maternal. She called the advent of her baby a whim, a caprice. Then she decided to call her daughter by that name. Somehow I always felt it suited her.'

'Do you intend to stay long at Milverton, sir? The next time you see Miss Elsa I am sure you will find her better.'

'I am returning home tomorrow. My wife will be anxious until I return but she was not well enough to bring with me. I am glad we have had this talk, my dear, and glad also that Thorn has found a young woman who is both sensible and understanding. My daughter will be happy with you, I am sure.'

I rose to my feet as he did; then he took both my hands, holding them closely within his own. 'Bless you my dear, and thank you for what you are doing for Elsa.'

I wondered as I mounted the steps from the hall if Thorn ever thought that I might be curious about Caprice. He knew now that I remembered her but he would probably think it was none of my business, any more than it was my business to wonder about his relationship with Lucy St Clare.

13

The long, glorious months continued and the windows of my room were opened wide, letting in the scents of summer. It was late August and the village children were on holiday so that the sounds of their voices could be heard from the meadowland beyond the wall. We spent long hours walking in the parkland or sitting in the sunken garden at the side of the house. The sunlight was reflected in the mullioned windows and even the old wing seemed to take on a mellow look.

There were days when Mr Thorn took Elsa with him round the estate and there were other days when horses were saddled for us to ride decorously along the paths and over the short, clipped grass but always within the boundary of the park. Elsa rode well. Not with the easy, careless grace of Caprice or Rowena, but competently, unafraid. I, too, was becoming more expert and there were times when I rode other horses besides the placid mare Betsy. Once or twice I would ride out alone towards the fells, taking the same bridle paths I had taken with Elliot, but when I came within sight of Mower Gap I was afraid to venture further, even on days when the sunlight turned the fells into patches of blue and gold and it did not seem possible that they should still hide a dark secret. Each day I called to see Miss Judith. Pregnancy was a distressing business for her, alternating as it did between sickness and bouts of dizziness. I never stayed with her long since she seemed to prefer to lie back in her chair with her eyes closed and the curtains drawn to shut out the sunlight.

None of the friendships of my childhood had renewed themselves. Emily told me it was because I was now living at the Hall and, although I would have liked to visit some of my old friends, after a time it ceased to trouble me, and if I visited the village at all it was to see the vicar or take tea with Mrs Merryweather. I had long epistles from Aunt Maud telling me about her church activities, admonishing me not to get sunstroke, informing me that Aunt Beatrice and Uncle David had departed for Bognor where they would most likely catch pneumonia. She always ended her letters by urging me to take a holiday in Medchester before the summer was over, despite the fact that the city sweltered under the hottest weather for years. I had no wish to go to Medchester. I was enjoying myself in Gleave now that Elsa and I were happy together. Her tantrums had become fewer and Agnes went away for two weeks to stay with her mother in Sutton so I had a good excuse for staying where I was.

In the afternoons we liked to sit on the lawns which sloped away from the rose gardens towards the mere. Here the servants served us with afternoon tea and all around us only the song of the birds and the steady droning of the bees accompanied our repast. Occasionally I would look up at the house where Mrs Lytton could be seen sitting at the open window of her room. She seemed to be watching us and I would wave to her. I called in often to see the old lady but she appeared inceasingly withdrawn. I thought it might be because her new nurse had none of Celia's bright chatter, although she cared for the old lady's comforts admirably.

I whiled away much of the time by knitting for Judith's baby. Elsa watched me with interest, so much interest that I wondered if she would allow me to teach her to make a contribution to the baby's layette. I had to leave her for a few moments to fetch another ball of wool but on my return I found that she had pulled my stitches off the needle and that the little garment I had been knitting was ground into the soil by her heel. I looked at her reproachfully but she turned her head haughtily away. That was the last time I did any knitting in her presence or broached the subject of her taking up the pastime herself.

It was September now and in the evenings there was an autumnal chill in the air. Once more the morning mist drifted over the parkland and in the fields around Milverton the men were working from dawn until dusk to gather in the harvest. Soon the leaves would be falling. Already they were turning to colours of scarlet and gold in the forests behind the house and with October would come the scent of woodsmoke from all over the area. It was one of the scents of England I loved best. I reflected that soon I would have been a whole year at Milverton; already the heather was past its best and the bracken was turning golden on the distant fells.

It was a rare, golden day when I drove the pony and trap into the village to purchase wools for myself and others for Mrs Lytton. As always on dry, pleasant days like this, the pony was full of himself – ears pricked, high stepping hooves, his long, feathery tail impatiently swishing the flies from his flanks – and I rejoiced in his air of well-being and of mine. Both the Misses Phipps came to the counter to enquire about my health, but I did not linger after I had made my purchases, and was very conscious that two pairs of eyes followed me up the street.

As I turned to cross the road I saw a gentleman who looked vaguely familiar walking towards me. He was dressed in country tweeds and carried a stout walking stick. As he drew nearer he took off his hat and with a smile on his face came towards me, holding out his hand. I allowed him to shake hands with me, but he must have seen the puzzlement on my face because he said, 'You do not remember me, Miss McAllister?'

'I'm afraid not,' I said hesitantly. Please forgive me, your face is familiar and I feel I should know you but I am not sure.'

'The day you came here, almost twelve months ago. Did we not meet on the train?'

My face cleared. 'Oh, but of course. How are you sir?'

'I am very well, and so are you, judging by the roses in your cheeks and the jauntiness in your step as you crossed the road. You appear to have settled down very well to your new life. How is Mrs Lytton and the poor young lady you came to care for?'

'About the same, I am afraid. I wonder sometimes if either of them will ever be any different.'

'It is very sad, but they are lucky to have found a young woman who cares about them.'

'Well, Mrs Lytton has a nurse, you know, and Miss Elsa also has a maid who came with her from her own home. I am only her companion and there are indeed times when I think I am entirely superfluous to the workings of the household.'

'No, no, I am sure that is not the case. You are a young woman of intelligence and resourcefulness. Mr Lytton will have seen that for himself.'

I didn't answer him. How did this stranger know I was a young woman of intelligence and resourcefulness and, if he knew so much about the Lytton family, why didn't he call on them?'

He must have read some of my thoughts because he looked down at me with ill-disguised amusement. 'This is a small community my dear and people talk. I have heard that Mr Thorn holds you in high regard and that his wife's progress pleases him.'

I was thinking of something to say in answer to this statement when I saw the vicar approaching us along the street.

'Here is Mr Fellows, sir, but you will know him of course?'

'Actually no,' he replied. 'The friends with whom I am staying are not good churchgoers and, I am afraid, neither am I. I will leave you now so that you can converse with the vicar in peace. No doubt we shall meet again when next I am in Gleave. I wish you good day, Miss McAllister.' Smiling, he raised his hat, then he walked briskly away from me in the direction from which he had just come.

I started after him in amazement. His departure had been so sudden that I wondered if he wanted to avoid the vicar for some reason or other. I was spared from further ponderings by Mr Fellows's voice saying, 'A gentleman admirer already, Lottie?'

I laughed. 'Nothing of the kind, vicar, merely a gentleman I met on the train the first day I arrived at Milverton. I wonder who he is staying with and why he suddenly rushed off like that when he saw you.'

The vicar threw back his head and laughed. 'Clergymen and policemen tend to have that effect on people.'

'Well, he did say he was no churchgoer. I wonder where he is staying. Have you ever seen him in the village before?'

'I'm not sure, but you know how absent-minded and

short-sighted I am. Are you letting that imagination of yours run riot again, Lottie?'

I had the grace to blush and was glad that Mrs Merryweather opened the door not then, having seen us pass her front window.

It was early evening when I headed back for Milverton. The nights were drawing in, already a mist hung low over the fields and there were lights in cottage and farm windows. Just as we rounded the lane with the gates of the house on our left the pony shied and I all but lost the reins. I looked back quickly to see what had scared him, surprised to see a man standing on a little hillock by the side of the road. The broad brim of his hat was pulled well down over his face, but still I recognized him, and I watched as he hurried back along the road in the direction of the village. My friend of the train and of earlier that afternoon was returning from his walk on the fells and I wondered what he was doing wandering about the lanes at an hour when most people would be sitting down to their evening meal. At Milverton we dined late, but I could think of no other large house in the immediate vicinity and the villagers ate high tea promptly at six o'clock. He knew much more about me than I knew about him, and I racked my brains to try to remember if he had ever told me his name.

As I drove the pony and trap into the stable yard I met Mr Thorn dismounting from his horse, a large black stallion, which he invariably rode and which terrified me because of his rolling eyes and nervous vitality. He waited for me to dismount from the trap, holding out his arm to assist me, and when my eyes met his I wondered if he was displeased with me in some way. As far as I knew, I had done nothing to incur his displeasure, but his eyes regarded me sombrely. Although he held the side door open so that I could pass into the house before him, he did not smile, but afforded me only the briefest of nods before he strode off towards his study leaving me to mount the stairs, perplexed.

I decided that I would not take the silks into Mrs Lytton until the following morning. She would not be needing them that evening and I felt suddenly tired. Nancy came in with my dinner tray, and I was glad to see that the meal she had brought was a light one, cold meat and salad with fresh fruit to follow. Later I read a little but I could not concentrate on my book and promptly at ten o'clock I was ready for bed, so tired that I fell asleep immediately.

I awoke sharply. The room was in pitch darkness but I was aware of a strange pounding in my ears which I did not recognize as the thumping of my own heart. I lay rigid, not daring to move, my eyes tightly closed now, my hands clenched together under the bedclothes and all around me the impenetrable darkness. If only I could reach out my hands to find the matches on the table besides my bed, but I knew that I must not move, that I must remain in the dark with my eyes closed, feigning sleep. Somebody stood beside my bed. I could hear gentle breathing and I could smell the faint, elusive perfume of honeysuckle which told me that whoever stood there must surely be a woman. There was no sound but I could feel my flesh creeping with terror and the hairs at the back of my neck pricked.

I lay as one dead, praying that I would not sneeze and wishing with all my heart that I had the courage to leap from my bed and challenge whoever stood there in the dark to declare themselves. I felt a soft breath against my face and I knew if I could only reach up my hand I would find a woman's face bending over me. Then, horror of horrors, I felt a hand on my brow, a touch as light as gossamer, as fleeting as the kiss of a fallen rose petal, and while I waited in agony for what was to come next I was astounded to hear the opening of my door and the small click as it closed behind her.

I was trembling, my teeth chattering in my mouth, the perspiration of fear trickling down my limbs, but at last my shaking hands groped for the matches, snagging my nails, breaking innumerable matchsticks before I could light the candle. The room was empty, as I knew it would be. The candlelight played on the high, ivory ceiling and over the polished furniture. The door was closed, but I crawled from my bed to turn the key in the lock.

I was so cold that my teeth were chattering again as I hurried into my robe. When I consulted my watch lying on the table beside my bed I was amazed that it was only one-thirty. The pale, flickering candlelight provided me with enough confidence to walk over to the window but I was afraid to look out in case there was someone in the old wing watching me. It took all my courage to put out the flame and pull back my curtains. It was a clear night. The almost full moon shone into my room, making it nearly as light as day. It shone, too, on the windows of the old wing, but although I stood shivering at my window for the best part of half an hour I could see nothing in the windows opposite my own. At last I returned to my bed, but the first rosy light of dawn was in the sky before I slept again.

My mirror the next morning showed me a face hollow-eyed and unusually pale. I felt tired, as though I had not slept at all, and wondered what I should do if I was taken ill at Milverton, amongst people who were neither kith nor kin to me. Promptly at ten o'clock I made my way to Miss Elsa's rooms. Agnes stared at me sharply, 'Are you not well, miss?' she whispered, so that Elsa, who was still eating breakfast, could not hear her.

'I slept badly, Agnes, and perhaps I have a cold coming on. No doubt I shall improve as the day goes on.'

'Well, if you don't, miss, I should go and have a lie down. If Mr Thorn comes here I will explain your absence.'

Agnes cleared away the breakfast things, and I had just settled myself in my chair opposite Elsa with a book opened in my lap, when a commotion was heard in the hall outside the door. The next moment it was flung open and a young man stood there, a tall, laughing, handsome young man who reminded me of Mr Thorn as he had once been when there were things for him to laugh about. He walked briskly across the room and picked up Miss Elsa as though she weighed no more than a piece of thistledown, and proceeded to waltz around the room with her while she laughed delightedly in his arms.

I was never more conscious of my heavy eyes and woebegone expression, but when Agnes came into the room to see what the noise was about he put Elsa down in her chair and took both of Agnes's hands in his. Only then did he turn his gaze in my direction and I rose shakily to my feet to stand miserably beside my chair.

'This is Miss Carla McAllister, Miss Elsa's companion,' Agnes said. 'This is Mr Jeremy, miss, Mr Thorn's youngest brother.'

He had only been a young boy, about my own age, the last time I had seen him riding his pony along the village street in Gleave, but I remembered his gay, laughing face and his bold, dark eyes which seemed to be searching all the time for mischief. I tried to smile at him, but my mouth no longer obeyed me and my limbs were trembling so much that I had to grasp the back of my chair for support. I saw him regarding me anxiously, then the room blurred and seemed to spin before my eyes as I sank to the floor in a dead faint.

I remembered nothing more until I awoke in my own room. There were voices in the background but my eyes had great difficulty in focusing and I could not be sure if it was candlelight or sunlight which played upon the ceiling. A man stood besides my bed, a man I had not seen before, and with him was Miss Judith and Mr Thorn. I struggled painfully to sit up but Miss Judith came and pressed me back against the pillows.

'Don't get up, Carla,' she said firmly. 'This is Dr Birch and you have a virus which is going to keep you in bed for several days. A lot of the villagers are suffering from it.'

My eyes filled with tears and I looked at Miss Judith helplessly. 'I don't want to be a nuisance,' I croaked.

'You won't be,' Miss Judith said gently. 'Now concentrate on getting well. I won't be able to come to see you again, Carla – the doctor has forbidden it because of my condition – but Mrs Lytton's nurse will come to see you and the servants are very good.'

Mr Thorn came to stand beside my pillow but all I could murmur was, 'I don't want to be a nuisance'.

'You will be less of a nuisance if you obey the doctor's instructions until you are well again. You will be well cared for and when you are better perhaps you should go to your aunt in Medchester for a few weeks.'

'But I don't want to go to Medchester,' I wailed. 'I just want to get well and resume work. I shall go to Medchester at Christmas. I hate Medchester.'

'Well, we will see later on,' he said, and all the time, even in the midst of my sick misery, I knew that here I had come up against an implacable opponent. He would have his way, I would go to Medchester.

I remember little of the next few days except for the morning when miraculously the ache had gone from my limbs and only the dryness in my throat remained. The doctor made me wait another two days before I was allowed to get up, but it was not until the fifth day that I was able to get dressed. I had lost so much weight that my skirt fell over my hips and around my feet. I had to fasten it with a pin and when I looked in the mirror I was appalled by my thin face and lacklustre hair. Nancy assured me that I would soon put on flesh when I returned to normal food. With her help I washed my hair, which at once made me feel more confident.

I had been up almost a week when Mr Thorn came to see me, shortly before dinner one evening. He sat down in the chair opposite mine, his eyes never leaving my face. Then he smiled.

'I am glad to see you looking more like yourself, Miss McAllister,' he said conversationally. 'I really think that by the weekend you will be able to travel.'

'Travel!' I echoed. 'Travel where?'

'You need a change of scenery. I have written to your aunt explaining that you have been ill and that you are to spend a few weeks with her until you are fully recovered.'

'But I am well now, Mr Thorn. If you knew my aunt you would know that I would much rather stay here. She will fuss and lecture me about all sorts of things and I shall hate it, even though she always means to be kind.'

'Nevertheless I propose that you should go. Two weeks in the care of your aunt will work wonders. You will return in time for Christmas and be able to join in our festivities.'

I opened my eyes wide.

'Oh yes, I have decided that this old house has been gloomy long enough. There will be guests here and I have decided to revive the Christmas Eve Ball. I seem to remember that the last time you attended a ball in this house you arrived uninvited in a flurry of snow, dragging young Elliot in with you. This time, Miss McAllister, you will both receive an official invitation. I will let you know when I hear from your aunt and if I have business in Medchester I will personally deposit you on her doorstep.'

He rose from his chair and, after favouring me with his most casual, impersonal smile, he left me alone to rage against his arrogance and visions of my impending visit to Aunt Maud.

By the end of October my skirts once more sat upon my hips and the colour had come back into my cheeks. I saw Miss Elsa every afternoon and had started to read to her again. I was touched when on my first visit she presented me with a small pin cushion that she had made herself. It was beautifully fashioned from pale blue velvet and I believed she was genuinely pleased to see me. Agnes informed me that the doll's house had remained closed for over a week and it seemed as though her interest in it had genuinely waned. I heard that Miss Judith was visiting friends in the south of England and was not expected to return for another week, but Mrs Lytton received me graciously, insisting that I take a box of chocolates from her tray and a freshly embroidered handkerchief from the supply she kept beside her chair. It was after one of my visits to Mrs Lytton that I met Mr Jeremy.

He waylaid me in the hall, standing boldly in front of me, his dark eyes filled with laughter and a merry smile on his lips.

'I don't believe it,' he said, his eyes teasing. 'How can that little mouse I saw in Elsa's room the morning I arrived have suddenly become such a beauty?'

I eyed him gravely, struggling to keep the laughter from my eyes. I already knew something about Mr Jeremy's way with women and I was determined not be unduly flattered by it.

'Are you better?' he asked solicitously.

'Yes, thank you, I am quite well now.'

'Did you get my flowers?'

'I got a great many flowers, Mr Jeremy. Everybody has been so very kind, I can't begin to tell you how grateful I am.'

'But did you get my flowers?'

I laughed at his persistence. 'Yes, and they were beautiful as. . . .'

'I know, as were the others. Well, I'm glad to see you up and about. But you're not ready for work yet. Why don't you let me take you driving up on the moors? The fresh air would bring some colour into those pale cheeks of yours.'

'It is very kind of you, Mr Jeremy, but I have work to do. Besides, I am going to Medchester to stay with a relative the day after tomorrow so I need to pack my things and prepare for my journey.'

'And how are you getting to Medchester?'

'By train from Feltham, I believe.'

'Very well then, I'll drive you into Feltham. The horses could do with a fair journey. We could get off immediately after breakfast, have lunch in Feltham and then I could see you on your train.'

'It really is kind of you, but Mr Thorn has business in Medchester and has already said that he will take me there.'

'The devil he has! Oh well, it's the story of my life when it comes to Thorn and me. The man is never satisfied. How long will you be away?'

'Two weeks, that is all.'

'You will be here over Christmas?'

'I believe so.'

'Well, that is excellent. The house will be full of people Thorn has invited. I'll be glad to have you around the place. I hope Thorn has had the good sense to invite you to the Christmas Eve Ball?'

'Yes, he has.'

I moved as though to leave him but he leaned forward, placing his hands against the wall, one on either side of me, barring my path. He was so close that I could smell the scent of tobacco on his clothes.

'I don't care who you dance with before the supper dance, Miss McAllister, but the supper dance is mine. Don't forget.'

'I won't forget,' I answered him, laughing.

'By the way, what is your name? I can't go on calling you Miss McAllister, as though you were my governess.'

'My name is Carla, but I would rather be called Miss McAllister.'

'Good Lord, why?'

'Because I think your brother would prefer it, and he happens to be my employer.'

He lowered his hands, and allowed me to run up the

steps from the hall, but it was not until I reached the second landing that I turned round. He was still watching me, his dark eyes laughing impudently, and behind him stood the dark figure of his brother, scrutinizing us both with stern eyes in an unsmiling face.

14

I stood in Aunt Maud's little parlour looking out of the window until the carriage bearing Mr Thorn turned the corner into the main road.

For almost half an hour he had dominated the little room with the charm of his presence and even Aunt Maud had not been proof against it. Her severity had melted away like a summer storm as they chatted amicably together on all manner of things while I stood tongue-tied, listening to their talk. She was not nearly so friendly later that evening, however, when I told her I intended to stay at Milverton over Christmas. She fussed over me and pampered me with special dishes, but I also had to suffer her strictures on how to take care of my health. Stout, leather shoes and woollen clothing were to be the order of the day, with plenty of warm, stodgy meals to keep out the winter cold.

Aunt Beatrice arrived at the weekend bearing gifts of chocolates and fruit and as soon as Aunt Maud left us to go to visit one of her friends we made coffee and sat drinking it before the fire in the sitting room.

'Your uncle and I had dinner at a new restaurant last week, Lottie. It was our wedding anniversary,' she began, 'and who do you suppose we saw dining just a few tables away?'

'I can't think.'

'Elliot Cliffe and Miss Rowena, that's who. I thought she was living in London.'

'I thought so too. She has friends in Medchester; perhaps she was staying with them.'

'I don't think Elliot saw us, in fact I'm sure he didn't. He had eyes for nobody but Rowena, and I must say she was looking very pretty.'

I was silent, for I felt the old anxieties washing over me again. I was sorry for Elliot, sorry that neither of them had the sense or the will to forget the old enchantment, sorry because I would not see Elliot on this visit. It would only make me irritable and impatient to see his woebegone face. I had no doubt that Elliot would be invited to spend Christmas at Milverton, indeed Mr Thorn had intimated as much, and of course Rowena would be there. The prospect of seeing them together at a time when family ties were closest troubled me. Elliot and I might laugh together at the memory of that other Christmas Eve, but it was Rowena his eyes would be searching for amongst the dancers. It was not for me to worry about Elliot or even to blame him. I had always been honest with myself and now I thought about how much I was looking forward to the Christmas Eve Ball. I dreamed of Mr Thorn's arms holding me as we waltzed to the music, feeling their steely strength, seeing his eyes, dark and sombre, looking down into mine, imagining the warmth I saw kindled there. At such times my honesty frightened me, filling my heart with unknown fears from which I knew I must run.

Aunt Beatrice was watching me closely and I realized that she was waiting for me to answer a question to which I had not listened.

'I'm sorry, Aunt Beatrice, what did you say?'

'Gracious girl, you were miles away,' she laughed. 'I was asking if you would like to spend Sunday with us so that you could come to church with me in the evening. We are hoping to have a well-known Scottish medium with us for the day, a Mr Ferguson.'

My reluctance must have appeared very evident for she said, 'Were you very disappointed in Mrs Findlay, dear?'

'Well, she promised me evil and that is something I can live without, but I believe now that she told me about the past and not about the future. How can there be evil in a household which has shown me nothing but kindness?

'I don't know, Lottie, but it will do no harm to come to the church with me. You will enjoy the service. The people are very friendly and will make you welcome. The church will be full because Mr Ferguson is well thought of in spiritualist circles. I don't suppose he will get round to everybody. He will only speak to those people whose message is important and must be told.'

She was watching me so anxiously that I gave her a little hug.

'It will be lovely to spend the day with you,' I told her, 'and of course I will go to church with you.'

When I told Aunt Maud what I proposed to do she merely sniffed her disapproval and on Sunday morning she saw me depart with a frown which spoke more plainly than the words of her displeasure at what she called tampering with the devil.

I had thought the church would be a spooky place with sombre incantations and flickering candlelight, but it was bright and happy with a full congregation singing familiar hymns. After two hymns and several prayers, a tall, silver-haired man rose to his feet and came to stand in front of the altar. His voice was pleasant and held only the slightest hint of a Scottish burr.

'I propose to come among you but do not be disappointed if I do not have a message for you all. My time is limited, but please be quiet while I am speaking and pray for me so that I might help those most in need.'

He moved slowly along the long lines of pews, singling out first one person then another. Sometimes it was difficult to hear his voice, but as he drew nearer to us I could hear some of the questions he posed and could only think them unimportant if not banal. He addressed an elderly woman sitting two pews in front of us, asking her if she knew of a Mary in spirit, and immediately she nodded her head, her eyes raised in shining anticipation waiting for more, eyes that were filled with tears. I felt impatient. How many of us do not know a Mary or a John, a William or a Sarah? But then he spoke to her of other matters, private family matters, and the woman was smiling, suddenly happy, convinced.

He moved back and all at once his eyes met mine. I found that I must look at him, that I could not tear my eyes away. It was almost as though he placed cords around me, holding me captive, and in the silence all I could hear was the pounding of my own heart.

He spoke slowly. 'There is a woman standing beside me, I cannot see her face and she does not give me her name, but maybe you know a woman who wears a curious ring upon the third finger of her right hand? Your mother perhaps or even your grandmother? I am only guessing at this because somehow I believe her to be a much younger woman, although the setting in the ring is very old.'

His face and his voice were puzzled as he looked towards me for confirmation.

'I will describe her ring to you since you seem in doubt,' he said. It is a large, green stone, I don't know whether it is an emerald or jade but it is set in a peculiarly twisted, heavy, gold setting. Would you remember anyone who might have worn such a ring?'

I shook my head. I had never known my mother or either of my grandmothers, but I certainly would have remembered a ring such as the one he described.

He was silent for such a long time that people began to look at us curiously. When next he addressed me his face had grown quite pale and his voice came to me faintly as though from a great distance.

'She is describing to me a house,' he said. It is a large, beautiful house with tall, graceful rooms and mullioned windows. It stands amidst scenery of wild splendour and is built from the same stone as the crags close by. She is showing me a room furnished in rich velvet where ruby is the predominating colour. From the windows of this room I can see rolling fells. Do you know of such a room?'

'I know of such a house but I cannot recall the room you speak of.'

He frowned, his head inclined as though he were listening. Then, not speaking to me at all but to someone invisible to me, he said, 'Very well, my dear, the house is not important, only the warning you bring her.'

Again his dark eyes fixed me with their penetrating stare. 'She tells me of some great wickedness which occurred in this house and which could happen again if you are not very careful.'

'But the wickedness is past, it was over a long time ago and it did not happen in the house, but on the moors away from the house.'

'She is telling me it is not past, it is there now, just as it was there then and if you are not careful it could destroy you as it destroyed her.'

My voice trembled for I was very frightened. 'What must I do then?' I whispered. 'Am I not to return there?'

'She tells me that you must return there because you are bound in honour to do so and also because your heart commands it. She tells me that you will search for the truth and find it, but in so doing you, too, could put your life in danger.'

'Please, ask her who she is that she comes to warn me of this danger.'

Again he spoke to that unseen being. 'You heard the question, my dear, the lady asks who are you?'

I waited, hardly daring to breathe, but the silence in the church told me that all those present waited also and at last he shook his head saying, 'She became so faint that I could not hear her but she was laughing softly and she said you would know her as a Fan . . . that is all I heard. Fanny perhaps, or Fiona, do those names mean anything to you?'

I shook my head, dazed, and the medium, after one long stare, moved on to the next person.

The only Fanny I had ever known was a girl in the village years ago, a big buxom girl married to a local farmer and, even if she were dead, she would hardly be likely to seek me out to warn of impending disaster.

As we walked towards the horse-drawn tram terminus after the service, Aunt Beatrice asked, 'Lottie dear, do you think you should go back to Milverton? That is two warnings you have had – one from Mrs Findlay and now this one. They can't both be wrong.'

'Did you ever know anybody with a ring like that one?' I asked curiously.

'No, never. Aunt Maud has your grandmother's ring. It is not valuable, opals and small seed pearls, and your other grandmother's ring went to another of her daughters, not to your mother.'

As I kissed her good-bye, I could not helping noticing her worried face and I gave her a little hug saying, 'Don't worry, I can take care of myself.'

I waved my hand as I started out across the road. It was a chilly, damp night with the mist making tiny globules on the hair not covered by my hat and I had to lift up my skirts to avoid the wet pavements. I was glad when I finally arrived in streets which were better lit – at least they dispelled somewhat the shadows which in my imagination had pursued me along the quiet avenues of the new suburb surrounding the Spiritualist Church. I had no difficulty in picking up a cab so early in the evening and soon I was shaking the damp from my coat in the warmth of Aunt Maud's lobby. She had not been back long and for once I was glad of the disapproval which prompted her to ask no questions. We chatted for a while and after our nightly cup of cocoa I pleaded tiredness. Then I kissed her on the cheek and escaped to my room.

I pulled back the curtains, letting in the light from the street lamps outside as well as the moonlight which had dispersed much of the drifting mist. My mind was too active for sleep as it went over the events of the evening, but try as I would I could not put a face to the woman whose name could be Fanny or Fiona. Whoever she was she was right about two things. I would go back to Milverton because I had a duty to do so, but I would also go back because my heart compelled it. I would go back though my life be forfeit and my heart break in my breast, for already it was in jeopardy and I would not heed her warnings.

For a long time I lay in my bed, my mind too active for sleep, but the sound of the wind in the branches of the chestnut trees which lined the road lulled me gently, then suddenly I was wide awake, sitting upright in my bed with my hands clenched against my breast. What had I always thought about Caprice's name, what had her father said to me? That her name was a romantic whim, a fantasy, and as I sat there with my mind in turmoil and my heart hammering I was convinced that I heard the light amused sound of a woman's laughter mingling joyfully with the night wind.

I felt so well now that all I wanted was to get back to Milverton and take up the pattern of my life. Aunt Maud tried to dissuade me from going back too soon, so I knew I would have to be strong with myself. I wrote to Mr Thorn telling him of my decision and received a short letter in return informing me that I would be met at the station if I caught the two-thirty train out of Medchester.

On the morning of my departure Aunt Maud had me out of my bed at the unearthly time of five-thirty. We were eating breakfast at six o'clock and the entire morning stretched before me interminably. I had packed the evening before so after I had cleared away the breakfast dishes I decided I would walk in the park for a little while. It was dry and I wrapped up warmly against the chill wind which swept down from the moors. The fallen leaves crunched under my feet and blew against my face but the walk exhilarated me, bringing a sparkle to my eyes and warm, rosy colour into my cheeks. Across the lake, which in summer was busy with boaters, the freshening wind had whipped up the water so that it bubbled and boiled under a pale, wintry sun, and I retraced my steps reluctantly, knowing that my aunt would fret and fume until I returned in case I should be too late for my train. In fact, I caught the two-thirty train with time to spare and it was once more a winter's night when I stepped down from the train on to the station platform at Gleave. It had been raining, and there were great puddles the length of the station platform. The light from the gaslamps outside the waiting room did little to dispel the gloom. I wondered if George would meet me with his disgruntled old horse, and I was, therefore, pleasantly surprised to be hailed by a cheerful voice and to see Mr Jeremy come striding down the platform to take up my case and propel me with his arm under my elbow towards the station exit.

He kept up a steady stream of conversation all the way to Milverton, handling the high-stepping pair of horses with consummate ease. As we approached the house I could see lights glowing in many of the rooms above the hall; all at once there seemed a new liveliness about the great, stone house.

I no longer felt a stranger as I stood beside Mr Jeremy, waiting for him to open the front door. In the hall, chandeliers were lit and there were lights on the landings above showing up Miss Elsa's portrait in all its ethereal loveliness. As I mounted the stairs I paused to look up at it and caught Mr Jeremy's eyes watching me speculatively.

'How lovely she is,' I murmured, 'and how sad that she should be as she is.'

'She knows you are coming, in fact she sat on the window seat all afternoon looking down the drive.'

A warm glow filled my heart. I truly wanted Elsa to look upon me as a friend. Outside my room I took the case from him and his dark laughing eyes looked impudently into mine.

'I am not, I take it, invited into the holy of holies?'

'I may not entertain men in my room Mr Jeremy. That is a rule in all the best establishments.'

He threw back his head and laughed. 'At least you will remember that you promised me the supper dance at the Christmas Eve Ball?'

'I did no such thing,' I retorted. 'You demanded it as a right, and I may not be able to agree to it.'

'Why not? Or can it be that you have somebody else in mind?'

'I may be otherwise engaged.'

'With whom?'

'I may be expected to help in some way. I am not a guest in this house Mr Jeremy, I work here.'

'On the night of the ball you are a guest. Miss Elsa will have her husband to look after her.'

'Miss Elsa will be at the ball?' I asked, in some surprise.

'Of course. This is the first ball in this house for many years and Thorn does not wish her to remain in her room while music is playing downstairs and people are enjoying themselves. Besides, the doctor says that such things could stir old memories which might jerk her into reality.'

I nodded, somewhat distractedly; then, thanking him again, I let myself into my room. There was a glowing fire burning in the grate and the curtains had been drawn to shut out the cold misery of the night. I sank down into one of the easy chairs, not even bothering to light the gas lamps or take off my outdoor clothing.

Was that why Thorn had decided to hold the ball? In the hope that it might revive happier memories in his wife's distorted mind and return her to some semblance of normality? Suppose she did become well again? There would no longer be any need for me to remain at Milverton and the mere idea of leaving it filled me with dismay. Where would I go? What would I do?

I had called Elliot weak and foolish in his infatuation for Rowena but I was a hundred times worse than he. I should be wanting Elsa to get well. I was her companion and supposedly her friend, yet all I could think about was how her improvement might affect me. I loved her husband. I would remain here, content to see him occasionally and to receive the odd kind word from him, but how could I bear it if Elsa recovered enough to be a wife to him in word and deed? Such a prospect filled me with an anguish that brought the hot, salty tears into my eyes and sternly I told myself to be strong, that I must face up to the world as it was and not as I would like it to be.

The first thing I noticed when I resumed my duties in Elsa's sitting room the following morning was that the old wing had been added to the doll's house.

15

During the weeks leading up to Christmas the house and its occupants reflected a joyous new life and I knew that however long I remained at Milverton I would forever remember these days of rare pleasure.

Logs were cut in the park and brought into the barns and every hod besides every fireplace in the house was replenished two and three times a day. Christmas trees, giant spruces, were felled in the forest, and the largest was taken down to the village hall while the other, only a little smaller, found its place in the hall at Milverton, where all the family as well as the servants helped to decorate it with shining baubles and glistening tinsel. We walked into the parkland to collect holly heavy with scarlet berries, and into the forest itself to take the mistletoe which circled the trunks and branches of the giant oaks. There was no snow as yet, only hard, silvery frost which turned the fields and parkland into a shimmering wonderland.

The guests began to arrive the day before Christmas Eve and we sat on the window seat in Miss Elsa's room watching their carriages approaching the house along the long drive through the park. Agnes informed me that these people would be the house guests. On Christmas Eve others would arrive for the ball, people who lived closer at hand, old friends of the family as well as business associates and professional men with their wives and families. Invited also would be many of the local farmers and their wives over whose land the hunt, of which Mr Thorn was master, regularly hunted.

We brought out gown after gown for Elsa's inspection but she chose to remain indifferent. Then, on the morning of Christmas Eve, a huge box was brought up to her sitting room bearing a label from the most expensive dress house in Medchester. I knelt with Agnes on the carpet while our eager hands busied themselves with the string. Our cries of delight brought Elsa over from the window; I felt sure that even she could not fail to be impressed with the gown we now brought out of the box.

The skirt fell from a narrow, boned bodice into an apron front under which the skirt fell in heavy folds to the floor. It was of oyster satin, embroidered with seed pearls and silver bugle beads. With it went a chiffon stole, also in oyster and similarly embroidered. I ran my hands over its perfection and I, who had never owned such a gown, held it against me so that Elsa could see the effect. I wondered if Mr Thorn himself had chosen the gown for his wife or if he had merely asked the shop to send their most expensive and exclusive model. Perhaps Lucy St Clare had chosen it to save him the inconvenience.

Elsa was to rest during the afternoon so I took the opportunity to drive down to the village in order to make some last minute purchases. I passed a group of village children who were sitting on the stone wall to watch the unaccustomed activity at the hall and I was reminded nostalgically that once I too had been a child such as these. I had only one call to make in the village and, although Mrs Merriweather pressed me to stay and take tea with her, I handed over her Christmas present explaining that I must get back quickly in order to prepare for the evening's festivities.

I spent the rest of the afternoon wrapping my gifts for the family and servants at Milverton. In spite of being so often accused of having too much imagination, my gifts showed a lamentable lack of it as they lay scattered across my bed. Chocolates for the servants and Mrs Bamber, even chocolates for Elsa, simply because I couldn't think of anything more appropriate and because I knew that she adored them. I had chosen a small picture for Agnes made out of spring flowers on a dark green, velvet background and framed in narrow gold. It was pretty and I thought it would give a homely touch to her unadorned room. For Mrs Lytton and Miss Judith, I had bought pottery bowls filled with delicately scented pot pourri, and there were cigars for the men, purchased in Medchester at the best tobacconist I could find.

By the time I had finished wrapping them I was dismayed to see that it was almost dark. Hurriedly I collected them in my arms, remembering that Miss Judith had told me they should be placed around the tree in the hall. I was so busy finding homes for them all I did not hear Mr Thorn until he spoke to me. With warm colour flooding my cheeks I turned round to face him.

'I see you have been told that family and servants, as well as guests, receive their gifts from the tree on Christmas morning.'

'Yes sir, Miss Judith told me.'

'Are you looking forward to the ball?'

'Very much indeed. I hope that the weather stays fine for those who have to travel a long way.'

'Yes. December is not the best month for travelling in these parts.'

How hard it was to find words and how stilted they sounded when they came! I never had any difficulty with other people but his face was an inscrutable mask and with his dark eyes regarding me gravely it was torture trying to find something to say to him which was not foolish. In desperation I blurted out, 'Miss Elsa's gown is very beautiful, Mr Thorn. She will look lovely in it.'

'No doubt,' he said, 'and you Miss McAllister, do you also have a new gown with which to dazzle the young gallants who will no doubt besiege you for a dance?'

'My gown is not new but at least I have only worn it once. At a dinner I attended with my father in London.'

He smiled and I was glad to see it was not the customary smile which never quite reached his eyes.

'Then your life has not been entirely spent in musty museums or in the dust of the Sahara? Are you quite sure you know nothing of the gardens of the Winter Palace at Luxor or the view of the Pyramids from the Mena House Hotel when the moon is full?'

'Quite sure, Mr Thorn. The gown was worn at a dinner of the Archaeological Society in London where I sat listening to learned old men discoursing on the dead past, with my ears straining to catch the music from the ballroom and my feet tapping out the tune underneath my chair.'

He laughed, genuinely amused. 'Then we must see that

you do not tap your feet in vain this evening, Miss McAllister. I have invited several most presentable young men who will not allow you to lack partners.'

Our eyes met and held for several seconds before he turned away, leaving me staring after him.

I wished that every encounter I had with this man did not leave me feeling bemused, my face blushing as I watched his head incline to hear my fumbling attempts at conversation.

Back in my own room I removed my rose-coloured gown from the wardrobe and spread its rich folds across the bed, examining it for any minute damage it might have sustained from constant packing and unpacking. I found my evening bag and slippers, then I took a bath and washed my hair, kneeling on the rug before the fire to dry it. It was still damp when, after a little knock on my door, Agnes entered, carrying a tortoiseshell box in her hands.

'I came to see if you would like me to dress your hair, miss. I received some training as a lady's maid and before any of the balls at Sutton I used to dress Miss Caprice's hair, as well as Miss Elsa's when she came home to England.'

'Oh Agnes, that is kind of you, but won't you be busy with Miss Elsa?'

'I shall have the time before she wakes up. I've left Mrs Lytton's nurse keeping an eye on her and it shouldn't take long. I have a pad of silk in my drawer. It polishes the hair so prettily, I'll go and get it, your hair will be dry before I get back.'

I lifted up the slightly damp hair towards the fire, allowing it to fall through my fingers loosely, drying as it fell. It smelled delicately of perfume as it hung silken and warm around my face and there was a warm, happy glow in my heart as I waited for Agnes to return.

I sat on the stool before the dressing table watching her brush my hair with long steady strokes, finally polishing it with the silken pad she removed from the pocket in her apron. My hair shone like burnished gold and I watched, fascinated, as she coaxed it into twists and curls with the aid of pins, encouraging the ends to curl upwards, bringing a heavy ringlet forward so that it hung over my left shoulder. My eyes held a startled look as they gazed into the mirror. Was it really *my* face, that pure oval out of which gazed wide, grey eyes?

Agnes opened the box bringing out several little jars which she placed on the top of my dressing table. 'You will find something amongst these to bring out the colour in your cheeks, miss. Artificial light alters your colouring, so do not be afraid to use them. They belonged to Miss Caprice. See, here is the initial of her name on the top of every jar.'

I took one from her and sure enough a large ornamental letter C was embossed on the lid with a pattern of leaves and flowers. Agnes favoured me with a brief smile which made her plain, rather severe, face suddenly charming; then she wished me a pleasant evening and was gone.

Happily I experimented with the creams and lotions contained in the little jars, intrigued by those containing creams in pale rose or deeper carmine, a little afraid of the jars containing khol. But then I knew something of khol, for had not the queens of Ancient Egypt used it to enhance the beauty of their eyes thousands of years before? In spite of my preoccupation I was not unaware of the crunch of carriage wheels on the drive below and the increasing sounds of chatter and laughter from inside the house. I was excited by the prospect of the night before me, excited and not a little afraid as I pulled my dress over my head, trying not to disturb the hair which Agnes had been at such pains to arrange.

My arms and shoulders gleamed creamy white above the rose-coloured velvet, and the heavy, rich folds of the skirt billowed about my feet. I fastened the amulet around my throat so that it fell just short of the neckline. Its gleaming gold and enamel glistened against my skin; suddenly my image seemed to have taken on a strangely alien look. The amulet was too exotic a thing against this dress and hastily I removed it, fastening to my shoulder the filigree rose which seemed more appropriate. It seems immodest as I write now, but the truth is that if ever I had a right to be called beautiful it was at that moment. The bloom of the velvet warmed my face and the khol I had applied to my eyelids made my ordinary, grey eyes gleam and sparkle. The dainty heels on my dancing slippers gave me an unaccustomed stature.

Yet, as I hovered on the landing overlooking the hall, I felt a strange reluctance to go further. The music had started. I felt that the haunting violins and cellos were penetrating every corner of the house with that sweeping waltz tune. I wanted to go down, but as I watched the dancers whirling round, I also wanted to take to my heels and run back to my room.

From my position in the shadows of the second landing I could watch the activity in the ballroom unobserved. There were girls everywhere, girls in pale, delicate colours, girls in satins and voiles, in chiffons and taffetas. Agnes had caught my hair back with a large ebony and diamante slide, a beautiful thing which I assumed had also once belonged to Caprice. The women in the hall below wore flowers or feathers in their hair, and here and there a tiara could be glimpsed sparkling under the lights from the chandeliers. Then I saw Elliot, standing alone near the window which once we had almost fallen through and, taking my courage in both hands, I descended the stairs.

I was aware that I was being started at. Compared to most of the women there I was singularly unadorned, and against their pale delicate draperies the richness of my velvet gown must have stood out like a beacon. The women eyed me curiously, whispering behind their fans. They smiled, parting to allow me to pass through their little groups, for the music had temporarily stopped. I had almost reached Elliot's side when I felt myself being spun round to face a boldly handsome Jeremy in sombre evening dress, his face alive with laughter.

'There you are! I've been waiting for you, but I must say the results have been well worth it. We are about to do an eightsome reel.'

'Then I'm afraid you must find another partner, Mr Jeremy. I have never done an eightsome reel in my life.'

'There's nothing difficult about it, Carla. Do as the others do and you'll soon get the hang of it.'

I had no choice, and before I knew it we were in the middle of the dancers while I tried desperately to follow the steps, my ears buzzing with simulated Scottish cries, loud enough to shatter the crystal chandeliers. I loved dancing and I soon found myself at one with the dancers, whirling when they whirled, echoing their exuberent shouts, laughing up into Jeremy's face as we spun with his arm around my waist.

After the dance was over we joined Miss Judith who was sitting with her husband at the edge of the ballroom. Her pregnancy was advanced now but the intricate cut of her gown disguised it very well. It was a delicate, pale blue embroidered in silver, against which her flame-coloured hair glowed, dressed high upon her head. I looked towards Elliot, hoping that he would join us, but he was looking up towards the staircase with such an air of anticipation on his face that I followed his glance. Miss Rowena stood alone below Elsa's portrait, slim and lovely in deep sapphire blue, a tiara on her dark red hair and long, diamond earrings in her ears. She had obviously paused for effect, one hand resting lightly upon the balustrade, inviting the admiration of those watching her and I regretted inwardly that Elliot should show so plainly how much he adored her.

She moved from group to group, dazzling those solid, north country people who laid so much store on class and wealth with her careless display of it. She was completely charming and utterly condescending. I wondered where her husband was spending Christmas and if the effeminate Mr Chalmers was his companion. I drew Jeremy with me so that we might stand beside Elliot before Rowena reached him, but it was Jeremy she invited to dance with her, laying a sisterly arm around his waist after giving Elliot and myself the briefest of smiles.

Elliot looked at me miserably and I could not resist snapping, 'Elliot, do try to look a little less like a deserted spaniel. Smile at me and let these busybodies see that you don't care any more.'

'What happens if I *do* care?'

'Smile, just the same. Try not to wear your heart on your sleeve.'

He put his arm around my waist and we drifted into the dance. 'It's so easy for you Lottie when you don't care for anybody under the sun, difficult when you do. Besides I was never as strong as you.'

'Fiddlesticks, Elliot! Of course you are as strong as me. Anyway, now that we are dancing together you might at least pretend to enjoy it.'

He laughed, his face cleared, and we danced happily until a sudden hush descended upon the room. We looked up to find out why and saw Mr Thorn and Elsa descending the stairs.

They walked slowly, his arm under her elbow. There could not have been a single person in that great hall who did not feel that here were two of the world's beautiful people. They were both tall and slender, he darkly handsome in his evening dress, she silver-fair from the top of her shining head to her satin evening slippers. Her gown fitted like a sheath, its silver beads catching the light as she moved. But her face was the face of a marble statue, as coldly beautiful and as expressionless. Thorn acknowledged his guests as they descended the stairs but Elsa looked straight ahead as though she moved in a trance. Chairs had been placed where they could watch the dancers and as they took their places I looked up towards the balcony to see Agnes looking down at them with intense anxiety written on her face.

I danced often with Jeremy, with Elliot, and with other men who asked for my dance programme, flattering me with their eyes but whose names I have long since forgotten. Once, as I whirled past Mr Thorn's group, I caught his eyes watching me with a slight smile upon his lips. I wondered if he was thinking that the little companion was enjoying herself, but some time later, when I told him what I had read into his glance, I was surprised to learn how wrong I had been.

Supper was served on long tables in the dining room under the glow from tall candles standing in silver candelabras, and it was a feast worthy of the servants and kitchens of Milverton. Jeremy gave me no choice as he claimed me for the supper dance and we sat together in the dining room, balancing plates on our knees, drinking wine from glasses which we placed at our feet. I discovered then that I, too, knew how to tease and enchant when faced with the bold admiration in his dark eyes and the way his hand lingered round my waist and around my shoulders. There were many looks cast in our direction but I was enjoying myself, careless of anything these people might say.

I danced with Mr Stephen, discovering for the first time his quiet charm, seeing the obvious difference between him and his two brothers, and noticing how his face broke into a shy smile each time we passed his wife's chair. I made it my business to approach Miss Elsa to enquire if she were enjoying the ball, but she answered me not a word, sparing me only a long, straight look from her incredible blue eyes. It was almost an hour before I looked across to her corner again, but she was no longer there, nor was there any sign of either her or Mr Thorn in the ballroom.

It was well past midnight before I saw him again, standing alone beside the lighted tree, watching the dancers. He was holding a glass in his hand and I wondered if he were thinking of other Christmases when he held Caprice in his arms, her dark eyes looking into his, her gay, vibrant face teasing, laughing. He turned his head and caught my eye. Then, heaven help me, he put the glass down on a small table and strolled slowly in my direction.

'You are looking enchanting this evening, Miss McAllister,' he said, 'and that gown is indeed a pretty colour.'

I knew that I was blushing furiously as I gathered my scattered wits together. A waltz was playing. It was music I loved, haunting and full of melody. Despite myself my feet had been tapping in time with the music and now, before I was aware of it, we were dancing, his hand firm against my back as he guided me expertly away with the rest of the dancers, his dark eyes smiling into my own.

I knew that many watched us as we danced and that heads turned to stare, but I did not care. This was the moment that I had dreamed of, the only moment in all this joyous night that had any real meaning, and once, just once, when other dancers crowded in upon us, he drew me closer into his arms so that his chin rested upon my hair and my body relaxed against his. Then for no reason at all I looked up into the darkness above where the lights from the chandeliers hardly reached and there I saw a pale figure leaning over the balustrade. Her eyes chilled me as no others had ever done. Elsa was watching us with cold preoccupation. I shivered in his arms as though the door

227

had suddenly blown open to let in a blast of frosty, night air. He followed my gaze, looking upwards into the shadows; then almost immediately he drew me towards the edge of the floor and gently released me. With maddening composure he bowed, his eyes suddenly sombre.

'I believe you are something of a witch, Carla McAllister,' he said, 'for I had not intended to dance with any woman here. Now if you will excuse me I shall retire to my study where I can drink a glass of brandy, undisturbed by flights of fancy.'

He smiled coolly, impersonal once more, and I watched his tall figure walking away, pausing now and again to speak to the people he met as he went.

I looked up into the shadows. She was still there, sitting on the stairs like a forlorn child, her silver-fair hair falling in great waves on to her shoulders. I could see now that she had discarded her ball gown and was clad in a robe over her night attire. Her eyes looked into mine accusingly and a feeling of such intense compassion stole over me I ran up the stairs to kneel by her side, my arm encircling her shoulders.

'Elsa, you will catch cold sitting here alone. Come, I will return with you to your room and see you safely in bed.'

She did not look at me, but I could feel that her slender body was stiff and unyielding. Agonizingly I wondered how much she had been hurt by the sight of me dancing ecstatically in her husband's arms. We sat together for what seemed hours but despite her indifference I was reluctant to withdraw my arm. I was relieved when eventually Jeremy looked up and then came running up the stairs to join us.

'I thought you were not enjoying yourself when you left so early,' he said to her, 'and now here you are peering at us like a child who has been sent to bed early without her supper. What are you doing here, and where is Agnes?'

'I am here, Mr Jeremy,' came Agnes's voice, and we looked up to see her standing on the landing, fully dressed but breathless, as though she had been hurrying.

Elsa allowed Jeremy to raise her up and lead her back towards her room, but she did not give me a second glance.

'I'll see to Miss Elsa, sir,' Agnes said, and placing her strong young arms round her mistress's waist she drew her away. Jeremy came to stand beside me and we watched until they had turned the corner.

Jeremy's expression was reproachful and the unfairness of his words brought the tears to my eyes. 'I am never quite sure how much Elsa understands or how much she pretends not to understand,' he said, 'but since you are the only woman in the house my brother has elected to dance with it has created quite a stir. It was apparently not lost upon his wife.'

As I walked down the stairs beside him I suddenly felt that every eye in the room was upon me, accusing, and Jeremy's eyes too were filled with such hostility that I knew his words had been meant to hurt me.

I could almost hear the whispers of the women behind their fans. Mothers of pretty daughters from county families asking other mothers who I was. As I caught sight of my reflection in one of the long mirrors my rose-coloured velvet seemed to turn to scarlet beside the pale, frilly dresses of the other women. Only Rowena had dared to wear a deeper shade, knowing full well that she would stand out in sophisticated isolation amongst her brother's guests, whereas I, heaven help me, was forced to wear a different sort of gown because I had no other.

Jeremy was determined to make me suffer and left me standing alone as he danced away with a girl in a white, frilly dress wearing a bunch of violets in her hair and another at her waist. He was flirting with her, looking down into her eyes with maddening impudence and she simpered up at him, laughing shrilly, fluttering her long eyelashes. Disconsolately I wandered down the corridor and into the conservatory but here I beat a hasty retreat when faced with soft laughter from behind the potted palms.

The orchestra struck up the strains of a polka and it was then that I discovered that, although the women might look upon me with acute disapproval, the men did not. Suddenly I was surrounded by an army of young men, all demanding that I dance with them. Without more ado I allowed a handsome young man wearing officer's evening dress to lead me on to the floor. I knew that I was being stared at again but I no longer cared. I danced the last waltz with his younger brother. We danced well together and he let me see quite plainly that I had his whole-hearted admiration. But when he asked if he might call upon me, I explained that I had little time, that Miss Elsa required a great deal of attention. He walked with me to the bottom of the stairs, and I saw that his eyes were upon the portrait of Elsa at the top of the first short flight.

'She is very beautiful,' he said. 'Will she ever recover, do you think?'

'We can only hope so and do the best we can for her,' I replied. Then after saying goodnight once more I left him.

The lights had been left burning in the corridors but they were dimmed and away from the laughter in the hall the house seemed singularly quiet. As I turned the corner to go towards my room I drew in my breath sharply.

A woman was letting herself into the corridor from the old wing and I watched as she turned round to lock the door behind her. It was so dim in the corridor that her face was hidden from me. I knew she had not seen me as I moved forward quickly in case she should escape towards the back of the house. My heavy skirts swished around me and nervously she turned, one hand against her breast. Even now I could not see her face, then she stepped forward into the light. I caught my breath, dismayed, for I had expected the night visitor to the old wing to be Rowena, if only because it was a safe retreat for a tryst with Elliot. But it was Agnes who faced me now in the flickering light from the candle she carried in her hand.

'Oh, miss, you startled me,' she said. 'Is the dancing over then?'

'Just over, although there are people still in the hall. Agnes, what are you doing here? It is almost four o'clock in the morning and you are still fully dressed?'

'A house party of this size makes a lot of work for the servants, miss.'

'I know, Agnes, but none of the guests are sleeping in the old wing.'

'No, miss, but furniture has been removed from it for some of the guests' bedrooms. I was merely trying the door to see if it was locked. Many of the floorboards in there are unsafe, I didn't want any of the young people falling through them.'

She could have been speaking the truth, of course. The

young people would be all over the house searching for privacy so that they could carry on their flirtations away from the prying eyes of the older guests, but I knew that Agnes was ill at ease and not once had her eyes met mine. She moved as though to pass by me but I stood in her way, willing her to return along the corridor with me. Together we walked back until we reached the door of my room, then she wished me goodnight, obviously anxious to be gone. I laid my hand upon her arm to detain her.

'If you will come into my room for a moment, Agnes, I can return the things you lent me earlier. I have them ready, I shall not keep you longer than a moment.'

She stood within the doorway while I lit the gas lamps, then she watched as I replaced the little jars in their tortoiseshell case. I smiled as I handed it to her and for a few moments she stood with it in her hands looking down at it, an inscrutable expression on her calm homely face.

'They are very beautiful, Agnes, I suppose they now belong to Miss Elsa?'

'Not these, miss, the colouring of the two girls was very different and although you are blonde you do not have Miss Elsa's fairness. I was sure the creams would be right for you.'

'I am very grateful Agnes for the loan of them. If they are not Miss Elsa's, where do you keep them?'

'In one of the drawers, miss. Most of her things belong to Miss Caprice, her jewellery, many of her furs and clothes, almost everything except the jewellery she was wearing on that last morning of her life.'

'You were surprised about the locket. Did you think she was wearing that on that morning?'

'I wasn't sure, miss. I hadn't seen it for a long time, so naturally I was surprised that Miss Elsa should have it.'

Her eyes now met mine without flinching, but her feet moved a fraction of an inch towards the open door.

'What sort of an engagement ring did Miss Caprice wear? Believe me Agnes, I have a very good reason for asking this question. It is not simply idle curiosity.'

'It was a sapphire, miss, surrounded by diamonds. Beautiful it was on her long slender fingers, but she was fond of jewellery and knew what suited her, rings in particular.'

'She had others, then?'

'Oh yes, miss, but they are now kept in the safe for Miss Elsa.'

'Agnes, was there one special ring which she always wore? Please bear with me. Tomorrow I will find the opportunity to tell you why I am asking these questions now.'

She was silent for so long that I thought she was not going to answer me, but perhaps there was something in my face, an intensity which made her tell me the truth.

'There was her grandmother's ring, she always wore that.'

'What was it like?' I asked hoarsely.

'It was very valuable, miss. An emerald set in heavy, twisted gold. She wore it always on the third finger of her right hand.'

Suddenly I felt my legs go weak under me and I had to grope behind me for the back of a chair to cling to. She stretched out her arm to steady me and from a long, long distance I heard her voice anxiously asking if I was feeling ill. She was watching me with considerable concern on her good honest face and I cried, 'Oh Agnes, there are so many things I do not understand and I am very afraid.'

'But there is nothing for you to understand or fear, Miss Carla. You are new to Milverton, why do you make mysteries where none exist?'

'Agnes, will you come to my room tomorrow? It is Christmas Day. There should be plenty of opportunity for you to leave Miss Elsa with others.'

'It is Christmas Day today, miss.'

'Heavens yes, so it is. Today then, will you come to see me today and I will tell you why I asked about the ring? I need an ally so badly and I have nobody else I can turn to. Tell me one thing, did you truly care about Caprice?'

She stared at me out of her straight, brown eyes for what seemed a lifetime before she answered my question, but her voice was so steady, calm and honest that I could not doubt her answer.

'I adored her, miss. Others who professed to love her were quick to believe ill of her but I never did. I loved her then and I love her now.'

She had told me all I wanted to know. As she moved towards the door I saw her shiver, and for the first time I realized how cold it was in my room. The fire had long since gone out and it could not be far from dawn.

'Here, take my shawl,' I said, draping it around her shoulders. 'You can return it to me tomorrow but it will help to keep you warm on your way back to your room.'

After she had gone I pulled back the curtains and looked out into the night. Below me the frost sparkled on the holly bushes and on the ivy at the side of my window and, although the stars had gone, the parkland glistened under its covering of frost.

It was Christmas morning and the house at last was quiet. I looked at my watch and was not surprised to see that it was going on for five o'clock. In just over three hours Nancy would be in to light my fire. The bedwarmer was only slightly aired as I climbed into bed. I pulled the bedclothes round me, snuggling down in order to find some lingering warmth. My mind was still too active for sleep and over and over again I lived my experiences of the evening. I wondered idly why Mrs St Clare had not been present at the ball, then forgot her immediately in the memory of my waltz with Thorn, and it was while thinking of him that I fell asleep at last.

16

The normal friendly sounds of the morning woke me; voices and dogs barking, church bells over the clear, frosty air, and the sounds of carriage wheels on gravel. I stretched my limbs luxuriously between the sheets then sat up to look at my watch. It was almost nine-thirty and the empty firegrate yawned back at me, dark and forbidding across the room, unlit and not even laid ready. I knew there were several extra guests in the house but they had brought servants with them. By this time on normal mornings the family would have finished breakfast and all over the house fires would be burning merrily in their grates. I hurried into my robe and looked at the empty firegrate unhappily. There was a little coal in the hod from the night before as well as a few blackened cinders in the grate but there was nothing with which I could be expected to light a fire myself. The water pitcher was also empty so I decided to dress and complete my toilet later.

I wore my black, velvet skirt and lace blouse, and looked round for a shawl to drape round my shoulders before remembering that I had wrapped it around Agnes's shoulders the night before. I put on the shawl Aunt Maud had knitted for me, and went to hang up my ball gown in the wardrobe. But as I took it down the skirt seemed to hang strangely on its hanger and on closer inspection I saw that it had been slashed from the bodice to the hem of the skirt. Trembling, I sank down into one of the chairs with the gown cradled in my arms, asking myself who could have done this spiteful, dreadful thing. Who had come into my room in the dead of night without disturbing me, carrying a knife which they could easily have plunged into my breast, only to mutilate my poor, beloved gown?

My mind flew to Elsa who was not responsible for many of her actions. Agnes had been late going to her room and I knew that she was a light sleeper. Agnes had often told me she slept with one ear attuned to Miss Elsa's movements next door and if Elsa had left her room for a single moment I was sure Agnes would have heard her and followed her. Rowena would never be my friend, but why should Rowena want to harm me? She had Elliot. She had nothing to fear from me and she knew it. Not for one moment could I suspect Judith or Mrs Lytton and I refused to believe that any of the servants would sneak up to my room on such an errand.

Sadly, I put the gown at the back of my wardrobe in order that it would not face me every time I opened the door, but I could not stem the hot, salty tears that rolled down my face. A strange feeling of foreboding was with me as the time moved on and still Nancy did not come. Perhaps there was sudden sickness in the house. I wondered about old Mrs Lytton and about Miss Judith who had only a short time to wait before her child was born.

I had made up my mind to go down to the hall when my door was flung open to admit a distraught and tearful Nancy who almost knocked me off my feet.

'Oh, miss,' she cried piteously, I'm that glad you're up, I haven't forgotten to light your fire, but it's Agnes, miss, we don't know where she is.'

My eyes opened wide with surprise. 'But she can't be very far away. She was with me at four o'clock this morning.

'We're all a bit late this morning, miss, but I took the tea tray to Agnes's room about nine o'clock. I always take the tray to Agnes and she serves Miss Elsa but there was nobody in her room and the bed was made just as though she'd never slept in it.'

'Does Mr Thorn know?'

'Mr Bamber said he wouldn't worry him about it just yet in case she turned up soon. If she's walked down to the village in this weather she'll catch her death and that's for sure. Besides, why would she want to do that with the shops all closed and Miss Elsa on her own up there?'

'Could she have gone to church, do you think? It is Christmas morning and I heard the bells ringing for early service while I was getting dressed.'

'Bless you no, miss, she wouldn't walk down to the village to go to church. She goes with the rest of us, when it's convenient.'

Personally I didn't see any difference in walking down to the village when the shops were open and walking down on Christmas morning to attend the church service but I kept my thoughts to myself and told Nancy that I would go to see how Miss Elsa was.

Miss Lytton's nurse was there and told me that Elsa was still asleep. 'I can't understand it, she's sleeping as though she's been drugged but perhaps it's just as well. She'll be in a right state if she wakes up and Agnes isn't back.'

The key had been left in the lock leading to Miss Elsa's bedchamber, so I turned it and went in. She was sleeping like a baby, oblivious of our worries, one hand under her cheek, her silver-fair hair spread out like a fan on the white pillow. I tiptoed across so as not to wake her and entered Agnes's room which adjoined it.

I had only been in there once. It was not a large room but it was well-carpeted and pleasant, with the window overlooking the meadows. A smaller window at the back looked on to the stable yard but all was quiet there. The bed was made and the whole room was impersonal in its tidiness.

On the table beside the bed stood a small clock and on the dressing table rested a hair brush, comb and mirror. I looked round curiously, wondering what she had done with my white shawl. Quietly, not daring to make a sound, I opened the wardrobe door. Inside hung several dark dresses and a dark blue coat, the only coat I had ever seen her wearing, but there was no sign of my shawl and I could not tell if any of these dresses had been the one she had worn the night before. I wondered idly if she had returned the little jars of cream to Miss Elsa's room or if she had placed them in the chest of drawers in her own room but I was reluctant to pry and closing the wardrobe door quietly behind me I returnend to Elsa's sitting room. She had not stirred and I saw no point in sitting beside her bed until she awoke.

I waited another half-hour before there was a timid knock on the door and Kate came in bringing two cups, saucers and a coffee pot on a tray.

'Oh, bless you Kate!' I exclaimed. 'Miss Elsa isn't awake yet and I thought I would let her sleep on. Is there any news of Agnes?'

'No, miss. She's not in the grounds. Hoskins and Painter have searched the park from end to end. You don't suppose she's gone up into the fells do you, miss? She spent a lot of time up there when Miss Caprice went missing?'

'Good gracious, Kate, Agnes is far too sensible to go walking on the fells on Christmas morning with frost on the ground and snow not far away. She's probably in one of the rooms somewhere and most likely fallen asleep in a chair and forgotten the time. It was very late when she went to her room.'

'But she didn't go to her room, miss.'

'Well, we don't know that do we, Kate? You had better go now or Mrs Bamber will come looking for you and blame me for keeping you chattering when there is extra work to be done. I'll see if Miss Elsa is awake and ready for her coffee.'

She cast me a long, melancholy look before scuttling away.

I did not immediately go to see if Elsa was awake. I sat in the window seat for a few moments, afraid to face the agonizing thought that something dreadful was once again going to happen. At last I busied myself with the cups and saucers on the tray and was just about to pour the coffee when the door opened again, this time to admit Mr Thorn and the doctor. I was startled by their sudden appearance and by Mr Thorn's abrupt question, 'Is my wife awake yet?'

'No, sir. At least she wasn't five minutes ago. I was just about to take her in a cup of coffee.'

'You may leave it for now,' he said, and with a curt nod to the doctor, he went to stand beside the window looking out across the park while the doctor went into Elsa's bedroom.

I sat down on the chair beside the fire contemplating his uncompromising back, wishing that he would turn and say something to me, anything to dispel the anxieties which whirled about my head. In only a few seconds the doctor was back holding an empty glass in his hands.

'This glass was beside Mrs Lytton's bed and she is very heavily sedated. Did you notice the glass this morning, Miss McAllister?'

'Why yes, Doctor. I assumed it had contained the milk she always drinks at night.'

'Is it usual for her to take a sleeping draught?'

'I don't think so, but then I don't really know. Agnes sees to her bedtime drink. All I can say is that she is normally awake long before this.'

The two men exchanged significant looks. They were silent for several moments, then Mr Thorn looked at me across the room. He smiled, his smile singularly sweet and at odds with the severity of his earlier expression.

'Have you had anything to eat today? I understand they forgot to light your fire and take in your breakfast.'

'No sir, they didn't forget but they were rather later than usual. As you can see, I have just been served with coffee.'

'Go to your room and I will see that lunch is sent to you. My mother's nurse will look in on my wife from time to time.'

I wanted to ask him about Agnes but the words stuck in my throat. He had not mentioned her to me and I doubted if he would wish to discuss her at that particular moment.

I didn't want to remain in my room after I had eaten my lunch. I could tell that it had been prepared in a hurry and in no way resembled the traditional lunch one might have expected on Christmas Day. However, it warmed me and stopped the pangs of hunger which had been plaguing me since earlier that morning.

Outside the house the parkland was deserted and a white ground mist swirled over the grass hiding the mere from my view. Making up my mind suddenly, I put on my coat and threw a long woollen scarf over my head. I was wearing stout, walking shoes and warm, woollen gloves and felt capable of facing anything the elements could do to me. I used the back stairs and soon was letting myself out by the side door into the little garden underneath my room.

I walked briskly, my hands thrust deep into the pockets of my coat, but even so the damp, freezing mist took away my breath, forming jewelled globules on my hair as my feet tried to avoid the icy puddles along the drive. My mind was in a turmoil. Where could Agnes have gone in the early hours of Christmas morning while the rest of the household slept? Had she returned to the old wing and was even now waiting to be released from some door which had unhappily locked behind her? She had evidently expected to be away some time because she had seen to it that Miss Elsa was heavily sedated and not likely to awaken in her absence. I strode doggedly down the drive, at every twist and turn expecting to come across her tall, angular figure hurrying back to the house. The drive opened up before me, weird and lonely in the swirling fog but there was no familiar figure to take me running towards it; hands outstretched in welcoming relief.

I reached the wide, stone gateway at last and looked down the road, debating whether I should go on towards the village or return to the house. Morning service at the church would have been over long ago. I could not believe that Agnes had gone off alone to take part in it when Milverton was occupied by a houseful of guests and there was much to do.

Miserably, I turned and retraced my steps. Now and again I told myself that there were footsteps walking quickly behind me, pausing when I paused, running when I ran, but they were illusions, echoes of my own footsteps in the thickening mist. I paused near the turn in the drive believing that I had heard the sounds of galloping hooves but moved on, thinking that I must have been mistaken. Then I heard them again, galloping at a terrifying pace along the drive. I peered through the gloom but could see nothing until he was almost upon me and I had to leap towards the bushes for cover. The horse shied so that the rider had to use all his skill to control him, then recovered as they galloped away down the drive. In that brief moment I recognized Mr Jeremy riding his horse as though all the hounds of hell pursued him and with such a look of grim determination on his face that my feet took wings and I fled, gasping and spluttering, towards the house.

I let myself in at the side door and ran up to my room, my fingers already fumbling with the buttons of my coat. It took but a minute to change my shoes and remove my outdoor clothing. What could have happened, I wondered, to send the son of the house on such a desperate errand?

The servants were seated round the large kitchen table on which they ate their meals, all except Mr Bamber, who was in urgent conversation with the groom and one of the stable lads. Kate and Nancy had their arms around each other, sobbing quietly. It was only when they saw me standing there that Nancy leapt from her chair and came running towards me, the tears pouring down her cheeks.

'Oh, miss, it's horrible, it is. Where have you been? I came to tell you but when you weren't in your room I thought something had happened to you too.'

Mrs Bamber got up from her chair and came striding towards us. She pulled Nancy away from me, not unkindly, but with determination, and in her sternest voice said, 'Now pull yourself together, my girl, such carryings-on will get us nowhere. There's guests in the house and the fires in the rooms upstairs will want attention. Come with me, Miss McAllister, I have something to tell you.'

With my heart beating painfully I followed her stiff-backed figure in its heavy, black dress down the passage towards her room, a room which for once looked rather less than impeccable. Mrs Bamber was never a lady to waste words and she did not do so now.

'Agnes has been found, miss. She was in the cellar under the old wing, although what she was doing there I can't imagine. She must have fallen down the stairs.'

'Is she hurt, Mrs Bamber?'

'She's dead, miss.'

I stared at her with my mouth open stupidly, wondering if I had heard her aright. 'Oh Mrs Bamber, how terribll! But I was with her at four o'clock and she was on her way back to her room. I put my shawl around her shoulders because she was cold.'

There was a strange expression on Mrs Bamber's face. 'So that's where the shawl came from. I said it wasn't Agnes's shawl, she never owned anything as fine as that. It was the shawl they spotted when they searched the cellars. White, wasn't it? At first they thought it was one of the guests. She must have fallen from top to bottom. Her neck was broken.'

I was trembling as I said, 'I saw Mr Jeremy riding his horse down the drive and looking so stern I thought something must have happened.'

'Yes, but Mr Jeremy's riding his horse down the drive had nothing to do with Agnes. It's Miss Judith. He was going to ask the doctor to return here.'

'Miss Juditt! But it can't be the baby, she has months to go yet.'

'If she loses this one it will be the third she's lost. The shock of hearing about Agnes won't have helped, but she insisted on hearing the news and Bamber had no more sense than tell her. I tell you miss, it's as though God had laid a curse on this house and all the people in it.'

I shuddered and at that moment the words of Mrs Findlay and the Scottish medium came back to me only too vividly.

'Who is with Miss Elsa?'

'She's all right, miss. I hear the doctor gave her an injection to keep her under, but goodness knows how she'll take on when she misses Agnes.'

'Is there anything I can do?'

'No, miss, I don't know that there is.'

'But I must do something. I can't just sit in my room with all this hanging over us.'

She looked at me without speaking for several minutes, then she said, 'Most of the guests are leaving tomorrow, they'll not forget this Christmas Day in a hurry, I'll be bound. Mr Thorn has given orders that the meal is to be served in the dining room as though nothing had happened but it will be a sorry meal unless I'm very much mistaken. If you care to go down into the kitchens, miss, cook will let you help with the tea things and it will take your mind off what has happened.'

I was too late to help with the trays since the servants had already taken them to the guests' rooms. Nancy and Kate were not in evidence and cook stood over the snivelling kitchen maids scolding them soundly.

She came eventually to sit opposite me at the kitchen table, bringing with her a large Christmas cake from which she cut two enormous slices, pushing one of them across the table to me on an enamel plate.

'Really cook, it looks delicious, but I couldn't eat a crumb.'

'Get it down,' she scolded. 'A little thing like you wants

building up. Why it's not so long since you were ill yourself and you've not had much food today. That lunch was nothing to go walking in the cold on.'

It was easier to eat the cake than to argue, so I swallowed it obediently while she sat watching me with a stern eye from the other side of the table.

'That's better,' she said, after the last crumb had gone. 'Now, a strong cup of tea with plenty of sugar is what you need.' She picked up the teapot from the top of the stove and poured out a cupful of tea.

The strong, sweet brew warmed me but it also did something else. Suddenly I felt the tears rolling down my cheeks, hard, racking sobs shaking my shoulders, and I laid my head on the table and wept. For Agnes, and Judith and for poor Mrs Lytton lying in her bed listening for somebody who might tell her all that was happening in her once happy home, and for Elsa, sleeping her drugged sleep oblivious to everything that had happened. But most of all I wept for Thorn whose cold, stern face had looked at me only that morning without emotion but whose words had been kind and whose smile when it came had been strangely sweet.

Cook left me to cry alone and I was glad of it as she shepherded the two staring kitchen maids from the room. At last there were no tears left to cry and I pulled myself wearily to my feet.

My room looked cheerful with the leaping flames from the fire lighting up the soft colours in the chintz covers and the rich, red bloom of the mahogany furniture. I drew the curtains against the damp mist, surprised to find that it was already dark. I was glad to light the gas lamps, wondering how I was going to spend the next few hours before it was time to seek my bed. I had never in my life spent a Christmas Day such as this one and there had been some strange ones in my life. In a while they would bring my evening meal and I knew now that I was not going to be able to eat it.

In fact, it seemed as though Nancy brought my tray almost immediately.

'I've only got a few minutes, miss,' she said, 'but I thought you might like to know what's happening now.'

'Oh yes, Nancy, I do.'

'Well the doctor's here with Miss Judith but we can't get anything out of Mrs Bamber. Cook hasn't been told anything so if you ask me nothing's happened yet either one way or the other.'

'I was told Miss Elsa was still asleep and that I needn't go to her.'

'That's right. The doctor brought a couple of nurses with him, that's three we've got now and a right lot of looking after they want.'

'Has anything more been said about Agnes?'

'Well yes, miss. Mr Bamber says there will have to be a trial and Mr Thorn has sent for the police.'

'A trial! Do you mean an inquest?'

'Yes, that's what I meant, but I couldn't think of the word. Do you think they've sent for the police because they think somebody pushed her, miss?'

'Oh, Nancy, of course not, who would do such a thing? No, they have sent for the police because it is necessary at a time like this.'

'We can't think what she was doing in the old wing to fall into the cellars, but then Agnes was always a funny one, secretive like, not a bit like Kate and me. Funny that she was still wearing your shawl miss.'

My heart jumped in a frightening fashion. Why had Agnes returned to the old wing after she left me? Because Nancy was gazing at me curiously I said, 'She promised to return it to me today. Poor Agnes.'

'Well, she won't be returning it now will she, miss? Mrs Bamber says it's all dirty from lying on the cellar floor but I don't suppose you'll ever want it back, will you?'

I didn't speak, and after a moment she gave her silly little curtsey and left me alone. I was shivering. Had somebody mistaken Agnes for me in the dark of the old wing, seeing only the white shawl which I had worn at the ball? Had that lonely and horrible death not been intended for Agnes at all? And which of the people at Milverton would be horrified when they realized the mistake they had made?

It was much later that night that I heard the sounds of carriage wheels upon the drive. I did not know if they were the wheels of the doctor's carriage or those of the guests already departing for their homes. Sadly I wondered how many of those people who only the night before had laughed and danced their way towards the dawn were left.

There was no sleep for me that night. I lay with my eyes open thinking about Agnes's body lying in one of the deserted bedrooms and poor Miss Judith surrounded by nurses as the doctor tried to save her baby. All through the night I thought I heard doors opening and closing and voices whispering somewhere in the house, but I stayed in my bed with my door safely locked on the inside.

I was up and dressed by the time Nancy came in at seven o'clock and from the dark circles under her eyes I knew that she hadn't slept either. It was Boxing Day. Outside a dismal, icy drizzle was falling and when I looked out of my window I could see no further than the steps which led down towards the Italian gardens. It seemed as though the entire world stopped short at the edge of the formal gardens and that the sweeping fells and rugged hills were part of a dream world I had only known in my imagination. In spite of the welcoming blaze from my fire the freezing cold seemed to seep into my room through the windows and I pulled my knitted jacket closer about my shoulders. I didn't want to make a nuisance of myself in the kitchens when the servants were at their busiest but at the same time I chafed at the enforced inactivity.

I tried to read but could not concentrate on books I had read many times before. By the time Nancy came back with my breakfast tray I was almost at screaming pitch. One look at her face told me the worst.

'She's lost it, miss. The doctor's given her something to sleep her and he's left a nurse in charge. Poor Mr Stephen doesn't look as though he's slept a wink all night.'

'I don't suppose he has. Oh Nancy, this is simply terrible.'

'It is that, miss. When Miss Judith wakes up and finds there's to be no baby there'll be no doing any good with her.'

How helpless I felt. I was desolate for the woman who had probably been my only friend since my arrival in this house, yet I could not console her for the loss of her child. I

244

could only show that I grieved with her.

Soon after nine I made my way to Miss Elsa's room and found a young nurse sitting in front of a blazing fire in the sitting room, a breakfast tray before her, her shoes off and her feet up on a small footstool. There was no doubt that she was enjoying unaccustomed luxury. Elsa was still sedated, so, after a desultory exchange of information about the family, I turned to go, feeling more frustrated and helpless than before. Disconsolately, I wandered down into the hall, surprised to see the Christmas tree still standing forlornly surrounded by the parcels that nobody had had the courage to open. The door between the library and Mr Thorn's study was open and as I closed the library door I heard Mr Thorn's voice call out, 'Is that you, Stephen?'

I crossed the room and walked into his study. He was standing at the window staring out into the bleak morning outside. The dog Laird lay stretched out in front of the fire and although he did not get to his feet he gave a whimper of welcome and thumped his foolish tail against the hearthrug.

Mr Thorn did not immediately look round. Even as he stood with his back towards me I was aware that he wore an air of dejected defeat. He turned his head to see who stood beside him and I thought I saw a sudden wariness in his eyes. He moved away to stand behind his desk.

'I am sorry, Miss McAllister, I thought it was my brother. I am afraid you find us a very unhappy household. Perhaps that is something we shall need to talk about.'

'I don't understand.'

He stood looking at me broodingly and I felt the first faint stirrings of unease. I ached for him to take me into his confidence but I was surprised when he reached out a hand, gently laid it against my face, and said, 'Was it only just over twelve months ago that I looked into your eyes and thought then that this house and the people in it might defeat that bright look of courage I saw in them? You were so sure, so confident then that you would be able to withstand all that might happen to you here.'

'But I have been happy here.'

'No, you have never been happy here. If you insist that you have, then you do not know what happiness is. I wonder if you have ever been truly happy in your life.'

'I believe that I have. I have tried to be happy.'

His voice was very tired. 'One does not try to be happy, Carla, believe me I know, because once I too was happy. It seemed to me then that the future stretched out bright and beautiful in front of me and I could see no end to it.'

'But nothing is forever. Perhaps you are right and I have never known the happiness you speak of. But I still feel that I have been happy here. I have come to love this old house and the people I know here.'

I could not keep the tremor from my voice; to my shame the tears filled my eyes and rolled slowly down my cheeks. I was embarrassed, impatient with my emotion, and I searched in my pockets for my handkerchief only to find that I did not possess one. He smiled a little and handed me a large, clean, white one from his own pocket. Quite unable to prevent myself, I sank into a chair, sobbing quietly. He let me cry without attempting to comfort me, and at last I was able to pull myself together, only too bitterly aware of my tear-stained face and red-rimmed eyes.

He was watching me closely and there was the greatest kindness in his face as he rose from his chair, and held out his hand to raise me up. I was aware of the scent of cigar smoke from his fingers and the clean smell of the soap he had used that morning. He smiled at me gently, and I will never know what power prevented me then from throwing myself into his arms.

'Tell me now, Carla McAllister, why you have always seemed so curious about Milverton and its people? Why in some strange way you seem to belong here. And why you were so amazed when I showed you the portrait of my wife, and later when you met Mrs St Clare in the drawing room.'

'I thought Caprice would be your wife. I had seen you with her so many times when I was a schoolgirl growing up in the village. I had heard you call her "darling" and seen you waltzing with her that night Elliot and I nearly fell through the window. I didn't know then that she was dead. I simply believed that you had married somebody else and that Caprice was now Mrs St Clare.'

He looked at me so long and searchingly that my face flamed.

At last he answered me. 'And now you know that Caprice lies dead somewhere out on the fells, that she did not love me enough, and that many of the miseries of this house can be laid at her door.'

'I do not believe it. She did love you. Nobody could pretend a love like that. How can you believe the things they say of her?'

His unhappy, ravaged face looked surprised at my vehemence, then the shutters came down again and the old cynicism was there, stronger, oh much stronger, than before.

'Your loyalty to Caprice does you great credit, Miss McAllister, but I can assure you that it is entirely misplaced.'

His face softened again and his voice was kind.

'You should not stay here at Milverton. You are young and lovely; that wide-eyed courage should not be destroyed by other people's misfortunes. I would advise you to get back into the world of the living as soon as you can. I have many friends and business acquaintances in Medchester, or even in London if that is preferable. I am quite sure that some suitable employment can be found for someone with your talents.'

'But what are my talents sir? You will search long for them and not find any.'

'Cheerfulness, loyalty, intelligence.'

'Those are qualities, Mr Thorn, not talents. Am I to understand that you are sending me away?'

'Do you not think it is for the best?'

'But what of Miss Elsa? She has already lost Agnes. I don't flatter myself that she cared for me in the same way, but we had grown closer together in recent months, and surely to lose both Agnes and me at the same time can only add to her confusion.'

'I don't know, but no doubt the next few weeks will tell us. Early in the New Year we must talk again. In the meantime, think over what I have said to you this morning. I will not send you away, Carla, but my advice would be for you to go.'

I could think of nothing else to say and the ache in my throat, even if I had been able to think of something, would have prevented it. I moved towards the door knowing that he was watching me, but as I opened it to go out into the hall I heard his voice.

'Miss McAllister,' he said, 'remove the servants' presents from around the tree and distribute them. It will give you something to do. I was looking forward to seeing your face as you unwrapped yours yesterday morning, now it seems I shall be deprived even of that small pleasure.'

I did not turn round but closed the door gently behind me. I had to make several trips to the kitchen with the parcels, leaving those intended for Agnes with Mrs Bamber, then returned to the hall to pick up my own gifts. I was surprised to see how many there were, and spent over an hour opening them in the privacy of my own room. There were small inexpensive presents from the servants. From Mrs Lytton there was an embroidered tablecloth which she had no doubt done herself, and from Miss Judith and her husband delicately perfumed notepaper and envelopes. Jeremy, like Rowena, had sent me chocolates, hand-made and exclusive, but I seemed to know instinctively that the last parcel I opened contained Mr Thorn's gift, and Miss Elsa's too of course. It was an evening bag, exquisitely embroidered in petit point, its clasp in the shape of a filigree dragonfly and I knew that he had chosen it himself. Miss Elsa's name was on the card but she had had no part in its selection.

17

They took Agnes's body from the house on the fourth of January in a plain, elm coffin made from trees on the estate, and I was told that she was to be buried in the little churchyard at Sutton which had been her home. The police had been and gone, but as far as I could tell, discovered nothing new.

Elsa was dressed now during the day and my visits to her room took up the old familiar pattern. But now, instead of Agnes there was a brisk, unruffled nurse sitting on the window seat, reading one of the love stories she revelled in, while Elsa once more knelt before the doll's house in the centre of the floor.

The nurse's name was Jennie and she was only staying until a replacement could be found. She herself had told Elsa that Agnes would not be returning to her, but had received only a long, cool stare by way of a reply and the subject was not mentioned again.

There were other changes, too, in the air. Elliot had said good-bye and returned to Medchester, and now Miss Judith was talking of leaving Milverton permanently, convinced that she would never bear a living child in her brother-in-law's unhappy house.

On the sixth of January I woke up to a clear, frosty morning with the sun sparkling on the frozen mere and I asked if I might take the pony and trap into Gleave to make one or two purchases. It was an excuse to get out into the fresh air more than anything else, and Mrs Lytton was quick to hand me a list of embroidery silks she required from the Misses Phipps.

I enjoyed that drive along the narrow country lanes and after I had purchased the materials from the draper's I walked along to Mrs Merriweather's cottage where she welcomed me gladly with cups of steaming coffee.

She told me that all the village had been agog at the news of yet one more tragedy to strike the Hall and prayers had been said in the church for the Lytton family and all who lived there. The villagers had talked of nothing else and newspapers had been exchanged from one house to the next in case some item of news was reported more vividly in one paper than another. The letters were becoming more urgent in their endeavours to persuade me to return to Medchester but I was equally determined that I would not leave Milverton until Mr Thorn decided to send me away. As we stood looking through her cottage window I started with surprise as I caught sight of a figure I knew walking briskly along the road.

'Do you know that gentleman?' Mrs Merriweather asked me.

'Yes, I travelled with him on the train the first day I arrived here, but I do not know his name.'

'He spends a lot of time here,' she said. 'Nearly every day I see him walking the village street from end to end and they do say he spends a lot of time walking the lanes around the Hall and further afield, up on the fells. You wouldn't catch me walking on the moors in this weather with the mist likely to come down when you least expect it and the grass slippy with frost. There's some who say he could be a policeman keeping his eye on the goings on at the Hall.'

I could see that her curiosity was well and truly aroused and, lest I be accused of gossip by my employer, I decided to say a hasty farewell to her. Then I set off up the village street to where I had left the pony and trap. We drove at a brisk pace along the lanes. The pony was glad of the exercise and the cold wind against my cheeks brought a sparkle into my eyes. I looked this way and that in case I should encounter the strange man who had been my travelling companion, but it was only when I rounded the last bend before reaching the gates of Milverton that I saw him striding out in front of me. He moved to one side to allow us to pass and I reined in the pony so sharply that he looked up, startled.

He raised his hat and smiled at me. I was struck again by the calm urbanity of his manner. He looked like a benign cleric or a city lawyer with his broad, pink face and shining, bald head, but his eyes in that smooth, clean-shaven face were like blue icicles.

'Good morning Miss McAllister and a Happy New Year to you,' he said genially.

I said that I was surprised to see him walking the country lanes on a wintry morning.

Quite unabashed he said, 'Ah, but it is good for the constitution, and too much Christmas fare has played havoc with my girth.'

'You are staying with your friends, sir?'

'Actually no, not this time. I am at the inn.' Then he went on, 'I was sorry to hear of yet another tragedy to strike the Lytton household. I suppose you would be acquainted with the young lady?'

'Yes, I knew her.'

'I take it her funeral has already taken place.'

'I believe so, in the village where she was brought up.'

'Ah, at Sutton.' He shook his head sadly. 'Very sad, very sad, and how is Mrs Lytton accepting the loss of her maidservant?'

'You seem to know more than you pretend, sir. Agnes was Miss Elsa's personal maid but it seems to me the villagers know the business of this household better than those who live in the house.'

My voice was sharp, defensive, and by his amused expression I could tell that he was aware of it.

'Well, my dear, it has all been in the newspapers, but when you have lived in the country as long as I have you will know that a tale never loses anything. There is little to do in a village but gossip and read the newspapers.'

'And to walk the fells and the country lanes around Milverton which you, sir, seem to be fond of doing.'

'Why should it bother you, my dear? I am a lonely old bachelor with time on his hands. I like walking the fells and the lanes around Gleave. I know people here, and the city can be a very lonely place at Christmas time when families are close.'

I bit my lip in exasperation, angry with myself. My outburst had been unforgivable.

'I am sorry, sir, if I appeared rude, I had absolutely no

right to question your motives in walking the lanes so close to the house but there has been so much gossip and I think the family have had enough to bear without the extra burden of prying eyes and gossiping tongues.'

He smiled down at me, but his eyes did not smile.

'Your loyalty does you great credit, my dear. Allow an old bachelor to give you some advice, however. In a household which over the last few years has been prone to accidents and sudden death be very wary. Do nothing foolhardy, and at all times be vigilant for your own safety.'

He raised his hat and, after favouring me with a long unsmiling glance, he left me to go striding up the lane in the direction of the moors. I gazed after him in astonishment not untinged with alarm. He had given me a stern warning. For once that bland face had been shorn of its customary smile and the seriousness of his mouth had matched the humourless look in his eyes.

Thoughtfully I drove the little trap into the stable yard and Painter was there to help me dismount. I was startled to find Jeremy waiting for me near the side door, leaning indolently against the wall in his riding clothes. He had a strangely twisted smile on his handsome face. I wanted no harassment from him, but it was obvious he was not going to let me pass easily.

'Where have you been hiding yourself these last few days?' he asked.

'I haven't been hiding myself, Mr Jeremy, I have been busy, that is all.'

'I suppose all the village is buzzing with talk of the Hall and its occupants?'

'I don't know, Mr Jeremy. I am not in the habit of discussing anything which happens here with the villagers in Gleave.'

'Very commendable of you, but I can assure you the gossip goes on, and it is not confined to the villagers. Aren't you the slightest bit interested in the talk that my brother chose to dance with his wife's companion when he so blatantly ignored the other guests in his house?'

I could feel my face flaming with colour as I turned to look up at him. His dark, boyish face was petulant, sulky, and for the first time I saw how like Rowena he was. He was as handsome as she was beautiful and both of them had that same spoiled awareness of their attractions. I had not allowed him to flirt with me, but had treated his advances with humour, refusing to be flattered by them.

Now, like a spoiled child, he was peevish, wanting to strike back because for that one, brief moment I had allowed my feelings for his brother to show in my face.

'You are being ridiculous, Mr Jeremy. It is a pity the people who are gossiping about us have nothing better to do with their time.'

'You show your feelings plainly, Carla. Why else should my brother think of sending you away?'

'Oh, that is unkind!' I cried, hurt and trembling but unable to move away from him as I stood with my back against the wall. 'Why are you trying to hurt me like this? I danced once with your brother and you talk as though we had committed a crime.'

'And what of Elsa sitting on the stairs watching you?'

'You are being unfair. Many men danced with women who were not their wives. I cannot think that Elsa cared either one way or the other. She is not like other women.'

'Carla, you are a fool if you think that Thorn will ever care for you. He will never put his wife aside, and whatever heart he has or ever had lies somewhere out on those fells with Caprice.'

I pressed my body back against the wall, frightened by his dark, angry, young face and cruel words. But his arms came round me like bands of steel and, although I struggled until the breath left my body, his lips came down upon mine until I felt I was drowning, with my heart hammering in my ears.

From a long way off I heard Thorn's voice, his words falling like drops of ice and Jeremy let me go so that I almost fell and would have done so but for the wall behind my back.

'If you must conduct yourselves in this fashion, I hardly think the stable yard and an audience of grooms is the right setting.'

The two brothers faced each other across the passage with open hostility. Thorn's face was haughty, dark with anger, and Jeremy's flushed, the face of a naughty schoolboy discovered in the middle of some misdemeanour. With a toss of his head, his whip striking angrily against his riding boots, he disappeared into the house and slammed the door behind him. I raised my eyes to Thorn's pleadingly, but with a curt nod he held the door open for me to enter the house.

My fingers were trembling as I took off my outdoor clothes in the quiet of my room, but I was angry too. Who were these Lyttons that they thought they could ride roughshod over other people's feelings and expect them to be grateful for attentions they had neither sought nor hoped for?

It was only later when my anger was spent that I realized fully how vulnerable my position was at Milverton. I was quite sure now that Thorn would send me away at the earliest opportunity, particularly if he thought there was something between Jeremy and me. I did not know how much of our conversation he had heard, but if he thought he was being gossiped about because of me that could only hasten my departure.

I must try to forget Thorn Lytton and my best opportunity to do so was to get away from Milverton. Jeremy's words had been spoken in anger but I recognized the truth of them. Thorn would never put his wife on one side, even though she was no real wife to him and, although he might say he hated the memory of Caprice, he had not forgotten her, nor would he. I could only wait now for the result of this morning's work, and hope that it would not be long in coming.

The days of January came and went, however, without a summons to Mr Thorn's study. I carried on with my duties, I drove down to the village on my days off and shopped for Mrs Lytton, but not once did I see Mr Thorn, although I heard his voice from time to time.

It was Elsa's birthday on the fourth of February and I went to her room early with the large box of chocolates I had bought for her. I had almost reached the door when I encountered Mr Thorn leaving it. He stood on one side so that I could pass in front of him but there was no smile of greeting on his face and the words good morning died on my lips. He merely bowed his head gravely and closed the door behind me. After that I realized my days were still numbered and I silently prayed that my departure might be soon.

The young nurse was still with us because no replacement had yet arrived, but there was a subtle difference in Elsa's behaviour. She refused to walk in the park with me even when the days were fine. She would not be read to and nothing I said or did could coax her away from the doll's house and the constant changing and rearranging of the furniture.

I saw no point in sitting with Elsa watching her play with her toy while the nurse read her interminable love stories. On that day, the fourth of February, I decided to walk in the park, even though it was cold. If I wrapped up well the fresh air would be preferable to the treacherous draught from the windows in Elsa's room. As I turned the corner into the corridor which led to my room I was dismayed to find Jeremy standing outside my door. I turned to flee but he caught sight of me and came striding down the corridor to meet me.

'I went to Elsa's room,' he explained, 'but the nurse said she thought you would be with my mother. I decided to try your room first.'

'What is it you want?'

He smiled – the engaging, asking-to-be-forgiven smile of a small boy who had been caught with his fingers in the candy jar – but instinctively I steeled my heart against the charm of it.

"I want to talk to you, Carla.'

'We can talk perfectly well here, Mr Jeremy.'

'That's just it, we can't. Five minutes, that's all I ask, on opposite sides of the room, I promise.'

Opposite sides of the room it was, and he stood looking at me, his mouth twitching with suppressed laughter but when my face remained grave and unsmiling he said, 'I came to apologize, Carla, for my behaviour the other morning.'

'Very well, I accept your apology. Now perhaps you will leave?'

He looked surprised, but when he took two steps towards

me I skipped behind a chair, placing it firmly between us.

'Good heavens girl, I'm not here to rape you,' he said in an exasperated tone of voice. 'Surely I'm not the first man who's attempted to kiss you, with or without your approval?'

'You took advantage of my position here. Even now I expect your brother thinks I gave you every encouragement and is only wondering just how soon he can conveniently get rid of me without worrying his wife too much.'

'That bothers you, doesn't it, Carla?'

'Yes, it does. It would bother you too if you had very little money. I have tried very hard to make a success of caring for Elsa and if I am forced to leave because of your stupidity or arrogance, call it what you will, I do not think I shall ever be able to forgive you.'

He stood looking at me, then the sulky frown reappeared on his face, the face of a spoiled child who had been denied his own way.

'I knew Thorn was in the stables, I saw him dismount from his horse only a few minutes before you came back with the pony and trap. I wanted him to see us.'

'But why?'

'Because all my life he has been held up before me as a pattern I should follow. It was always Thorn who got the prettiest girls, Thorn who was everybody's idea of a country gentleman, Thorn who would one day be master of Milverton. I suppose I've been jealous of him, and that night when I saw your eyes worshipping him I wanted to hurt you both, you for your stupidity, Thorn because he is Thorn.'

'You cannot expect Thorn to suffer through me. He has no feelings for me either one way or the other but you have succeeded in making me suffer. Because of your jealousy for your brother I shall lose my position here and what good will that have done you?'

'You were so damned indifferent, Carla, so upright and proper, that you became a challenge, but then on the night of the ball I saw that you didn't respond to me because it was Thorn you wanted and that in itself made me want to punish you.'

'You have let your imagination run away with you, Mr

Jeremy. Just because I am not in the last attracted by you, and because you are very spoiled and something of a womanizer, you have behaved like a child who doesn't particularly want the toy he is offered but can't bear to think that the toy doesn't want him.'

I thought at first my words had made him angry. Indeed I was appalled at my own audacity in the way I had upbraided him, but he threw back his head and laughed, his laughter ringing out across the room until I caught hold of his hand.

'Stop it, for heaven's sake,' I cried, 'or you'll have everybody wondering what you are doing in my bedroom.'

'You needn't worry,' he said impudently, 'my brother is in Feltham to see what can be done about a permanent nurse for Elsa.'

My heart sank. 'If he is successful I shall not be needed.'

'Well, that's for him to decide, but don't look so despondent, he won't cut you off without a shilling. Thorn always honours his obligations, even if it means inconveniencing the rest of us.'

'What do you mean about inconveniencing the rest of you? Has my being here done that?'

'Not *you*, my dear girl, *Elsa*. If he'd had Elsa put in a sanatorium like we wanted him to do when she first became ill we'd have been spared a lot of inconvenience. Then there's my mother. She doesn't improve, so surely she'd be far better off in a convalescent home somewhere among old people like herself.'

'I fail to see how you are inconvenienced either by Elsa or your mother. Your brother pays my salary, he also pays for the nurses and all the other expenses. All you are required to do is call in to see them from time to time, which, I might add, isn't very often.'

He threw back his head and laughed again. 'Oh Carla, I love you. So small and slender and spirited. I wouldn't blame my brother if he kept you on as his companion and brought a hundred nurses in for Elsa.'

But before I could think of an apt rejoinder he left me, and I swear I heard him chuckling as he walked down the corridor. For the rest of the afternoon I tramped about the estate, walking with my head lowered against the biting wind, with my hands thrust into the deep pockets of my coat, a warm, woollen scarf covering my hair.

'So Mr Thorn was in Feltham looking for another nurse ! Very well then, I would anticipate my dismissal by handing in my resignation in the morning. I had no idea what length of notice he would demand of me but one thing was sure, I would not allow him to do anything in the way of finding me other employment. That night, more for something to occupy my time than for any other reason I started to put my things together, placing them back in the drawers in such a way that they would be easily packed later. I would have to ask Mr Bamber if my trunk could be brought from wherever it had been taken but there was plenty of time for that.

It was with considerable dismay therefore that I learned from Nancy, when she served my breakfast next morning, that Mr Thorn had gone early to Medchester and would not return until late that evening. I had worked up my courage to no good purpose and the day stretched before me much as any other day.

Shortly after nine o'clock Elsa's nurse came to my room. She did not wait for an invitation to take the easy chair opposite mine, but sat with her feet curled under her, accepting gratefully the cup of tea I offered her.

'I believe Mr Lytton's gone into Medchester for the day?' she said.

'Yes. I wanted to see him myself but I was too late.'

'Well, I wanted to see him yesterday but he was over at Feltham. The top and bottom of it is I simply have to go into Feltham myself today. I'm getting married in the summer and stuck out here in the wilds means I'm getting nothing done.'

'I don't suppose he'll mind for a moment if you go. I will look after Miss Elsa and if I have any difficulty Mrs Lytton's nurse or Mrs Bamber will lend a hand.'

'I would be grateful, Carla, but I can make it easy for you. I propose to give her a sleeping draught in her morning coffee, only a very mild one, but that way she'll be no trouble until I get back.' She pointed to a pile of parcels besides my dressing table.

'You look as though you are packing.'

'Yes, I shall probably be leaving soon so I have been getting one or two things together.'

'I can't say I blame you. Mr Thorn looks at me as though he doesn't know I'm alive – in fact the whole house gives me the creeps. I shall be leaving here about half past ten. Mr Jeremy has promised to drive me to the station. Just keep an eye on her from time to time, that's all that's necessary.'

I smiled to myself after she had gone. Mr Jeremy had lost no time in ingratiating himself with the nurse.

Later that morning I went to Elsa's rooms. The sitting room was empty and the doll's house closed up in the centre of the floor. In her bedroom I found Elsa stretched out on her bed sleeping peacefully. It was warm in her room but I added more coals to the fire, placing the fireguard safely around it before I left.

I stood in front of the doll's house looking down at it, then, making up my mind, I turned the little key and opened the front. She had changed much of the furniture in the rooms so that they looked entirely different, but no amount of chopping and changing could disguise their beauty or the exquisite proportions of the miniature furniture. I tried to open up the front of the old wing but it seemed to be stuck. At last, with the help of a small pair of scissors which I found in the sewing box, I managed to prise open the doors.

I sat back in amazement for this was not the old wing as I knew it. The corridor level with my room with its tall, glass windows was a ballroom and round the edges of the room were placed small, gilt chairs and there was even a dais and a small orchestra surrounded by miniature potted palms. Every room in the wing was furnished, as exquisitely and completely as the rooms of the newer part of the house, but nowhere was there a room as described to me by the medium in Medchester. Quietly, not daring to make any noise, I closed the doors. I felt relief but also a vague disappointment.

The day now stretched long and empty before me, a grey, wintry day when distances were shrouded in mist and a lowering sky promised torrential rain or snow before nightfall. Sure enough, after lunch, the rain started – hard driving rain. The wind was up, too, lashing the branches of the trees so that even the spindly branches outside my window tapped mournfully against the panes.

I stood looking out, miserably chilled, watching the raindrops chasing each other down the panes. Opposite me the old wing seemed more sinister than ever with its dark, soaked stone and dripping trees lashing their branches viciously against the cold, empty windows – windows which rattled ominously even without such a gale as this one.

I do not know how long I stared at the desolate old wing or when the idea was born in me, but it seemed that some power outside myself drove me so that in the end I had no will of my own. There would be no peace for me at Milverton until I knew the secret of the old wing for I was convinced there was one, a secret compelling enough to entice a visitor in the hours when the rest of the household slept, sinister enough to have lured Agnes to her death. There would never be a better time than this quiet afternoon when the master and Mr Jeremy were out of the house. Mrs Lytton hardly constituted a problem and Elsa I could discount since she was fast asleep in her bed.

As soon as luncheon was over the Bambers always retired to their sitting room and seldom emerged from it before five. Nancy and Kate had gone out and Cook liked to sleep in her chair until it was time to prepare tea. I was restless as I watched the clock, willing the fingers to move faster. Promptly at half past one I carried my tray down to the kitchen, pausing on my way to try the door leading to the old wing. It was locked. In my mind's eye I visualized Mr Bamber's keys hanging on a nail in the corridor outside the kitchen door. I had often wondered why they were not kept in his room or in the kitchen itself, but then Milverton was not overburdened by people as curious as I.

The fire in the kitchen grate roared halfway up the chimney and Cook sat before it in her rocking chair, snoring gently, her head hanging forward on to the starched, white bib of her apron, her hands idle in her lap. In the scullery beyond I could hear the kitchen maids whispering and giggling together, but Mr Bamber and his wife had already retired to the privacy of their sitting room and the kitchen itself looked as tidy as a new pin with the luncheon things already cleared away and the hard, wooden table scrubbed clean. One of the girls took my tray at the scullery door and I could tell from her expression that she would rather attend to it herself than have me interrupt whatever was causing the amusement in there.

I tiptoed across the kitchen, closing the door quietly behind me, holding my breath for a few moments in case Cook's slumber had been disturbed, but there was no sound behind the closed door. I could hardly bear to look towards the hook where I knew the keys were normally hung in case they were not there, but when I saw them, thick and bulky against the white wall, my heart lurched with suppressed excitement. I reached up to take them, praying silently that they would not jingle loud enough to bring Mr Bamber out of his sitting room, but they were heavy in my hands and thankfully I managed to conceal them in the soft folds of my skirt, holding them against me so that they would not rattle.

Attached to the larger bunch was a smaller one on a separate ring but joined by a length of cord. These, I thought, were the keys for the old wing, but my fingers trembled as I tried first one and then another until only two were left. I was on the verge of panic when I heard a sharp click and to my utmost relief the doorknob turned in my hand.

In the daylight, even the grey, stormy daylight of this winter's day, the corridor looked much larger and I could well believe that it had once served as a ballroom. The chandeliers had been taken down and there was now no means of lighting it except by portable lanterns, but I heard no scuffling sounds from the skirting boards and, if bright, inquisitive eyes watched me, I steeled myself to believe they had gone and would not return. Once there had been the pattern of their feet on the dusty floors, but now the floor had been swept clean, perhaps when the furniture was removed from some of the rooms or when the police inspected the rooms after Agnes's death.

I wasted no time in moving along the length of that corridor and through the door which stood open at the end of it. The rooms smelled musty as only old, disused rooms can smell, and in the room where I had stood in the dark, terrified, not knowing who stood beside me, I could smell again the insidious odour of rats, constricting my throat muscles until I could hardly breathe. The dark, damask wallpaper, once beautiful, gave the room a dismal look, and the heavy, grey skies outside the window did nothing to relieve it. I was glad to move out into the corridor beyond.

The passage was narrow and dark and I trod gingerly, unhappily aware of the creaking floorboards under my weight. The light came fitfully through the door I had left open behind me and I expected to find the door in front of me securely locked as it had been on that other night. To my surprise, the door opened easily at my touch and once more I was in a square hall, almost identical to the hall outside Miss Elsa's rooms in the new wing. Stairs descended from it and others climbed upwards – uncarpeted stairs, thick with grey dust and the pattern of small claw-like hands. I coughed. My throat felt dry and swollen and the echo of that cough sounded eerily throughout the void above and below me. This time I was convinced that I heard a squeaking and scuffling in the shadows and my flesh crawled as my ears strained for other sounds. Only the empty silence surrounded me and after a few moments I looked round the hall with interest.

There were light patches on the walls where once portraits or pictures had hung and although the gas jets still protruded there were no mantles on them. As I looked around the dismal setting I wondered anew what possible attraction this old disused building could offer, but I knew that it had enticed Agnes as it had enticed me and one other whose identity I did not as yet know.

Opposite me was another door, a stout, freshly painted door, and I reasoned that beyond it must be windows which overlooked the distant fells, windows which marked the end of the house. My hand trembled as I reached out for the knob to open the door, but this time it did not respond to the touch of my fingers. The door was locked and if I wished to enter I must find the key. I tried several without success, but after the third or fourth attempt I heard a click and on turning the knob I found it opened easily as though the lock had been recently oiled.

Inside that room I gasped with amazement at the sight which confronted me. I was in a large room with two enormous bay windows which looked out on to fells and moorland. But it was not the size of the room or the beautiful proportions of it which astounded me, it was the fact that it was furnished as though its occupant might return at any moment. Rich, ruby-red, velvet curtains hung at the windows, their pelmets edged in pale blue. A beautiful Chinese carpet covered the floor and the chairs and couches were also covered in ruby-red velvet or palest blue. There were priceless, walnut chests around the room and on them rested beautiful vases and other ornaments. Upon the walls hung oil paintings in ornate frames and watercolours whose freshness defied description.

Then I saw that there was another door and, like a child in the Arabian Nights, I opened it to go into the bedroom beyond. This room too was furnished in shades of rose and palest turquoise and over the large ivory and gold bed was thrown a counterpane in heavily quilted, turquoise satin to match the drapes at the windows. Another door led into a bathroom and beyond it was an austere man's dressing room, all looking as though they had been furnished yesterday.

I returned to the bedroom, looking round me entranced, unable to believe that in this lonely, derelict part of Milverton one suite of rooms alone retained something of the beauty of the rest of the house. On the dressing table lay a heavy silver and ivory toilet set and I caught my breath sharply at the monogrammed letter C picked out in gold. Heavy, crystal jars and bottles still sparkled in the light from the windows and I knew that these had been Caprice's things. This furniture had been intended for her and Thorn, but why had he kept it all these years in all its original perfection unless he loved her still?

Quietly, not daring to make a sound, I opened the doors of the wardrobe. They were filled with her clothes. Ball gowns in rich satins and brocades, dinner gowns in velvet, while in another were her outdoor clothes. Summer dresses in lawn and sprigged voile, capes trimmed with fox, and casual clothes for walking the fells or sitting in the gardens. In the millinery chest lay her hats. Wide-brimmed picture hats trimmed with tulle flowers or ostrich feathers, small toques ornamented with osprey. I found her shoes also and without a second thought pushed my foot into an exquisite confection made from blue satin edged with diamante. It was obviously an evening shoe, an exquisite thing but a size too big for my own foot. Caprice had been much taller than I. It was Aladdin's cave. The drawers were still filled with her underclothes, heavy satin and crêpe de chine appliquéd with lace, negligées of floating chiffon, night-dresses as light as gossamer, and when I held them up against my face I could smell the perfume, elusive and delicate – Caprice's perfume.

All sense of time seemed to leave me as I knelt on the floor tenderly replacing her underwear in the chest from which I had taken it. Then suddenly my heart became a dead thing and I thought I knew at last who came to the old wing in the dead of night. It could only be Thorn, coming to look at the things they had chosen together, at the rooms which had been furnished with loving care in readiness for a life they would share. These rooms represented a shrine built for Caprice to last as long as Milverton would stand, left amid others no longer in use, like the tomb of some long-dead pharaoh in a desolate valley, furnished at the moment of his death to await that other moment when his spirit would return from its wanderings to enjoy again all the things he had loved most in his lifetime.

I could imagine Thorn standing in these silent rooms, lost in his private misery. Did he stand here heaping curses upon her memory or did he lie on that exquisite bed in silent anguish for what might have been?

I crouched on the rug, shivering, aware for the first time that I was very cold. I wondered how long it was since a fire had glowed in that cream, marble fireplace. A sixteenth-century firescreen stood in front of the empty grate. It was a French period piece, filigree gold on small, golden claws; on the front was a picture of a shepherdess being serenaded by a handsome, young prince in a powdered wig, his long, delicate fingers idly plucking at the strings of the lute he held in his hands. The carpet felt icy cold to my touch and I wondered if the charm of this room and the priceless things it contained would crumble into dust if they were ever exposed to air and sunlight.

I looked at my watch. It was almost three o'clock and I

panicked then. Suppose Mr Bamber had looked for his keys and found them gone? Suppose they came looking for me and found me here? I jumped to my feet, looking round the bedroom quickly to see that I had left everything in its place, then without a backward glance I went through the door into the room beyond, closing it quietly behind me. I went straight to the door ahead of me, hurrying a little now and not bothering to look again at the exquisite proportions of the sitting room. I was surprised to find that the door was locked. I could not remember locking it behind me. Surely I had been too surprised by what confronted me to think of locking the door? Luckily, I still had the bunch of keys and my fumbling, trembling fingers hastened to find the one which would open the door.

Quite suddenly I had the strangest feeling that I was being watched. I stood facing the door but there were eyes boring into the back of my head. I only wanted to open that door and run, regardless of creaking floorboards, back to the safety and familiarity of the corridors I knew. I was afraid to turn round, afraid of what I might see, but as I heard at last the click of the lock I also heard the sound of light, silvery laughter in the room behind me. I spun round, cold and terrified, my heart thumping, my face flaming to face whatever menaced me, either of this world or that shadowy, supernatural world of which I knew nothing. It was, therefore, with the utmost amazement that I saw Elsa sitting in the chair beside the window, her elegantly slender body curled up amongst the deep velvet cushions. She was laughing softly, her china-blue eyes amused, her entire attitude one of delighted mischief.

18

I could not keep the relief out of my voice and my racing heart became calmer as I walked across the room to stand beside her.

'Why Elsa,' I said smiling, 'I thought you were sleeping.'

'Obviously,' she answered.

I looked at her uncertainly, surprised by her answer and the tone of her voice. It had not been what I expected.

I held out my hand, 'Come, shall we go back together,' I coaxed.

She continued to smile at me, ignoring my extended hand. Then in a tone which I had never heard her use before, she said, 'What are you doing here, Carla?'

It was a question any member of the household might have asked, but I had not expected it from Elsa. Elsa's questions were never posed like those of an adult woman. Usually they were asked petulantly in the voice of a little girl who expected to be pampered.

I continued to look at her doubtfully, until she said, 'I have asked you what you are doing here, Carla.'

There was a tremor in my voice, put there by the new fear in my heart. 'I shouldn't be here at all, Elsa, but I was curious because I have seen a light burning in these rooms. Come, shall we return now? It is cold in here.'

Her voice mocked me, as did her eyes. 'You have seen everything you came for, then? Is there nothing else you care to look at? Surely my sister's poor belongings have not so quickly exhausted your interest?'

I was silent, only too well aware that she was taunting me cruelly. She rose to her feet in a graceful movement and stood looking down at me. I had not realized that she was so tall, but the face which had always seemed like that of an angel seemed somehow different now. If Miss Judith or Rowena had discovered me where I had no right to be I would have expected their faces to register displeasure, but not Elsa, who had never seemed to care what went on around her. Now I looked into her cold, blue eyes and haughty, alien face with fear.

She walked into the centre of the room and pointed out several articles of furniture, asking in a conversational voice if I liked them, giving me exact details of their value and their age. Then she asked, 'You like beautiful things, do you not, Carla? All the things you see here were chosen for their beauty, many of them made specially for the day when my sister Caprice would be the mistress of Milverton. Some of them are not to my taste, although without exception they belong to me.'

'Not to Mr Thorn?' I ventured.

She laughed. 'What would he want with things which would only remind him of Caprice? Come, let us go into the bedroom. Or have you already pried into the wardrobes, perhaps even tried on the clothes you found there?'

She swept on ahead, and miserably I followed in her wake. She flung open the wardrobe doors, asking me to stand forward so that I could see better. It was then that I tried once more.

'I confess, Elsa, that I did look into the wardrobes, mainly because I was surprised to find them here, but now it is so cold. Can we not return to your room and have tea?'

'Tea! You make it sound so civilized, Carla. I have a much better idea. Let us look through the drawers in the wardrobe here to see if we can discover together any of Caprice's little vices. You admired her very much, didn't you? And rightly so. She was very beautiful.'

She dragged me behind her, forcing me to kneel on the carpet while she emptied the drawer, then she jumped to her feet and started bringing out one gown after another, holding them in front of her so that I might see the effect.

'Unfortunately none of these would fit you, Carla, since you are much smaller than I. Still, since you will never have the opportunity to wear such a gown, the notion is a foolish one. Come let us look in this chest now and see what is left.'

We knelt together and one by one she passed over the articles she had heaped upon the floor, periodically taking others out of the chest.

'My sister kept her souvenirs in here, and now and again I look at them — not because I loved her. You must not for one moment think that, but it amuses me to think that they are now mine.'

I wanted to tell her not to be bitter, to forgive Caprice for what she had done to her, that Caprice was dead and could hurt her no more, but the words would not come. This strange, new Elsa terrified me as no person in my whole life had terrified me and I prayed silently that this was a dream, a nightmare from which I might awaken at any moment, and that in the morning I would find Elsa still a child. Fascinated, I watched her long, slender fingers smoothing and stroking the things she removed from the chest and I knew that this was no nightmare but terrifying reality. I wanted to jump to my feet and run, but she was between me and the door and I had already had a taste of her strength from the bruises on my wrist when she dragged me into the bedroom.

The things had belonged to Caprice; they were possibly her most treasured possessions for many of them had been with her since childhood. There was a small, ivory fan which had been made for a child, and a rag doll, decrepit now and soiled from much handling by small fingers, and another doll with a sweet, vapid face and eyes which closed when she was laid flat.

'I had a doll like this,' Elsa said, 'but my doll had fair hair like my own. When it broke I asked Caprice to give me hers but she took it away. I have it now though. Her name is Lucinda.'

She handed me a shawl wrapped in soft tissue, beautifully knitted and so soft that it felt like a piece of thistledown in my hands.

'It was her shawl as a baby,' Elsa explained. 'She was keeping it for her own baby, hers and Thorn's.' Then she laughed, and the sound of her laughter was false, taunting, mocking the dead Caprice.

I was shivering, but whether from fear or cold I didn't know. I watched her fingers undoing the ribbons on a large packet and then she was handing me photographs. I recognized her father and another photograph which I assumed was Caprice's mother – a lovely, laughing woman holding a small child with dark shining ringlets and a bright beautiful face. There was several photographs of Thorn and the last one she showed me was of herself, a fair demure little girl about ten years old.

'I cannot imagine why she kept this,' she said, 'my sister never liked me.'

She handed me a pile of dance cards. 'You will see that Caprice never lacked dancing partners. No doubt she kept these so that she could remind herself of all the men she could have married if she had not married Thorn.'

'But these are only dance cards Elsa, nothing more.' I ventured.

'See, look at this one,' she said, thrusting one into my hands, showing me that against every dance was Thorn's name.

Impulsively she slammed the things back into the chest in no sort of order, not even bothering to wrap the baby's shawl which Caprice had treasured so lovingly and for so long.

She rose to her feet pulling me up after her. 'Come,' she said, 'there is something else you should see, unless of course you have not already looked at them.'

Miserably I followed her across the room towards a small white and gold chest standing against the wall between the two windows, and for the first time I noticed the bunch of keys she carried in the pocket of her skirt. The keys looked new, a small bunch of them, and when she saw the surprise on my face she explained, 'I had these keys made in the first year after I came to Milverton. Nobody knows I have them.'

A small key unlocked the chest and my heart turned over as I watched her remove the small tortoiseshell case which lay on top of the first drawer. I knew that case – it was the one I had handed back to Agnes in the small hours of Christmas morning. Now I knew that she must have returned to the old wing to replace it in this chest. Elsa was watching me closely, and again the expression on that beautiful porcelain face frightened me.

'You have seen this case before haven't you, Carla? Did they do you justice these creams and lotions which once belonged to Caprice? How kind it was of Agnes to lend you something which was not hers to lend.'

'She meant no harm by it. She was only being kind.'

'I thought you had borrowed them yourself, because you were always sneaking and prying into things which did not concern you. I thought it was you returning them here, it was so dark in the passage yonder and all I could see was your white shawl.'

I looked at her in dismay, my mind not daring to face what my heart told me was true. Elsa had been the last person to see Agnes alive while we had all thought she was sleeping her drugged sleep in the early hours of Christmas Day. She was watching me closely, a strange secretive smile on her lips.

She turned to replace the make-up chest in the drawer, slamming the door but not bothering to lock it.

'I wanted to show you some of my sister's jewellery. Much of it is in the safe in Thorn's study but there are some pieces I kept back and I look at them from time to time. I am bored now and it is cold.'

'Oh yes, Elsa, it is very cold. Should we not go back so that I can replace Mr Bamber's keys before he misses them?'

Her eyes swept over me with contemptuous amusement. 'I will replace the keys. Mr Bamber will not dare to question the mistress of the house.'

I followed her out of the bedroom into the sitting room, praying that this time I would be allowed to return with her to the safety of familiar rooms and corridors, but outside the sitting room door she held my wrist while she turned round to lock the door behind us.

'There is just one more thing I want you to see, Carla. It is in the attic and was placed there a long time ago. Your curiosity should be rewarded, you came here hoping to solve a mystery. It would be a pity to find only half what you came for.'

She took my arm in a grip from which there was no escape and then she dragged me, struggling painfully, back along the corridor until we reached the stairs. I was no match for her strength and with my feet slipping and sliding on every step I was hauled behind her up the stairs. I know that near the top I caught my flailing arm against the balustrade, sending two of the rods clattering down into the regions below. The sound of their falling echoed eerily in the emptiness around us, so loudly that I felt sure they must be heard all over the house. There was a smell of rotting woodwork and at every step I thought our weight upon the stairs would send us careering downwards into the cellars below.

At last we reached the landing above but still she did not let go of my arm and it ached from the steely strength of her fingers. Again she produced the small bunch of keys, inserting one of them into the lock of the first door we came to. We were in a large attic illuminated by a skylight and although the centre of the floor was empty, like all attics every bit of wall space was taken up by discarded furniture, old trunks, unwanted toys, even a big rocking horse which had no doubt once been much loved by the children of Milverton.

Elsa drew my attention to a large picture standing against a wall. Only a little of the wide ornamental frame could be seen – the rest of it was covered by a dust sheet, but she tugged the dust sheet sharply so that it fell away, revealing in the fading light a portrait of Caprice.

This was how I remembered her best. She had been painted wearing her blue, velvet riding habit. On her head was a small tricorn riding hat, its ostrich plumes falling from the brim on to her shoulders; there was a riding crop in her hand and on her lap sat a small terrier dog.

Fascinated, I looked at the face that had haunted my childhood; at eyes which had the velvety lustre of violets, at the passionate red mouth and the porcelain texture of her skin. One long, narrow hand rested lightly on the small dog, and in her smile was all the gay, provocative humour I remembered.

'How beautiful she is,' I murmured, and as I spoke I felt Elsa's hand tighten upon my arm.

'Yes, I suppose she was beautiful, very beautiful. This portrait was to have been placed where mine is now at the head of the stairs. They were painted by the same artist and when Caprice's portrait was relegated to the attic my father gave my portrait to Thorn so that it could take its place.

'Elsa,' I cried piteously, 'why are you suddenly so different? Why have you pretended all these years, when

271

your life could have been so wonderful? It is not Caprice you are punishing, it is yourself.'

She threw back her head and laughed, but there was no humour in her laughter and quickly I snatched my arm away and ran towards the door. She came after me, pinioning my arms above my head against the door and, try as I would, I could not free myself. Her face was close against mine and as I looked into her eyes I knew that she was indeed mad, with a madness more terrible than anything I had seen in the other Elsa I had known and cared for all those months.

'You stupid little fool,' she hissed, 'if only you had kept your place and remembered why you were here, instead of giving yourself airs and prying into things which did not concern you. Don't think I didn't see you looking at Thorn with those wide, innocent eyes of yours, but it's done you no good has it? When Caprice died she took everything of Thorn I ever wanted with her. The man I married was a stranger to me.'

At first the meaning of her words didn't signify anything. I was more troubled by my aching arms and her nails biting into my flesh. Then I realized what she had said and with dismay in my heart I stammered, 'You wanted Thorn?'

She released me so suddenly that I almost fell, and then she began to tramp about the room, talking all the time, while I stood with my back against the door listening to her with increasing horror.

'Of course I wanted him,' she said, 'and then I began to hate that milksop of a boy who had followed me so devotedly all the way from India. I only wanted to be rid of him, but all summer long he pestered me, until in the end I could have screamed with rage.'

'They said Caprice took him away from you.'

She paused in her tramping to look at me, then once again she threw back her head and laughed. 'No woman could have taken him away from me. Besides, what would Caprice want with him when she had Thorn? She came to stand before me and her voice dropped to little more than a whisper.

'Shall I tell you what happened that afternoon, Carla? You deserve to know after all your poking and prying, and I can tell you because I know you are not going to repeat it to a living soul.'

I was blabbering now, assuring her that she could trust me, that I would never betray her confidence, but she only looked at me in an amused sort of way, at length holding up her hand to silence me.

'I would like to be able to trust you, Carla, but if I let you go from here I will never be sure, will I? The story is a long one. I should think you will be more comfortable sitting in this chair here.' She swept whatever was lying on the chair on to the floor and pushed me into it. The upholstery smelled musty and there was a cloud of dust which tickled my throat and my eyes. She perched herself on the edge of a trunk, facing me, and I could tell from her face that her thoughts were no longer with me.

'It was so glorious that summer,' she began. 'My mother was not well so we always seemed to be at Milverton – Caprice, Perry and I. There was so much going on here – dances and picnics and lots of young people. Caprice was to be married in the autumn. She needed to be at Milverton in order to see to the suite of rooms she had chosen in the old part of the house. She wanted the rooms to overlook the fells. She loved the fells and whenever she wasn't packing and unpacking she was out on her horse riding over the moors. I remember it was August and the weather was warm, glorious as it had been all summer, but it was quiet around the gardens and the stables because the men were out in the fields helping with the harvest. I felt so lazy. It was too hot to go cavorting over the moors on horseback and I just wanted to be left alone to laze in the garden. Perry wanted to ride and, when we saw that Caprice's horse was already saddled and waiting for her, I went into the house to ask her if she would ride with him so that I could be left in peace. She wasn't in any of the downstairs rooms so I looked in her bedroom. She wasn't in there either but there was a pile of underclothes on her bed which she had obviously just taken from a parcel which had arrived from London. I picked up a nightdress and held it against my face – it was so soft and smooth, but I longed to rake my nails through the lace so that she would never be able to wear it lying in Thorn's arms.

273

'I turned round when I heard her at the door. She was watching me, and I remember wondering if she knew how much I hated her, how much I had always hated her. She was wearing that riding habit you can see in the portrait there and that same silly little hat. She looked so beautiful and elegant, so sure of herself and happy too, that I ached to wipe that cool, assured smile off her lips. It was her eyes though, those dark, pansy eyes that stupid men raved about; they were filled with pity. I knew at that moment that she pitied me because she knew I was in love with Thorn.

'She walked towards me and took the nightdress from my hands, then she asked if I would like to go with her to the suite of rooms she had chosen in the old part of the house to look at the furniture which had arrived that morning.

'I followed her and when we crossed the landing I could see that her portrait had already been put in its place where mine is now. I think it was then that I knew I could never let Caprice become Thorn's wife. Only I didn't know how easy it was going to be.

'This wing was furnished then, although Thorn had workmen in it decorating and attending to damp and rotting woodwork. The rooms you have already been in were just as you have seen them today and she was like a child let loose in fairyland as she took me round, careful that I should see everything. I remember that she was standing with her back towards me looking out towards the fells and I saw on her desk a narrow, silver paperknife. I picked it up and then I went up behind and plunged it into her back. She turned to look at me and I cannot forget her eyes. They were so surprised as she backed away from me saying 'No, Elsa! *no!*' I stabbed her again and again, I don't remember how many times, until in the end she lay on the carpet with the front of her riding habit blood-stained and horrible and her eyes wide open and staring. I knew that she was dead. I took the thick paper wadding that had come wrapped around the furniture and put it around her body as best I could – I was so afraid of the blood staining the new carpet, you see – then I dragged her along the corridors and into a room where I was sure they would never find her. There was an old settle in that room and I managed to put her into that. She was very slender, you wouldn't think she could be so heavy, but I lifted her and all the front of my dress was stained and wet with blood. It was lucky that it was Saturday and the workmen had gone home for the day. The kitchen, too, was quiet – like earlier today when you took the keys away. There was a fire in the grate, even though it was August and so terribly hot outside. I burned the paper bit by bit in the grate, then it was all over.'

'And they have never found her?' I heard my voice murmuring.

'How could they when they searched the fells and ignored the house? I must tell you the rest of the story and then you will have heard everything.

'As I ran upstairs from the kitchens I heard Perry calling to me from the hall. I couldn't let him see me with blood on my dress so I ran quickly to my room calling out to him that I would not be long. I hid my dress at the bottom of a drawer until I could dispose of it and I changed into my riding habit. I told Perry I had been unable to find Caprice and although he wanted us to wait for her I said that we should go, that obviously she did not intend to ride that day. I took her horse and there was nobody who saw us leave. We rode out on to the high fells where in spite of the sunlight the wind was sharp and fresh and we left our horses and climbed almost to the summit of Mower Gap where we sat on the grass above the tarn looking back towards the house. I thought about Caprice lying in the settle in her blue riding habit, her face pale in death and the blood drying on her breast, but he was going on and on about the life we would have together in India and I felt if he didn't stop I would go mad.

'A flock of wild geese flew over our heads and he got up to walk to the edge of the crag, his eyes following their flight. I knew I had to think quickly about what I must do. If Caprice did not return by nightfall they would search the house and Perry would remember that I had gone inside to look for her and kept him waiting in the stableyard. If they found her body they would know I had done it. At all costs I must make it appear that Caprice had left the house with Perry and not returned.

'I remember how still it was up there on the fells. Perry was staring after the geese, his hand raised to shade his eyes from the sun and he did not see me walking up behind him. All he felt was the strength of my hands against his back and all I heard was his cry as he plunged downward on to the rocks below. I looked over the edge. He was lying with half his body on the rocks and his legs in the reeds at the swampy edge of the tarn. He didn't appear to be moving but of course I had to go down to make sure.

'I knew that he always carried his service revolver. I had ridiculed him about it for, although it may have been necessary in the hills of India, it seemed strangely out of place in the quiet lanes of England. As I touched him I thought he groaned a little but I could not be sure, and I sat beside him for an hour or more. It was so cold down there beside the tarn. The crag cast great, blue shadows where the sun could not reach me and after a while I could bear it no longer and I went to feel his heart. It was still. I knew he was dead.

'I shot Caprice's horse because I knew he would return to the stables and I never wanted to see him again. Besides, she loved him so it was only right that he died. I fired another shot into the tarn, then I left the revolver near Perry's hand. I was clever, too. I remembered to wipe the revolver on my coat first.

'I rode back to the house on Perry's horse. I knew he would find his own way back to the stables if I left him outside the gates and I ran the remaining distance until I could let myself in by the side door.

'It was so quiet in the house, as quiet as a tomb.'

She paused in her tale, then she giggled a little.

'But of course it *was* a tomb, wasn't it, with Caprice's body lying upstairs in the attic? I saw one of the servants crossing the hall so I stepped back in the shadows and he did not see me. I was glad, though, when I reached the safety of my own bedroom.

'We all waited dinner for them. I remember sitting in the dining room with Mr and Mrs Lytton, Thorn and Rowena. The dusk was coming on and Thorn was angry, apologizing to his parents for their lack of consideration. Then they started to get anxious and one of the grooms came to tell

Thorn that Perry's horse had returned to the stables without him. After that there was no talk of dinner, although I was so hungry. Thorn organized search parties to go out on to the fells. There were dozens of them, carrying lanterns and farm gates in case either of them had been hurt.'

There was silence and I could tell by her face that she was thinking of that night. I, too, saw in my imagination the procession of men carrying gates and lanterns with Thorn striding ahead of them, anxious and afraid of what he might find.

I had to ask it, but surely it was not my own voice I heard, hoarse and stilted.

'How long was it before Thorn asked you to marry him?' I asked her.

'We grieved together, Thorn and I. He for Caprice and I for my sister and my fiancé. Sorrow drew us together and I knew that I only had to wait patiently for that day when he would know he could marry no other. He did not love me, right from the start I knew that, not even on the first night of our marriage when he played the husband and made a pretence of caring. I believed that time was on my side, that one day he would cease to hold me in his arms and think of Caprice, that it would be *my* beauty which would excite him, *my* charm which would hold him. At first I refused to believe it but as the weeks and months went on I began to realize that he would never love me. He came less and less to my bed. He tried to hide it, but I knew that there was something in me he found offensive. It was as though he couldn't bear to touch me, as though something within him knew what I had done but refused to recognize it, and I began to hate him. I was as beautiful as Caprice, as intelligent as Caprice, and he could not love me. Very well then, I decided, I would be more than a wife to him. I would be an encumbrance too great to be borne. His standing in the county, his proud name, that aloof, handsome face of his, tied inescapably to an idiot wife until one of us died. In time, Carla, I came to relish my role because I knew how much it made him suffer.'

She was watching me now, a twisted smile on her face, marring the icy, classical perfection of her face.

'You are shocked are you not? Be very sure that no

stupid, ineffectual little companion is going to take from me what is mine. If Caprice could not do it, what chance have *you*?'

I recoiled before the venom in her eyes but I could not put my fears into words. If this woman had been capable of murdering her sister and her lover, she would not hesitate to dispose of me. These old walls were stout, no screams of mine would reach the people going about their everyday duties in the rest of the house. Elsa was enjoying my misery.

'I looked into your room before I came here,' she said softly. 'I saw that many of the drawers were empty as though you had already made up your mind to leave. When I go back there I shall empty the rest of them and take away everything I can. The servants will be busy in the kitchens, they will not see what I am doing and I locked my bedroom door so that the nurse cannot go in there.'

'What are you going to do with me?' I croaked.

She laughed, fumbling with the keys in her hands. 'I shall leave you here, Carla, but do not worry, you will be in good company.'

For a moment I shrank back in my chair. Then, as I watched her walk away from me towards the door, I made one last try. I rushed towards her so that she spun round surprised, then contemptuously and with her superior strength she gave me a push which sent me sprawling on to the floor. Before I could struggle to my feet she had opened the door and let herself out of the room. I heard it slam in all its finality. Then I heard the key turn in the lock. I did not even waste my energy at that moment by pounding on the door.

The daylight was fading as I sat in the old, velvet chair with my head in my hands. I raised my eyes to look at Caprice's portrait. Most of it was in shadow. Only her face seemed to look out at me across the darkening room; whether it was a trick of the light or not I do not know but I could swear her eyes were filled with a strange compassion.

What had Elsa meant when she said I would be in good company? I felt the hairs at the back of my neck rise and I looked round the room fearfully. Suppose Caprice's body lay in one of these old chests on which books and other bric-a-brac had been heaped. Plaster busts of ancient heroes stood cheek by jowl beside worn-out toys. There were old trunks bearing labels from exotic places as far distant as China and Malaysia, and then as my eyes roved round the room my heart gave a quick lurch. My trunk stood across the corner with its labels from Egypt, Greece and Persia. Surely if my trunk had been brought here as recently as twelve months ago Caprice would not be in this room?

My heart lifted. If Thorn found a nurse for Elsa and they discovered my things had been packed and were gone, they must remember before long my old trunk for the rest of my things, but *how* long? I could be dead from cold and starvation days before they remembered it and Elsa was clever. I wondered idly how long it would take for me to die from starvation, and if Elsa would come when I was almost dead to drag my body to that other room where she had left Caprice.

More than anything I was aware of the cold. It entered my whole body, numbing my hands and feet until they no longer seemed a part of me and I struggled to my feet to pace about the room in an attempt to warm myself. Before me stretched the long night without a light of any kind and I began to look around for something to cover myself. After rummaging behind an old chest I came across a pair of heavy, brocade curtains. I shook them out, coughing and spluttering in the cloud of dust which came from them, and wondered which would be the greater misery, to sit and shiver under the damp feel of them or curl up as best I could without them.

I could do no more now. In the morning I would look round this grim room for anything I could find to force the lock on the door, and with the hope that springs eternal I reassured myself that I would survive the night. In the morning, I resolved, I would look for some means of escape, even if it meant piling up old trunks and furniture high enough to break the skylight above.

I had no means of knowing the time and at one stage I thought I heard rain pattering down steadily on the skylight, and a scuffling sound which filled me full of dread. There was no moonlight to penetrate the inky blackness of my prison but so amazing is the resilience of the human body that I slept, only to be rewarded by excruciating pain in my limbs when I awoke, cramped and miserable in the first, cold light of day.

Blinking, I looked round the dismal attic, incredulous until the awful truth dawned upon me and I remembered why I was here. All the horrible moments of the previous afternoon came flooding back to me. My throat was sore, like the throat which heralds a coming cold and I forced myself to uncurl my limbs so that I could walk up and down, flapping my arms against my sides to restore the circulation and warm me a little.

As I moved about the room the eyes in Caprice's portrait seemed to follow me and I paused in front of it. She looked so serious. I had always seen her laughing, her eyes gay, but for this portrait which had been meant to stand above the hall she had somehow managed to compose her features into a dignified maturity. I found myself talking to her, asking her to help me. Through the agency of two mediums her spirit had tried to warn me of approaching evil if I returned to Milverton, and now that the evil was here I had no armour against it.

I could visualize what had happened the night before in my absence. Elsa would have packed my belongings in my small case and taken them from my room. With Nancy and Kate out of the house she would have no fear of being disturbed and in any case the servants would be busy with the evening meal. I wondered why the sleeping draught the nurse was supposed to have given her had had such little effect, then I recalled how heavily she had been drugged the morning after Agnes's death. Elsa was no doubt familiar with sedatives and clever enough to fake sleep if it was required of her.

There were tears in my eyes when I thought about Thorn returning from Medchester to be informed by the Bambers that I had left the house. He would be furious with me, disappointed that I could so lightly leave my charge, sneaking away like a thief in the night without so much as a farewell to those who had been kind to me. For a while I wallowed in self-pity, then suddenly my heart lifted. They would know in the stables that I had not left by carriage. But then they would suppose that, in my new found spirit of independence, I had walked into Gleave, carrying my suitcase with me. Thorn would be incensed by my ingratitude and by my desertion of the woman he had paid me to befriend. His pride would not allow him to make enquiries in the village about my whereabouts.

The attic was becoming much lighter now and I saw from my watch that it was almost eight o'clock. I set about moving things away from the walls, throwing them on to the floor in order to make as much noise as possible, enthusiastic with my task until my eyes fell upon a large trunk standing against the wall with all sorts of objects piled on top of it. For a plit second my heart turned over as I wondered if this might be the trunk containing Caprice's body, but it was very heavy, too heavy for the skeleton of a woman and I decided that it was probably filled with old books. Old chairs, bundles of magazines, empty cardboard boxes had all been piled on top of it and these were quickly removed. I could not repress a cry of joy when I found a door hidden behind the bric-a-brac. I had to move the trunk to get at the door but try as I would I failed to drag it one inch. A rusted old padlock secured the lid firmly in place.

I battered the lock with old books and rolled up magazines but still it held, then in desperation I looked round for something heavier. My eyes fell upon a marble bust – I think it was of some long-dead Greek philosopher – but it was very heavy, so heavy that it took all my strength to reach it down from its pedestal, and I had to roll it rather than carry it over to the trunk. For a few minutes I stood there panting, struggling to regain my breath. Then, with all the strength I could muster, I lifted it as high as I could and brought it crashing down upon the lock on the trunk. It fell with a resounding crash upon the floor and rolled the length of the room but, joy of joys, the lock was broken. I listened. The noise the falling bust had made was loud enough surely to have awakened the dead lying in the little churchyard in the village, but my straining ears heard no opening and closing of doors, no voices raised in disbelief outside the attic door.

I was trembling a little as I raised the lid of the trunk, but, as I had thought, all it contained was old dusty volumes in faded leather bindings. I started to remove them one by one, dropping them on the floor with as much noise as possible, until I suddenly remembered the fragile state of the floorboards and became less enthusiastic. I could not believe that the noise I had made could have gone unheard in the rest of the house, but then when I remembered the size of it and the densely carpeted corridors which muffled every sound, my hopes faded.

It was not difficult to move the trunk once the books had been taken out – and now the door was fully revealed – a solid, panelled door with a white, china doorknob, a doorknob moreover which made no response to my eagerly turning fingers. It was locked with the same finality as the door behind me. Tears of frustration filled my eyes. Surely I was not to be beaten now after all my efforts of the morning? Determination lent me added strength and once more I picked up the marble bust, using it as a battering-ram to splinter the wood on that solid door. After the first few strikes I was exhausted, however, and sank to the floor until I could recover my breath and my strength before starting the next onslaught.

I hammered and listened, then I hammered again, and the sheer futility of my puny strength against that solid door made me so angry that at last I used all my strength to throw the bust against the door. To my utmost amazement I was rewarded by hearing a resounding crack as the wood splintered. I looked round to see if I could find something with which I could make a hole in the door large enough to insert my hand to try to open it from the inside but I only had books with which to pound upon the damaged woodwork until my poor hands became blood-raw and painful. At last I could get my hand through the door, but there was no key on the other side and weary with frustration I realized that I would have to go on pounding until there was a hole large enough for me to crawl through.

It took the best part of three hours and by that time I had neither the strength nor the will to go further. I sat on the floor gasping for breath, but for the first time since I had been lured into this terrible place I was warm.

I did not hurry. I was so sure that when I climbed through the hole into the room beyond I would find another door leading out into the corridor and freedom. I was hungry. It was now almost twenty-four hours since I had eaten anything and there was a gnawing pain in the region of my midriff. It was this feeling of hungar which encouraged me to go on and painfully I crawled through the hole I had made, tearing my skirt and bruising legs and ankles already painful from when Elsa had dragged me after her up the steps leading to the attics.

This room I now entered was smaller than the other and it, too, was lit by a skylight. I was surprised to find very little in it. My first thought was to look for another door but there was none and the disappointment was so great that I leaned against the wall, sobbing with frustrated anger. I had been so sure that this door would be my means of escape. It was useless to beat upon the other door. It was of stout, thick oak, dark with age, and any puny attempts to batter it down would have been doomed at the outset to disappointment.

Through a blur of tears I looked round the attic. The things in it were of a much older period than those in the other room and they were sadly in need of repair. There were two easy chairs which had once been beautiful, but their legs were broken, the damask which covered them was faded out of all recognition and the padding in the backs and seats hung out in several places where it had been pulled out by vermin as a lining for their nests.

An old, brass fender lay along the skirting boards, green with age, and there were old lampshades and old discarded workbaskets. I wondered why they had not been given away or thrown out as rubbish by a family as wealthy as the Lyttons, but then thought that perhaps they had merely been placed in the attic to await repair and then forgotten. The floor was covered by a layer of dust and apart from the claw-marks left by rats no human foot had trodden it for many years.

My eyes roamed round the room until they found the settle and for one terrible moment I thought I was going to faint I felt so sick. I moved towards it slowly, drawn against my will, and now I could see that it was made from old, dark oak, heavily carved and standing on four feet carved to represent the claws of a big cat. My feet took me an inch at a time and I was conscious that my hands were hurting until I realized that they were so tightly clenched against my breast that my finger-nails were biting into the flesh. I was trying not to think about Elsa's cold, pitiless face describing to me the events of that afternoon in the late summer, but at the same time my lips were pleading, praying that the settle should be empty. I could see now that the lid was slightly open and something seemed to be sticking out from under it, hanging downwards against the side of the chest. Fearfully I leaned forward to see what it was. Then, oh dear God, I realized that it was a hand, a long white skeleton hand, and on it, hanging loosely on the bleached bone, a heavy ring, curiously wrought and bearing a large, green stone. I had found Caprice.

I do not remember crossing the floor or climbing out through the hole I had made in the door into the other attic. I only remember sobbing wildly as I dragged back the trunk to stand in front of it, piling back the heavy books, standing furniture, old chairs and stools on top of it so that the door was hidden from my sight. I had loved Caprice but I could not spend the night aware of that gaping hole and the gruesome thing behind it. Elsa had not been referring to her portrait when she promised me that I should spend the night in good company.

I knew now that I could expect no mercy and in a last desperate bid to be heard I pounded with my two fists against the door crying for help until my voice was hoarse and my body exhausted. Nobody came. I wondered if Elsa had known that she had trapped Caprice's hand when she closed the lid, or if Caprice had died later after struggling to lift it. I willed myself not to think of such things, there was enough horror in the present without thinking about the evils of the past.

I could not think straight any more. I knew now that Elsa was mad with a madness so clever and so devious no sane mind would be able to follow the tortured twists and turns of her mentality. I prayed for release until I found myself babbling like a terrified child. I had no hope left and I wondered if I too would go mad before I died. Now I prayed that I might die quickly instead of by the long, lingering death she had planned for me.

The pitter patter of rain had ceased on the skylight above me and it was growing dark. I could only just see the hands of my watch and was astounded to find it was only two o'clock. I looked upwards but the skylight was strangely dark and with despair I realized that the rain had turned to snow or sleet. If it continued there would be no daylight in the attic while the snow covered the skylight.

Time no longer meant anything for it was dark all the time. My limbs ached and the cold was so intense that I curled up on the floor, whimpering like a tortured animal. Hunger and thirst were one now but they had no portion in my ultimate misery and I cannot say if I heard or only imagined that I heard Elsa's voice outside the door, taunting me softly that I would soon be dead and the echo of her laughter growing fainter and fainter as she left me to my fate.

19

The air was filled with sounds. Men's voices, sharp orders and there was light – bright, piercing light, which hurt my eyes. I could feel hands touching me, then strong arms lifted me so that I moaned at the hurt they caused my cramped and aching body. Every step caused me untold agony but I can remember now the rough feel of tweed against my cheek and the faint aroma of tobacco. I couldn't see, it seems my eyelids were stuck together by all the tears I had shed, and I could not cry out because my tongue felt huge and swollen between my dry, cracked lips.

Stupidly I wondered who carried my aching body down the steps and the long corridors of the house but eventually I could feel myself being lowered on to something soft and there was warmth, the most blessed warmth I have ever known. The voices continued but I could not hear the words they were saying. The next moment something warm and very sweet trickled down my throat. I coughed a little, reaching up my hands to grasp whatever was being held to my lips, but almost immediately a deep, langorous feeling filled my entire being as they laid me back against my pillows. I remember nothing more.

I do not know how much later it was before I opened my eyes again, but I do know that until my dying day I shall remember how wonderful and beautiful were the ordinary, everyday sounds I had taken for granted all my life. Rain pattering against the window, birds singing in the rafters, the barking of dogs, and men's and women's voices whispering about me. I lay there, not daring to open my eyes, wondering if perhaps I was dead and if I opened them I would only see angel faces looking down at me. I tried to move my legs under their coverings but, although at first they felt as if they did not belong to me, after a few moments they became free and I was able to clench and unclench my hands. Slowly I turned my head and almost immediately I heard a woman's voice saying, 'Nurse, I think she is coming round.'

I could not focus my eyes at first and there seemed to be a strange haze in the light which tortured my eyes, then all at once I was aware of a face peering down at me, a woman's face under a starched white cap with eyes that were kind and a mouth which smiled.

'Don't try to talk dear,' the face said, 'there will be plenty of time for talking when you are well.'

I turned my head away and then I saw Nancy, Nancy with the tears coursing down her cheeks and I too was weeping, for I could taste the salt on my lips.

After that first moment of waking, they tell me, I recovered quickly. I was young and my constitution was strong. I had excellent nursing and soon I was able to sit up in my bed. My heart was filled with questions but nobody spoke to me about my ordeal and I gathered the doctor had forbidden them to speak of it to me. The nurse's name was Mrs Levens and I was told that Mr Thorn had obtained her services during that fateful afternoon when he visited Medchester.

Nancy and Kate came often to sit with me, as well as Mrs Bamber, but none of them stayed too long and my questions were parried by soft words and the promise that there would be time for talk when I was better. One morning Mr Thorn came. He stood at the end of my bed looking down at me and because I had not looked into a mirror for many days it was a good thing I was not then aware of my transparent hands and thin, white face. We talked pleasantries. About the promise of spring and the return of the swallows, about the new foal in the stables and the kittens produced by Mitzie the cat. After he had gone I could feel the treacherous, frustrated tears in my eyes again, and I brushed them away impatiently. It was time they stopped treating me like a child, time they told me how they came to rescue me and what had happened to Elsa.

Miss Judith came and she, too, avoided all mention of my miseries in the old attic. She did say, however, that she and Mr Stephen were now happily settled in their own home and that I must go over to see her whenever I felt equal to the journey. There were flowers and fruit in my room from the greenhouses and each day some new magazine or book was brought for me to look at.

My health improved so rapidly that I was soon able to sit in my chair before the fire. Nancy washed my hair and that alone considerably improved my appearance, and although I was painfully thin I was eating well. Both the doctor and the nurse were delighted with my progress. None of this helped my frustration. I had quite made up my mind that at the first opportunity I would demand to see Mr Thorn and acquaint him with the full facts.

I was sitting in my chair with my hair brushed and shining and with a firm resolve in my heart that I would speak to Mr Thorn that very night when there was a knock on my door and Elsa's nurse came into my room.

She came in confidently, unconcerned, taking the chair opposite me and, fixing me with her pert, bright eyes, she said, 'I'm glad you're feeling better. You've never seen such a scare with the whole household looking for you.'

My heart raced. Here was someone willing to talk, nay anxious to talk, however taboo the subject was supposed to be.

'Did they think I had left the house?' I asked her.

'They did at first. I don't know all the details and I don't suppose I should be talking about it with you, but I'm leaving on Saturday so I don't really care if I am hauled over the coals. I think it's awful how they've hushed everything up.'

'I don't know what you mean.'

'Well, when I ask any questions, I'm simply told that you got locked in the attic by mistake and couldn't open the door it was so heavy. Mrs Bamber's out now and so is Kate – it seemed like a good opportunity to come in to see you and find out a few things for myself.'

'Well, it is true I got locked in the attic and couldn't get out. What else are they saying?'

'Well Mrs Bamber's a cagey old bird and no mistake, but she says you'd packed all your other things and taken them down to the village and you must have gone up to the attic to look for your trunk, that the door slammed behind you and because the lock was faulty you couldn't get the door open again.'

'I see. What am I suppose to have done with the keys?'

'Well, they were Mr Bamber's keys, weren't they? Besides, they were in the lock outside the door.'

'In the lock!' I cried incredulously.

'So they say. He'd been looking everywhere for them.'

I was stunned. Obviously nobody knew the truth of the matter and although they had nursed me carefully and been kind to me they could have no great opinion of one who meant to leave the house at a time to suit herself and was not averse to borrowing the butler's keys without his permission in order to busy herself in the old wing.

'I say, I hope I haven't upset you. You are looking quite pale.'

'I expect I am still feeling a little weak. How is Miss Elsa?'

'I'm glad to be leaving, I can tell you. The night they found you she finally went over the edge and now there's no doing any good with her. The doctor keeps her sedated most of the time.'

'I see.'

'Mrs Levens has been brought here to look after her when I'm gone but I can't see there being much for you to do when you're well enough to go back to work.'

'No, I expect I shall have to seek another post. Do you remember the afternoon you went into Feltham, and you said you would be giving Elsa a sleeping draught? Did you give it to her?'

She puckered her brow in an effort to remember. Then suddenly it cleared. 'Yes, I gave it to her in some warm milk after breakfast, I left her drinking it while I took the breakfast tray down to the kitchens.'

'How was she when you came back?'

'Sleeping like a baby. I needn't have worried after all, but I wasn't late and Mr Jeremy met my train.

'I wonder how they came to search for me.'

'Well, I don't really know. I remember we all thought you'd left of your own accord so I don't really know what put the idea into Mr Thorn's head to have the house searched. It was Mr Thorn who carried you down from the attic and Mr Jeremy who rode into Gleave to fetch the doctor. Bamber said if you had stayed there another day you would probably have been dead, from cold, hunger, fright. I can tell you it was a night to remember.'

I shivered despite the warm glow from the fire.

'You said that was the night Miss Elsa got worse?'

'Yes. She started screaming and throwing things about. It took three of us to hold her while the doctor gave her an injection. She's the last mental patient I shall nurse I can tell you.'

Elsa had known they were looking for me and she was afraid. She had faked a childlike insanity for so long that she would not be defeated by it now. As I sat staring into the fire after the nurse had left me I heard again her calm, faintly amused voice relating to me the tale of her old wickedness.

I could walk about my room now with slow, halting footsteps, but every day they were becoming steadier and soon I was hoping to walk as far as the kitchens and into the library perhaps.

Mr Jeremy came to see me – a quiet shame-faced Mr Jeremy, who brought me chocolates and flowers and talked to me about dogs and horses. Not once did he speak of my intention to leave Milverton, and I felt that inwardly he blamed himself for my anxieties about my future.

I had no doubt that Elsa had returned to the attic to leave the keys in the lock of the attic door, and bitterly I wondered if I would have any armour against her when the full story was told. She had not swallowed the sleeping draught the nurse had left with her, any more than she had swallowed it on the night Agnes met her death, and for the first time I genuinely wanted to leave Milverton, to get away, right away into the fresh air and the clean, blustery wind.

It was several days before I fully realized that only Elsa and I knew the true story of Caprice's death. They told me that Elsa was constantly sedated but I knew of two other times when she was supposed to have been sedated and I also knew something of her iron will. I troubled the servants by my fetish for keeping the door locked but I knew she would have no hesitation in killing me to stop me telling the truth. Her madness was a sickness but it was also a loophole, and my first tentative steps outside my room found me looking this way and that, my ears strained for any unusual sounds. I am convinced that the servants thought my sojourn in the attic had made me a little mad also.

As the days wore on I became more confident. My door was kept locked in accordance with my wishes and I confined my walks to the kitchens and Mrs Bamber's room. I was feeling much stronger now and anxious to get fully dressed so that I could venture out into the park when the weather was fine. Mrs Bamber assured me that there was plenty of time for that, but I did not see why they should continue to cosset me now that my employment had come to an end.

One day, shortly after lunch, I decided that it was time I visited Mrs Lytton. She had sent me flowers during my illness and messages written in her neat handwriting and now I was rewarded by seeing her welcoming smile as I took my seat beside her chair.

She started to write as soon as I sat down and when she handed me her pad the words she had written caused me some dismay.

'You must take care, Carla. Be vigilant.'

She was regarding me with sad, steady eyes and I could not help wondering how much she knew or suspected. I rose to my feet, saying that I would allow her to rest and return to my room where I had letters to write, but as I spoke to her I saw her face change from friendliness to terror. She shrank back against her cushions with dilated eyes and I spun round to find Elsa standing in the doorway looking at us with the utmost malignancy.

She advanced into the room, her hands behind her back, her steps measured, and I stepped back, wondering which way I could run to evade that purposeful stalking, as of a predator after its prey. I ran towards the windows but she came after me, bringing her right hand from behind her back and I saw that she carried a long, curved knife which she must have drawn from its sheath, for there were many of these weapons hanging on the corridor walls throughout the house. The old lady had risen from her chair and was trying to reach the door but Elsa held her struggling until she became limp in her arms. Contemptuously she allowed her to fall to the floor, then she continued to come after me and when I remembered the maniacal strength in those long, steely fingers I knew I would have no armour against the hatred I saw in her eyes.

She stood between me and the door. She was laughing, so softly but so venomously that it frightened me more than the knife in her hand, but even as she held me with the knife poised above my head I wondered desperately if Mrs Lytton had only fainted or whether she had had a heart attack.

Elsa's hand was on my shoulder, hurting me cruelly, but I knew that my puny pressure on her arm could not keep the knife from my breast for very much longer. By the mercy of God, I heard footsteps running across the hall and next moment Thorn was there, followed by Jeremy. He caught her arm and for one terrible moment I saw it flash downwards towards his face, then he had overpowered her and the knife, bloodstained, lay on the carpet. It took both Thorn and Jeremy to hustle her, protesting obscenely, from the room and I wondered how badly she had hurt him.

I crouched besides Mrs Lytton. Her face was waxen pale, but to my joy she still breathed. I did not want to risk lifting her on my own but next moment her nurse was there as well as Mrs Bamber and together they carried her to her chair.

That night Mr Thorn sent for me.

I found him standing on the hearthrug in his study looking down into the flames. He stood very still but there was about him such an air of defeat that my heart ached for him. He looked up as I entered and the great dog left his place on the rug to rub his head against my knees.

Thorn pointed to a large, leather chair drawn up in front of the fire saying, 'Sit there, Miss McAllister, where I can see you.' Unhappily I wondered if I had imagined that he had ever called me Carla.

When I drew closer to him I could see that he wore a dressing upon his right cheek and I exclaimed in consternation.

'It is nothing,' he said irritably, 'a scratch, that is all, it could have been much worse. Tell me, Miss McAllister, what were you doing in the attic of the old wing?'

Although I was astounded by the abruptness of his question, I parried it with one of my own. 'First, Mr Thorn,' I asked, 'will you tell me how you came to look for me there?'

He frowned. 'I will tell you. Nancy reported to Mrs Bamber that your belongings had gone from your bedroom and that your hand luggage was missing. Your outdoor garments had been taken from the wardrobe and naturally we assumed that you had left the house. I questioned Painter and the stable hands but they confirmed that you had not left the house by carriage. The afternoon was fine and we naturally assumed that you had walked into Gleave since your case could not have been heavy. To be frank I was annoyed with you and so no search was made for you in the house. My brother Stephen, who was having dinner with me, pointed out that you could not possibly get a train out of Gleave that day for Medchester and so we assumed you would be spending the night with friends in the village. I was so very angry with you, Miss McAllister, that I decided if you were as desperately anxious to leave Milverton as that I would make no effort to prevent you.'

'Why, then, did you search for me?'

'Mrs Bamber informed me that your wardrobe was still filled with your clothes and that your trunk was in the attic. Either you would have to ask for them to be sent on to you or you would return to collect them. Either way, since you had not had the courtesy to provide me with a forwarding address, I decided to do nothing. That morning I had to go into Gleave to meet a business associate, and we lunched at the inn. Dining there was a man I had met many years before and he came to my table to make himself known to me again. We talked about you, Miss McAllister.'

'About me!'

'Yes. He told me he had travelled with you on the day you arrived to take up your appointment and had seen you several times since.'

'Was he a big man with a bald head and a smooth, clean-shaven face?'

'Yes. His name is Colonel Fielding, late of the Indian Army, an uncle of the young man who was once engaged to my wife.'

My eyes flew open in startled surprise, and one more piece of the jigsaw fell into place.

'That is why he knew so much about Milverton, ' I said softly. 'He said he had friends in the vicinity but I always felt it was more than that.'

Thorn smiled a little then, his old taunting smile. 'When I told Colonel Fielding that you had left us in somewhat of a hurry he seemed surprised, then he told me how vehemently you had defended both me and my family, and he could not believe that disloyalty was one of your besetting sins. Because of his words I decided to ask your friends in the village if they had seen you. I visited Mr Fellows, the vicar, and together we went to see a Mrs Merriweather who informed me that she had not seen you for several days. It seemed that you had disappeared without a trace and it was your friend Colonel Fielding who urged me to search further, and my mother who begged me to search the house.

'Your mother!'

'Yes. I found her very frightened and as soon as she saw me she handed me her pad on which she had written the words, "Search the house". You know the rest, but now I want to know what you were doing in the old wing. I cannot believe it was your trunk you went to find.'

I told him everything. From the night I arrived at Milverton and saw lights in the windows of the old wing in the dead of night, and heard the sound of a woman's laughter while the rest of the household slept. I told him how I had stood in the darkened room shielded by the cutains, not knowing that it was Agnes who had come to stand beside me. Indeed I kept nothing back until that morning when I removed Mr Bamber's keys from the kitchen wall. Then my voice faltered.

'If you were so interested in the old wing of the house, why did you not ask me to show it to you, that way there would have been no danger of finding yourself locked in.'

'May I go on, sir?'

'By all means, but you must surely have been disappointed in the rooms of a house which have not been used for a great many years.'

'One suite of rooms is still beautifully furnished, sir, and have been left as if they were to be occupied tomorrow.'

His face flushed darkly.

'I know about those rooms — it was a foible of my wife's in the early days of our marriage that they were to remain as they are. I never visit them and nor does she to my knowledge. No doubt Bamber sees that they are kept clean although I gave instructions that they were to be sealed off when the floorboards became dangerous in the corridors.'

'The door was locked, sir, but I entered with the aid of Mr Bamber's keys. They are beautifully furnished and apart from the cold could have been used as frequently as the rooms in this part of the house. I believe now that Agnes kept them clean. The wardrobes are filled with gowns and the chests are full of underclothes. On the dressing table are the toiletries which belonged to Miss Caprice and when I looked at them I wondered if the rooms were a shrine to her memory, or a museum for posterity.'

He was angry and for the first time I did not care. I had suffered in this house, as a result of my curiosity it was true, but even now he did not know the extent of my suffering nor who had caused it.

His dark face was hawk-like and angry as he asked, 'And what conclusions did you reach?'

'There was not time to reach a conclusion. When I returned to the sitting room to let myself out by the door, your wife was waiting for me.'

'My wife!'

'Yes, Mr Thorn. But she was not the Elsa I had come to know over the last few months. This was a very different Elsa who confronted me. She could talk intelligently and calmly, though with a greater madness than any she had shown to me before. I had to stand before her while she made me listen to a tale of great wickedness and then, when it was told, she informed me that she could not allow me to remain alive to repeat it. It was Elsa who locked me in the attic and she took me there on the pretext of looking at the portrait of Caprice which is in there.'

'You are accusing my wife of locking you in the attic? But the keys were in the door !'

'Then she returned to put them there. You look at me as

though you do not believe me, and I know it is hard to believe ill of one who is close to you. Nevertheless I can prove that the things Elsa told me were true. Go back to the attic, but do not go alone. Take Mr Bamber with you, for what you will find there will cause you much distress. Behind the trunk and the pile of old chairs you will find a door which I managed to splinter, making a hole in it large enough to crawl through. In that attic there is an old settle and if you will open it you will find all the evidence you need to enable you to believe my story.'

'But what in heaven's name is in there?'

'Caprice is in there, where Elsa put her on that afternoon Caprice was supposed to ride out on to the moors with her lover. That boy was never her lover. How could you ever have believed that she ceased to love you? Elsa wanted you and she killed Caprice to get you. She must always have been mad, mad or evil, I do not know the difference as yet.'

He was looking at me with such bewilderment I thought he must surely be thinking that I too was mad, then slowly his expression changed and with quick strides he was pulling the bell rope besides the fireplace.

In answer to his summons Mr Bamber came and the orders he received sent him hurrying in search of lanterns to light their way into the old wing.

'Stay here,' Thorn commanded, 'and I will ask Mrs Bamber to remain with you until we return. There is a key in the lock, use it.'

In silence Mrs Bamber and I sat together, one on either side of the fireplace with the dog lying between us, his sad intelligent eyes perplexed, as though some of our anxiety stirred his canine sensitivity. Now and again I saw her look at me questioningly but I continued to sit looking into the fire; my ears straining for sounds to indicate that they might be returning. It was not for me to inform Mrs Bamber why she had suddenly been summoned to the sitting room, or why her husband had been instructed to accompany Mr Thorn into the old wing. She would know soon enough.

It seemed like a thousand years before we heard Mr Thorn's voice outside the door telling us to unlock it.

I shall never forget his face, for in that moment when I opened the door he seemed to have aged twenty years.

There was dust on his hair and on his shoulders, but the dust was no greyer than his face. Never again do I want to see such tormented anguish in the eyes of another human being. I held out my hand to take his arm and I could feel him trembling as I pushed him down into a chair. The dog whimpered, laying his head on Thorn's knee, his dark brown eyes looking up at him sympathetically, and Mrs Bamber hurried to the table to pour out a stiff glass of whisky which he drank neat in one quick gulp.

He sat with his head in his hands and after a quick look at me Mrs Bamber left us, no doubt to see if her husband would inform her of the results of his night's work.

I sat opposite him, quietly, not wishing to intrude on his misery, but it was a considerable time before he could pull himself together enough to sit back in his chair and meet my eyes.

'It was Caprice?'

He nodded, opening the palm of his hand to let me see what he held. It contained two rings, her engagement ring of diamonds surrounding a large sapphire and the emerald in its curious setting.

We stared at each other for several moments before I asked, 'What will you do?'

He seemed by a determined effort to pull himself together. 'First thing in the morning I must send for the police. This is not something which can be hidden.'

'And Elsa?'

'I do not know. I am sorry, Carla, but you will be asked to give evidence and it could be very distressing for you. Once again the village will be crowded with reporters, it will be in all the newspapers, but remember that you will be on oath to tell the truth. You must spare neither myself nor my family nothing in the telling of this tale. For Caprice's sake, the truth must be told.'

'The truth will not bring her back.'

'Nevertheless, it must be told. Men have looked at me in pity because they believe the woman I loved had played me false. In this house her name was never mentioned – at first because they knew it would give me pain and later because her name spelled such wanton wickedness all the ills which befell us were laid at her door. You believed in her, Carla.

Why? You scarcely knew her.'

So I told him how right from the very beginning I felt I had been drawn to Milverton for some other purpose besides the duties he was paying me for. I told him about the messages I had received from the two mediums in Medchester and finally I told him how my lonely imaginative childhood had seen in Caprice an elusive rarity, a radiance which had coloured my most impressionable years. As I talked I saw his eyes soften and much of the pain left his face.

'Are you trying to tell me that you believe it was Caprice's spirit who came to warn you and to ask you to find out the truth?'

'I know you find that hard to believe, as I did, but she warned me of evil and I found evil. She said it was still here in this house and that it had not died with her because she had never been the perpetrator of it. She asked me to find out the truth and now that I have done so I pray to God that her spirit can find peace at last.'

I rose from my chair and he rose also so that he stood looking down at me, his face still wearing a strangely bemused expression.

He held out his hand and gently touched the side of my face.

'Your time in this house has brought you little happiness Carla, yet on that first evening when I found you asleep in the library you seemed even then to be a part of Milverton. I remember how resolute and determined you were to make a success of the position I was offering you, but even then I was afraid it would defeat you.'

'There were times when I was happy here.'

'No, Carla, as I told you before, that was never happiness, you were only a little less unhappy. Lately when I have looked into those level, grey eyes of yours I have seen again that little girl Caprice and I found hiding in the rhododendron bushes. I remembered your thick, gold pigtails and your starched pinafore and those ridiculous, black-ribbed, woollen stockings, for that little girl's face wore the same wide-eyed look of courage. You will need to draw upon a little more of that courage in the next few weeks, my dear. Caprice will have to be buried, probably in the churchyard at Sutton where they buried Agnes. You will be talked about and stared at, the police will be here asking their questions and after what you have already gone through I wonder if you will be able to face more.'

'I shall face it, Mr Thorn. Whatever happens in the future the worst is clearly over. What will happen to Elsa?'

'I do not know.'

'But they cannot take her to prison.'

'She killed Caprice and she tried to kill you. She killed the man who loved her, and she destroyed my hope of happiness. Can we really afford to be generous and ask the courts to show her mercy?'

'But if she is insane they cannot take her life, can they?'

'Perhaps not. There will be a wealth of evidence in support of her insanity and no doubt she will be able to hide behind it in this instance as she has so many times before.'

'Will they take her away?' I faltered.

'Oh yes, they will take her away, and what becomes of her after that. . . .' He shrugged his shoulders, afraid to finish the sentence he had started.

There was no pity in his face for the woman he had married but how could I blame him for that? She had taken the life of the woman he loved and by her act she had robbed him not only of Caprice but also of his faith in her, diminishing his manhood, robbing him of his pride.

Miserably, without looking at him again, I turned slowly away and left him alone with his thoughts.

20

As Thorn had predicted there were giant ordeals to overcome during the weeks that followed. An inquest on Caprice's remains proved that she had met her death by knife wounds and in due course her funeral took place on a clear spring day in the little churchyard at Sutton. Her father attended the funeral – a tired, old man burdened by grief – but not her stepmother. She, poor lady, suffered a stroke from which she never recovered and went to the family vault a week before Caprice.

I only saw Elsa once. She walked down the staircase at Milverton between two police constables followed by a nurse from the sanatorium where they were taking her. She was calm, her lovely face as childlike and innocent as a girl going to her first ball. Thorn was not there to see her leave but as she passed me in the hall she looked straight into my eyes and I trembled. I saw no madness in her eyes, no wildness, only bitter amusement and as I turned away to walk up the stairs I heard Miss Judith who had been standing beside me, draw in her breath sharply. She too had seen that strange look of sinister humour and I wondered if she thought as I did, that Elsa did not deserve to cheat death.

There was nothing left for me at Milverton. I realized that when I left the crowded courtroom in Feltham on the last day of the inquest. I had sat between Mr Thorn and Mr Jeremy every day of the hearing, aware of eyes boring into the back of my head, acutely conscious of the silence when I took my place on the stand and began to speak. Not once did Thorn raise his head to look at me but I answered the questions put to me simply and truthfully as he had asked me to do.

There was a sudden burst of conversation when he took his place on the stand, but it was immediately silenced by the stern voice of the magistrate. The verdict was not unexpected, indeed there could have been no other, but the reporters left their places to rush out into the lofty corridors and we were left to follow at a slower pace.

I stood in the late afternoon sunlight in the midst of a crowd milling round the little square outside the courtroom. I saw Miss Judith's face, bewildered and a little frightened, and I had no doubt that my face too wore those same expressions. People were coming from all directions to shake hands with Thorn as he elbowed his way through the crowds and we followed closely behind, not wishing to be separated before we reached the safety of the carriage.

The story was a sensation in the papers, particularly the local press, for here was a prominent county family involved in something more serious than scandal, and splashed all over the front pages were pictures of Milverton and the Lyttons. Side by side were pictures of Caprice and Elsa, with such sordid headlines as: SISTER MURDERS SISTER FOR LOVE OF COUNTY SQUIRE. Thorn tossed them aside angrily, in fine contempt at their sensationalism, but he could do nothing to prevent their publication. Even my picture appeared on the front page of the Medchester Gazette after I had given my evidence, along with veiled insinuations of intrigue. I wondered what the aunts would think about it. Already I was receiving frantic letters urging me to leave Milverton at once and return home. I could only reply that it was not yet possible to do so.

The day after the inquest I received a summons to go to the study and there I found my companion of the train standing with Mr Thorn, looking out through the window. They turned as I entered and Thorn said, 'You remember Colonel Fielding, Carla? He is leaving for the south tomorrow morning and has asked to see you so that he can say good-bye.'

He went out of the room, leaving us together and I indicated to the colonel that we should sit in the chairs facing each other. He seemed different somehow, but then I had always regarded him as a sinister creature, prowling about the countryside on peculiar errands. Now in the bright sunlight of a spring morning he appeared to be what he was, a country gentleman and a retired army man.

For a few moments only we discussed ordinary things – the weather and the promise of Easter, the views from the windows and the longing for summer. Then, when I felt there must surely be something else this man wished to say to me, he leaned forward in his chair, his deep-set eyes suddenly serious. 'I feel that in some ways I have deceived you, Miss McAllister, but you will understand there was nothing else I could have done. Now I intend to tell you why I spent so much time in Gleave where, alas, I have no friends with whom I can stay.'

'So you lied about your friends, sir,' I said, but there was no reproach in my voice.

'I shall ask you to forgive me for that, my dear, but perhaps I had better start at the beginning where all good stories start.

'As I told you, I am a bachelor and much of my life has been spent overseas – Egypt, India, the Far East, but mostly India. I had only one sister, also married to an Indian Army officer, and Perry was their son. His parents were killed in an uprising in the north of India and suddenly I found myself the guardian of a schoolboy in England. We had met, of course, from time to time, but it was a responsibility I hadn't asked for and one which worried me not a little. We corresponded, and when I took leave in England my house was his home. I was his godfather so I naturally took an interest in the boy's future and tried to advise him on a career without appearing to be too dogmatic on the subject. His mother had always hoped he would choose the diplomatic service but his father, not wishing to be in the least insistent, wanted him to go into the army. I decided to let the boy choose for himself. I was not surprised, therefore, when he wrote to me to say it was to be the army and after giving him my blessing I continued to watch his progress with interest. I won't bore you with the details of his career but the eventual outcome was that he arrived in India as a second lieutenant with the Forty-Seventh Lancers stationed at Lahore.

'There was a fair distance between us. My regiment was stationed near Calcutta and at that time he seemed as remote as he had been in England. We wrote to each other as before and from what I could gather he was entirely happy with the life he had chosen.

'I was considerably surprised, however, to receive a letter from General Langham inviting me to spend a few days holiday as his guest in Lahore. It was to be the usual thing. A tiger hunt, pig-sticking and regimental balls, and I could not help but wonder why he had suddenly invited me. I barely knew the gentleman and my nephew was a very junior officer, hardly likely to have captured the notice of the top brass so early in his career. However, I had a few days' leave due so I advised the general that I would be delighted to accept his invitation and that I would be arriving by train at such and such a time.

'I had an idea that Perry knew of my visit but even so I wrote to tell him of the invitation and asked him, if possible, to meet me at the station. He was almost the first person I saw as I stepped down from the train, looking very bronzed and happy, and with him was one of the most lovely girls I had seen for a considerable time. Amongst that crowd of dark-skinned men and women on the platform and Englishmen with tanned faces she seemed somehow ethereal. I remember that she had on a pretty, frilly thing in white and a big, white hat with streamers under her chin, not unlike the hat she is wearing in her portrait on the landing yonder, and she carried a white parasol. When he introduced her as Elsa Langham the reason for my invitation suddenly became clear. I was the boy's only living relative, and it was necessary for me and the Langhams to get to know each other if these two young people were serious in their intentions.

'The holiday was a success. They entertained me royally and to this day I have nothing but affection for the General and his wife. I do not know when I started to worry or when I began to watch Elsa more closely. She was charming and sweet-natured, lovely to look at, invariably friendly, but there was some subtle something which disquieted me. Perry adored her and thought her little less than perfect but there were times when I saw a hurt in his eyes as though she had said something particularly unkind, and others when I was conscious that behind her beautiful sweet smile there was only emptiness. I noticed other things also. At the balls and garden parties the young officers only stayed with her for a time before they moved away to dance with less pretty girls, girls they were content to remain with. She seemed to have no women friends, at least I never saw her with any. I told myself that I was a silly old fool. I had had little to do with women and didn't understand them too well. All the way back to my bungalow in Calcutta I argued that the girl was all right and that the lad had done very well for himself in finding such a treasure.

'After a few months Perry wrote to tell me that he was returning to England with the Langhams so that he and Elsa could marry in the little church in the village where she was born, and he hoped I would be on leave to attend the ceremony.

'I had not had any real leave for quite some time and I felt it a bounden duty to see my next of kin married, whatever my private thoughts might be. I have a house on the Sussex Downs, an old manor house which has been in my family for a long time and which I hoped one day would be Perry's. It is a lovely old house, not nearly so grand as this one, but one day I intended to put down roots there and, well, I won't bore you with such matters, in any case I digress from my story.

'I invited Perry and Elsa to spend a few weeks with me and it was then I think I began to see the real Elsa. She would go off by herself across the downs leaving Perry alone and miserable and I saw that beautiful face could grow suddenly petulant and sly. I have seen her cruel with animals too. My old dog Susy refused to go near her and she tormented kittens until her hands were a maze of scratches.

'By then I would have given anything to prevent their marriage, but the young seldom listen to the advice of their elders, particularly if it is against their desires. Later in the summer I was invited to Sutton to spend a few days with Elsa's parents and it was there that I met Caprice. How I wished that it had been this girl Perry hoped to marry! She, too, was beautiful, but her smile was gay and open and she was loved by all who knew her. She swept Elsa and Perry along in her wake all through that summer and I learned that Caprice and Thorn were to be married before Elsa and

Perry.

'I do not rightly know what happened between those young people after I returned to my home in Sussex, but I know that I could not believe the things I was told. I could not believe that Caprice had transferred her affections from her fiancé to Perry, and although Perry admired her he was besotted with Elsa, so much so that he did not seem to have any life of his own outside hers. Believe me, my dear young lady, since the day of my nephew's death I have followed the fortunes of the Lytton family so closely that nothing that has happened over these last few weeks has come as any surprise to me.'

'How long after the tragedy did you stay in these parts Colonel Fielding?' I asked him.

'Long enough for the inquest, that is all. Then I took my nephew's body back to Sussex and buried him with his grandparents.

'It took me a long time to settle and at first it seemed to me that my little manor house had no purpose any more. Then I returned to India to finish out my term. I have been retired seven years now but even when I came back finally to live here I couldn't erase that old tragedy from my mind. I learned that Thorn Lytton had married Elsa but I could not think that marriage to her would compensate him for the loss of that beautiful vital creature he had been engaged to. I was alone in the world and I came back increasingly to these parts to learn what I could about this house and the people in it. I was fascinated by Milverton and the Lyttons. Gleave and those dark hills held me in such a spell I had to come back to them again and again. I walked those moors until I knew every stone, every place where the walls crumbled, every burn and every clump of heather, but every time I climbed the fells my rambles always ended below Mower Gap. Sometimes I climbed upwards to stand on the edge looking down towards the tarn below, but I could never be sure, if I were not subconsciously looking for Perry's lost revolver or the girl's body. Although I knew very well constant searches over the moors had revealed nothing, I searched in the clumps of coarse grass and the leaves of the bracken and once I saw foxes and carrion crows pecking at something at the edge of the tarn. I was afraid, but I made myself go down to see what they had found but it was only a dead ewe left there after the winter snows.

'That is the end of my story, except to say that when I saw you on the train that afternoon, so young and resolute, so extraordinarily vulnerable, I wanted to warn you. I was troubled about you, I wished you did not have to earn your living in the company of one such as Elsa.'

'I have to thank you, Colonel Fielding. It was you who first begged Thorn to seach for me, you and his mother.'

'I am glad, my dear, that I was able to be of service.'

We were both silent for several minutes until he asked, 'Have you decided what you are going to do now?'

'I shall probably go to my aunt's house in Medchester, then I must look for work. Surely in all that busy, bustling city there is something I can do.'

'Will you be happy to leave?'

I turned away, my lips trembling, and when I looked at him again he was watching me with an expression of such kindliness on his face that I wondered how I could ever have thought him sinister.

'Will you allow a tired old bachelor who has had little experience with women to give you some advice, my dear?'

'Of course, but you said yourself the young rarely heed the advice given to them by those who are older and wiser.'

'Do not delay the return to your aunt's house too long. Soon it will be summer. When I was in Medchester recently there was an air of expectancy in the city streets, like the awakening to life after the long winter. In just a few weeks the childen will be sailing their boats on the lakes in the parks, the bands will be playing in the bandstands and the barrows will be piled high with flowers on the city streets. You are young and lovely. In time you will forget all that has happened to you here and somewhere there is some young man who waits to come into your life with the express purpose of making you happy.'

'You make it all sound very simple, sir, but I know it will not be so. I know the sort of person I am, I do not think I shall lightly forget Milverton or the people I have known here.'

'Not yet perhaps, but you will. Let me see, how old are

you, twenty-three, twenty-four? It is a magical age to be with all the world in front of you, whatever the torments of the past.'

I looked down at the floor. I could not answer him then because my throat ached with suppressed tears and he took my hands in his and held them for a few moments before he released them.

'I know why you are unhappy, my dear. I have watched you in the court-room these last few days, I have seen you looking at Thorn with your heart in your eyes, living his pain with him, wishing you could shield him by your love and your loyalty, but his burden is one he must bear alone. He is not for you, Carla. The scars will remain long after the wounds are healed and, whatever her sin, Elsa is still his wife. You must look elsewhere for your happiness. This is the advice he would give you, or he is not the man I think he is.'

'He will not need to give me this advice, sir, he is not aware of me as a woman.'

He smiled then. 'He is indeed a strange man if he is not, and here am I, a prosy old bachelor, telling you so.'

I walked with him to the door and stood watching his tall broad-shouldered figure marching down the drive. He would not come back to Gleave again, his mission was over. All those long years he had come back winter and summer alike, walking the fells, searching for any small thing other searchers had failed to find, listening and watching and hoping for a miracle to bring to light anything which would restore his faith in a kinsman he had loved. Now he would go away knowing that his instincts had been right about Elsa and about so many other things also. He looked back at the bend in the drive and I was glad that I had stayed at the door to acknowledge the wave of his hand before I turned to go back into the house.

I did not know what to do with myself. I had no appetite for walking, yet the prospect of sitting about the house held no attraction for me either. Wearily I climbed the stairs towards my room and for a long time I stood looking out of the window towards the fells where patches of sunlight mingled with dark blue shadows. I seemed to be standing outside myself, watching a pale girl in a blue dress with her eyes fixed sadly on a view she could not expect to see for very much longer. I was in limbo – that strange place between reality and fantasy – and my heart was immeasurably sad.

I was thinking to myself how stupid and foolish men and women could be when it came to love. If Perry had not loved so blindly he would have seen Elsa's imperfections for himself as others had seen them, and if Thorn had only loved a little more and with greater trust he would have known Caprice could never have left him of her own free will, however much the evidence spoke against her.

My trunk and my small valise stood forlornly together in the hall, waiting for the coachman to load them into the carriage. I had said my farewells to the servants and to Mrs Lytton. Nancy had wept a little and I had comforted her by promising to write to her as soon as I was settled. Mrs Bamber had thrust a packet of sandwiches into my hands to eat on the journey. Jeremy was to drive me to the station in Feltham and there was now only Thorn to speak to before it was time for me to leave.

He stood behind his desk, his hands idle before him, his thoughts far away. It was one of those spring days when a light, soft rain fell on the dark soil, the sort of rain which makes the English countryside so lush and green and, already on the grass which sloped away from the driveway, gold and purple crocuses ran riot towards the tarn. He looked up as I paused on the other side of his desk, then he came round it to greet me. He did not take my hands but we stood staring at each other like two people who had much to say but could not find the words with which to say it.

I was the first to speak. 'I am leaving now, Mr Thorn. I have come to say good-bye.'

I did not know if it was regret or pain I surprised in his dark eyes but he did not immediately answer me. Instead he picked up an envelope from the top of his desk which he pressed into my hands.

'Please take this, Carla. It is inadequate I know, but you will not wish to find employment immediately. Let your aunts take care of you for a while. Better still, find somewhere on the coast where you can get a taste of sea air to bring back the colour into those pale cheeks of yours. When you are ready to seek employment do not be afraid to write to me and I will do everything within my power to help you.'

I nodded miserably, afraid to speak, but now I only wanted to get away before he saw the telltale tears in my eyes. I bent down to make a fuss of his dog, then quickly I turned and stumbled towards the door, fumbling with the knob through a mist of tears. He was beside me, turning me to face him, holding my hands while the hot tears rolled down my face, then suddenly I was in his arms and he was holding me against him, breathing my name against my hair.

'Oh Carla, Carla,' he was saying, 'Leave this sad, old house and its sad people. Get out into the world, meet new people, see new places.'

'Please don't talk to me of new people and places,' I said between my sobs. 'I don't want to leave here, I don't want to leave you. You are part of my life.'

He held me so close I could feel his heart beating against mine. His chin rested on my hair while his hand came up to stroke it.

I had no dignity now as I entreated him between my sobs not to send me away, offering to stay at Milverton just to be beside him regardless of what the world might say, and although he held me close not one word did he say until my passionate pleading was done. Then he held me away from him and I knew when I looked into his sad, grave face that I had lost. He would not let me stay, the conventions binding us were stronger than the feelings we had for each other.

He put both his hands on my shoulders and held me away from him, looking down into my eyes.

'You would have me keep you here and have the whole county whisper about you Carla? You know what they would say? Once more Elsa would be the deceived, unhappy girl who was first driven to murder, then to madness. It would not be Caprice this time who was thought to be the evil spirit spreading her dark shadow over Milverton, it would be you they would cast in this role.'

'But, it isn't true! You know it isn't true. Why should we

care what they say when we know the truth?'

'Then I must care for you, my darling. You are such a child, Carla, a brave, courageous, headstrong child, and I am far too old for you. What if I let you stay? I may never be able to marry you. Physically Elsa is strong and madness is not a malady one dies from. For good or ill she is my wife and do you really think we could live in this house together without caring what those outside might say about us? No Carla, I must ask you to forget about Milverton and the only way to do so is to fill your life so completely with other things there can be no room left for old memories however good or bitter they happen to be.'

I turned piteous eyes upon him and although his face was grave his eyes were very tender.

'What will you do now that you are alone?'

'Work, Carla. Work very hard. The estate needs a great deal of attention as well as the house itself, particularly the old wing of the house. You must not worry my dear, life will not stop because you and I have gone our separate ways.'

I stood in the shelter of his arms with my head resting upon his breast, then I said plaintively, 'You have never kissed me. Will you not do so now before I go?'

He bent his head to kiss my mouth, tenderly at first, as he might have kissed a child, then I felt his arms tighten around me and our lips crushed and clung together as though our kiss was eternal, that nothing past or present had any meaning for either of us. It was during that kiss, in the midst of its heady ecstasy, that I knew I could not stay.

He put me away from him gently but in my bemused state I stood swaying drunkenly, feeling like a lost soul away from those strong, sheltering arms. I watched him open the door and step back to allow me to pass before him. It was as though I watched an actor performing a part in a play, as if his actions had no connection with me at all. With tears streaming down my face I stumbled out into the hall. I did not look back, but it was several minutes before I heard the library door close behind me.

The ride to the railway station in Feltham was taken in silence which neither Jeremy nor I seemed disposed to break. He waited with me on the platform until the train arrived, handing me and my valise into the compartment after he had seen my trunk safely aboard the guard's van, then he bent and kissed my cheek.

The last view I had of him was standing on the station platform, bareheaded, his dark hair stirring in the wind which swept along its length and I continued to watch him until the bend in the line hid him from my view. He had looked so like Thorn as I first remembered him that once more the stupid, treacherous tears blurred my sight.

I was alone in the compartment and for a while I gave myself up to the luxury of tears. I gave no thought to the warm, spring sunshine and the vista of the distant fells outside the window. I felt brittle, drained of emotion, as though all the world's sufferings were nothing compared to mine. Then when I thought of all the sad, lonely people there were who were ill and hungry and without hope, I felt ashamed. I was young and strong and I was returning to people who loved me. Time would help me to forget Milverton and its tragedies, time and distance. But, even as I had those thoughts, the rhythmic sounds of the engine in my ears and the banks of blue lupins on the railway embankment seemed to mock my new found composure.

21

At first the aunts lectured and exclaimed upon my appearance, saying that I was too thin, too pale and too sad, but they waited for me to tell them about my ordeal in the attics of Milverton, purposely refraining from asking any direct questions until I was ready to tell them. I didn't want to talk about it, I had no wich to keep memories alive which were painful to me but, in the end, because I thought I owed it to them, I told them a little of the horrors of those last few weeks before my departure. They listened for the most part in silence. Occasionally Aunt Maud would express her shock and Aunt Beatrice would weep a little, but when the tale was told I asked that it should never be spoken of again, that it was an experience I wished to forget and they kept their promise.

They did more than that. They asked their friends not to speak of it either, and even Dora, who came round to see me the morning after I arrived, had been admonished not to speak of it until I was ready to tell her.

They made me eat far more than was necessary and they took me to concerts and church fêtes, anything to help me forget, but Aunt Maud put her foot down when I suggested looking for work. She said it was too soon and that she would tell me when she required to supplement her income by anything I could earn and it was impossible to argue with her. So, I walked in the park where the band played every Saturday and Sunday, I watched the children sailing their boats on the pond and young lovers strolling arm in arm along the paths. It was at such times that I realized how solitary I had become. There was no young man beside me, his arm about my waist, his eyes looking down at me with tenderness and, when I saw the children run laughing towards their parents, the scene became blurred by the tears which came too readily to my eyes.

Summer arrived. I became godmother to Dora's baby and took a job in the local museum. I learned not to think of Thorn and Milverton, but the ache of loneliness in my heart did not diminish, and every now and again some small thing would bring the memories, with all their old pain, rushing back upon me.

Nearly two years passed in this fashion, and now it was autumn again. I had always loved the autumn, perhaps because I was born at the beginning of November, but the mere sight of chrysanthemums on the barrows in the city streets and the Michaelmas daisies in the park had the power to fill my heart with pain. They reminded me of Milverton. Always in the autumn these flowers had filled the huge copper urn in the hall, their heavy, showy heads exotic against the dark oak panelling, their warm strange scent clean and sharp like the scent of the sea across the dunes.

From the windows of the museum I watched the park attendants sweeping up the fallen leaves and once more the scent of woodsmoke drifted across the grass. At Gleave now the mist would hang low across the countryside at eventide, thinning out here and there in the lights from farm and cottage windows, and whoever walked along the drive which led to Milverton would hear the dry leaves crunching under their feet in that warm, scented darkness. In the forest behind the house the trees would be alive with colours of red and gold and on the moors the heather would long since have gone, leaving the bracken golden and brittle against the hillside.

The only opportunity I now had for walking through the park came on Saturday afternoons when work was finished for the day. I looked forward to this time to myself, when I did not have to make conversation and could listen to the crisp leaves crunching under my feet, my cheeks cold and rosy in the sharp autumnal breeze.

All the people I met were warmly wrapped up and the children ran ahead of their parents, laughing as they bowled their hoops along the paths or searched the branches of the horse-chestnuts for conkers. The time for sailing boats on the lake had gone and now the waterfowl had the lake to themselves, even the little boating pond had been drained of its water and was a mass of dried leaves. At the wooden café besides the lake shutters had been put up and the chairs taken in and the ice-cream seller had moved his pitch to the bridge across the river.

My walk took me beside the boating lake and through the sunken gardens, now strangely dismal with the rose trees already pruned in readiness for their next blooming and the doves huddled together outside their dove-cotes waiting for the children with their bags of corn. The main entrance to the park lay ahead of me, deserted except for the solitary figure of a man who walked slowly towards me. At first I did not take much notice of him, but then I thought he seemed familiar but it was only when he raised his hat to greet me that I realized it was Elliot Cliffe who waited for me along the path. I ran forward to meet him, my hands outstretched in greeting.

'I didn't want to stray too far from the gates,' he said, 'in case you decided to leave by a different route. I didn't want to miss you.'

'Oh, Elliot, it is good to see you,' I cried. 'How are you?'

'Well enough. I went to your aunt's house but she said you were at the museum until one o'clock. She said you would be walking through the park today with the weather being fine.

'I am glad to see you Elliot. It has been a long time, considering we both live in the same city.'

'Yes, it doesn't seem possible that we haven't run into each other at some time or another. You look well, Carla.'

I took his arm in a friendly fashion. 'I hope you are going to come back to my aunt's house to have lunch with us?'

'Well, I was rather hoping you would come and have coffee with me. I know a little place in Brunswick Street just round the corner from here. I would rather say what I have to say there than at your aunt's house.'

'You sound very mysterious.'

'I don't mean to. Will she mind you being late home for lunch? She knows I have come to meet you.'

'She might fuss a bit.'

We had no difficulty in finding a small table well away

from the rest of those still lingering over their lunchtime coffee. It was a pleasant café, with red and white check tablecloths and brown earthenware pottery. I watched Elliot closely as he spoke to the waitress. He seemed thinner, and his face had a restless, haunted look about it as though he had suffered in some inexplicable way since our last meeting.

'Well, Carla, and what verdict have you reached?' he asked, smiling gently at me.

I realized then how hard I must have been staring and blushed. 'You're thinner, Elliot, have you been ill?'

'No. I say, do you mind if I call you Lottie, I can never remember you prefer to be called Carla, and we are after all old friends?'

'Call me Lottie if it makes you feel happier. Now tell me why you suddenly want to see me after all this time.'

He smiled, his sweet remembered smile. 'Yes, well I won't keep you guessing, Lottie. I have come to say good-bye.'

'Good-bye! Why, where are you going?'

'I am emigrating.'

'Emigrating!' I wish I didn't need to repeat everything he said to me like a parrot but I couldn't believe that this was Elliot saying good-bye, telling me he was leaving England for some unknown country.

'I am going to Canada. A friend of my father's has a practice .in Hamilton, Ontario, and he's offered me a partnership. He's getting on in years and there is nothing for me here in England.'

'But you have a practice here in Medchester, your friends are here and your parents, even if they do live miles away. Why on earth have you suddenly decided England has nothing to offer you?'

'Well, I've been thinking about it on and off for a long time now, but something has happened to make me make up my mind finally. I'm not going without thinking about it very carefully first.'

'It's Rowena, isn't it?'

I saw the shadow cross his thin, sensitive face and his eyes clouded with such misery that I reached out my hand across the table and laid it on his.

'It's finally over between us. It was never any good and it was foolish on my part ever to think it could be any different.'

'But I thought she still loved you?'

'Rowena doesn't know what love is,' he said bitterly, and I recoiled from the disillusionment in his voice.

'She was always here after that weekend in Gleave. Sometimes she only came up for the weekend, at other times she stayed weeks, sometimes a month. At first she stayed with Lucy St Clare, then she bought a house not far from the surgery and spent a small fortune renovating it to her own taste. I begged her to divorce her husband but she always had some excuse or other to stay married. She said it would distress her mother who was far from well. Then her husband was ill, then she was afraid of the scandal it would cause, but she kept me hanging on. I was as much her property as her pet dog. In the end my practice began to suffer and my partners got so exasperated that they gave me an ultimatum: do my fair share or get out. Rowena didn't care. When has Rowena ever cared about anything or anybody except Rowena? She and Jeremy were cut from the same mould, only I didn't have the sense to realize it until it was almost too late.'

'She knows you are going to Canada?'

'No, but she wouldn't care if she did.'

'When did you last see her?'

'About a month ago. She came up here to take some things from the house. I didn't even know she'd sold it until she appeared at the surgery with several things which were mine.'

'But when did it start to go wrong? I was so sure after that weekend you spent at Milverton that she wanted you back, that she would leave her husband eventually and turn to you.'

'Well, in the end she has left both her husband and me. It started in the summer when she went back to attend Ascot. I didn't see her for weeks. I wrote to her but she didn't answer my letters and then when I was at my parents' home for a short holiday I saw pictures of her taken at Ascot in the *Illustrated News*. Her husband was not mentioned, it was always: "Lady Wheeldon and her escort Prince Ludwig of

Prussia". You can imagine how the gossip writers pounced on that sort of scandal.'

He took his wallet out of his breast pocket and pulled out a newspaper clipping which he passed across the table to me. It was a picture of Rowena – a lovely, laughing vibrant Rowena, elegant in her long, sweeping gown and a large picture hat crowned with silk flowers. Beside her stood a tall man of military bearing with a dark clipped moustache and a monocle. He was wearing the uniform of a high-ranking Prussian army officer and, although they were surrounded by a group of laughing onlookers, they appeared to have eyes for nobody but each other. The wording underneath the photograph informed me that Lady Rowena Wheeldon had recently received a divorce from her husband Lord Wheeldon and was expected to marry Prince Ludwig of Prussia early in the New Year.

I handed the picture back to him without words. For a few moments neither of us spoke, then Elliot said, 'Rowena will enjoy being a Prussian princess, Lottie, and we can both see that he's a handsome chap.'

There was so much bitterness in his voice that my heart ached for him and I hastened to assure him that the prince's brand of allure in no way captivated me. 'He looks stiff-necked and overbearing,' I said stoutly. 'Rowena will not get all her own way from that gentleman.'

He smiled at my rush of loyalty. 'You don't change, my dear. I remember you years ago when the village lads used to play tricks on me because I'd been sent away to boarding school and spoke with a strange accent. You always sprang to my defence, and you were so small and fearless.'

'You'll forget Rowena in time when some nice girl comes into your life. I think you're wise to go to Canada. It's a new life, a fresh start, all sorts of wonderful things are going to happen to you.'

'Perhaps. And now that I've told you all about my troubles, how goes it with you? Do you like your work and have you forgotten that ghastly experience at Milverton?'

'I haven't forgotten it but I try not to think about it. Do you ever hear of Milverton and the people there?'

He was watching me very closely and under his steady regard I could feel the colour flooding my face, wishing I

317

had left my question unsaid.

'I spent all last week at Milverton. I resigned my practice a month ago and since then I've been trying to clear up everything outstanding as well as make preparations for my journey to Canada. I invited myself to Gleave but as always I was made very welcome. The worst part of it was seeing Milverton again. It opened wounds which were beginning to heal, but I couldn't help it. I could see Rowena everywhere. In the park, on those confounded moors, in every corner of that big, rambling house. I don't think I shall ever be able to go back there, Lottie, there are too many memories.'

'My father always said one should never go back.'

I wanted to ask about Thorn, I wanted it so badly that my hands underneath the tablecloth clenched until I could feel my nails biting into the flesh. The backs of my eyes pricked with tears.

'Do you ever think of the people you met there?'

Dear God, did I ever think of them? Only every day of my life ! I nodded miserably. 'Yes, Elliot, I am always thinking of them, especially on days like this one when the park is filled with the scent of woodsmoke and the moors stand out stark and brooding on the outskirts of the city. I hope they are all well.'

'Judith and Stephen seem happy enough now in their own home and a new baby is expected sometime in the spring. You'll be glad to know Mrs Lytton is very much improved, but apart from that everything is much the same.'

I wondered why he didn't speak of Thorn and all the time I was aware of his eyes watching me closely.

'I'm so glad for Miss Judith and her husband. They need this child badly, I hope nothing goes wrong this time. Have there been other changes?'

'Well, Jeremy has gone off to South Africa. He's joining some chap he was with at Winchester in a tea planting venture. Of course Jeremy has always maintained that Milverton would never be his, so how could he be expected to have much interest in it? They're alike, Rowena and Jeremy – restless, unpredictable, uncaring somehow.'

I felt my eyes watching him with feverish excitement.

Why, oh why, didn't he stop talking about Rowena and Jeremy and tell me about Thorn? I didn't care about Rowena or what she was doing with her life, I cared even less about Jeremy and his tea planting venture, but I did care about Thorn. I wanted to know about Thorn, but it seemed that Elliot would not mention his name unless I mentioned it first.

I could hear .the tremor in my voice, despising myself for the emotion which caused it. 'And Thorn?'

'Thorn is well. He has done a great deal of work on the estate with the help of his new estate agent and is busy making changes to the house. This new man he's got is a splendid chap, very reliable. He's been a great help to Thorn these last eighteen months and Thorn has worked himself to a standstill. I can understand that, Lottie, there's nothing like hard work to help one to forget things.'

'And has he succeeded do you think?'

'Perhaps, to a certain extent. You knew of course that Elsa was dead?'

I could feel my heart lurch sickeningly in my breast and I stared at him with wide astonished eyes.

'You didn't know did you? It was in all the papers.'

'I didn't know, and nobody told me.'

'Don't your aunts know?'

'I don't know, if they did they never told me.'

'And Dora?'

'Nobody told me, Elliot. What happened to Elsa?'

'You knew of course that she was in a private sanatorium for the insane. It was evening and she was waiting for her nurse behind the door of her room. When the young woman entered with the tea tray, Elsa grappled with her, stole the keys, and locked the nurse in her room, then she ran out on to the landing and the cries and thumps on the door made by the nurse brought other nurses running to see what was happening. Elsa was at the top of the stairs by this time and she must have caught her foot on the extreme edge of one of the stairs; she plunged from top to bottom and when they got to her she was dead. Her neck was broken.'

'Oh, Elliot, that is terrible ! Was there another inquest?'

'Yes. They brought in a verdict of misadvanture. I know

the whole thing was reported pretty fully in the local papers but perhaps not in Medchester. Maybe for once the journalists thought they had had enough.'

'Poor Thorn having to go through all that wretched business again. Was he very unhappy?'

'At the opening of old wounds, yes. At the loss of Elsa, how could he be? Thorn never loved her. If she had been a normal woman I have no doubt that in time they would have made something of their marriage, but he should never have married her. It was never right to put her in Caprice's place.'

I looked down at the tablecloth miserably, seeing its red and white checked surface blurred and shimmering. Concerned, Elliot leaned across the table, his voice urgent.

'Go back to Milverton, Lottie. Let Thorn see how much you care for him. It's not too late.'

'How can I ever go back? Do I stand on the doorstep and say, I'm here if you want me. If he had been in the least interested in me don't you think he would have made some effort to come to me?'

'He probably thinks you have found somebody else. Lottie, my dear, you are not talking about a boy in the throes of his first love affair. Thorn is a man, a man moreover who has suffered more than most in the name of love. It will take years for the scars to heal, perhaps they will never do so.'

I thought about Colonel Fielding's words to me before he left the house and I recognized the truth of Elliot's words. He was looking at me from across the table with tender compassion and I wondered why we couldn't have fallen in love. We were much of an age and able to talk easily to each other. He smiled, his singularly sweet smile.

'I know what you are thinking, Lottie. I don't think there was ever a time when I didn't know what was going on behind those wide, grey eyes of yours. If you want Thorn, bury your pride. Go to Milverton, let him see that you care enough.'

'I could go next weekend.'

'Then you must. Pride is a small thing to lose for a lifetime of happiness.'

'You think I could make him happy?'

'Do you?'

'I would spend a lifetime trying.'

'Then there is nothing more to be said. Next weekend you go back to Milverton and don't let anything or anybody try to stop you.'

'There's Aunt Maud.'

'Its your life, Lottie – not even Aunt Maud can live it for you.'

'I wonder if I shall have that special kind of courage when the time comes.'

'You will have. Now let me pay for these coffees and return to your aunt's with you. We shall be in her black books if the lunch has spoiled.'

It was only after Elliot had gone that I started to worry about what I should tell Aunt Maud. I would not lie to her, but I dreaded her forthright and bitter reproaches. She would view my return to Milverton as unmitigated folly, opening everybody's mouths she would call it, as though there hadn't been enough gossip already. Cowardly, I left it until the very last minute before I told her, but I remembered her expression of astonished disbelief all the way to Gleave.

'You know what they'll say in the village, Lottie, when you turn up again?' she had said spitefully.

'What can they say? Surely I am entitled to visit people I liked at Milverton, or anywhere else for that matter without people turning my visit into something wrong.'

'Gleave is a small community and villages are full of gossips. You've made a new life for yourself, it doesn't do to rake over the past. You've got a nice job at the museum and a good home here. What do you want going back there for?'

'Please, Aunt Maud, let me do things my way. I promise not to be secretive or difficult. You may have no fear that I shall disgrace you in any way.'

After that she had offered no more words of reproach or instructions on my code of behaviour. She did, however, allow me to kiss her cheek before I departed and I escaped with such a feeling of relief I could hardly believe my good fortune.

22

It was one of those golden autumn mornings when the sun shone out of a clear, blue sky scudded with white clouds, when the cattle grazed placidly in the fields, and the broad, gentle English river which the train followed for several miles rippled and sparkled in the sunlight. There were fishermen along its banks, the hawthorn bushes were bright with red berries and the brambles heavy with fruit. The little train chugged contentedly between banks of grass and bracken which had already turned golden and soon the countryside took on the familiar aspect of stone walls and stone farmhouses leading upwards towards the sweeping fells. I was alone in the compartment, and I sat in the corner facing the engine where I could catch my first glimpse of Mower Gap rising clear and menacing beyond the pasture land and and the purple, shadowed moors.

I knew my face was intense as my eyes searched for the landscape I both feared and loved, and there was an ache in my throat when the little train rounded the bend and there, high above everything else, stark and breathtaking, the rocky fell rose crag upon crag to its majestic summit. Below it the tarn sparkled as the sun fell upon it and under the bridges we passed over ran narrow country lanes, their hedgerows bright with the tints of autumn. The reservoir was low after the long, hot summer but the water was as blue as the water on some Alpine lake and as I looked upwards a flock of wild geese flew down to settle on the water.

I was the only passenger to alight from the train at Gleave and the chill breeze which swept along the station platform made me glad of the foresight which had prompted me to wear a warm coat. I looked into the waiting room but there was no sign of life, so I sauntered towards the station entrance. It was about ten minutes' walk into the centre of the village and Milverton lay a few miles further on. I had given no thought of how I was going to get there and hoped that old George would be in his customary place outside the station. There was no sign of him, however, and I decided to walk in the direction of the village. I had only gone a few strides when I heard a voice say, 'If yer lookin' for George 'e'll be back in a jiffy.'

I looked up to find the station master standing high on the banking tying up his dahlias. He had not bothered to attend to the arrival or the departure of the train.

'T'wind in t' neet blew 'em down,' he informed me.

I stood watching his efforts to secure the flowers and sure enough in a little over five minutes I heard the rumble of cab wheels on the cobbles and the steady clip-clop of the hooves of George's patient old horse. I went back into the station and inserted a coin into a chocolate machine. The horse should be rewarded, I thought, feeling pretty confident that a bar of chocolate would be a new experience for him.

If George was surprised to see me his rheumy old eyes showed no sign. He made no effort to get down from his perch on the driving seat, but sat with his cap pulled well forward to shield his eyes from the sunlight, his long whip over one shoulder, his attire as tattered as it had been on our first meeting. I walked over to his horse and after breaking the chocolate into smaller pieces held them out to him on the palm of my hand. He took them gently and I'll swear there was amazement in his soft brown eyes.

'He's noan 'ad choclit afore,' George said, 'ad noan like 'im to git used to it.'

I decided to ignore that remark. 'Can you take me up to Milverton?'

'Ay, it'll cost twopence moer as it's Satdey,' he said.

I climbed up into the cab without answering him, then off we set towards the village. The village high street was busy with shoppers, but nobody seemed interested in George's cab. No doubt he was a familiar enough sight outside the inn and I had a vague sensation that the horse slowed his pace as we passed this establishment. The door of the cottage which had once been my aunts' had been newly painted, a dark unimaginative brown, and I could not help wondering what sort of people lived there now and if 'Old Pear' still stood guardian over the garden at the back of the house.

As we drew nearer to the gates of Milverton I decided I would not travel all the way by cab. It was a beautiful day, indeed I could not think that there would be many more such days in what remained of the year, and I wanted to savour every dip and every curve in the long drive leading to the house. I tapped on the window signalling George to stop, then I opened the door and jumped down on to the roadway.

'I think I'll walk the rest of the way, George,' I said in answer to his suprised stare. 'How much do I owe you?'

'I'll 'ave to charge thee t' full price, miss. It's noan my fault tha's decided to walk.'

'That's all right, but it's such a lovely day I feel like walking.'

I handed him a ten shilling note and watched as he counted out my change in the palm of a grimy hand, then I handed him back the twopence extra he had asked for and a sixpenny tip which he pocketed with something approaching a smile.

'Will thee want me to come back fer thee?' he asked.

'I don't know George. They're not expecting me.'

'Well, if I'm noan busy I meght 'ave a ride up later in t' day. Thee meght noa what thee's doin then,' he said, and with that encouraging remark and a crack of his long whip he turned his horse and cab round in the middle of the lane and drove off towards the village.

I walked slowly, every bend and twist in the road recalling half-forgotten memories. There was the stone wall we had sat upon as children so that we could better observe the activities of those we had been told were our betters, and there, too, was the path sloping downwards towards the shrubbery, which had added to the impetus of that errant ball. The rhododendron bushes were bare of their blossoms but their leaves shone dark and glossy bearing little relation to the forlorn shrubs I was accustomed to seeing in the gardens of city houses. I could see the mere now, sparkling and blue, and the short, clipped grass sloping upwards towards the formal gardens in front of the house. Soon the bend in the road would bring me my first view of Milverton and as I reached it I paused so that I could take in every aspect of its mellow stone and the sun shining on the panes of the mullioned windows. Smoke curled lazily from several of the chimneys and in the great stone urns along the terraces geraniums still bloomed.

It was so beautiful and so peaceful that my throat tightened and there was a blur before my eyes as the memories came crowding back one after the other. There was no sign of life around the house and on consulting my watch I saw that it was just after one o'clock. No doubt the gardeners would be eating their lunches in the barn set aside for them within the stable yard, and the family too would be at lunch. I could well imagine those workmen gathered round the huge, oak table scored and furrowed by the years, mottled with huge knots in the wood, held steady by six stout wooden legs. They would be laughing together, chatting in their broad north-country accents, their teeth biting into thick hunks of bread and cheese, washed down with mugs of strong tea or home-brewed ale.

From somewhere beyond the stables a dog barked and I wondered if it was Laird out with his master on the estate. Probably not. Now that Laird was old he preferred the warmth of the library fire and the feel of the soft rug under his ageing bones. I had seen his limbs twitching as he slept and wondered if he was dreaming of a chase across the snow-covered moors under the moonlight as he hunted for his old enemy and common ancestor, but Laird had been a past master at closing his ears to the sound of the wind as it swept across the moors and the pattering of rain on the library windows.

I walked faster now, wondering if I had been observed from the windows of the house, and as I neared the terrace I instinctively raised my eyes to see if Mrs Lytton sat in her customary place at the window of her room. I could not see her but even so I stood for several minutes before I found the courage to lift the heavy, brass knocker on the door, listening to the sound echoing hollowly through the lofty hall behind. It seemed an eternity before I heard the steady sound of footsteps approaching the door, then it swung open to reveal Mr Bamber's majestic countenance. For a moment he stared at me, then his face lit up with an unexpected smile which did much to restore my flagging confidence.

'Why, Miss Carla,' he said, and there was now no mistaking the pleasure in his voice. 'Come in, come in, I expect you are wanting some luncheon.'

'Oh no, Mr Bamber, I had something in Medchester before I left.'

'That must have been some time ago, miss. Come up to our sitting room and I'll tell Mrs Bamber you are here.'

I followed him to the back of the hall but as we passed the bottom of the stairs I could not help looking up to where Elsa's portrait had hung. Instead of it there now hung a portrait of Mrs Lytton, a very much younger Mrs Lytton, and a portrait which had obviously stood there when she was the mistress of Milverton. Mr Bamber's eyes followed mine.

'The master had Miss Elsa's picture removed, miss. It was sent to her father at Sutton, along with the portrait of Miss Caprice from the attic. The old gentleman asked for them.'

I nodded wordlessly. I could imagine the old soldier staring at the pictures of his daughters, grief-stricken by the tragedy which had linked their lives. He was old. When he looked at those portraits of his daughters, both beautiful, both so different, I hoped that he would forget the tragedy of their lives and remember the days of their childhood when they were carefree and joyful.

Mr Bamber was speaking to me, but I had to ask him to repeat his words, I had been so immersed in my own thoughts.

'I was saying, miss, that that is a portrait of Mrs Lytton painted for Mr Lytton just before their silver wedding. It is the only portrait in the house large enough to fill the empty space and it hung their originally.'

'I thought so, Mr Bamber. It is a beautiful portrait and has every right to be there. How is Mrs Lytton?'

'She is very much improved, miss, indeed you will be surprised how much improved she is when you see her. Mr Thorn is not home for luncheon, but he will be home for dinner this evening. No doubt you will join him.'

'Well I don't know, Mr Bamber. Perhaps Mr Thorn has

other plans.'

He took me straight to their sitting room, telling me to sit down and wait for his wife to come to me.

Nothing in the room had changed. It smelled of furniture polish and lavender. Everything was in its place and the fire burned brightly in the grate in readiness for their afternoon nap. The room was at the back of the house overlooking the moors and I stood for a time looking out until I could hear footsteps approaching the door.

Mrs Bamber herself brought in my luncheon tray and stood over me until every particle of food had been eaten. Then we sat together across the table and talked. Eventually, after we had discussed Elsa's death, I plucked up enough courage to say,

'I hope I may see Mr Thorn for a few moments before I leave?'

'There's nothing to stop you staying the night, miss. You can have your old room. Nancy will light a fire and air the bed for you.'

'But wouldn't that be causing an awful lot of trouble, Mrs Bamber?'

'It's no trouble at all, miss. We have the same number of servants as we had when all the family lived here, and then both Mrs Lytton and Miss Elsa gave us a great deal of trouble. They don't have half enough work to occupy their time and when they haven't enough to do that's when they get into mischief. You stay the night and let the girls wait on you for a bit.'

'Perhaps Mr Thorn should be consulted first?'

'Eh, bless you, Miss Carla, he won't mind. He won't even know you are here unless he sees you himself. Mr Thorn has never interfered with the way I've run this house and I don't suppose he'll start now.'

As she hurried away to instruct Nancy what do do with my room I wondered how I would have coped with tragedy. Would I have done what Thorn had done, involve myself in endless hours of toil so that there would be little room for anything else? Or would I have done like Rowena, who had jumped on a merry-go-round that never stopped? I suppose sufficient money did help to cushion one against life's disasters but no amount of money could restore Caprice to life or bring back the past.

I waited for Mrs Bamber to return to her sitting room, then I asked if it would be convenient for me to visit Mrs Lytton, or should I wait until later in the afternoon.

'She doesn't sleep in the afternoon now like she did,' Mrs Bamber said. 'She'll be glad to see you I know because her nurse has gone into the village and she'll be alone for most of the afternoon.'

I knocked lightly on Mrs Lytton's door, and knowing that she would not be able to call me to enter I opened it and went in. She was sitting before the fire looking into the flames, her embroidery idle in her lap. She looked up as I entered and immediately her face broke into a smile. She put her embroidery down on a stool at her side and held out her hands to me. I took them in my own and bent forward to kiss her cheek.

'How well you look Mrs Lytton!' I exclaimed, then my eyes searched the room for the writing pad so that we could converse together. It was not in its customary place on the writing desk beside the window and I felt her take hold of my skirt to pull me back.

'There is no need to search for my writing pad, Carla. I am able to talk to you.'

I stared at her in startled disbelief, my eyes open wide, then I sat down weakly on the chair beside her.

'But this is marvellous!' I said at last. 'They told me that you were much better but they didn't say you had found your voice. When did it come back?'

'It came back a long time ago, Carla, but I pretended that it had not.'

'But why?'

'Because I was afraid. Like old Emperor Claudius who pretended he was a fool because he feared for his life at the hands of his nephew, I pretended I couldn't speak because I was afraid of Elsa.'

'You suspected Elsa even then?'

'No, at least not of murder. The feelings I had about Elsa were less substántial than that. She was welcomed here as Caprice's sister. She was very pretty and the two girls seemed happy enough togther. There were times, however, when I found Elsa looking at Caprice when she thought they were unobserved, slyly, resentfully. Those big, blue eyes of hers could look so cold. I came to the conclusion that Elsa was jealous of Caprice but I couldn't understand why. She had a loving fiancé and parents who were devoted to both the girls, but one night I saw her looking at Thorn. Caprice was playing the piano. Like Judith she was very musical and a joy to listen to. Thorn was standing behind her so that he could turn over the pages and the room was full of guests. I remember that night because I felt so happy with all my family around me as well as a number of our good friends and I turned my head to smile at those nearest to me. Elsa was sitting with her mother near the wall but with such an intense expression on her face that I turned away quickly to see who she was staring at. She was looking at Thorn. After that I watched them often when they were together and I realized that it was Thorn Elsa wanted and that she hated Caprice because my son loved her.

'I knew Caprice intended to go riding the afternoon she died. She came into my room soon after lunch wearing her riding habit, she had brought some underclothing with her which had arrived from London that morning and I asked her if it wasn't a little hot to go riding. She laughed and said it would be cool on the fells and that Sultan needed the exercise. That was the last time I saw her. She was so gay, so very much in love, and I heard her going down the corridor singing to herself, completely happy. Later I heard her calling to Elsa to come upstairs and see what had arrived during the morning.'

She was silent for awhile, brooding over her memories and I was reluctant to disturb the tenor of her thoughts. I knew the subject was painful to her, yet I felt she wanted me to know the truth.

At last she spoke again.

'This was a happy household until that terrible day when they brought that boy down from the fells, then after that nothing was ever the same again. My husband had a heart attack and died shortly afterwards, then I had that terrible stroke. For weeks I was helpless, unable to move and it is true I did lose my power of speech but it came back to me with the use of my limbs. Before then I was told Elsa was to marry Thorn.

'They came together to tell me they were to be married and I remember lying in my bed like a rag doll with the tears rolling down my face. You see, Carla, I had loved Caprice so much. She was so beautiful and had such grace, but she was kind too. I'm not saying she was perfect, she was too high-spirited for perfection. She was a flirt, a tease, a piece of quicksilver, but she was young and youth is a time for such foolishness. She filled this house with so much laughter that everybody adored her, family and servants alike, then on that terrible day we all felt cheated, disillusioned, unable to love or trust again.

'Nobody suffered more than Thorn, and I suffered for him. From having everything in the world to look forward to, he had nothing. Almost overnight other troubles came thick and fast, one after the other.

'Because of my illness I knew nothing of things going on around me. My children were dutiful, they came to visit me but they were forbidden to say anything which might worry me, so instead they talked about the weather, the goings on in the village, the harvest, and during that time also Thorn and Elsa comforted each other. Ill as I was, I sensed that Thorn had changed. The gay, happy boy I remembered had turned overnight into a cynical and bitter man and I knew that the man Elsa would marry was not the man Caprice would have married.

'It was a quiet affair. It could hardly have been otherwise, but almost from the first I knew that he wasn't happy. Elsa was quite well then, at least she seemed so, but one afternoon I heard them quarrelling. They had the same suite of rooms you remember over the main hall and my own room was close by. They were quarrelling because Elsa insisted on keeping the rooms Caprice had chosen in the old wing exactly as they were and Thorn could not understand why. He said it was morbid, unnatural, and he left her screaming with temper. I do not know if the matter of the rooms was ever discussed between them again but we both know that they were kept furnished as though Caprice lived in them. I often wondered if Thorn ever knew that Agnes cared for them.'

I raised my eyebrows. 'I wondered if it was Agnes who

kept them looking so beautiful.'

'Yes. She was Caprice's maid you know, but she came to Milverton with Elsa because, like me, she sensed that we did not know the full story of Caprice's death. Like poor Colonel Fielding who came back year after year when others had all but forgotten the story in case he discovered something others had missed. Poor Agnes, she was not proof against Elsa as I was and happily, as you were also.'

Again there was silence in the room and from the expression on her face I could tell she was reliving the past all too poignantly. Then she spoke again.

'Early in her marriage Elsa would come to see me every day, but as the weeks passed and I was unable to converse with her she would talk at me, not to me, mocking my affection for Caprice until I came to dread her visits. She was obsessed by Caprice, so much so that I sensed a wildness in her, an instability that frightened me. I knew there was something terribly wrong with my son's marriage. Thorn didn't seem to want to be with her, and he used his own bedroom more and more. That told me and the rest of the household that all was not as it should be between two newly married people.

'She would come into my room and stand at the bottom of my bed, just watching me. There was a slyness about her, an evil if you like. I felt I could not stand her visits any longer and one day when the nurse came in she found me cowering against my pillows with Elsa standing over me, laughing. After that Thorn put a stop to her visits and my rooms were changed.

'When I could walk a little the nurse put my chair in the window so that I could look out across the gardens. Elsa spent much of her time sitting in the garden and she would look up at my room, never taking her eyes off me and it was then I made up my mind about what I must do.

'I thought at first that she resented me because I knew of her jealousy for Caprice and that she had wanted Thorn for herself. But now that I know the full facts I have wondered if she was afraid of how much I knew. I had been the only member of the family to remain in the house that afternoon and I suppose I could quite easily have seen Elsa ride out on Caprice's horse. They were alike in stature if not in colouring but something told me then that as long as I remained unable to speak I was safe.'

She leaned back in her chair wearily and I wondered if she was tired by her long narrative and if I should have allowed her to continue. But soon she spoke again.

'I wonder sometimes if my two younger children are lost to me now but I hope that it is not too late for Thorn to find happiness.'

I could not speak of Thorn to his mother, not, at least, about his happiness, and hurriedly, before she could speak of him further, I said, 'Mrs Bamber has said I might stay the night Mrs Lytton. If you agree I would like to do so.'

'My dear child, of course you must stay. You must not think of going back to Medchester tonight. I don't know if Thorn will be in for dinner. Sometimes he eats at the inn, sometimes he tells me that he has eaten when I know very well he has not, but he is usually in the library at about eight o'clock. He will be glad to see you, I know.'

I could feel myself blushing under her steady regard and after a few moments she said, 'I wonder if you have enough courage, my dear? You are so young and Thorn has not been a young man for a very long time. I fear he may have forgotten how to laugh and enjoy life. Are you strong enough to change things and wise enough to accept what you cannot change?'

'I think so, Mrs Lytton.'

'Do you love my son?'

'Yes, I love him. One day I will tell you about the strange fate which seemed to bind me to this house and the mission I was given to discover the truth. I may never be able to erase Caprice's memory from his heart but I feel I could go to him with her blessing and her help.'

She looked at me without speaking for so long that I wondered if I had been presumptuous and said too much. Then she drew my face down to hers and kissed my cheek.

'Have you brought a change of clothing?' she asked. I was taken aback by the question.

'No, I thought I would be returning home tonight.'

'Go to Rowena's room. The wardrobe is full of gowns she has decided not to take with her and the drawers are bursting with her underclothes. Don't be afraid to take whatever you need for the night, and choose the prettiest gown you can find. I want you to make yourself beautiful for my son.'

I bent forward and kissed her cheek again. 'I will let you see the gown I have chosen. I would like it to have your approval.'

I went directly to Rowena's room, surprised to find it aglow with the late afternoon sunlight. The room had been polished and dusted after her last visit but it seemed entirely impersonal now. Rowena was not a tidy person and whenever I had caught a glimpse of this room through the open door there had been articles of clothing thrown on the bed and shoes hurriedly kicked off on the moss-green carpet. The wardrobe contained six gowns but, as Mrs Lytton had said, the chests were filled with beautifully embroidered silk and satin underwear. I selected a night-dress and robe in heavy blue satin, then turned my attention to the gowns.

I wondered how Rowena could have dared to leave such dresses behind. To my mind it was highly unlikely she would find anything more superior in Germany. There seemed to be countless numbers from which to choose, but at last I selected a gown in black velvet. It had a long, narrow bodice and sleeves that were tight to the elbow, then fell away to reveal the lower arms. The graceful skirt was slender at the front but fell away into great folds at the back. The neckline was cut low but it was edged with a band of sable and there was sable, too, round the edges of the sleeves. I knew as I held it up in front of me before the long mirror that it flattered my fine, fair skin and heavy, blonde hair. I completed the ensemble with a pair of black, silk slippers. I needed no jewellery, the rich fur should not be asked to vie with the sparkle of gems.

I took the things I had chosen back to Mrs Lytton's room so that she could give me her opinion. When I held the gown against me she said, 'It does you more than justice, Carla. I never liked Rowena in black but she bought a great deal of it after her husband's uncle died.'

'Perhaps she intends to send for them,' I said doubtfully.

'I don't think so. I know my daughter very well. Rowena

has never had any thought for money, she will discard her gowns as cheerfully as she has discarded her lovers. You need not look so shocked my dear, I know more about my daughter's affairs than the family give me credit for.'

It seemed strange to be wandering along the corridors of Milverton now that I was no longer part of the household. My eyes lit up with pleasure on entering my room. There was a bowl of late summer roses on the dressing table and the fire danced and crackled in the grate. The room looked just as it had on the morning I left it but I noticed that several new books had been placed in the bookshelves and whoever had laid the fire had set out clean towels and fresh water in the pitcher.

I still had several hours to kill before Thorn's return. I couldn't don my new finery and hang about waiting for him; on the other hand, I could not ask the servants to serve me in the dining room in solitary state. I decided I would eat dinner in my room but by this time I was beginning to have second thoughts about the wisdom of my visit. I looked out into the garden which skirted the old wing, surprised to see that already half the stonework had been cleaned and now matched the rest of the house. Squaring my shoulders I made up my mind that I would see for myself the changes that had been made. The late afternoon sun hung like a crimson ball in the western sky and I realized that if I wanted to see the rooms in the old wing before twilight I would have to go immediately. In spite of the renovations I was reluctant to spend one single minute there after dark.

The knob on the door responded instantly to my touch and I looked round the wide corridor with delighted surprise. Velvet drapes in rich, figured velvet hung at the tall windows, their pelmets edged with heavy fringes and the floorboards under my feet had been cleaned and polished until they shone. On the dais at the head of the room stood a grand piano as well as numerous music stands. Small gilt chairs and tables, and velvet-covered sofas in pale blue were ranged along the walls. Once more this wide corridor had become a ballroom and now there was no dust marked by tiny hands. The skirting boards were new and shining along the walls and overhead four crystal chandeliers, identical to those in the other rooms of the house, hung suspended from the ceiling.

This is what is must be like, I thought, to discover an unrifled tomb and wander enchanted through chamber after chamber in search of the ultimate perfection. Everywhere there were thick carpets under my feet and satin damask papered the walls. The room where Agnes and I had held our breaths behind the curtains were unrecognizable. Gone was the dark blue wallpaper, replaced by pale turquoise and on the floor from wall to wall was a new Chinese carpet in shades of blue and rose. The heavy, dusty, velour drapes had been replaced by Chinese silk and the room smelled fresh, as though the decorators had only recently completed their work.

I stood with a beating heart for a long time before I found the courage to enter the rooms Caprice had furnished, but I forced myself to enter. The carpet, the curtains, the furniture were as I remembered it. Perhaps the furniture had been rearranged slightly but that was all. The deep velvet chair where Elsa had sat still stared at me across the room and so weird was the feeling of unreality that came over me I leaned back trembling against the door.

Sternly, I made myself go into the bedroom beyond and here again everything was as I had last seen it except that now Caprice's toilet things had gone from the top of the dressing table and only the heavy, cut-glass jars and bottles remained. I opened drawers and cupboards but they were empty. Nothing of Caprice remained in these rooms now.

I stood at the door looking back at the beautiful bed which Caprice and Thorn would have shared, at the view through the windows which Caprice had so loved, and I could feel the back of my throat prick with unshed tears, but it was only when I reached the door leading to the corridor beyond that I felt the first sensation of fear. My hand had been on the doorknob that afternoon when I heard Elsa's voice in the room behind me, and I could hear it now – taunting, high and clear in the empty room. Quickly I spun round to gaze back at that velvet chair, but it was empty, merely a chair, beautiful but impersonal. My heart was beating painfully in my breast as I stumbled out into the corridor pulling the door shut behind me. I stood for a few moments to allow the fear to pass, reflecting painfully on how one's imagination can play tricks. Then, squaring my shoulders, I went on to see the rest of the wing. Elsa had not been able to defeat me in life, and I was determined that she should not defeat me now that she was dead.

Some of the rooms were still locked and I thought that these rooms had probably not yet been touched so I retraced my steps to the hall where the steps led down to the kitchens and the others led up to the attifcs. I willed myself to climb up those stairs and as I reached the landing the door of the attic stood open before me. The walls had been painted with fresh white paint and in the light coming from the skylight they had taken on a faintly pink hue from the setting sun. The old rocking-horse was still there, retained no doubt for purely sentimental reasons. But many of the trunks and pieces of broken furniture had gone. Gone too was Caprice's portrait and there was now no door leading from this attic into the next. The attic which had been Caprice's tomb would remain closed for as long as Milverton would stand.

There was nothing more for me to see and purposefully I made my way back through the old wing and the other part of the house to the rooms that had been Elsa's. My hand was trembling as I turned the knob on the door but I forced myself to open it and enter the room. I stood in amazement in the centre of the floor with the door open wide behind me. It seemed to me that every trace of Elsa had been deliberately removed from that room. The furniture, the carpet and drapes at the windows, the colours, even the fireplace was different. It was the same in the bedroom beyond and in the smaller room which Agnes had used. The drawers and wardrobes were empty but more than anything it was the doll's house I missed. Without it the sitting room looked enormous, its proportions elegant and uncluttered. I had always thought that somehow the doll's house had a life of its own. I was afraid of it, and now that it had gone the memory of Elsa seemed to have gone with it. At last I could look at the beauty of the room without thinking it sinister.

It was dark outside but a pale misty moon shone over the parkland, shimmering in the waters of the lake. I had eaten my evening meal and wondered how long I must wait before I could go down into the hall to see if Thorn had arrived back. I had almost lost courage and decided to go to bed. when I heard the distant clatter of horse's hooves along the drive.

I stood on the staircase with my ears straining to hear any sound from the direction of the library but all I could hear was the sonorous ticking of the grandfather clock and the thumping of my own heart. I was about to go on when I heard a faint click from the drawing room door then firm footsteps crossing the hall in the direction of the library. Only one chandelier burned at the top of the first landing and the wall lights in the hall below. Much of the hall lay in shadow and only one ray of light streamed out from the open library door. I was halfway down the stairs when I heard a sound and next moment Laird was there, peering up at me. There was menace in his stance until suddenly he recognized me and the low growl in his throat became a shamefaced grimace and he wriggled his body in an attitude of greeting.

Thorn's voice came from the library. 'Laird, where are you? Come here, old boy.'

Instead he came to me, loping up the stairs, thrusting his long shaggy head into my hands. Thorn came to the bottom of the stairs. Our eyes met over the dog's ecstatic body, mine filled with pleading, his with astonishment.

He was the first to gather his wits. 'Why, Miss McAllister,' he said, 'this is a pleasant surprise. Come into the library and join me in a glass of sherry,' and my heart sank dismally.

I passed in front of him, the dog at my side, and heard the door close with a sense of finality behind us. He moved over to a tray of drinks standing on a small table near the wall and in a matter-of-fact voice said, 'Perhaps you would prefer something else. Whisky or brandy?'

'No, thank you, Mr Thorn, sherry will do quite well.'

He poured sherry out for me and a brandy for himself, then he brought the drink over to my chair. He smiled down at me, the faintly humorous, taunting smile which twisted my heart.

'You should have let me know you intended to visit us, Miss McAllister, and then I would have made a point of being at home to have dinner with you. I must ask you to forgive my riding habit but I have been over at Colonel Hesketh's and he insisted I stay to dine with him. I must say you are looking very beautiful; it is a pity there was no one to enjoy sitting opposite you at the dining table.'

'I dined in my room, Mr Thorn. Your mother said I might stay the night and this is Miss Rowena's gown which she kindly said I could borrow.'

'Then it does you justice. You are looking well, charmingly well. It is apparent that your life in Medchester agrees with you.'

I did not answer him. He had stated a fact, he was not looking for a reply. We sat before the fire, he on one side of the fireplace, me on the other, and the dog sat beside my chair his head against my knee.

'You have evidently made a conquest,' Thorn remarked. 'Laird is particular where he gives his affection, or at least I had thought so until I learned he had been foolish enough to sire a litter of puppies on Painter's old bitch Dolly. He should have had more sense at his age.'

I sat stiffly in my chair, my hands clasped together in my lap. Had I come all the way from Medchester to listen to talk of Laird's prowess as a sire for Dolly's offspring? How much longer could I remain to watch his cool, impersonal face and listen to his banal attempts at conversation?

'I have been round the house since I arrived,' I ventured. You have made great improvements to the old wing, the rooms are beautiful.'

'You liked them, did you? Well I must say I am quite pleased with what has been accomplished so far but there is still much to do. You had apparently no fears of entering the old wing?'

'Yes, I had fears, but I told myself I should overcome them.'

'That was very brave of you, but it is the only way. If you fall off a horse you should get right back on and ride him. If you are afraid of shadows you should face them. But then I never doubted your courage, Miss McAllister.'

'What happened to the doll's house?'

'I sent it to a museum in France. I heard about it from a friend of mine. It is a museum which specializes in toys of all descriptions and they were glad to have it.'

'They must have been, sir. It was very beautiful.'

'An expensive toy, but it would have been a pity to let it deteriorate in some dusty attic where most likely it would have been forgotten in time. Children will see it now and children will know how to enjoy it.'

'I was happy to see that Mrs Lytton is so well and that her speech has returned.'

'Yes indeed, that was splendid news.'

For a few minutes we did not speak and he sat watching me, warming the brandy glass in his hand. He was the first to break the silence.

'It is nice of you to come to see us again, and during the weekend when I am sure there are so many more enticing things to do. I am sorry you will not be able to see Judith, unfortunately we do not expect them this weekend.'

'No, I am sorry. I did not come to see Judith.'

He raised his eyebrows, maddeningly, and there was no denying the cynical amusement I saw in his eyes as he sat leaning back indolently in his chair, idly turning the glass in his hands.

'I dare not assume that you came to see me, Miss McAllister?'

From that moment I wanted to escape from the room, to flee across the hall and up the stairs to my room, anywhere away from this man with the cool, aloof expression on his face and the indifference which showed all too plainly that he had forgotten that morning when he made me believe he could love me.

I could not mention Elsa, her name would stick in my throat. She was dead but her death had caused him little sorrow. No, it was Caprice, always Caprice, dead, too, but chaining him to her still.

Stiffly I rose to my feet, putting my empty glass on the table beside my chair. I was afraid of the emotion which would cause my voice to tremble but its coldness surprised me, and I was grateful for the sudden spurt of courage which allowed my eyes to meet his unflinchingly.

'I'll say goodnight then, Mr Thorn. I shall be leaving early in the morning. There is only one train into Medchester on Sunday.'

'I will see that you are taken into the village in time to catch it.'

'There is no need, Mr Thorn. I have already arranged for George to collect me.'

For a moment we stared at each other like two polite strangers. We did not exchange handshakes or even smiles of farewell but when the library door closed firmly behind me with resounding finality I ran with all the speed I could muster across the hall and up the stairs towards my room. Then in an agony of weeping I threw myself across the bed, staining the silken coverlet with my tears, with black despair in my heart.

I do not know how long I lay spreadeagled across my bed. I only know that when I finally put my feet on the floor I felt cold and stiff. The fire had long since gone out and with shaking fingers I lit the gas lamps above the fireplace. I applied cold water to my eyes, miserably aware of my woebegone face in the mirror. I removed Rowena's gown and the slippers I had borrowed, leaving them in the wardrobe. My teeth were chattering, as much from despair as from cold, and I slipped my arms into Rowena's robe which did little to warm my heart or my shivering limbs. I couldn't lie in my bed and sleep, not with the memories of my interview with Thorn still ringing in my ears and I went to the window and pulled back the curtains. The earlier mist had gone now and the moon shone clearly out of a deep blue sky busy with stars. The house was silent. By this time all who lived here would have retired to their beds and even Laird would be stretched across the door of Thorn's room where I had often seen him.

I took off the robe and carefully folded it. If I left it on the bed Nancy would remove it in the morning and return it to Rowena's room. It had been a mistake to come and as I hurriedly pulled my travelling dress over my head it seemed that I could hear my father's voice telling me it was unwise ever to go back unless one is prepared to face regrets and disillusionment.

All these thoughts were running through my head as I tied up my hair. Then, with my straw hat firmly upon my head and my shoes underneath my arm, I turned off the gas and let myself out into the corridor. The moonlight illuminated it enough for me to tiptoe down the stairs and across the hall. It fell across the polished surface, shining upon suits of armour and portraits of Lyttons long dead but I had already decided I would not risk opening the heavy front door.

I went through the conservatory, warm and pungent

with the scent of soil and rare, exotic plants, then I fumbled with the bolts on the side door. I was wearing gloves, but in my haste I bruised my fingers, and I am ashamed to say I gave little thought to burglars or trespassers as I left the door unlocked behind me.

There were no lights burning in any of the windows but I kept to the shadows of the shrubbery, until I felt I was out of sight of the house, then I took to my heels and ran. I don't know how far I ran before I was compelled to stop, gasping for breath, but now the azalea bushes and rhododendrons lined the drive. It was darker here. The moon barely penetrated through the tracery of branches and from somewhere close at hand I heard the mournful cry of an owl and a scurry in the bushes from some small, nocturnal animal. I waited fearfully until I regained my breath, then I ran on towards the gates.

The lane leading into the village lay ahead of me, like a shining stream in the moonlight and I kept to the middle of the road. The only people I was likely to meet were poachers in search of Mr Thorn's birds or his salmon, but I met no one. It seemed even the village ne'er-do-wells were unwilling to embark on their exploits so early on the sabbath. The little high street was deserted. The inn had long since closed its doors to late Saturday night revellers and there was only one light burning in an upstairs room along the street, probably in the home of some sick person receiving attention or a child unable to sleep.

The distance was telling on me now. My feet were blistered and aching from the long walk down the drive and the country lane which followed and the station was still some distance away. The church clock struck two as I passed the village hall and miserably I realized I had five hours to wait before I could board the milk train into Medchester. I was sobbing quietly to myself by the time I reached the station, filled with self-pity and hurt from my tired feet. The station gate had long since fallen off its hinges but I knew there was a seat on the platform which spurred me on.

With little hope of success I tried the waiting room door, but to my profound joy it was open. The room smelled strongly of carbolic and cold tea but I didn't care, at that

341

moment those scents were as dear to me as all the perfumes of the orient. Gratefully I sank down on to the cold, horsehair bench, leaning my head back against the wall. I closed my eyes, though I knew full well sleep would not come. My heart was too immersed in its problems for sleep, but somehow I had to pass those few hours until I could hear the train thundering into the station.

Aunt Maud was at church when I let myself into the house. When she returned I was sitting in front of a fire with a book on my knees as though I had been reading. She was not to know that I had not turned a solitary page and I was determined that no hint of the turmoil in my heart should reach her.

It was all over. Milverton and Thorn, Elsa and Caprice. I would not go there again, never as long as I lived. I would never again see the mist sitting on the summit of Mower Gap like a white, woolly cap or the dark, rolling beauty of the hills against a threatening sky. Henceforth I would order my life in known everyday channels. I would attend to my work and make it my whole life, I would make new friends wherever I could and see less of Dora. Dora reminded me too much of Gleave.

Somehow or other I got through the next week and once more the weekend loomed ahead of me. The prospect of a day and a half's holiday with nothing to do with it filled me with dismay and I wondered if it would always be like this, dreading Saturday morning and longing for Monday to arrive.

I took my time on the way home, kicking the dried leaves under my feet, pulling my coat collar closer around my throat to keep out the first really icy blasts of the approaching winter. The scents of winter were all around me. The cold damp of rotting vegetation and the scent of chrysanthemums, the smell of hot, roasting chestnuts and small potatoes and the river smells, more pungent at this time than any other. As I turned out of the main thoroughfare into the tree-lined street where I lived the leaves flurried towards me like a snowstorm and I had to hold on to my hat to keep it on my head.

I opened the front door and called out as usual, 'It's me

Aunt Maud.' Then I shrugged off my coat, leaving it hanging on the hall stand before I went through into the kitchen.

There was a plate of thinly cut bread and butter and a bowl of stewed pears waiting to be carried into the dining room. I did not know what else was on the menu but as I was looking round for something to do Aunt Maud flustered into the room. Flustered was the right word. Two bright spots of colour burned in each cheek and she was stammering a little in her confusion.

'Lottie, take off your apron, you have a visitor in the parlour.'

'I have a visitor!' I exclaimed.

'Yes, do hurry, he's been waiting more than an hour already. You're later than usual.'

She gave me a little push towards the parlour door and when I opened it I saw Thorn standing on the hearthrug looking down into the fire. He turned quickly as the door opened and we were staring into each other's eyes, my own face aflame with colour.

I don't know how long we stood without speaking, his eyes searching my face and still I couldn't move. He had hurt me, long and deeply he had hurt me, and in my heart I could only think that his visit was to be a continuation of that hurt. He had come to chide me because I had left his house ungraciously in the middle of the night without so much as a farewell to his mother and others who had been kind to me, to steal away like a thief in the night, leaving the doors of the conservatory unlocked for any intruder who cared to enter. I could feel the hot tears rise to my eyes and ashamed of them I used the back of my hand to brush them away. Then suddenly he was beside me, his arms around me, holding me against him as though he would never let me go.

I let my body go limp against his, aware of his lean strength and all the time he was kissing my tear-stained face and trembling lips so that all I could say was 'Why, Thorn? *Why*?'

He told me then that he believed I had found someone else, and Thorn who had already been hurt so much, whose scars were deep and still raw, felt only bitterness towards

343

me that I had found consolation so soon. On the morning after I left Milverton the servants found my bed unslept in and Rowena's gown hanging in the wardrobe. My few belongings had gone and Mr Bamber reported my absence at breakfast. Thorn immediately sought his mother to ask if she was aware that I had left the house and then, angry with him, she told him the truth, which sent him to Medchester in search of me. All week, he told me, he had fretted because he must wait until weekend to see me but he was afraid to write to me in case I felt I could not forgive him.

'Oh Carla, my darling,' he murmured against my hair, 'I love you, I shall never allow you to leave me again. When will you marry me?'

My eyes opened wide as I struggled out of his arms.

'Thorn, are you quite sure it's me you want to marry? I'm not of your world. I know nothing about being the mistress of a house like Milverton or the handling of servants. Please Thorn, don't do anything too quickly before you have had time to think; there are so many other girls you could marry and find happiness with.'

'My dear girl, don't you think if I'd wanted such a girl I would have had her mapped out for me long before this? It's *you* I want to marry, you Carla, with those wide, grey eyes and that tender mouth that can be so determined and full of humour. We'll get married quietly, in Medchester by special licence, and you can do all the shopping you need to do in London after we're married. We'll go abroad for our honeymoon – France, Italy, Greece – there's so much we need to do and see together.'

'Can we go to Egypt do you think, or is that too far?'

He threw back his head and laughed. 'We can go to the moon, my darling, but yes, by all means let us go to Egypt. Do you remember that night in the village hall when you talked to the villagers about Egypt? That was the evening I first began to fall in love with you, seeing you standing so lovely and forlorn, so alone with the light turning your hair into the colour of a young cornfield, in front of all those people you had known since childhood. It took courage, Carla, and for the first time for many years I saw courage in a girl and loved her for it.'

'Oh, Thorn, there are so many things we need to say to each other, but not yet. What about your mother, does she know you have come here?'

'She knows and she is delighted, as are Stephen and Judith. I shall need to talk to your aunt. She looks a most formidable lady.'

'She is, but you won't let her dissuade you will you?'

He laughed. 'Oh Carla, it seems as though I haven't laughed with a woman for so long. We are going to have such fun, you and I.'

He swept Aunt Maud along as I have never seen any person do it before. I found the utmost difficulty in taking it all in, but he was there, strong and real in the little parlour, and I didn't in the end care whether we had her blessing or not.

At the end of November, on a dull, grey morning, Mr Fellows married us very quietly in Aunt Maud's church. Our only guests were my aunts and uncle David, Stephen and Judith, and Dora and Peter. Thorn's mother sent us her blessing but she was not able to make the journey into Medchester. I was glad that we did not have time for long farewells after the wedding breakfast, but our little handful of guests stood on the station platform until we could see them no more. Aunt Beatrice wept copiously and once I thought that Aunt Maud looked away so that I would not see the emotion in her eyes.

EPILOGUE

They are almost over, the long sun-filled days and clear, starlit nights.

From our balcony in Aswan I can sit looking out across the gardens towards the river – the most romantic river in the world – while below me the water swirls and boils between the shining, black rocks which appear like great, prehistoric beasts waiting to emerge from the deep. In the hotel gardens palm trees rear their graceful heads against the sky, and the air is filled with the perfume of jasmine.

It has been a lazy day for us, the last before we board the train which will take us to Alexandria and the ship which will carry us home. The late afternoon sunlight has turned the white walls of the little town to gold and already in the west the sky is changing to colours of crimson and orange, all the tragic glory of an Egyptian sunset. A flurry of doves comes sweeping down the sky to alight on the dovecotes across the river and, as I wait for that moment when the figures of men and women and beasts become merely silhouettes against the sky, I can see Thorn walking towards me through the gardens from the direction of the town. He looks very youthful with his shirt sleeves rolled up over his slim, brown arms, his clean-shaven face bronzed by these last few weeks in the sunshine of Egypt. He looks relaxed and happy, as I first remember him and I am glad, knowing that I have restored that look of serenity into his face.

Since that dismal November morning when we left England behind us we have made our leisurely way through Italy and Greece, historically coming backwards into time and now it will soon be over. We have danced until dawn, until the morning mist swirled about the river and the stars paled, but we have not slavishly followed the army of tourists with their sketching pads and fly whisks, for I knew better than they what marvels we must see.

347

I have been glad to have been my father's daughter so that I could show to Thorn all the wonders my father showed to me, and read for him, however haltingly, the writings on the walls of the great temples. I would be happy for this time to go on for ever, for every golden morning and every silver night to stretch onwards and outwards towards the limits of time, but I know in my heart that this cannot be. We are not of this land, Thorn and I. Our future lies amongst the rugged hills where the climate is unpredictable and the seasons more sharply defined. Now, when I think about returning there, I cannot always prevent the small chill of fear which creeps into my heart.

Thorn's mother has written to say that the alterations to Milverton are complete and our furniture which we ordered in London is in our rooms. Thorn has told me that as soon as we return I must sit for the portrait which is to take its place at the head of the stairs and I worry a little when I think of those others which have hung there before it. He has already said that he wants to see me in the rose-coloured velvet which I wore on that fateful Christmas Eve and I have not had the heart to tell him that it hangs mutilated in my wardrobe.

We never speak of the past, not even in our most quiet moments. It is as though our lives only began on that bleak, misty morning when we watched the shores of England drop below the horizon and even now I am afraid of the fragility of the bonds which bind him to me. I am his wife and I shall return to Milverton with him, but it seems that the dark spectre of the past lies brooding over the house, anxiously waiting for the sounds of our carriage wheels upon the long, twisting drive. I am being fanciful I know, but then, as Thorn told me long ago, Milverton is a house which lends itself to fantasies.

One day I will speak to him of Caprice but it will not be yet. When I see him now, watching me from across the balcony, with a warm smile on his lips and tenderness in his eyes, I know that he loves me. Once I saw him look at Caprice with that same tenderness and my heart aches for that beautiful, high-spirited girl and the empty, bitter waste of it all.

I pray that one day there will be that between us which

will allow me to speak her name freely, perhaps on some long, winter evening when we are together at the end of the day, when I can be sure that his eyes are warm with peace, and his mouth is set in lines of contentment, or perhaps on the day he holds our son in his arms and we both know that Milverton is safe at last for those who will come after.

'Still writing, Carla?' he teases me. 'What can you possibly be writing to bring that sad, frightened look into those grey eyes?'

He holds out his hand as though to take the book from me but I close it firmly and lay it on the table beside my chair.

'One day I will let you read what I have written,' I promise, 'but not yet. Anyway it is almost finished, when we get home to Milverton I shall not write again.'

'You said home, Carla. It is the first time I have heard you speak of Milverton as home and I wondered if you were still afraid. It will be home for us my darling. There are no longer any shadows there to frighten you.'

We stood together looking out across the Nile towards the sun setting gloriously behind the western hills, and when I looked up into his dark, handsome face I found it filled with a great strength. I lifted up my arms and we clung together with a mounting passion that satisfied my soul, while high above us the warm wind from the desert rustled and sighed through the palm fronds.

One day we shall speak of Caprice. Her sad, wandering spirit is at rest now, and surely she must keep faith with me as I have kept faith with her. In the years that are before us Thorn belongs to me and I plead with her silently to let him go. I must learn not to fear the remembered beauty of her face or the passions of other years.